NO LONGER PROPERTY OF
THE SEATTLE PUBLIC LIBRARY

THE WAY SPRING ARRIVES

AND OTHER STORIES

THE WAY SPRING ARRIVES

AND OTHER STORIES

EDITED BY YU CHEN
AND REGINA KANYU WANG

A Tom Doherty Associates Book • New York

This is a work of fiction. All of the characters, organizations, and events portrayed in these stories are either products of the authors' imaginations or are used fictitiously.

THE WAY SPRING ARRIVES AND OTHER STORIES

Copyright © 2022 by Tordotcom Publishing

All rights reserved.

Edited by Ruoxi Chen 陈若熹 and Lindsey Hall in collaboration with Storycom

Designed by Gregory Collins

A Tordotcom Book
Published by Tom Doherty Associates
120 Broadway
New York, NY 10271

www.tor.com

Tor® is a registered trademark of Macmillan Publishing Group, LLC.

The Library of Congress Cataloging-in-Publication Data is available upon request.

ISBN 978-1-250-76891-9 (hardcover)
ISBN 978-1-250-76893-3 (ebook)

Our books may be purchased in bulk for promotional, educational, or business use. Please contact the Macmillan Corporate and Premium Sales Department at 1-800-221-7945, extension 5442, or by email at MacmillanSpecialMarkets@macmillan.com.

First Edition: 2022

Printed in the United States of America

0 9 8 7 6 5 4 3 2 1

COPYRIGHT ACKNOWLEDGMENTS

"The Stars We Raised"
Copyright © 2017 by 修新羽 (Xiu Xinyu)
English translation © 2022 by Tom Doherty Associates
Translation by Judy Yi Zhou
Originally published as 逃跑星辰 in March 2017 by *Master* (大家)

"The Tale of Wude's Heavenly Tribulation"
Copyright © 2011 by E伯爵 (Count E)
English translation © 2022 by Tom Doherty Associates
Translation by Mel "etvolare" Lee
Originally published as 五德渡劫记 in May 2011 by *Odyssey of China Fantasy* (九州幻想)

"What Does the Fox Say?"
Copyright © 2022 by 夏笳 (Xia Jia)

"Blackbird"
Copyright © 2020 by 沈大成 (Shen Dacheng)
English translation © 2022 by Tom Doherty Associates
Translation by Cara Healey
Originally published as 黑鸟 in 2020 in *Asteroids in the Afternoon* (小行星掉在下午) by Imaginist—Guangxi Normal University Press in Guilin

"The Restaurant at the End of the Universe: Tai-Chi Mashed Taro"
Copyright © 2016 by 吴霜 (Anna Wu)
English translation © 2022 by Tom Doherty Associates
Translation by Carmen Yiling Yan
Originally published as 宇宙尽头的餐馆之太极芋泥 in August 2016 by *Zui Novel* (最小说)

"Baby, I Love You"
Copyright © 2002 by 赵海虹 (Zhao Haihong)
English translation © 2022 by Tom Doherty Associates
Translation by Elizabeth Hanlon
Originally published as 宝贝宝贝我爱你 in August 2002 by *Science Fiction World* (科幻世界)

"A Saccharophilic Earthworm"
Copyright © 2005 by 白饭如霜 (BaiFanRuShuang)
English translation © 2022 by Tom Doherty Associates
Translation by Ru-Ping Chen
Originally published as 嗜糖蚯蚓 in 2005 by *Magic Fantasy* (今古传奇·奇幻版)

"The Alchemist of Lantian"
Copyright © 2005 by 白饭如霜 (BaiFanRuShuang)
English translation © 2022 by Tom Doherty Associates
Translation by Ru-Ping Chen
Originally published as 蓝田半人 in August 2005 by *Magic Fantasy* (今古传奇·奇幻版)

"The Way Spring Arrives"
Copyright © 2019 by 王诺诺 (Wang Nuonuo)
English translation © 2022 by Tom Doherty Associates
Translation by Rebecca F. Kuang
Originally published as 春天来临的方式 in 2019 in *No Answers from Earth* (地球无应答) by Hunan Literature and Art Publishing House in Changsha

"The Name of the Dragon"
Copyright © 2007 by 凌晨 (Ling Chen)
English translation © 2022 by Tom Doherty Associates
Translation by Yilin Wang
Originally published as 应龙 in April 2007 by *Fantasy World* (飞·奇幻世界)

"To Procure Jade"
Copyright © 2013 by 顾适 (Gu Shi)
English translation © 2022 by Tom Doherty Associates
Translation by Yilin Wang
Originally published as 得玉 in May 2013 by *Super Nice Magazine* (超好看杂志)

"A Brief History of Beinakan Disasters as Told in a Sinitic Language"
Copyright © 2018 by 念语 (Nian Yu)
English translation © 2022 by Tom Doherty Associates
Translation by Ru-Ping Chen
Originally published as 衡平公式 in 2018 in *Lilian Is Everywhere* (莉莉安无处不在) by Bofeng Culture in Beijing

"Dragonslaying"
Copyright © 2006 by 沈璎璎 (Shen Yingying)
English translation © 2022 by Tom Doherty Associates
Translation by Emily Xueni Jin
Originally published as 屠龙 in July 2006 by *Magic Fantasy* (今古传奇·奇幻版)

"New Year Painting, Ink and Color on Rice Paper, Zhaoqiao Village"
Copyright © 2020 by 陈茜 (Chen Qian)
English translation © 2022 by Tom Doherty Associates
Translation by Emily Xueni Jin
Originally published as 年画 forthcoming in *West* (西部)

"The Portrait"
Copyright © 2003 by 楚惜刀 (Chu Xidao)
English translation © 2022 by Tom Doherty Associates
Translation by Gigi Chang
Originally published as 画妖 in December 2003 by *www.rongshuxia.com* (榕树下)

"The Woman Carrying a Corpse"
Copyright © 2019 by 迟卉 (Chi Hui)
English translation © 2022 by Tom Doherty Associates
Translation by Judith Huang
Originally published as 背尸体的女人 in December 2019 by *Flower City* (花城)

"The Mountain and the Secret of Their Names"
Copyright © 2019 by 王诺诺 (Wang Nuonuo)
English translation © 2022 by Tom Doherty Associates
Translation by Rebecca F. Kuang
Originally published as 山和名字的秘密 in 2019 in *Morning Star Award-Code*

"The Futures of Genders in Chinese Science Fiction"
Copyright © 2022 by Jing Tsu 石静远

"Translation as Retelling: An Approach to Translating Gu Shi's 'To Procure Jade' and Ling Chen's 'The Name of the Dragon'"
Copyright © 2022 by Yilin Wang 王艺霖

"Is There Such a Thing as *Feminine* Quietness?: A Cognitive Linguistics Perspective"
Copyright © 2022 by Emily Xueni Jin 金雪妮

"Net Novels and the 'She Era': How Internet Novels Opened the Door for Female Readers and Writers in China"
Copyright © 2022 by Xueting Christine Ni 倪雪亭

"Writing and Translation: A Hundred Technical Tricks"
Copyright © 2022 by Rebecca F. Kuang 匡灵秀

THE WAY SPRING ARRIVES AND OTHER STORIES

TABLE OF CONTENTS

1

The Stars We Raised
逃跑星辰

Xiu Xinyu 修新羽
Translated by Judy Yi Zhou 周易

The Stars We Raised

By Xiu Xinyu
Translated by Judy Yi Zhou

All autumn long, we searched for baby stars. Our scavenged treasures would be carefully placed in gauze-sealed glass fishbowls. The tiny rocks were still soft, their glow a faint green. They couldn't yet fly: all they could do was worm around at the bottom of the bowl.

We would make a clearing in the sea of endless leaves to claim our share of the hunt. The brightest and softest baby star always went to Captain Wang, our class president appointed by the head teacher. Even outside the classroom, he acted like our leader and enjoyed the perks fully. He would split the rest of the baby stars among us. I would usually receive a yolk-sized one, but Jiang Yang would only ever get nail-sized pieces—dull and fragmented. That was the way it should be: after all, he was the smallest of our group, and the quietest, trailing behind everywhere we went.

Only kids with nothing better to do and the most stubborn scientists had the patience for this: going to whatever lengths to train a star, and believing that they might succeed.

We would have about four months. We would wipe the baby stars with melted snow, hoping the pristine water would wash away the dullness and make them shine more brightly. Some thought the icy cold air would make their baby stars stronger, so they would swaddle them with wet gauze and set them outside their windows to freeze. Others, under the belief that their baby stars could learn to understand simple commands, would cup them in their palms, hold them up like offerings, and talk to them every day.

No matter what we did or did not do, however, the stars always grew up. They became larger and lighter, and by the following spring, when the fields came back to life, the stars' translucent fluorescent green would turn an opaque grayish brown. That was when our parents would try to get us to grind them into dust and sell them.

Parents always seemed to know exactly what they wanted from the start, as if their plan had been for the stars to grow up then be turned into dust and sold for money all along. When baby stars grew up, they became clumsy, boring and ugly, looking like nothing more than an ordinary rock. What's more, if we didn't tie them up with rope, they would float around slowly, making a nuisance of themselves.

It was only many years later that I found out when it all started: one summer over a decade ago. Some people had seen stars circling about in midair. They seemed to only appear in a few small cities at the horse latitudes—about thirty degrees north and south of the equator—including several villages in the United States, Australia, and China. At first scientists were not aware of this phenomenon, and nobody told us what to do. So some folks took things into their own hands, before they could be stopped.

When the stars first descended upon villages in Anhui, herds of journalists swarmed and dug up every possible detail surrounding them. Some Taoist priests had swung dirt around in the air while chanting mantras at the stars, and some crackpots had thrown themselves to the ground and kowtowed repeatedly until their foreheads bled.

Yet nothing happened.

And that was the best way it could have turned out. People tried everything they could to communicate with the stars slowly drifting through the air, but nothing worked. Only after several years were the scientists willing to admit that the stars were completely harmless. A few years later, scientists found a use for these stars: after they were ground into powder, the stardust could be made into a superior cement additive. Most started to think of it as nothing more than an ordinary natural resource, save for one or two cities that thought it would be a good gimmick to build a theme park with stardust cement.

If these stars had a message, no one knew what it was. We didn't know where they came from or what kind of force sustained their constant flying. Perhaps there was some kind of magnetic or energy field—we just didn't know.

Growing up in such a village, we were used to seeing stars hovering in the mountains. We often gathered under a street lamp to show off our stars, each of us carefully reaching into our pockets to bring out the baby star we had been training. Unsurprisingly, Captain Wang's baby star would always be bigger, brighter, rounder, smoother, and softer than the others. He was the class president, tall and handsome, the pride and joy of his family since birth. Why shouldn't his baby star be the best too?

That was why we all kept our silence when he stamped down on Jiang Yang's baby star, throwing all his weight on it. None of us tried to stop him.

That day had seemed pretty unusual from the start. We would often set up a small hurdle on the ground with tree branches and stones, then we would excitedly cheer on our stars as they squirmed, struggling to make their way across the hurdle. Jiang Yang normally wouldn't participate in this game. And in our village, secrets didn't exist. Everyone knew everyone else's dirty laundry: Jiang Yang had no mother and his father found a city job long ago, so he had always lived with his grandmother. She was a scary old lady, twig-thin and dry like a raisin. When she looked at you, she stared with such menace. In winter, she would wrap Jiang Yang in thick cotton coats. No way would she let her darling grandson out at night.

But that evening, remarkably, Jiang Yang did come out, and he was even zipped up in a brand-new red jacket. He almost seemed happy, if a little shy.

"My baby star is super fast," he promised, reaching into his pocket for it. It was still tiny, but it glowed with a dazzling light. Its light wasn't even the usual fluorescent green—it looked kind of pale. Who would have known that a baby star could be this bright!

"How'd you do it?" Even Captain Wang couldn't help but marvel. He squatted down and scooped up the baby, squeezing it in his hand.

Jiang Yang stuttered as he explained he didn't know how this had happened, but he quickly realized that nobody cared. By then, we could all see that Captain Wang didn't plan on giving back the star anyway.

At this, Jiang Yang lost his mind and started wailing, digging his nails into Captain Wang's wrist, pinching him. Captain Wang spat, then tossed the little star on the ground and stomped on it, snapping, "Your star is sick, you know that?! It's radioactive, that's why it's so bright. It'll make you dumb. And it will never grow up. You know why? Because it'll use up all its energy before that!"

Jiang Yang leapt to cover the star with his arms, forgetting all about his new jacket. Captain Wang's foot had nowhere else to land, so he stepped on Jiang Yang's torso, furnishing the new jacket with a few fresh boot prints. Jiang Yang didn't flinch. He stayed on the ground until those of us watching got bored and started to leave. Then he quickly stood up, clutching his star. I vaguely remember Jiang Yang still crying when he left, while we went on playing amongst ourselves. The particular cruelty of children gave us the unique power to turn a blind eye to all the miseries thriving in our own lives.

Jiang Yang never joined our games again. Nor did he ever show us his star.

Come spring, when we were heading back to school, our parents would strike deals with star buyers to make our stars disappear once and for all. Of course, we were livid, and would get together to brainstorm ways to forestall this despicable act.

"But I don't wanna!" the girl with the braids would cry. "I didn't raise my star just to sell it off."

Captain Wang didn't think it was that big of a deal. "Look at these stars," he would say, "they are so ugly. That means the training failed. Who cares if these failures got sold? We'll get another chance next year."

The cries usually died down in a few days, after we had filled our pockets with the candies our parents gave out to make up for our losses. Besides, it was spring, when the earth awakened with its streams of fish and trees of birds.

All the stars we had failed to train were sold. Except for Jiang Yang's. But I only pieced this together later. Since I was younger than him and lived nearby, I would run into him often and sometimes we would speak.

That day after school, as I walked by Jiang Yang's house, I saw him standing outside the door in his red jacket, which now appeared a bit worn. He was getting ready to say something, but shut his mouth right before words came out.

I stopped and looked back at him. He remained silent. Just as I put one foot up in the air to start walking again, I heard his shy yet crisp voice behind me. "You all sold your stars?"

Once I nodded, he continued, "Do you . . . want to come see my star?"

Jiang Yang's grandmother, practically coddling him, hadn't let him climb trees or play in the farm fields with us. As a compromise, she had agreed to let him hold on to his star to keep him company. He kept the star at home and diligently tied it to one end of a strip of cloth. The other end of the cloth strip was knotted to his bed. The strip was long enough for the star to enjoy a little freedom, swaying and floating in the air. Jiang Yang even carved his name on the star, claiming ownership.

I didn't know what there was to see about this star, but Jiang Yang kept inviting me over, and I felt bad turning him down, so I went a few more times. These visits seemed to greatly encourage him, so much so that he eventually decided to take the star out on a walk. At this point, the entire village learned that Jiang Yang was still raising a star.

Jiang Yang walked solemnly at a very slow pace. Adults were amused by this bizarre performance, and they gathered in small groups to point at him, laughing all the while. But Jiang Yang kept his gaze dead ahead, as if the whole world was muted and everything dimmed in his eyes except his star, which he would glance up at on occasion.

We tagged along behind him, waiting to see what would happen next. Captain Wang was the only one unmoved. He stood in front of his house with a puppy in his arms and looked at us like we were a bunch of fools. Then he sallied forth at Jiang Yang, "My dad told me all about it: your dad is lying to you. He's got a new wife in the city and doesn't want you anymore. Even your trained star won't bring him back!" That was when we noticed Jiang Yang's father indeed hadn't come home for Lunar New Year.

Jiang Yang didn't argue back. He just kept on walking, but his solemn parade became a dejected plod. His fingers clung to the strip like a drowning man clutching at a straw. The star dragged along behind him, as if it were depressed too.

That night I knocked on his door, asking to see the star. The scrawny old lady who answered stared at me for a very long time before letting me in.

Jiang Yang was ecstatic. That night, he had so much to say.

Jiang Yang told me that his father was making airplanes in the factory. For kids like us, growing up in this stagnant, middle-of-nowhere village in the South, those airplanes were something we only saw on TV. Occasionally, we got to see the long white trails the airplanes traced across the sky. We looked up to Jiang Yang's father, and our reverence even cast Jiang Yang in a certain light of awe in our eyes.

Jiang Yang said he wanted to become a pilot when he grew up, so that he could reach faraway lands and even the sky, where he would get real close to the clouds, the stars, and the moon. More importantly, pilots could probably make a lot of money, then his father wouldn't have to work in the factory every day anymore, and he would be so proud of him.

"If I don't make the cut as a pilot, I'm going to raise stars."

"But what does that even mean?" I found it a little ridiculous. "These things can grow up on their own, even if nobody takes care of them."

"It's not the same," Jiang Yang replied without looking at me, lowering his gaze to that little rock he had been fiddling with.

After a long pause, Jiang Yang revealed a secret: "My star has been successfully trained."

Since he wasn't allowed to play outside, he had been reading his textbook aloud to the star and talking to it, day after day. He truly believed that as long as he didn't give up, one day the star would understand him.

Under the dim yellow light, he buried his head in a textbook with curled pages and painstakingly searched for quotes, particularly those with reference to stars.

"From the towering temple perched atop the mountain, I could pluck the stars."

"Stars drape over vast open fields; the moon rushes on—and the wide river runs."

He enunciated each word slowly, a syllable at a time, with a perfect accent.

Maybe because of my presence, his voice was louder than usual. His grandmother rushed in to check on us. Once she confirmed that I was not bullying her precious boy, she stomped off.

But Jiang Yang didn't seem to have noticed anything; he kept on reading poems out loud, followed by an intent "hello" to the star. He said, "Did you see? The star jiggled! It always does when you say hello, try it yourself if you don't believe me."

So I also said, "Hello." The star really did jiggle—it was obvious. But these stars were always jiggling and rocking, who knew if it actually worked?

Things appeared to be going well for Jiang Yang. Then one day, his star went missing.

No one knew what happened, but we all heard the cries from Jiang Yang's house, which went late into the night until he lost his voice.

At first, it seemed he suspected his grandmother, who must have made a secret bargain and sold it. Then again, star buyers wouldn't be here this time of the year. His next theory was that someone stole it, but who would bother stealing something that could be found everywhere? It was true that this star had been trained. But only the two of us knew about that.

I hesitated for a long time before knocking on his door that night. I thought it would be good to comfort him. The door didn't budge. Maybe he also found me suspicious, or maybe his grandmother didn't want anyone near him.

I knew a line had been drawn, and I never tried again. Later, I heard that Jiang Yang had run to a cement plant in the neighboring village and started talking to piles of stardust at the top of his voice. Maybe it was more like yelling. He thought the powder of his star might be in there somewhere, and it might give him a sign. However, the piles of powder remained the same dreary grayish brown. Jiang Yang, on the other hand, was dragged home in tears by his grandmother after getting a beating.

After his star's disappearance, Jiang Yang stopped raising baby stars. A few years later, the rest of us moved on as well. We were all in middle school now, and our days were flooded with homework. We were older, wiser.

Among the things we came to understand: No city kids had ever bothered to try raising stars. They had all sorts of toys, like transformers, dolls, and stuffed animals. City people had thought of stars as strange objects with a mysterious composition and unknown origins, so it would be best to keep the children as far away from the stuff as possible.

What we also came to understand was that these stars could never be trained. A star's coming of age was the process of slowly getting uglier. Their brightness would gradually mute, their warmth vanished, and their softness charred. They would become coarse and dim, like snowballs sprinkled with coal dust, or ball-shaped wet sponges that have frozen. Eventually, they would manage to float up in the air and even fly, but they sure were hideous. And the same thing would happen to us too, as we grew up.

I started to get acne, and though I shot up in height, my limbs were flimsy and I would fumble as I moved. Jiang Yang was close to my height, but his face was paler, and he was quieter than me.

He used to be a year above me, but he had to repeat the year because of his grades. He would always be tucked away in one of the back corners of the classroom. Perhaps Captain Wang had a point about the bright star having radiation; because Jiang Yang, who had raised a star for so long, looked sickly pale all the time. People in the village said that Jiang Yang's father hadn't been making airplanes in Shenzhen after all, but rather putting together cheap model planes in a toy factory, the crappy kind sold by street vendors. The pay was so low that he would have to work more than ten hours a day just to save a little bit of money to send home. In recent years, he might not even have managed that, because Jiang Yang never showed up in new clothes anymore.

Captain Wang was no longer the class president—he had been promoted to captain of the school basketball team. He was not only tall and good at studies, but he also managed to win every single fight he got into, and he would get into them often. Rumor had it that he had been passing snacks to his little girlfriend in seventh grade through the back window of her classroom. She was the prettiest girl in the whole school. Almost all the boys were obsessed with her.

I wasn't in the same class as Captain Wang, and we wouldn't hang out much. But the following spring, something big happened.

Captain Wang's and his girlfriend's parents showed up in school, and they were fighting right outside the front gate. It took us a while to figure out what had happened: Apparently, the young lovers had a stargazing date in the mountains. On their way back, Captain Wang fell, broke his leg, and cracked some ribs. He was going to have to lie in bed for six whole months.

"Your daughter insisted she saw a blue star and our boy went over to look, that was when he broke his leg!" Captain Wang's overbearing mother barked. "Since when are there blue stars?!"

It was the seasoned village head who came up with the idea of getting a Taoist priest involved. The person that arrived was a bony, middle-aged man. He held a swishing sword, and right in front of the school gate, started a fire with sheet after sheet of paper covered with spells written in strange characters.

"Your boy is possessed," concluded the Taoist priest. Then he muttered, "The guest star is shining extra brightly, while the host star wanes."

He continued with conviction, "Someone in the village must be raising stars in secret and using them to cast an evil spell on your boy. It's something I've only read about, using a baby star to curse someone . . . People are capable of terrible things." What he said had the chill of truth: when the stars first arrived over a decade ago, some villager's eldest daughter killed herself by drinking pesticides, and the devastated mother followed by hanging herself.

We all knew that Captain Wang used to bully Jiang Yang. And that nobody was as good at raising stars as Jiang Yang.

"Jiang Yang? Sounds familiar, our kid probably received a love note from him at some point." The girlfriend's mother added, "Young people can be so jealous sometimes . . ."

The next thing we knew, Captain Wang's father stormed into our classroom, yanked Jiang Yang out of his seat like he was picking up a chick from a brood, and roared, "Was it you, you wack job? Was it?"

Jiang Yang did not speak. He lowered his head and hunched over. How did a lanky guy like him shrink into something so small?

Furious, Captain Wang's father rummaged through Jiang Yang's desk drawer, shoving all his books on the floor, and even flipped his school bag upside down to empty it of everything. Who would have thought, a few shiny baby stars actually fell out. Only then did we realize that Jiang Yang was still raising stars without anyone knowing.

He was caught red-handed. The dean contacted Jiang Yang's family, and the group waited in the dean's office for a solution. Jiang Yang's grandmother appeared. The old lady looked even more scraggly than I remembered, and her hair had turned completely gray. But her eyes were gleaming, and she wielded two butcher knives in her hands.

"Where is he?" his grandmother thundered. "Where did you hide those damn stars?"

Jiang Yang kept his head down and did not make a sound. Those of us who flooded the hall for the show kept quiet as well.

The dean instinctively shot a look at the office desk where the "criminal evidence" was spread out, sending the grandmother straight there, her knives flung high in the air. She was going to chop those baby stars into pieces.

It was common knowledge that baby stars were indestructible. Their makeup was different from grown-up stars, so they were not as dry or light. Instead, they were soft and resilient, but could not be penetrated by any hard or sharp objects.

Jiang Yang must have been scared out of his wits, because he lunged forward and blocked the knives with his own hand.

Blood dripped down the blade, splattering onto the floor. The old lady shuddered and tossed the knives aside.

At this point, the dean, who had been keeping out of the way, was propelled by a surge of courage to open his mouth for the first time. "Hurry to the nurse's office," he blurted, and he even gave Jiang Yang a nudge. Jiang Yang froze for an instant, then stumbled out.

We never found out whether he went to the nurse's office.

I didn't see Jiang Yang again for a long time after that. People said that he dropped out of school and went to Shenzhen to look for his father. Captain Wang eventually returned to school with a cast and crutches. A few months later, the crutches were gone, and he seemed to have fully recovered. His cockiness never fully recovered though, perhaps because of the fright. It was a good thing for the rest of us.

After I left for college, the only time I would come back was during Lunar New Year.

New stars had been appearing steadily in recent years, and the village had even developed an elaborate set of star-mining standards. The mountains were now blocked off all year, except in winter, when the government paid the village to hire a bunch of locals to collect grown-up stars all at once. For young people who came back once a year, it was a good seasonal job for extra cash. It worked out for everybody.

But my family had made a good enough living this year that my parents didn't want me to go out to the mountains in the cold. One day, I set off a bundle of firecrackers in front of my house, and as the crackling and smoke died down, I found Jiang Yang watching me from his front door. He stood in a large gray sweater, a lot taller than the boy in my memory. His frame seemed more muscular too, less frail. Perhaps Shenzhen had toughened him up a bit. But he still wore that same hesitant look on his face. It was indecision that would incense an older relative and score him a round of insults like "How useless!" or "What a waste of space!"

I had heard many rumors. That his father never did come back, that his grandmother got gravely sick, and was wasting away at home with no money for treatment. Everyone in the village would say it was because of Jiang Yang's stars. He had been raising stars for so long that he must have gotten too close to the evil spirits and pissed off a god somewhere, and now he was paying for it.

"Happy New Year," I decided to say. He didn't respond, of course. I did not expect him to. I turned around and got ready to go back into my house. Just as my foot stepped over the threshold, I heard a tapping sound.

It was Jiang Yang. He was looking down, but his finger was tapping off-beat on the doorframe.

"What is it?" These days, I no longer had the patience to wait.

"I'm a little tight on money lately. Thinking of going to the mountains to make some cash," he said.

It was an indirect way of putting it, but I knew what he meant. He wanted to go hunt stars.

Over here, when people were coming up short, it was the first thing that came to mind. The mountain roads were difficult, and the government required labor forces to sign up in teams of two. People were supposed to find their own partner. I guess nobody wanted to team up with Jiang Yang.

I wanted to say no. But my eyes had a mind of their own—they found his hand on the doorframe, and the scar still distinctly visible on his finger. I didn't know what got into me, because what came out of my mouth was *yes.*

I kept it from my parents, pretending that I was going to a classmate's place in town. I went with Jiang Yang to pick up the supplies: plenty of sturdy bags, a portable star grinder, and face masks to protect our lungs from the bitter powder of ground-up stars.

We followed the narrow trail that led all the way into the mountains. Together, we fed all the stars we could find into the grinder.

There was so much I wanted to say to Jiang Yang, but the timing never seemed right. I wanted to ask him where on earth his father had gone. It had been the talk of town for so long at this point, and still no one had any idea. The way his father had vanished was just like his star, suddenly, without a trace. It unsettled us all.

Before I found the right moment for my question, Jiang Yang beat me to it with one of his own.

"There's something I've wanted to ask you." He kept his head down and his eyes focused on the trail as he spoke. "Back then, did you ever really believe that I managed to train that star?"

"Yes, really! I saw it with my own eyes, how it followed your commands," I replied hastily, even though my actual memory of the event was quite blurry and there was no other witness.

"You would believe anything." Jiang Yang turned around and looked at me for a second, a conspicuous smile spreading across his face.

Neither of us said anything more. Walking the trail became our sole focus.

The mountains were hushed. Once in a while, we heard a little crackling of dead leaves and branches getting crushed under our feet. When we came across fellow star hunters, we made some small talk and quickly went our separate ways. Enveloped by layers of ridges, we rarely caught a glimpse of others. The mountain range had no end in sight.

The stars in the mountains' outer rings were mostly cleared out. We had no choice but to keep going deeper into the valleys. We went so far that we had to bring our backpacks and grinder to camp. Jiang Yang pulled out a sleeping bag, basic tent, and stacks of hand warmers from nowhere. I had no idea where he had gotten his hands on this stuff. We were looking for a spot where stars gathered, but did such a place even exist? That night, we slept in a shallow cave scattered with abandoned plastic bottles and ragged blankets. We weren't the first star hunters to stay here.

"I mean, I don't know," Jiang Yang said, "but in the newspaper they mentioned that stars would often gather during the winter, maybe because they also feel cold and want to keep warm . . . The star I raised really enjoyed leaning on our light bulb at home. Maybe they like light."

He switched on the flashlight and pointed the light away from us, toward the entrance of the cave. "Let's leave it on like this and go to sleep. I've got quite a few batteries with me."

But how far could a flashlight reach? The light beam barely shone three feet. The only thing it revealed was the withered grass on the ground. For several nights in a row, we fell into slumber and woke like any other day. There was nothing to speak of.

Throughout the third night, swallowed in the frigid belly of the mountain, our sleep was light. Even though we stuck hand-warmer patches all over our bodies, our faces were exposed to the cold air. That is to say,

I was not entirely sure if I was dreaming that night, or if my memory was blurred by my overstretched nerves.

What I most clearly recalled was seeing a world bursting with clear light the color of an emerald. At the same time, someone might have been squeezing my hand.

"Look outside," whispered Jiang Yang.

I turned to the mouth of the cave and discovered that the woods and sky were no more. Stars. There were only stars. Tens of thousands of stars. All of them not yet fully grown, still giving off a faint, misty glow.

No one had seen so many stars all at once. Had they come to avenge their lost ones? Or were we cursed as well? The stars were so light, moving sluggishly. Who would have thought that they could contain death?

Lit up by the starlight, Jiang Yang looked even more dazed.

"Hello," he muttered, almost without realizing.

In that instant, I saw in him the stubborn child who spoke to his star time after time. I found the stars jiggling, in formation, as if they perfectly understood us.

Yet how could so many stars have been trained before?

As if they had received a command, the stars started to quiver rhythmically and spread out in an orderly manner, creating a space in the center. It was here that an even smaller star came into our view.

It was merely the size of a basketball. Stuck between being a baby and a grown-up, it was a "teenage" star. It could fly nimbly, but it still had the faint glow of a baby. Unlike the fluorescent green of the other stars, this star shone with a pale blue light, the color of a wintry moon.

The blue star. The ominous blue star that Captain Wang's girlfriend saw in the mountains.

It hovered in midair hesitantly. Then, as if realizing something, it started to slowly draw closer to us.

Stars had never attacked humans before.

"Run," Jiang Yang said in a low voice, as if afraid the stars would eavesdrop on us. "Run outside." He squatted down to pick up the star grinder, clasping it tightly. Then, step by step, he inched toward the cave's entrance.

The star followed behind. As if it were possessed. Or had fallen sick.

Perhaps Jiang Yang had done or said something he wasn't supposed to. Perhaps there was something special about the clothes he was wearing. He stopped moving and stood there, frozen.

I came up to the star. And before I knew it, I reached out to touch it. It was softer and smoother than I had imagined. I could feel it trembling, as if a soundless hum had been set off. I could feel an engraving of some sort, like a symbol. Like a fragment of the words "Jiang Yang."

From the towering temple perched atop the mountain, I could pluck the stars.

It jiggled almost imperceptibly, then reversed its course and slipped out of my hand.

"Jiang Yang." I took a step back and said quietly, "It's the star you trained."

Jiang Yang turned to look at me. The light from the stars sparkled brightly in his eyes, and his face seemed so young. His expression was that of a youth awash in sadness.

"Jiang Yang?"

He jerked forward without warning. I thought he was about to collapse. To my surprise, he reached out and shoved past the stars blocking his path, and ran all the way outside the cave. His unsteady figure waded through the sea of stars and at last dissolved into the dreamy luster.

I tried to catch up while hollering, but nothing stopped him. My cries echoed back and forth among the shallow and deep folds of the mountain ranges—I had never heard such a lonely sound. It was as if the world had been stripped bare and only I remained. Me alone, with those slow-moving stars.

He was nowhere to be seen. Flashlight in hand, I started making my way back down the mountains. The night air up here was bone-piercingly icy, and the wuthering wind flapped between the rugged edges of mountain valleys. My hands and feet just about froze. For a while, that particular star followed me at a slow pace, but then it realized that I no longer paid it any attention, so it gradually, slowly, little by little, flew back into the valleys. When I said goodbye, it jiggled at me gently. My eyes might have been playing tricks on me because I was cold out of my mind, but I wanted to believe that it really did jiggle. That Jiang Yang had truly taught it to trust him. That his star would answer his call.

I found Jiang Yang shivering under a streetlight at the base of the mountains.

The trail was tough. Every year there were people who would get lost at night, some who would break a leg, and some who would never make it back. When Captain Wang broke his leg and ribs on this trail all those years ago, even he'd had a flashlight in his hand. It was a miracle that Jiang Yang had run down the trail in complete darkness and made his way out in one piece. He had wrapped his coat around himself and curled into a small ball on the ground. He was a rather tall and skinny man by then, no longer the young boy he once was, and yet he could still shrink into something that took up so little room.

He seemed relieved to see me, as he loosened his arms and stood up from the ground. He looked calmer than I would have imagined.

"Thank goodness! How did you get down from up there in the pitch-black night?" I waved my flashlight at him.

"I . . . I sort of know the trail," Jiang Yang replied with difficulty. After spending so much time in the frosty wind, his voice was muted and his words slurred.

"Know the trail?"

"Not that well." Jiang Yang hastily drew a sharp breath, then said, "They were following me back there." His voice was leaden, and I felt a hole rip open in my heart. "They actually wanted to follow me . . ."

I interrupted him. "Jiang Yang, that was your star."

He didn't leap for joy or even seem amazed. He simply nodded and rubbed his hands together, hard.

"It could be," he said. "Maybe."

He didn't waste any more time, picking up the star grinder and gesturing for me to follow him. Then he turned and started walking toward the village. There was still some stardust stuck on the grinder. Under the flickering lamppost, the stardust glowed a faint blue. I stared at the machine as I took each step, and more and more strongly I inhaled a sharp bitterness. The smell of freshly ground stars, like a field of crops rotting in a snow-covered land, lost in the capsule of time. The smell of dead stars.

That was the last time we went hunting for stars.

The next morning, Jiang Yang came over to say goodbye. Luggage in hand, he said he was heading back to Shenzhen. A day of extra work meant a day of pay. He had never planned to stay long at home for Lunar New Year, anyway. His grandmother seemed to have recovered at long last. On the fifteenth day of the New Year, she stepped out of the house and bragged about her grandson to the neighbors for several days straight: he had enough money saved to buy her all this delicious food, and even a new jacket.

I never saw Jiang Yang again. Once or twice, I wandered into the mountains and saw a few lone stars. They looked gray and dull, drooping in the air. Not a trace of light around them.

For a long time after that night, I kept revisiting the scene in my dreams.

I heard Jiang Yang say, "*Run.*" Those stars really seemed to have understood him, and they jiggled in the cold night. Countless stars arose from the horizon, the earth veiled in their radiant light. They flew toward the sky. It was the most wondrous winter I had ever seen.

2

The Tale of Wude's Heavenly Tribulation
五德渡劫记

Count E
E伯爵
Translated by Mel "etvolare" Lee

The Tale of Wude's Heavenly Tribulation

By Count E
Translated by Mel "etvolare" Lee

West of Heaven's Temple, star, and pillars far, do rest stone stairs that moss curtain guards.
Ascend transcendent peaks of vast sky reach, to overlook humanity and setting sun be seen.
Flute of pine and chime of stone rise in myriad song, dappled sun rays paint the skies in five directions 'round.
To seek the verdant mountain, no road is to be found, only trills of bird, serenity, and babbling brooks resound.

"Escorting Refiner Zhang Back to Mount Emei" by Sikong Shu, poet of the Tang dynasty. A depiction of the fairy peaks of Mount Emei, transcendentally exquisite and ideal for contemplating body and mind.

Mount Emei. A mystical retreat where eminent monks and virtuous sages choose to seclude themselves. Here, they withdraw from the clutter of society and wholly dedicate their energies to refining themselves. Local flora and fauna also benefit from the inherent spiritual energy of the surroundings, awakening intellect and gaining awareness. Thus initiated on the path of enlightenment, many journey on to become immortals through the metamorphosis of cultivation.

It is said that a wild fox, hailing from the mountain's second peak, opened its eyes to good and evil after a fortuitous meal of a wandering monk's alms. This marked the starting point of its own trek to immortality, where modest achievements after five hundred years allowed for human form. His surname was Hu—in accordance with fox customs, as that was how the character for *fox* sounded—and he gave himself the name of Wude. Changming rounded out his courtesy name, and thus some called him Longcrow.

Born with jet-black fur, Wude was a bona fide black fox. Prior to his mental awakening, his favorite hobby was to visit farmhouses and steal chickens under the cover of night. Although he later grasped the error of his ways, the habit proved difficult to quit. Every time a fasting period concluded, he would procure two chickens from a random village or town, and sacrifice them upon the altar of his body.

Chickens were widely regarded as possessing the Five Virtues—civility, martial prowess, courage, benevolence, and trustworthiness—and also went by the moniker of "Commandant Longcrow." Hence, Wude elected to pay homage to the virtuous fowl by naming himself *wŭ* for the number five, and *dé* for virtue.

When Wude first attempted human form, he dared only reveal the fruits of his accomplishments to a creek next to his home. First it was a fox head and a human body, then a human body with foxy paws or furry legs. When he finally managed four complete limbs and clear human features, his pesky tail insisted on coming out to play.

He tried the transformation art again and again, but the results were never wholly satisfying. Coming up empty-handed after repeated brainstorming for possible solutions, he manifested a black hat and robes in defeat. Tucking his tail inside the outfit, he set off in search of guidance.

Five miles away by a thousand-year-old pine tree, there lived a green snake with an eight-hundred-year history on the path of cultivation. His name was Cangyuan and he bore an exceedingly gentle soul. He often extended advice and pointers to Wude. Being a self-made cultivator, the fox had no formal master to call his own. Therefore, the frequent exchanges gave rise to a deep friendship.

A palm-sized hollow amid the pine tree's roots presented an unassuming front to the typical eye. It seemed far too small to be good for anything, but cultivators like Wude and Cangyuan needed only to shrink themselves for entry. This was where the green snake called home.

Still far off in the distance, Wude glimpsed a man waiting in front of the hollow. The fox made haste and offered a cupped-fist bow in approach.

"Brother Cangyuan, what brings you out here?"

The gentleman in green robes smiled. "I happened to cast lots today and divined that you, my sage younger brother, would find some initial success on your path. Seeing that you would soon pay a visit to my humble abode, I wished to wait in welcome." He looked Wude over and continued with praise, "Your human form is of striking appearance and uncommon bearing—a sign that your cultivation runs deep. My greatest felicitations."

However, Wude hung his head and turned around, allowing the bushy tail to peek out for a cheerful shake at his friend.

"My face and limbs may be complete, but this final detail lingers stubbornly no matter what I do. I'm sure Brother Cangyuan knows just as well as I that it's one thing for foxes to flick our tails around when playing inside the mountains, but to do so in the world outside would scare the wits out of others."

Flabbergasted, words escaped Cangyuan for a long moment. The incongruous sight of a wagging fox tail extending from a human figure prompted him to yank out a few hairs. *It's real!*

Wude yelped in pain and whipped around, eyes wide. "B-brother Cangyuan, what was that for?"

"Don't be alarmed! Your foolish older brother was just a bit astonished. Judging from your appearance, it seems that you have yet to pass your heavenly tribulation?"

Complete bafflement blossomed on Wude's face. He was a minor spirit who'd only begun his journey after a chance encounter. Gaps in knowledge were a common occurrence for him, and it seemed another loomed over the horizon.

"All things in life have their destinies laid out accordingly." Cangyuan pulled his friend over to a seat on bluestone rock. "Those meant to be beasts on land are beasts on land. Those meant to fly as birds will fly as birds. Even humans can only be humans for the entirety of their lives. Cultivation allows us to break free from this cycle and defy heaven's will.

"Thus, it goes without saying that some suffering is necessary. The hardships of cultivation are a given, but we must also weather the jealousies of the heavens themselves. All of us must endure heavenly tribulations before our cultivation can advance to the next level. Though we emulate humans in taking their form, even they must brave a tribulation to seek immortality."

"Then, my tail can be concealed only after persisting through my tribulation?" Melancholy colored Wude's expression.

"Precisely."

"What is a tribulation and how do I weather it?"

"In my humble opinion, seeing as your path and mine are essentially the same, it will be a trial of thunder."

"Thunder?" Wude's mouth twisted. "Do you mean thunder and lightning from the skies?"

"Indeed, forty-nine bolts, to be exact. Each and every one of them is to land directly on your body."

Chills swept Wude's body and the icy grasp of fear closed around his heart. Color drained from his face to filter out through the bristling hairs of his tail.

"Even one or two ordinary bolts require sequestering in a cave for safety. Forty-nine bolts will cook me like grilled meat! Please hurry and impart the method to survive them, Brother Cangyuan. Surely you know of one. My endless gratitude will be yours."

"When undergoing a heavenly tribulation, one must fortify their internal energy and use whatever arts at their disposal, be it transformation or manipulation of the elements." Cangyuan lowered his head, brows furrowed in thought. "Recovery takes place automatically upon successfully passing the trial. Though the tribulations are harrowing, they are immensely rewarding for our cultivation. However, given the humble level of your cultivation, it would be a tall order to endure all forty-nine bolts by yourself. When I underwent my first tribulation, a senior advised that I combine my efforts with a peer and arrange ourselves in a formation for joint defense. Do you have a companion of your species, sage brother? Perhaps the dual cultivation method of the Taoist school will prove useful."

Cangyuan's suggestion shifted Wude's worry to joy. One of his best friends was a white fox who went by the name of Yuzhu and lived on the main peak of Mount Emei. Her cultivation ran four hundred years long and she was a perfect candidate. As it happens, this method was typically a precursor to marriage, as participants often became lifelong lovers.

Wude requested that Cangyuan divine when the heavenly tribulation would arrive. After learning that it would take place five days from now, the black fox took his leave and set off in search of Yuzhu.

The white fox lived only a day's travel away, a short trip in ordinary times. However, anxiety gnawed at Wude and worries assailed his mind. He deployed an earthbending art to flash through the distance and arrived in the next instant. He was greeted by a mountain cave beside a turquoise pond, fed by a lively creek—Yuzhu's residence. Fragrant grass waving in a lush field set the scene for tranquil serenity. This was truly an optimal place for cultivation. Sweet warmth prickled at Wude's heart upon his arrival.

There were only a dozen years of difference between his cultivation tenure and Yuzhu's. They'd trained and played together when they were still foxes. In fact, they were childhood sweethearts, and even now employed intimate terms of address for each other. Yuzhu had achieved human form faster than him, but her ears and tail still plagued her. This would be a wonderful solution for her as well. Not only would he resolve his worries about the impending tribulation, but he'd be able to spend time with the object of his affection.

Ah, good things really do come in pairs!

As the abacus of Wude's thoughts clattered madly away, a figure rose from the turquoise waters. Raven-black hair, flawless skin, clear eyes, red lips. The stunning view revealed itself to be a woman who could launch a thousand ships. But upon closer look, two furry ears upon her head clued him in to the fact that this was Yuzhu.

Wude's heart pounded fiercely as he bade her hello. An ivory-white robe manifested around Yuzhu with a turn of the body, and upon reaching shore, she materialized a stone table and a set of chairs.

"My tribulation is to arrive in five days." After an exchange of greetings, Wude cut straight to the point. "Will little sister Yuzhu render aid and take me as your cultivation partner, for better, for worse, for richer, for poorer, in sickness and in health? Your older brother will gladly dash his brains out on the ground in reciprocation."

However, the lady's slender brows knitted together and she hesitated. "Please don't fault me, brother, I know the might of the heavenly tribulation as well. My powers are weak and wouldn't amount to much if I helped, not to mention . . ."

Wude urgently pressed her to continue, nerves twanging loudly in response to the note of rejection in her voice.

Yuzhu blushed and mumbled, ". . . not to mention, I already have a dual cultivation partner. How can I bear to leave him behind and sail off into the sunset with my good brother?"

The tender question crashed into Wude like a bolt of lightning, as if his tribulation had arrived before schedule. Ears ringing and head spinning, he squeezed out a smile that proved uglier than tears.

"It's been but thirty years since we last saw each other. How could little sister seek out someone else as soon as you emerged from seclusion?"

"Brother, you too know that it's been thirty years." Yuzhu smiled despite the tone of censure from Wude. "Humans have a saying that the river flows thirty years to the east, and thirty years to the west. Through the ups and downs of life, the only constant is change. The times now are hardly the times then.

"My powers are weak and I too need to undergo my trial. Preparations had to be made. Jiulang has progressed far on his path and is true to me. I couldn't help but answer in kind. If I devote myself to good deeds in the future, then I might be so blessed as to reach immortality at the same time as him." The lady turned to the mouth of the cave. "Jiulang, do hurry out and greet Brother Wude!"

A fat civet came waddling out of the cave by the lakeshore, bearing round eyes that were a perfect parallel to a stomach as wide as a beer jug. Russet fur ran along his body and ended in a long, thick tail ringed with nine circles of white fur. His face split into a wide grin as soon as he glimpsed Wude. By the time he stopped in front of the fox, he'd transformed into a stocky, ruddy-faced man with a mouth full of gleaming teeth.

The civet greeted Wude enthusiastically, and casually imparted over the course of a few pleasantries that he possessed seven hundred years of cultivation. Since he and Yuzhu had joined hands as cultivation partners, they would weather their heavenly tribulation together and set up their formation in a few days' time.

Glum ruefulness flooded Wude's heart to see the loving couple dote on each other in front of him. Unable to bear another word of their sweet nothings and at a complete loss for what to do, he quickly took his leave.

He couldn't be bothered with the earthbending art on his way back and struck out on foot, slowly trudging his way home. Here he was, all by his lonesome while his childhood sweetheart had already found someone with whom to spend the rest of her days. These years of cultivation had been long and marked with difficulty, and it appeared that they would grow lonelier still.

Bereft of a master, he'd wandered lost on many twists and turns, and fallen flat on his face more than once. When he'd finally attained some small accomplishments, looming danger prevented him from grasping it in hand. If he didn't successfully weather the tribulation, he'd suffer becoming a mere wild fox again at best, or be dusted to nothing but ashes at worst.

A passing creek reflected the delicately sculpted features of a cultured gentleman. *But Yuzhu would rather lower herself to be with a fat civet!* She thought nothing of their years together and their shared memories. Ah, the world truly abounded with the cold-hearted!

Wude sank further into melancholy the more he considered things.

But, as anxious as he was about the upcoming trial, there was nothing to be done about it. The best course of action was to pay another visit to Cangyuan and see what steps there were to be taken. However, someone called out to him before he'd taken a few more steps.

Wude turned back to see Jiulang hailing him, transforming back into animal form as he ran. Wude remained where he was, giving the civet time to wipe at his sweaty forehead when he caught up.

"Please stay your steps, Brother Wude, this humble one has a few things to say. Yuzhu and I were inadequate hosts earlier, please find it in your heart to forgive us."

Still floundering in a vat of jealousy, Wude refrained from responding with anything other than a few grunts. The civet grinned broadly, reaching up to scratch his now-furry head with a claw, and swept clean a nearby rock with his tail. He invited the fox to take a seat before plopping down himself.

"Ah, this hits the spot," sighed the civet. "I never got why we had to take human form, anyway. If you ask me, even the heavens are boring. Damn, I'd take having a good time in the mountains over this shit any day!"

Displeasure set in at hearing the civet's coarse speech. "Since that is the case, why dual cultivate with little sister Yuzhu?"

Jiulang chuckled bashfully. "Since Yuzhu wants to be an immortal, of course I must stick with her." The irreverent civet turned serious again. "Brother Wude, I forgot to mention just now that I have an idea when it comes to the tribulation."

Wude's eyes lit up, but skepticism still swirled in his heart.

"The thunder tribulation is under the jurisdiction of the God of Thunder. He carries out his duties with the appropriate instruments whenever the hour for tribulation is nigh. What worries are there for a difficult trial, if Brother Wude sends up an official petition for leniency and presents some proper offerings?"

"Could I ask for an exemption instead?"

"You cannot."

"Then, a delay of the trial?"

"Not even a minute will be granted."

"Then, fewer bolts?"

"Not even one."

"Then, what's the point of petitioning the gods?" Wude deflated.

"Brother Wude is truly such an honest character." The civet beamed. "Just think about it: casting thunderbolts around is just an assigned duty. There's always room to maneuver when it comes to duties. No one would be able to withstand thunderbolts in quick succession, but what if the bolts were spaced out? What if some breathing space was granted? What a thought, a most interesting line of thought!"

Comprehension struck Wude. "Who should the petition be addressed to?"

"Addressing it to the 'Assorted Deities Under the Banner of the Venerated Celestial Who Disseminates the Sound of Thunder of the Primordials in the Nine Heavens' will suffice."

The civet's recommendation greatly lifted Wude's spirits. He bowed again and again with cupped fists, babbled a litany of gratitude and compliments, and only then reluctantly took his leave.

Making haste back to his residence, he carefully set brush to paper and sought prime specimens for the Three Sacrifices of chicken, fish, and pig. Setting up a table with fine incense and his offerings, Wude waited for an auspicious hour before bowing, kneeling on the ground and pressing his forehead down in a reverent kowtow.

The round of preparations extended deep into the night before he wrapped up. Having finally managed his Great Matter, the realization that he should update his reptilian friend didn't strike until he was ready for bed. Fatigue encroaching on his mind, sleep overtook him after he mentally inscribed a visit to his friend on the morrow.

The jade hare of the moon rests in the west,

while from the east rises the golden bird of the sun.

A most pleasant night of sleep refreshed Wude with high spirits. In fine fettle, he attired himself as a scholar and set out for Cangyuan's residence. He would first make a detailed recounting of everything that had happened yesterday, then seek out further guidance from his sagacious friend.

Free from worries, he was in a mood to stop and smell the roses on his morning stroll. But halfway up a hill, he rounded the bend and saw thunderclouds swiftly gathering at the foot of the hill ahead. He could almost taste the lightning snaking through the heavy clouds. Elsewhere reigned the burgeoning azure of early morning and a clear firmament, which only served to highlight the eeriness of that one patch of sky.

Shock gripped Wude's heart as he recalled all that Cangyuan had told him. *Are there other fellow Taoists undergoing their heavenly tribulation today? Why don't I go down and take a look?*

Making haste to the foot of the hill, he noted with a dry mouth that the thunderclouds were indeed more ominous here. They cast a large patch of shade on the sparse forest, draping the area in a sinister darkness. Wude didn't dare draw nearer, instead locating a hiding place fifteen meters out, behind some boulders.

He poked his head out, only to be startled by rolling thunder and crackling lightning that crept down like a silver snake to smite a pine tree. Weak at the knees from the rumbling roars, he tumbled into a seated position and clutched his head. Deafening pops and bangs frightened him so thoroughly that his tail refused to be concealed. It swept back and forth on the ground, as if to sweep away his nerves.

The area brightened after a few more claps of thunder. Wude reluctantly cracked open his eyes to see thunderclouds dissipate from the sky. All was as it'd been before, apart from the poor pine tree, still billowing black smoke with a heavily charred scent.

Was it a tree spirit who'd undergone its tribulation? While Wude's thoughts ran wild with speculation, the last thundercloud unraveled and sent a shadowy figure to the ground. The fox's eyes sharpened to see a strange vision—a monster more than six meters in height, sporting horns on top of a pig's face. The fleshy wings sprouting from its back were a good three meters long, while a tunic of deep burgundy covered the rest of its body, save for a leopard's tail. Rounded out by gold claws, the monster was both savagely peculiar and extremely awe-inspiring. Heart leaping into his throat, Wude cautiously wondered if this monster was the God of Thunder. He watched breathlessly as the creature fetched a blackened corpse from the pine tree—a macaque. Lost in thought while peeping, he failed to notice that the creature had sensed the additional pair of eyes. Enormous eyes swept his way, locking onto Wude with a piercing gaze.

Frightened out of his wits, the fox took off in the opposite direction. However, a string of fireballs came soaring from behind him—bolts of lightning in clear skies! They blasted the boulders to smithereens and sent rock chips flying everywhere. Wude hadn't even taken three steps before a sudden pain from his behind signaled that he'd been picked up and was now hanging by his tail.

A savage face with sharp knives for teeth set in a bloody, yawning maw boomed in Wude's face. "Whence does this little monster hail, skulking and creeping about like this?"

Two brisk shakes by the tail shook Wude right back into his animal form.

"And I wondered who would be so bold as to spy on the thunder god!" Peculiar cackling rang in the air. "It's a little fox! You don't look too big, but you'll serve as this seat's appetizer!"

Wude twisted and struggled at this, shrieking for his life. "Mercy, Grandpa Thunder God! Oh mercy! This lowly one was just passing by, and never dreamed of giving offense to such a great venerated one!"

The thunder god licked his wide chops with a long tongue measuring one-third of a meter. He leered. "I don't care if you were passing by or not. Anyone who offends this seat shall suffer the consequences!"

"Grandpa Thunder God, will my offerings yesterday possibly make amends for my offenses today? Please grant this lowly one a reprieve!"

That entreaty proved useful. One smack of the lips, and the thunder god discarded the fox, sizing up the small animal in a jumble at his feet. Wude scrambled back up, eyes wide from shock and still badly shaken.

"You're an interesting one, fox. When did you worship me yesterday? Why do I bear no recollection of this?"

Wude crouched low to the ground on all fours, prostrating himself with abject humility. "If Grandpa Thunder God will permit a report, this lowly one burned a petition last night to the Venerated Celestial, offering the Three Sacrifices in a plea for leniency in my upcoming thunder tribulation. Did Grandpa Thunder God not receive my offerings?"

"There are many thunder gods in heaven," harrumphed the thunder god. "Your sacrifices did not make their way to me. But count your lucky stars today, for this seat happens to hold jurisdiction over this mountain's thunder and lightning. Serve me well, and I might consider letting you off the hook."

Delight flooded Wude's heart, and he almost ground his pointy mouth into the dirt in thanks. "Thank you for your mercy, Grandpa Thunder God. This lowly one will carry out your every wish as my most ardent command!"

The thunder god barked in laughter and returned to the pine tree. He turned to Wude after kicking the macaque's corpse. "My duties for today are complete. Hurry and fetch ale and meat. If they are not tasty, I will fill my stomach with you instead."

Wude's eyes flitted to the macaque again and again as he screwed up the courage to ask, "Is the one who lies at your glorious divine feet one who just attempted their heavenly tribulation?"

"A mere monkey spirit. It's a pity he was unsuccessful. This will be your end too, little fox, if you fail to be a good host."

Repeatedly stammering, "Not at all, this lowly one wouldn't dare," Wude took his leave and sprinted to town. Bereft of alternatives, he transformed some leaves into silver bits, and used them to purchase a bundle of roast chicken and strong spirits. Concealing himself with an invisibility technique, he made quick time back to the side of a thunder god completely out of patience.

The divine one cursed and complained as he feasted on the offerings. Wude didn't dare breathe a peep and danced careful attention off on the side. Mouth watering profusely at the smell of roast chicken, the fox mutely looked on while the thunder god dug into the repast. Hard swallows of saliva would have to do for Wude, the agony of which could not be described in words.

Upon washing down the final bite with a swig of liquor, the thunder god deigned to ask, "Little fox, when is your thunder tribulation?"

"O mighty one, my tribulation is in four days."

Licking each of his golden claws clean, a thoughtful expression crossed the thunder god's face. "In that case, I will dally a few more days in Mount Emei, as opposed to hurrying back. What say you, little fox?"

How would Wude ever dare say no? A fawning smile creased his lips, and he expressed such delight that one would think he'd found a statuette made of pure gold.

Thus began Wude's days of servitude, so preoccupied with showing off the sights that he didn't even have time to return home. Over the next three days, the thunder god and the fox idled all around the mountain. They refrained from visiting heavily populated areas, instead preferring copses where fowl nested and land animals trod.

To see was to desire, and the thunder god's desire was Wude's directive. The thunder god bore a craving for mountain goat when he sighted gray wolves, and hungered for geese when he glimpsed sparrows. Ever since that first meal of roast chicken and liquor, the god demanded chicken at every meal.

Mouthwatering fragrances assaulted the fox's nose every time, but not even a bone was ever awarded to Wude. He grew used to the constant complaints of his stomach—his only companion apart from rushing to and fro as a divine errand boy. He busied himself with either exquisite preparations of mountain game or transmuting more silver to purchase alcohol and meat from town.

One day, the thunder god strolled to where dots of fuzzy white marked a green expanse. Looking down at the bunnies racing and frolicking in the grass, he licked his wide mouth and turned to Wude.

"Little fox, do you know what the tastiest part of a rabbit is?"

Wude looked down and answered respectfully, "Please enlighten this humble one."

"You are a fox, yet you claim ignorance?"

"This lowly one has always just haphazardly eaten my fill and never paid attention."

"The tastiest part is the ear. Skinned, steamed, sauced, and served with a cup of good wine."

Almost drooling, Wude bobbed his head rapidly in agreement. The thunder god beamed and pointed at the wild rabbits. "Go nab those little rascals, this seat hasn't had rabbit ears in such a long time . . ."

That day, Wude cleaned out the rabbits in this part of the woods. Finally slaking the divine one's hunger, the fox traveled to town to "purchase" more chickens and alcohol. But when presented to the thunder god, the jugs of ale sailed far, far away with a mighty throw.

"After drinking and partaking of rabbit ears this afternoon, how will the same suffice for dinner? Doesn't Mount Emei produce good tea? Go fetch some, on the double!"

Though Wude scraped and bowed his apologies, flames of fury roared to life in his heart. If there were any backbone to be found in him, he would've smacked his bundle of trash onto the big head in front of him. However, he instinctively hunched back down when he thought of the blackened macaque corpse and meekly went off in search of tea.

While Wude scurried around Mount Emei as a personal servant, someone on the other side of the mountain fretfully searched all over for him.

After imparting a sound plan to survive the thunder tribulation, Cangyuan saw neither hide nor tail of his friend again. At first, the green snake surmised that Wude had gone off to arrange a formation with the white fox. Worry crept in when three days passed without a word, and he paid a visit to Wude's abode.

A deserted residence greeted him; it looked like it'd lain empty for several days. Thoroughly beset by anxiety, Cangyuan asked around and obtained the white fox's address. He found Yuzhu on the banks of a lake, but the one by her side was a rotund civet rather than Wude. Mouth agape with surprise, the snake asked the merry couple if they'd seen his friend. When Jiulang conveyed everything that had taken place, Cangyuan's eyelid twitched forebodingly.

It was one thing if Wude managed to successfully bribe the God of Thunder, but what if some other manner of mischievous spirit took advantage of the fox in need? What if they swindled the trusting fox out of house and home, or worse?

The more Cangyuan's thoughts traveled down this path, the more his heart raced with concern. Recruiting a fellow Taoist in his search—a black bear named Yueya with eight hundred years of cultivation—the two looked all over the mountain for the next few hours, leaving no stone unturned.

Splitting up to cover more ground, the two finally found a black fox fishing in a creek on the main mountain peak. Cangyuan quickly performed a hand seal to send a verbal message through the air to Jiulang, while he approached calling Wude's name.

The black fox turned around. It was none other than his erstwhile missing friend.

Irritation supplanting his disquiet, Cangyuan adopted the tone of an older brother and launched into a lecture. "You've sent me on quite a wild goose chase, my good brother! Your tribulation is set for tomorrow, yet you're of a mind to sit here and fish?"

Two lines of tears streaked down Wude's black fur. Seeing Cangyuan was to see his savior. He threw down his fishing pole and burst into loud sobs, rather startling the snake.

"I followed Jiulang's instructions and sent up a petition and offerings to the heavens, praying that the God of Thunder would show me mercy. However, I was caught in the act of witnessing the god smiting a monkey spirit, and taken as a pageboy. I've been waiting hand and foot on Grandpa Thunder God these days, plying him with boundless food and drink.

"I catch rabbits if he wants their ears, I dig into bird nests if he wants wings. He said this morning that he has yet to taste the fresh fish of the mountains, so I set up a fishing spot here. Ai, not a single grain of rice has passed my lips for three days. It'd be one thing if I were fasting for cultivation, but I have to suffer the agony of watching him munch on roast chicken every day!"

Cangyuan's brows were tightly drawn together. "The God of Thunder is a righteous and proper god. How can he be such a glutton and a carnivore? Can he be a fake?" Misgivings grew when Wude relayed the ins and outs of their meeting. "This is highly suspicious indeed. Please lead the way, sage brother. Allow me to pry into the matter and ascertain the truth within."

Wude nodded rapidly. Cangyuan called upon his arts to fetch a few fish out of the water, so that his friend could adequately fulfill his duties. He then concealed himself and followed Wude to where the thunder god awaited.

The vaunted deity was still waiting in a copse of trees when Wude returned with the fresh fish. Not daring to draw too near, Cangyuan stopped roughly ten meters away and watched his friend skin and debone the fish.

When Wude picked up some kindling to light a fire, the thunder god solved that problem with a snap of the fingers. A dry branch now burning away merrily, Wude set up the fish over the flames and bustled off to warm some ale.

The entire sequence of events struck Cangyuan as deeply wrong, and he was about to slip away when he noticed Yueya surreptitiously hiding nearby. The two exchanged a look and retreated into the distance.

After he offered both baked fish and warm ale, Wude took advantage of a lull in his duties to convene with the two in a nearby outcropping of rocks.

"That useless plague lord glutton! He eats more than a pig! His mouth never stops chewing, so why hasn't he exploded from overfeeding yet?!"

Cangyuan offered a few words of comfort and reason. "The situation doesn't look right to me, that one shows none of the aura of a righteous and proper god. He's certainly very suspicious. Do you have any words of wisdom, Yueya?"

"There are many thunder gods in the heavens and they come in all shapes and sizes." The black bear stroked the white fur of his chest in thought. "However, I have a friend who's long ascended to immortality. He told me that whenever a thunder god calls upon his powers, he must do so through his treasures. They wield a drum of thunder in their left hand and brandish an awl in their right. Did this being carry those instruments when you first met him, Brother Wude?"

Searching through his memory, Wude shook his head. "He did not. Could they have been put away?"

It was Cangyuan's turn to shake his head. "The instruments of a proper god are no trifling matter. He wouldn't be able to call fire like he did just now if they are stowed away."

"I see." Wude's heart clenched. "Then the fish-eater is no thunder god at all!"

"There is an auxiliary branch of thunder gods called thunder ghosts," Yueya mused. "They number not among immortals and neither are they animal spirits. Though they too can call down thunder and light fires, their powers are humble. They frequently summon thunder and lightning to smite beasts for food, but to do so exhausts their powers. They are like regular spirits for ten days afterward. Wise brother Wude, have you seen him use any powers over the past couple of days?"

Wude shook his head blankly. He'd worked himself to the bone during this period of time, and truly hadn't witnessed that one display anything out of the ordinary. Fact and observation lining up with each other, the flames of rage in his heart were fanned into a veritable bonfire.

He wanted to explode! All of his toiling and tiptoeing on tenterhooks had been nothing but entertainment to that one! Blood rushing to his head, he was about to charge over and rain down his version of fire and thunder, but the snake quickly restrained him.

"Quell your anger, wise brother Wude! Although that vile spawn can't summon thunder like the gods, his fire-calling abilities seem perfected. Keep yourself from brash action!"

"It is your tribulation day tomorrow, sage brother. Wouldn't it be a waste of power if you tangled with that thunder ghost now?"

"So what of my thunder tribulation? I've been a plaything for that bastard for so many days! Am I to end up worse than that monkey spirit?"

Yueya stroked his tuft of white fur again. "I've also heard from my immortal friend that the thunder gods care deeply for their good reputation. Since this thunder ghost is deceiving and beguiling in their name, his capture is sure to make them happy."

Cangyuan clapped his hands together. "Yueya speaks truly! If you wish to avenge yourself and survive your tribulation, good brother, capturing this thunder ghost will prove immensely useful!"

The new train of thought slightly derailed Wude from his fury. He shook his black fur and carefully formulated a plan with his two friends.

Night gave way to day in the blink of an eye, and with it came Wude's day of heavenly tribulation. Early this morning, he sought out an empty clearing to receive his trial by thunder.

"You're a sharp one, little fox." The so-called thunder god flashed a grin. "Don't worry, this seat will not make things difficult for you."

Beet-faced with "gratitude," Wude inwardly stewed with anger. He led the thunder ghost to a grassy slope, one encircled by a bevy of mountain peaks and lush forests. The fox picked up various multicolored stones and laid them in a pattern of the eight trigrams. Each trigram consisted of three lines, broken or unbroken, and represented the different forces of nature. Once finished, he took a stand in the center of the pattern where safety can presumably be found. He bowed to the thunder ghost.

"This lowly one's life is in your mighty hands."

"Don't you worry about it," guffawed the thunder ghost. "Just sit down with peace of mind! When is your tribulation?"

"Isn't that Grandpa Thunder God's duty?" Wude smiled. "What are you asking me for?"

The thunder ghost's expression shifted and he huffed, "I am just testing you. If I undertook my duties on time while you loafed around in ignorance, wouldn't the lightning bolts smite you to death then?"

Wude couldn't be bothered with arguing and made his apologies. "When the hour strikes noon."

At the thunder ghost's nod, Wude sat down and settled into meditation. Meanwhile, strains of a mountain folk song danced teasingly on the wind. Faint and breezy, the melody slowly grew in volume, accompanied by the enticing waft of rich fragrance.

Nose twitching, glee stole into the thunder ghost's heart—this was a delicious bouquet of fine wine! He called out for Wude to fetch some for him, but no response was forthcoming to his summons. The sun high overhead indicated that it was near noon. Eyes screwed shut, the black fox seemed insensate to the world. There was nothing for it, the thunder ghost had to seek out the piquant libations himself.

A tall, stocky man heaving two jars of wine on a shoulder pole was found on a mountain path. Sweat poured profusely down his face. He'd temporarily set aside his burdens for a spot of rest against some rocks.

The thunder ghost leapt out in a frightful manner, screeching and caterwauling with claws extended. Seeing a horned monster in a burgundy wrap lunge at him, the man shrieked in horror and fled in abject terror. All thought of his goods having flown out of his mind, the man tripped and scrabbled frantically in the dirt to get away. How he wished he'd been born with another set of legs to run with!

The thunder ghost quickly hugged the two jars to himself, taking in a deep breath of the wine's sumptuous scent. He brought his spoils back to Wude's side, ready to drink to his heart's content. Ripping off the seal and dumping the contents of one jar into his mouth, he quickly chugged half of it in one mouthful. The wine's finish lingered on a prolonged note; there was no joy greater than this!

Wiping off his mouth, the thunder ghost fished out half a roast chicken from yesterday, tearing at the meat and drinking with gusto. Quaffing both jars in less than ten minutes, a now muddleheaded thunder ghost blinked slowly, fighting off the throes of sleep.

At this time, a head poked out from behind a rock—the strapping wine courier who'd fled earlier. Seeing the thunder ghost stagger around with an unfocused look, he pursed his lips for a whistle.

From a nearby grove of trees slithered a green snake as thick as a human wrist, slowly entangling the thunder ghost's feet and dragging him to the ground. The deeply meditating Wude suddenly sprang up as well, conjuring a hemp rope out of nowhere and rushing to bind their quarry.

Though the thunder ghost was properly tipsy, such a large disturbance roused him back to some semblance of sobriety. He struggled furiously, spittle flying everywhere as he cursed. "Treacherous and wicked! How dare you attack a divine thunder god! I'll have your heads for this, I will!"

"If you're a thunder god, then I'm the Jade Emperor, the highest emperor of all the gods! You've deceived me for so long and forced me into thievery so many times. It's me or you today!" cursed Wude.

In his animal form, Cangyuan hissed with a flickering tongue. "No need for further talk, good brother. Hurry and tie this fellow up."

Wude firmly yanked the ropes around the thunder ghost's arms, piling on the insults. "You damned filthy lout, eating me out of hearth and home for four days! All those chickens! I usually only have the luxury of one a month, but you had a veritable feast of them, and not once did you offer me any part!"

Although flailing as wildly as he could, the thunder ghost found he was unable to bring his strength to bear. When Wude tightened his bonds, Cangyuan loosened himself and flashed into human form. The wine courier ran over as well, returning to his black bear form.

"Did you enjoy those two jars?" Cangyuan smiled at their captive. "I added snake venom to the wine. It won't claim your life, just render you languid and listless. You'll soon be a puddle of weak lethargy."

Wude couldn't help but bring his foot down on the leopard tail flicking about on the grass. "Don't you know how to summon lightning? Why don't you call down a few bolts and hammer us to death?"

Pain from his tail being trampled upon drove the inebriated state out of the thunder ghost. His tunic suddenly expanded like a rubber ball and he opened his mouth, breathing a few fireballs right onto Wude and Yueya. When the smoke cleared the air, it left behind patches of burnt fur and bald skin, as both were in their animal forms.

"Beware, the scoundrel can breathe fire! Be careful, wise brother!"

Jumping in surprise, Wude quickly dodged to the side. Yueya, however, grasped the two wine jars and heaved them at the thunder ghost. They smashed to pieces on his forehead in spectacular fashion, and the pain drove his fury to new heights. Though he was tied up, he abruptly sprang up and shot off fireball after fireball.

As bulky as Yueya was, he still hopped and sidestepped adroitly, dodging most of the ones sent his way. Skilled in the arts of coldness and shadow, Cangyuan easily dispelled any fireballs that reached him. Only Wude ended up worse for wear with his lower cultivation. His fluffy tail was singed after a few fireballs struck glancing blows.

The sun continued its climb in the sky, dispassionately overseeing the battle below. Though the thunder ghost couldn't summon his namesake, its fire arts were never-ending. He suddenly belched out a small stream of flames and burned away the ropes constricting him. Cangyuan had infused them with his powers so they wouldn't break no matter the amount of force straining them. But they were ordinary material in the end, and thus highly flammable.

"Watch out, the fraudster's about to break free!" the green snake called out in warning.

The last of the ropes fluttered to the ground as ashes before he finished speaking. Unfurling his fleshy wings, the thunder ghost beat them vigorously, whipping up a forceful gale.

Two more empty wine jars appeared in Yueya's hands. "The hour has arrived, but the venom still lingers in his body! Now's our chance!"

Patches of thunderclouds suddenly scudded across the clear blue skies above them. The thunderclouds churned and roiled against one another, completely blotting out the heavens. Lightning occasionally zigzagged through, like silver snakes flicking their tongues.

Wude lifted his head, beset with acute paroxysms of dread. He sprawled boneless on the ground in a shivering heap, like someone had removed all of his muscles and strength. He knew that he should immediately enter a meditative trance and bring all facets of his mind to bear in deep concentration, but he couldn't move a finger.

Instead, he felt that his soul was about to shatter and scatter to the four winds. *This* was the aura of a true god. None of the trepidation and alarm he'd felt upon seeing the thunder ghost could compare.

Wude silently bemoaned his dire circumstances. This was his day of reckoning! Great pangs of sorrow rose in his heart, not at all alleviated by the tears staining his black fur.

Cangyuan and Yueya were still contending with the thunder ghost. Even though the cheat didn't have any great arts of his own, he lacked not for fireballs. An unceasing stream of them proved incredibly vexing. Cangyuan brought all of his strength to the fight to aid his friend, but the results weren't quite what he desired.

The thunder ghost also seemed to have detected which of the three was weakest and concentrated his fire on Wude. The fox's two companions blocked the vast majority of a great surge in fireballs, but could only watch helplessly as three of them made a beeline for the black fox curled up on the ground.

BOOM!

A thick bolt of lightning split the air, halting the three fireballs in their tracks. All combatants on the ground started, raising their heads upward unbidden.

Wude gawked through his tears, seeing a human face with a bird's beak peering out of the clouds. It was followed by an upper body that wielded the instruments to call thunder and lightning. Eyes gleaming bright as mirrors scanned the ground, looking first at Wude, then at the thunder ghost. With a wave of one hand, a bolt of lightning crashed into the thunder ghost and threw him to the ground, tunic in rags and charred all over. The thunder god up high waved another hand and reduced the thunder ghost to miniature form, collecting him into the clouds.

Cangyuan and Yueya pressed themselves to the ground, not daring to give the slightest hint of disrespect. Only Wude remained staring dumbly at the thunder god, completely oblivious to the meaningful glances that the snake shot at him.

After capturing the mischief-maker, the thunder god trained his eyes on Wude. A peal of laughter rang out from the pointy beak, rumbling across the sky in grand echoes, preceding a conversation that delighted Wude.

"Are you Hu Wude of Mount Emei's second peak, the fox spirit to undergo heavenly tribulation today?"

Wude bent over and touched his forehead to the ground. "That is indeed this lowly one."

"This degenerate has been falsely evoking the name of the thunder gods, plaguing people and spirits alike with indiscriminate fire and lightning. It is to your great merit that you have lured him here for me to capture."

Smiling beatifically, Wude kowtowed again.

"However, your sacrifice and petition a few days ago bore intent to meddle with official divine business. As such, merit and demerit balance out. Seeing as it is your first tribulation, I do not intend to pose undo difficulty upon you. However, you must henceforth conduct yourself with proper protocol and propriety."

Heart racing with nerves, Wude stammered out his agreement.

The thunder god slowly retired back to the clouds, which began brewing with agitated lightning. Wude quickly sat up straight, clasped his front paws together, and circulated his breathing evenly.

Crack after crack of thunder roared with each bolt of lightning that descended upon the fox. However, the silvery snakes of electricity struck the air over his head and skimmed his back, traveling down his rear into the ground. Even with this show of mercy, the tribulation quaked Wude's frame until he felt like he would fall apart. Aches and pains beset him all over.

When the forty-nine bolts finally concluded, it was already late in the afternoon—the hour of the monkey. With the departure of the thunder god, so too did the thunderclouds disperse. Wude sagged and then keeled over like a sack of potatoes.

Cangyuan and Yueya had been waiting impatiently off to the side. They ran to help him up, the snake offering a stream of felicitations while the black bear chuckled merrily. "Congratulations, wise brother, you've passed your tribulation! Your powers will be elevated from now on!"

Wude squeezed out a smile—though happy that his cumbersome tail was no more, he was also apprehensive about the future. Judging from the thunder god's words, the divine ones in heaven had committed his name to memory. He likely wouldn't have an easy time of things in his next tribulation.

Relieved that the ordeal was over, Wude had no inkling that his future would be marked with endless brain-wracking every hundred years to survive his tribulations. He fathomed even less that a scholar would one year unintentionally wander into his anti-thunder formation and take the brunt of the trial for him. Thus, owing the hapless scholar a monumental favor, the fox would have to enter the world of humans to pay it back.

But that is a story for another time.

3

What Does the Fox Say?
狐狸说什么?

Xia Jia 夏笳

This irreverent exploration of language and translation in flash fiction form was originally written in English by Xia Jia

What Does the Fox Say?

By Xia Jia

The quick brown fox jumps over the lazy dog.

You type this sentence word by word, and wait.

It will be fun, you think. They said you could input anything that popped into your mind, and this one came to you. It might be the most widely known English-language pangram, containing all twenty-six letters of the alphabet, commonly used to test typewriters, computer keyboards, and show fonts. Brief, coherent, but mostly meaningless. You've typed it thousands of times and never wasted your time considering how computers **understand** this sentence.

The algorithm analyzes this sentence and recognizes two nouns (fox, dog), three adjectives (quick, brown, lazy), one verb (jump), two articles (the, the), one preposition (over), and one punctuation (period).

A sub-algorithm called "metonymy" lists 2,785 words associated with "fox" (including "fire," "twenty-first century," and "Ylvis"). In the category of "fairy tale" (which is randomly decided), it picks out one noun (forest) and the first sentence of a picture book ("A fox lives alone in the dark forest").

The other keyword, "dog," is processed simultaneously. Within 0.21 seconds, two new sentences appear on your screen.

The quick brown fox lives alone in the dark forest.

The lazy dog feels sad about that.

How does a human author compose a literary work? That's an interesting question. Someone may have told you they only need to grasp those wonderful tropes and rhythms whispered in their ears, and then rearrange them in a reasonable way. They may have told you that all creative processes depend on two elementary functions: intuition and logic. The former triggers the first spark of inspiration, while the latter completes the rest of the work.

That's why a masterpiece always follows a magical opening, just like a ripple follows a pebble.

"Mrs. Dalloway said she would buy the flowers herself."

"Un jour, j'étais âgée déjà, dans le hall d'un lieu public, un homme est venu vers moi."

"列位看官: 你道此书从何而来?"

That's why you, a smart Homo sapiens, were invited to provide the first sentence.

Another sub-algorithm called "binary opposition" analyzes the first new sentence; then it produces a pair of opposites ("dark forest" versus "wide world"), which leads to the next sentence, extracted from "The Ugly Duckling."

I think I'd better go out into the wide world.

Unluckily, an "interruption" happens (the dog meets the fox), linking with a similar situation in "Little Red Riding Hood."

She did not know what a wicked creature he was, and was not at all afraid of him.

The fox, who is friendly and innocent, chooses the same lines in *The Little Prince* to greet the dog.

I am a fox, come and play with me.

An "interdiction" is addressed to the fox, from *The Lord of the Rings*.

You shall not pass!

The fox decides upon a "counter-action," as Alice in Wonderland did.

I think I could, if I only knew how to begin.

The dog, then, places a "curse" on the fox, as the sea witch did on the little mermaid.

You will not have an immortal soul.
Then what does the fox say?

People do believe that machines are incapable of creative thinking. In 1949, Sir Geoffrey Jefferson, an eminent brain surgeon, delivered an address challenging the claim that machines can think, asserting that, "Not until a machine can write a sonnet or compose a concerto because of thoughts and emotions felt, and not by the chance fall of symbols, could we agree that machine equals brain—that is, not only write it but know that it had written it."

A reporter from *The Times* telephoned Alan Turing. He answered, "I do not think you can even draw the line about sonnets, though the comparison is perhaps a little bit unfair because a sonnet written by a machine will be better appreciated by another machine."

Now the story is finally complete.

One day in the future, a quick brown fox lives alone in the dark forest.

"How wide the world is!" says the fox. "I think I'd better go out into the wide world."

A lazy dog meets the fox on her way. The fox does not know what a wicked creature he is, and is not at all afraid of him.

"Good morning," says the fox. "I am a fox, come and play with me."

"Go back to the shadow!" says the dog. "You shall not pass!"

"I think I could, if I only knew how to begin," says the fox.

"No you can't," says the dog. "You will not have an immortal soul. You cannot procure one for yourself."

"Is that all?" says the fox. "I am master of a hundred tricks, and in addition to that I have a sackful of cunning. I feel sorry for you."

Quietly and lightly, the quick brown fox jumps over the lazy dog.

The lazy dog feels sad about that.

Now you, smart Homo sapiens, answer me.

Do you feel sad about that?

AUTHOR'S NOTE

"What Does the Fox Say," my second story written in English, follows "Let's Have a Talk," which was published in *Nature* in 2015 (https://www.nature.com/articles/522122a). Both of them involve artificial intelligence and linguistics, and animals as well.

As a non-native English speaker, writing in a second language is just like playing an imitation game in some way. "What Does the Fox Say" tries to develop a kind of "algorithm" to "generate" a story, which involves my cooperation with search engines and translation software. The truth is, this very intertextuality is the dominant mode to create as well as to read most of the works in our time: quotation, collage, tribute, deconstruction, parody. At the same time, however, these works are created in the network of human communication, and their meanings are made within that. Even if it accurately retrieves the sources of every sentence, an algorithm cannot recognize the implication of "I know where it comes from." Only you, as a smart Homo sapiens, can decode and enjoy that subtle pleasure.

4

Blackbird 黑鸟

Shen Dacheng 沈大成
Translated by Cara Healey 贺可嘉

Blackbird

By Shen Dacheng
Translated by Cara Healey

The full moon rose one winter night, suspended above the building. In the courtyard, a few steps down the front path, a young woman waited for strawberries to be delivered.

She wore a small blue cap atop her head. As she stepped outside, she draped her coat around her shoulders, the front open, revealing her blue uniform underneath. Although her hands were hidden in her uniform's pockets, it was not long before the cold air brought a red flush to her cheeks. After a moment, she turned and looked at the sky, cap askew.

The golden moonlight shone in all directions, even as the wind blew dark clouds, strand by strand, past the moon's now-dappled face. She heard a bird murmuring in a tree in the courtyard, crying out sorrowfully.

The rest of the sky was clear. The dark clouds seemed to pour between her and the moon, floating up from the roof: the dissipating auras of the elderly.

The building was a nursing home, and at that moment the warm rooms were crowded with elderly patients. Too much age, concentrated in one place, grew volatile, forming the dark mist rising up to the sky.

She was used to the elderly auras. She worked in the nursing home. As a new nurse, she was often assigned this type of job. Specifically, the arduous, filthy tasks that shook one out of a comfortable routine. Just that night, one of the elderly residents had been eating voraciously, talking to herself, until she began choking on a bit of food and someone had to fish it out of her throat.

The sound of a motorcycle and its lights cut through the night. The delivery man had arrived.

"Mrs. An's strawberries," she said in response to his question, as she accepted the box of fruit.

"Mrs. An is still alive?" The young man sat astride his motorcycle, one long leg touching the ground, forgetting courtesy in his shock. He did a quick calculation in his head of how much time had passed since he'd last seen her. He'd grown up since then. As a student, he had often been required by his school to volunteer at the nursing home in place of punishment. Back then, in his young eyes, Mrs. An had already been ancient, so old that she seemed ready to pass on, as if she were oversaturated. He and the other young volunteers hadn't had much work to do, and they pretended not to see her. After graduation he hadn't been admitted to any of the top universities, so he'd joined the army. After his discharge, he'd been unemployed until his current job.

Even after all that, Mrs. An was still there on this moonlit night, craving the first crop of fragrant, late winter strawberries.

The delivery man pulled back his outstretched leg, and the motorcycle sped away, sewing up the cut it had rent in the night. The mumbling of the strange bird in the courtyard grew clearer. Unlike the calls of joyous, lovely songbirds, this was a sonorous chant. The shadow of the tree concealed the bird, unseen but all-seeing in the night. The dark clouds still floated on the breeze, sometimes dense and sometimes thin, in a vain attempt to cover the moon.

The largest room in the nursing home was used as a multipurpose recreation room. It was the residents' main living space, where they could interact with each other. On weekends and holidays, chairs were lined up in rows, and a screen was brought in to show films. Sometimes, there was a kindhearted artist who would come by and play the piano. That night was an ordinary evening, so there were only ordinary evening activities. These so-called evening activities were the same as daytime activities: playing cards, watching TV, chatting, that sort of thing, only after dinner. The frailer residents and those who weren't interested didn't participate, but the majority were willing to idle away the hours before bedtime scattered about the recreation room, mostly watching TV.

Occasionally, the nurses bustled among the elderly residents. They all wore blue uniforms. The women pinned stiff caps to the tops of their heads, though the men did not. The most senior nurses were allowed to wear fleece cardigans over their uniforms and two gold threads sewn on their caps. Even after the young nurse took off her jacket and returned inside to join her colleagues, she was still distinguishable by her red cheeks and by her eyelids, the tip of her nose, and her chin, which had turned pink in the cold.

A dozen or so elderly residents were eating strawberries. The strawberries were held in old, misshapen hands and placed in toothless mouths to be gummed slowly. With each lift of a hand there passed a long, slow moment, enough for the characters on TV to exchange a dozen lines. The residents struggled to finish what a young person could eat in one bite. The sounds of their mouths clicking and sucking filled the room.

Mrs. An was not among them. She ate her strawberries quickly, and after five or six indicated that she was done, and they should give the rest to her fellow residents. After the young nurse finished attending to the others, she again encountered Mrs. An, now in her bedroom. The light was very dim, and the heat was turned all the way up. The air was so hot and thick that it felt as though she had to push through it to deliver the evening's medicine. She found Mrs. An sitting in her electric wheelchair, wearing a red silk gown and nearly a full face of makeup.

The nurses often speculated that Mrs. An stayed up all night. Each morning, the nurses made their way down the halls, opening door after door to call those residents who were still mobile to breakfast. Whenever they opened Mrs. An's door, they would find her sitting in her wheelchair, expression and posture just as it was the night before. Her eyebrows, eyes, cheeks, and lips were fully made up, as if she had not washed her face, but simply painted on another, more colorful layer. Under her wool shawl, she wore a similar gown in another color. She had robes in every color imaginable, and changed them daily.

In the young nurse's first week on the job, she had gone to tidy Mrs. An's room for the first time. There the nurse saw the old woman's wardrobe and cosmetics, and softly asked, "Are these all yours?"

"What?" At that moment Mrs. An had been pacing up and down the room, torso centered, repeatedly spreading her crooked arms in opposite directions—doing light exercises to expand her chest. Her head was just as bent as the other elderly residents' due to atrophied bones and muscles, but other than that her physique was decent. A hairnet covered her hair.

The young nurse's face reddened, but she couldn't take her eyes off the old woman's colorful face. Their eyes met. Mrs. An's dark eyes, surrounded by wrinkles, seemed permanently raised toward her forehead.

The nurse summoned her courage. "Were you a famous movie star? I don't watch many movies, so maybe I just don't recognize you."

Mrs. An lifted her head slightly, and her frail neck began swaying left and right. Her vocal cords had lost elasticity with age, and it was only after the first few chuckles moistened her throat that she could intermittently laugh aloud. When her neck stopped moving, she tightened the belt of her robe, sat on a small chair with an embroidered satin cushion, looked at the mirror she used for applying makeup, and put on her wig. Only then was she fully armored. She grasped several strands of hair, twisting them around her fingers.

The nurse could see that her question had pleased Mrs. An. The old woman laughed. "Movie star? Not a chance."

Soon after, she tugged at her clothes and sat on the electric wheelchair she used to get around. One hand gripped the joystick as she glided out of the room, the young nurse walking beside her. The nurse had noticed that the other residents' manner toward Mrs. An was quite distinct. Some bowed their heads. Just a few days ago, the young nurse might have mistaken the gesture for an exercise to limber up, or shaking due to Parkinson's disease, but now she knew they were showing respect.

Some rolled their wheelchairs aside or hobbled, leaning on their canes, a few steps out of the way to let Mrs. An pass in the corridor. She sat in her chair and rode straight on, occasionally returning a smile to this woman or that man, as if she were a wealthy lady on tour, with the young nurse as her maidservant. Thus, the nurse could see, even without needing to be told by her coworkers, that Mrs. An was at the top of the nursing home's social hierarchy.

That night, back in Mrs. An's room, the young nurse noticed that the older woman's lips were especially red, as if she had been eating not strawberries, but something else. Not only red, but glossy, coated with a satiny gleam. The nurse entered and held out a square box, revealing a carefully measured dose of medicine. Mrs. An fished out the pills with her wizened finger. When she opened her mouth, sticky red threads of lipstick spread between her lips, not breaking even as the pills slipped past the strands and disappeared down the depths of her throat. The nurse thought of the delivery man's stunned expression as he exclaimed, "Still alive!" and shivered involuntarily.

She realized then that Mrs. An had been watching her the whole time.

The older woman drank a sip of water and shut her bright red lips. As she swallowed, the spider's web of wrinkles surrounding her mouth moved, a hunter stirring at its prey. The aide suppressed an uneasy feeling in the pit of her stomach and quickly left. She turned off the light, looked down at the square box in her hand, and then farther down at her white shoes. In the room's heat, a black substance had oozed under the door onto her feet. Mrs. An's elderly aura, trying to trap her.

"She's so strange!" she exclaimed to her colleague back at the nurses' office. "I felt really weird." She had wanted to throw up.

The nurses had tried to make the office look as different from the rest of the building as possible: decorated in mint green and pink, the doorframe and the windowsill, the desk and chairs, the mini-fridge in the corner, and the small mirror hung on the wall, everything just so. They would often gather there to drink sweet tea and gossip.

At night, there were usually only a couple of nurses on duty. That night, the other nurse was more experienced. At the young nurse's complaint, she replied, "Join the club. We're all scared. None of us like to go into her room to tidy or bring her medicine."

"Oh," the young nurse sighed, eyes downcast.

"Let me get you a cup of tea," the veteran nurse offered, hearing the dejection in the younger woman's voice. She herself was drinking tea and eating a late-night snack. She poured the tea and gestured toward a small plate of freshly-wrapped cookies that she had baked that morning.

The new girl had been working hard to gain the other nurses' approval to become a full-fledged member of their community. The veteran nurse knew she couldn't be so tough on her anymore. Or only a bit tough, balanced with kindness, like now. The girl would wise up any day now, and then everyone would have to split the hard jobs equitably again.

The young nurse knew she wasn't yet senior enough to complain, so she resolved to stop sulking. The two of them took off their blue caps and loosened their creased hair from the coils atop their heads, bobby pins dropping to the desk, just like two real friends sharing tea and a late-night snack.

By then it was nearly half past ten, and most of the building's residents were in bed. Even the night owls would turn in soon. But the night was far from silent. All night long someone would be up relieving their bladder, and the tinkling sound could be heard from one end of the nursing home to the other. Someone would cough, sneeze, groan. Someone would rattle their bottle of sleeping pills and swallow a small capsule, or secretly pop the cork of an illicit alcoholic drink, seeking the comfort of the bottle.

All kinds of inelegant noises. An ordinary night.

As they listened, the more experienced nurse shared tips with her younger colleague. First, she mentioned one resident. "He likes to grope us."

The younger nurse was unable to conceal her shock.

"You didn't know? He's always been creepy, and nurses would always complain about him. Now his hands shake too much. It takes time for him to lift them from his knees, so you can escape before he touches you. Hand him a napkin, an empty cup, anything to put in his hands. He'll take it out of habit. Then you can push his wheelchair aside and leave him to stare at the wall alone for ten minutes. That'll teach him to behave."

The veteran nurse mentioned another resident. Gentle and refined, he had the haughty air of an intellectual, but in the blink of an eye he would turn into the world's worst salesman. "Whenever he talks with you, he tries to convince you to read his four books. No matter what you're talking about, he'll always find a way to steer the conversation toward at least one of them. He wrote them all years ago when he was younger, and apparently, they brought him a bit of fame. Now he wants you to read them."

"That's already happened to me," the young nurse confirmed. "Even if I wanted to read them, I'm still not clear which four books he's talking about. I have the feeling even he doesn't know their titles. How do you all usually handle him?"

"We each have our own way," replied the other nurse. "Take me, for example. I'll randomly mention a bit of plot and say it was written well, or that the story was good. In fact, it's all nonsense that I make up on the spot. The author will say 'Oh, really? Do you think so?' He becomes bashful and deeply moved, and his eyes start tearing up. Do you know why? He's entirely forgotten what he wrote. He mixes up his books, his life here, the plots of the TV shows he watches every day, and he can't tell the difference. I'm telling you, making up nonsense always works. Or there are other ways too. You can grab any old book, even a diagnostic manual, flip to a blank spot, and ask the author to sign his name. Like I said, he won't be able to recognize that it's not his book; he's not even too sure of his own name. But whatever he scribbles, his handwriting won't be rusty. He'll fish out a felt-tip pen from his pocket—he always carries one—and sign. He's signed thousands of autographs since he got here. As long as he lives, he'll keep signing."

"No wonder!" The young nurse had always assumed that the many signatures in the diagnostic manuals had belonged to some doctor. At the thought of the author's plight, she exclaimed, "How awful!"

"It depends how you look at it," the experienced nurse replied. She returned to her gossip. The comedic, the disgusting, and the uncontrollable were all inevitable in old age. "You know, that's life."

"And Mrs. An . . ." Their conversation eventually returned to her.

"She refuses." The experienced nurse wrinkled her nose in disgust.

"Refuses?"

The experienced nurse lifted her head from her hand, glancing at the clock on the wall. It was already past eleven.

"Still a little over six hours until the end of our shift," the experienced nurse calculated. "Then we'll walk out, head over to the bus stop, and leave. But if you think about it, they can't leave. They've been shut in here because they're old. Death is the only way out. Mrs. An, she refuses this ending."

"But, that . . ." The young nurse wrinkled her nose in incredulity, unconsciously imitating her colleague. It was difficult to reconcile desire and reality.

"Old Mr. Groper and Old Mr. Author don't want to die either. No one especially wants to die, but we have no choice but to go forward. That's how it is for normal people."

"Oh, I see. But Mrs. An, she lingers."

"That's it. She's been lingering for twenty years at least, so we're afraid of her," the experienced nurse said bluntly.

In the many years that Mrs. An had lived in the nursing home, she'd had several close brushes with death. In the end, she always made a full recovery, even from extremely poor health. When the weather was nicest, when the temperature was warm and the wind gentle, when the barometric pressure hovered around one thousand hectopascals, and when the tulips and camellias surrounding the building were in full bloom, she could walk along the footpath out front. When she rode her electric wheelchair down the hall, the other residents parted to clear a path for her. They held her in awe because she had hovered so close to death.

She had lived for a long time in this nest of the dying, like the long-lived queen of an ant colony, and she had become their spiritual leader. They saved her the best spot in the recreation room, easily accessible and facing the TV, leaving her plenty of space, even if it meant they would all be a bit cramped. When new residents were admitted, they would each stop before her wheelchair, lean over to speak in her ear, and introduce themselves, in an attempt to curry favor.

"That's why she wears makeup," the experienced nurse said, running one hand down her face, fingers spread slightly. "She wants to preserve her appearance. One of the nurses used to say that she never washes it off. Every night she just reapplies a new layer on top of the old."

Their voices grew softer as they spoke, their heads leaning lower and closer. The young nurse was about to share her experience that night. Mrs. An's lipstick had been as thick as swamp muck. That wasn't normal, or at the very least, it wasn't hygienic.

Just as she lifted her head, her words were cut off by an abnormal silence. The sounds of the residents urinating, coughing, and groaning in their dreams, all the small, scattered sounds of the building, were swallowed up by silence. Immediately after, they heard a resounding boom in their heads, their eyes widening suddenly. The young nurse saw their two shadows creeping across the table, stretching as if their heads were being compressed in a photocopier.

They both looked out the window. It was as if that night's massive full moon had moved to shine directly on the building, suspended just outside the window. The silence that had muffled all other sounds had heralded its approach, and the following boom was the sound of its majestic light shining with all its might into the room. It had thoroughly obliterated the dark mist.

"I've never seen a moon like that," the veteran nurse murmured, words stretched out at half speed.

They both rose like sleepwalkers, as the golden moonlight suffused their office. Slowly, as if moving through water, they approached the window. Their hair floated from their shoulders and stretched behind them, keeping them an arm's length from the moon's craters outside the window.

They dared not touch the windowsill, for along with the moon had come another uninvited companion: a blackbird, hovering in midair.

The blackbird hung between the moon and the building, flapping its wings in place just outside their window, tail feathers straight. It was as big as their palms and strong, with a shrewd air. The blackbird's twin eyes drilled into the young nurse, then he tilted his head toward her companion, gaze darting back and forth between them. *He's passing judgment in the bright moonlight*, the younger nurse thought. The bird mumbled gravely, spread his wings wide, and flew away. He flew to the next window and again looked inside. The moonlight illuminated every room as the blackbird searched for his target.

Mrs. An had been sitting all night, resplendent, her silk robe draping to the floor, exquisitely luminous in the dark.

That night, before the young nurse had brought the medicine box, the fragrant taste of strawberries on her lips had already turned sour. Remembering how she had appeared in her youth, she remained incredulous that time had made her unrecognizable, even to herself. She had eaten strawberries back then. Had she thought they were delicious? She must have. Each fruit sacrificing its vitality, fresh juice spattering into her mouth, its sweet, tart flavor offered as a tribute for her to savor. She remembered that feeling. She had turned to the strawberries that night in an attempt to re-create it, but it was not the same.

The strawberries responded with apathy toward the elderly, perishing indifferently in her mouth, leaving her even more despondent. The sound of the other residents sucking the fruit had filled her with revulsion. With the press of a finger, she had steered her wheelchair away. As she left, the sucking stopped momentarily, adding insult to injury. She had returned to her room with a putrid taste in her mouth, as the strawberries she had swallowed decayed along with everything else in her stomach. She had painted her lips, layer upon layer, until the lipstick was too thick to wipe away. Then the young nurse had arrived, and Mrs. An had swallowed her pills while the nurse looked on. She had watched the younger woman's response carefully, observing her shudder as her clear, delicate skin flushed. The nurse had struggled to maintain the appearance of politeness, but she fled quickly.

After the lights went out, only the moon was left to attend her, bright and clear. Downstairs in the recreation room, she had observed the moonlight piercing through the windows, unnoticed by the residents, shining on their shoulders, hands, and bald heads.

Whenever the moon was like this, she would remember a story she'd heard years ago. These days Old Mr. Author could only peddle his books clumsily, but ten or fifteen years ago, before he had lost his memory, he'd been charming, wearing a suit that didn't quite fit and strong cologne to mask his growing odor.

Upon his arrival, he had hobbled up to greet her; the other residents had advised him to pay his respects to the one who had lived there longest. He had only been admitted the night before, relying on the pension he had set aside for his old age. During the afternoon recreation period, he approached her wheelchair, bent at the waist, and with a small smile told her his name and that he was an author. Though his features had grown slack, she could tell that he had been handsome in his youth, which might once have helped him sell books. He had pulled out a chair and sat down, not waiting for an invitation, and had dug out a felt-tip pen and out of habit written his name on a napkin.

A quarter of an hour later, they had decided to go outside for a stroll.

She had placed her hand in the crook of his arm, and he praised her excessively for still walking so steadily. In ten minutes, they made a slow circuit of the path. That day, the path had been lined with lush trees, and the flowers had just bloomed. The nurses, student volunteers, and artist who had come to wish them well must have thought they were simply taking a stroll, but actually, their walk had been a race. The other residents on the path had all lost, toppled one by one.

"What do you write?" Mrs. An had asked, ten or fifteen years ago. "About this kind of life?"

"Some. And also a novel based on local folk legends I heard in my travels."

"What's it about?"

"When the moon rises at its fullest and the night is lit bright, a small bird will be watching and listening, searching room by room for the oldest person," the author had said, panting with exertion. "And so, the oldest person, despite their best efforts to hide, will be found and killed."

Mrs. An had laughed at the story's preposterousness. At the time her vocal cords had been firmer than they were now, and her laugh had been strong and drawn out.

"That's a terrible story!" she had said. "Why does it end with death?"

"I don't know. It needed to end somehow." At that, the author pleaded exhaustion and asked to return inside to sit and rest.

These past few years, even as Mrs. An had seen the author growing weaker and more confused, his signature had remained clear and fluid. He seemed to be staying alive based on will alone.

She had gradually stopped sleeping through the night, as if she had already used up her lifetime's quota of sleep. She remained constantly on guard, and so was not startled when a bright full moon appeared abruptly outside her window. Nothing in the world could shock someone so old. The moon lashed ferociously at her body, but still she struggled, her four limbs pinned down. The blackbird flew to her window, stopped in midair, and then landed on the sill. She heard an indescribable call, and in the bright light, her last thought was of whether she looked good that night.

The moon retreated. Early morning had arrived. The residents of the nursing home opened their doors to a new day. Her appearance was the same as it was every morning, sitting on her electric wheelchair ready to start the day, but by now she had gone elsewhere.

No one could understand, for none had ever been so old. No one had refused death so patiently or for so long.

5

The Restaurant at the End of the Universe: Tai-Chi Mashed Taro
宇宙尽头的餐馆之太极芋泥

Anna Wu 吴霜
Translated by Carmen Yiling Yan 言一零

The Restaurant at the End of the Universe: Tai-Chi Mashed Taro

By Anna Wu

Translated by Carmen Yiling Yan

The Restaurant at the End of the Universe

Far away at the end of the universe, there was a restaurant, and its name was the Restaurant at the End of the Universe. From a distance, it looked like a conch shell spinning in the void of space.

The restaurant was sometimes big and sometimes small. The furnishings inside its walls changed often, as did the view outside its windows. It had a refrigerator that was always full of fresh ingredients; a cooking box that fried, baked, seared, steamed, and everything else; a clock that could regulate the flow of time within a modest area; and a melancholic android waiter named Marvin. A red lantern shone perpetually at the center of the restaurant.

Two people, a father and daughter, ran the restaurant. They came from a place called China on a planet called Earth. Going by the *Traveler's Guide to the Milky Way,* the father was an exemplary specimen of the middle-aged Earthling male—perhaps even a few deciles handsomer than the median. He was thin and black-haired, and there was a scar on his left wrist. He didn't talk much, but was well versed in Earth cuisine. If a customer could name it, he could make it. The daughter, Mo, looked to be eleven or twelve years old. She had black hair too, and big round eyes.

The nearest space-time hub was a small cargo station, a singularity primarily used for Earth shipping. Of course, as a singularity, only organisms with a civilization rating above 3A—capable of uploading their physical bodies into the network—could use it.

Few guests came. Most hailed from Earth, but there were the matchbox-sized three-bodied people of Alpha Centauri too; Titanians with their vast balloon forms, adapted to the atmosphere of Saturn; even dazzling silver Suoyas from the center of the Milky Way, twenty-five thousand light years from Earth. Intelligent beings of every shape and size might be seen in this restaurant's blurred concept of time and space: waving their antennae, dribbling their mucus, crackling and sparking their energy fields.

Virtual reality may hold infinities, but wander long enough in it and your soul feels a little lost. Every once in a while, people still want to put on a real body, eat a real meal, and reminisce.

There was a rule for everyone who ate here. You could choose to tell the owner a story; as long as it was interesting enough, your meal was on the house, and the owner would personally cook you a special dish. And you could eat while you thought of the countless civilizations rising and falling, falling and rising, at every instant and in every corner of the universe outside this restaurant, like the birth and death of a sextillion stars.

Tai-Chi Mashed Taro

WU LING

In the twelfth month of the fifth year of the Chongzhen Emperor's reign, I was with my lord at West Lake. For three days, the snow fell.

The first two days, my lord spent as usual: wrapped in an ash-colored fur coat, reading by the light of the window. Silver charcoal burned in the brazier; incense burned in the bronze censer—agarwood during the day, to calm the spirit while he read, replaced in the evenings by sandalwood, to accompany his flute and calligraphy practice.

The night before, he'd had the cook prepare a supper of white rice, West Lake vinegar fish, four-colored greens, tai-chi mashed taro, minced beef soup, and a small jar of piping hot osmanthus yellow wine.

"Wu Ling, this is your favorite, eat up." My lord nudged the dish of fresh, hot taro mash toward me with his chopsticks.

I didn't make a show of refusal for the sake of politeness; I swept half the taro mash into my belly. A thin layer of boiling hot lard gleamed over the surface of the taro mash, so it didn't steam, giving it the appearance of a cold dish. In fact, it was scalding, perfect winter fare.

The madam cook sat across the table from us, chopsticks at her lips, chuckling as she saw the way I ate. My lord was an unfettered soul; he always bade his servants dine at the table with him. After so many years with him, I'd grown increasingly lax myself.

By the time we'd finished eating, the snow and wind had let up a little.

My lord opened the window, then carefully polished his jade flute with a soft silk cloth. A pendant woven with silver thread hung from the flute, handcrafted by Miss Weirui of Caiwei Hall on the Qinhuai River. The pendant fluttered in the wind, a lovely sight.

The sound of the flute drifted out the window, carried far on the winter wind.

At dawn, just as the sky was brightening, I got up, ready to draw water for my lord's ablutions, only to find him sitting in front of the window.

The snow had stopped. Against the faint light of dawn, my lord seemed a silhouette cut from paper.

"My lord?"

He turned, quietly looking at me. A spark of elation shone in his eyes. He had a strange air about him, as if he hadn't seen me in a long time.

"My lord . . ." I was deeply uneasy.

"Wu Ling."

"Yes, my lord."

"Get ready for the day. Today, we're going to the pavilion at the lake's center, to gaze upon the snow."

I paused, but I wasn't surprised. My lord was an aesthete.

"Yes. My lord, what would you like to eat today? I'll have the madam cook prepare it."

"Whatever you wish. Bring some taros to roast at the pavilion."

"What . . . what about everything else? Wine? Sides? Which incense shall I bring?"

"No need, it's not important."

I was stunned. When had my lord Zhang Dai been one to partake of crude foodstuffs like roasted taro? *It's not important?* My lord had always taken the utmost care with the elements of his daily life.

But my lord's contemplations were beyond the ken of a simple soul like me. I hurried to gather the thickest furs and bade the madam cook to rinse and clean some taros. I prepared the little brazier of silver charcoal, and after further thought, packed some Orchid Snow tea anyway. Then I set off to find the boatman.

At breakfast, my lord's thoughts still seemed elsewhere. He ate only a few mouthfuls of rice porridge, leaving the sides of smoked bamboo shoots, cured fish, salted meats, and pickled vegetables hardly touched.

At noon, my lord and I stepped into the little boat and were rowed to West Lake.

The snow may have stopped, but the weather was only growing colder. Gusts of wind scoured the surface of the lake. The boatman was well into his seventies, white in both beard and hair, though he punted the vessel agilely enough. It couldn't be helped. In this kind of weather, only someone like him, without sons or daughters, without rice to put in the pot, would accept a job like this one. Commoners had a hard enough time just getting by; they had no interest in singing odes to the wind and moon, or coming here just to admire the snow.

"Wu Ling."

"My lord." I stood at attention.

"The cock crows as I lay on my pillow; my thoughts turn in the predawn tranquility. I think of my life, prosperity and opulence gone in the blink of an eye. Fifty years are naught but a dream."

Fifty years? Whose writings was my lord reciting?

Wrapped in a mantle of pure black fur, my lord said nothing more the rest of the journey. He remained standing at the helm of the boat, as if he didn't feel the cold at all. Who knew what he was thinking?

After an hour or so, we finally reached the pavilion at the lake's center. The boatman and I transported the brazier and everything else off the boat, item by item. My lord tipped him a chip of silver and sent him off with an agreement to meet us here at dusk, for the return journey.

"It's not that far off. Why make him go to the trouble of leaving then coming back?" I asked as I boiled water for tea.

"A guest is coming. It's more convenient to meet him without the boatman here." My lord gazed into the distance.

"Ah?" I followed his gaze. The white snow reflected the sunlight; the sunlight reflected off the lake.

In the distance, amid the vista of snowy white, a small black boat gradually steered toward us.

Mo

"Dad! I'm exhausted . . . Hey, what are you doing?!"

It was midnight and the restaurant was closing up. Mo wandered into the back kitchen, ready to give her father the puppy eyes, only to get an eyeful of the robot waiter Marvin's roly-poly head, detached from its body and set upon the kitchen counter, surrounded by a heap of spare parts. Dad was holding up one of Marvin's robot arms, leisurely polishing it.

"A spot of maintenance," Dad said evenly.

"I've been rendered useless," Marvin spoke in a lifeless whine.

"Ooh, fun!" Mo crowded closer, practically squishing her face against Marvin's. Marvin, disdaining her, went into sleep mode, the blue light in his eyes dimming.

Seeing Mo mischievously making to stuff Marvin's head in the sink, Dad was forced to step in. "We have a delivery gig today. Do you want to go?"

"What kind of delivery? When?" Mo instantly perked up. She spent most days stuck inside the restaurant and jumped at the chance to check out a different planet and era. Unfortunately, when it came to takeout, Dad rejected any orders he didn't consider interesting enough, so there weren't many opportunities.

Dad used the opening to rescue Marvin's roly-poly head and set it aside. He spread a painting out on the counter. Mo scooted over.

It was a Chinese watercolor painting, quite well made. Mo had seen many similar paintings in the database.

It seemed to be a snowscape, with distant mountains enfolded in white waters. A lone island lay on the water: a pavilion, two people, faint cooking smoke. Far away, a little boat rowed toward them, bearing a human figure the size of a bean.

On the upper right corner, there was also an inscription.

"In the twelfth month of the fifth year of Chong . . . Chongzhen's reign, I-I came . . ." It was archaic Chinese script, and handwritten; Mo read it haltingly.

"Deliver it there. The order's for tai-chi mashed taro. Do a good job making it, and I'll let you go." Dad rolled up the painting efficiently, not allowing Mo's gaze to linger.

"What do you mean, *there* . . . You're baiting my curiosity again." Mo could only smack her lips reluctantly and turn to prepare the dish.

Mo had never made tai-chi mashed taro before, but it was no challenge for her. After looking it up in the cookbook, Mo set about preparing the ingredients. She washed the taros, peeled and diced them, then added water and let them steam. She took out another steamer, cored some red jujubes, mixed them with white sugar, steamed them briefly, took them out, mashed them into paste, and mixed in bits of candied winter melon. At this point, the taro was nearly cooked through. She took them out, squashed them until they were fluffy, picked out the veins of fiber, and mixed in a touch of peanut paste—the recipe didn't say to include it, but Mo thought it would add a dash of fragrance. Finally, she arranged the taro mash and jujube mash into a yin-yang symbol on the dish, ornamenting it with a red cherry and a green ball of candied winter melon. As the finishing touch, she heated the wok, added lard, cooked it slowly until it was crystal clear and filling the room with its fragrance, then poured it atop the taro mash.

By now, Dad had finished cleaning and reassembling Marvin. He wiped his hands and came over. He tasted the taro mash, and nodded.

Mo took out the quantum food box, set its temperature and force-field parameters, and set the taro mash inside. The dish quivered a few times in the box, then locked into place as the forcefield sprang up around it. No matter how the dish moved and swayed, it wouldn't spill or touch the sides of the box.

Dad took out the painting from earlier.

"How do I get there? Is someone coming to pick me up?" Mo picked up the food box with her right hand, peering at the shop entrance.

Dad smiled cryptically. Catching her off guard, he took Mo's left hand and pressed it against the boat in the painting.

"Give the painting back to Li Jia at the Agency of Mysteries," Dad said.

Wait, what Li Jia?

White light flooded out from the boat. Mo startled, eyes widening. She didn't even have a chance to cry out before the piercing white radiance forced her eyes shut.

She wanted to yell, but forced down the urge—with a dad like hers, any resistance would only lead to worse consequences. Mo could only roar inwardly as an unknown force pressed firmly against her shoulders.

The white light faded. The painting on the counter was gone. Mo, too, had disappeared.

Dad sat down and directed Marvin to make him tea. He sipped it slowly. "This Longjing tea Li Jia sent is quite good."

Zhang Dai

Amid the vista of snowy white, not a sound could be heard. Time, too, seemed to slow. Behind me, Wu Ling carefully watched the fire in the brazier, preparing to brew tea. His expression was one of concentration, taut even in the apples of his cheeks.

From the fragrance, he was brewing Orchid Snow tea.

I'd invented this tea myself, with its profoundly complicated process of preparation. Before, I'd frequently told Wu Ling that the so-called way of tea demanded spring water and snow water, the correct temperature, high-quality leaves, a suitable time of year. It needed to be brewed properly and served in fine wares; ideally, it would be attended to with the music of flutes and zithers, the company of beauties. Poor, clumsy Wu Ling practiced endlessly, yet I frequently found fault with him anyway. Perhaps the person I'd been yesterday, at thirty-five, would have found fault yet again. But the person I am today would not.

Today was the fifth year of the reign of Chongzhen. Sixteen years earlier, I'd similarly taken Wu Ling with me as I toured West Lake.

That year, in the balmy third month, West Lake had been beautiful from shore to shore, in all its nature and artistry.

That year, I'd been nineteen. At West Lake, I'd met Li Jia for the first time.

At nineteen, I was an outrageous libertine. I loved fine houses, pretty maids, handsome boys, colorful clothes, gourmet foods, fast horses, vibrant lanterns, fireworks, opera, musicians, antiques, rare flowers and birds. On the shores of West Lake, under the high sun, in the arms of boat girls, I reveled with my society of poet friends in boundless pleasures.

Amid the rouge and powder, we scattered ornate verses like jewels across the floor.

Li Jia appeared one morning on the pleasure boat, dismissing the disheveled boat girl with an ingot of silver. I'd sent Wu Ling off to the Sunyang Winehouse a mile away to buy tai-chi mashed taro, lotus root soup flavored with osmanthus, and flat cakes made with pine nuts and sweet wine. Inside the cabin, it was just me and Li Jia.

The man was extraordinarily handsome, with the air of one above the mortal fray. I took him for an admirer. With my shirt still hanging open, I allowed him to sit down inside the boat and spread out a painting.

It was a watercolor—a snowscape of West Lake, practiced in technique, leaving just the right amount of blank space for the imagination. The work had a remarkable air of distance and vastness, a lonely sense of "seeing no precedence from ancients before me, and no succession from comers after me."

But what really astonished me was the small passage inscribed on the painting.

Gazing upon the snow at the pavilion at the lake's center

In the twelfth month of the fifth year of Chongzhen's reign, I came to West Lake. For three days it snowed; the sounds of birds and men disappeared from the lake. The evening of the next day, I rowed on a little boat with my furs and my brazier fire, and came to the pavilion at the lake's center to gaze upon the snow. The mist made a haze of white, the sky and clouds and mountains and waters were all white. Of the shadows on the lake, there was only the score-mark of the long levee, the dot of the pavilion, and the grass-blade of my boat bearing two or three grains of passengers.

At the pavilion, two sat on a rug across from each other, while a child heated wine to boil on the brazier. Seeing me, they were overjoyed, saying, "We didn't think there would be others like us on the lake!" They pulled me over and had me drink with them. I managed three cups before departing. I asked their names—they were from Jinling, visiting here. When I debarked, the boatman muttered, "It is not simply that you, sir, are a romantic dreamer—there are others who are fools like you!"

"Good!" I struck the table in exclamation.

The passage was extraordinary, displaying an intimidating talent wielded with elegant subtlety. It possessed a loftiness that could stand the test of time—truly, I'd felt it to my soul.

But wait, the inscription was signed Zhang Dai?!

At the time, I'd taken what the man said as nothing but mad ravings.

Such as the man claiming that his name was unimportant, and having me refer to him as simply Li Jia.

Such as him coming here on a tour from Jinling, when in fact, he wasn't from this era. Rather, he came from a place called the Agency of Mysteries, outside the vault of heaven.

Such as him having the ability to traverse time and space.

Such as this painting, this *Gazing upon the snow at the pavilion at the lake's center*, truly having come from my hand—I'd painted and written this at the age of eighty-seven.

Such as the Ming dynasty falling in just twenty-eight years.

Such as me living my final years in abjection, dying at the age of eighty-eight.

"All laws are one; all things are eternal. In your wild youth, you frittered away a lifetime's worth of good fortune. Never mind this lovingly crafted tai-chi mashed taro—in your old age, you won't even have taros roasted in coal to eat." Li Jia tapped the dish on the table, filled with cooled taro mash.

"Why would a sage with powers like yours fixate on an ordinary, insignificant mortal like me? Unless you harbor certain feelings toward me?" I thought it all so outrageous that I spoke with reckless brashness.

Li Jia laughed, delighted. "I like your *Gazing upon the snow*, and I like to play my games. I'm visiting you for the fun of it, that's all. What I've said today, you of course won't believe as a nineteen-year-old. But once you approach the end of your life, I'll take you back to the time you were thirty-five, West Lake in the fifth year of Chongzhen. In the parallel universe where I never appeared, you wrote *Gazing upon the snow* at the age of thirty-five."

"A madman, you're a madman . . ."

The morning mist of West Lake brought a chill, spreading quickly. I looked at this man, so handsome, so close to me, so solemnly stating his ravings. A deep terror seized me.

Perhaps he sensed my fear. Li Jia gave a chuckle, and left with the painting.

At nineteen, I sat dazed on the pleasure boat on West Lake amid the radiance of the third month.

At nineteen, I didn't know that the Manchurians a thousand miles away would soon assail the Ming dynasty's Great Wall, a silent, ravenous, vengeful army.

The songstress knows not the grief of a fallen country,

On the other side of the river, she still sings Back Courtyard Flower.

The pillars of heaven were about to snap. The Four Directions were about to rupture.

Wu Ling

The boat drew closer and closer. Its prow bumped gently against the island, casting ripples across the surface of the water.

From a distance, I saw two people step out of the boat. One was very tall, likely a man, while the other was shorter. The two followed the island path toward us. My lord looked away; he turned to sit, instructing me to bury the taros in the brazier to roast.

When he lifted the teacup, his hand was trembling.

"Brother Zhang, hope you've been well," the man called cheerfully as he entered the pavilion.

He appeared twenty-five or twenty-six, and about seven feet tall. His features were handsome, and he wore a mantle made of a silvery material I didn't recognize. His eyes burned like coals. Beside him was a girl of about eleven, likely his servant. Dressed in red, she carried a long wooden case in one hand, and a dark box in the other. Her complexion was snowy, her air lively. She was looking me and my lord up and down.

For some reason, the man seemed vaguely familiar. I thought carefully but couldn't remember when we'd met.

A gust of the north wind blew billows of snow from the leafless trees. The two visitors stood in the pavilion, looking like sages.

The man gestured for the girl to hand over the wooden case. I hurriedly took it and transferred it to my lord. However, the girl looked rather displeased at being ordered about like this, and gave the man a . . . scornful look? It seemed that this man was even more lenient than my lord, to tolerate such behavior from an underling.

My lord wordlessly opened the wooden case and took out a painting. I wiped the stone table clean and spread the painting across it.

The painting depicted a snowscape, seemingly West Lake itself.

"Wu Ling, we've met sixteen years ago." The man suddenly spoke to me, the picture of geniality.

A numbness streaked across my mind like lightning. I remembered.

That morning, sixteen years ago, I'd hurried back to the pleasure boat with treats from the Sunyang Winehouse, planning to make tea for my lord, right as a tall man came out of my lord's boat.

I knew my lord's predilections, of course, so I hurriedly lowered my head. As I passed the man, he turned to look at me.

He was extraordinarily handsome. His eyes held a burning light like coals. It wasn't an easy sight to forget.

"This servant remembers." I gave a small bow. So my lord had gone to all this trouble in order to reignite an old . . .

"Don't speculate wildly," my lord interrupted frostily.

The girl went *pfft*. She fought to hold herself back, found herself losing the battle, and then gave up altogether, laughing to her heart's content.

Setting aside the matter of propriety, that sound was real as silver, ringing bright in the space between heaven and earth.

Mo

The white light faded. I lay on a small boat, quantum food box by my right hand, a long thin wooden case in my left. I grumpily weighed the case in my hand, and knew for sure it held the painting.

I didn't have to ask to know the smiling man in front of me was Li Jia.

The Agency of Mysteries was an organization famed throughout countless multiverses. People said they could fulfill any desire, but you had to trade for it. What exactly you traded differed with every person.

I still remembered the author Ah Chen from last time. To acquire the ability to write like a grandmaster, he'd traded away his ability to love, and spent the remainder of his life in suffering.

All laws are one; all things are eternal—like many of the axioms of the universe, the motto of the Agency of Mysteries was cold and unfeeling.

If this Li Jia in front of me was from the Agency of Mysteries, then was someone going to make a bargain today?

"Hello, Mo. No bargains today—I'm just going to see a friend." Li Jia seemed to read my mind when he spoke. He nodded toward the distant island. "Right there."

Li Jia succinctly explained the full story to me.

. . . So that's why. Dad really did take interesting jobs.

Soon, we arrived at the island. We got off the boat and came into the pavilion, where Zhang Dai and Wu Ling already awaited.

Zhang Dai wore a black fur mantle. He had the air of a scholar, his gaze tranquil yet weary. By the reckoning of Earthlings, Wu Ling was about twenty-seven or twenty-eight, plump and sturdy. He also had a rather cultivated air, maybe from following Zhang Dai around for so long.

According to Li Jia, Zhang Dai was thirty-five this year, but his consciousness was eighty-seven years old. Li Jia had made the switch yesterday, and it would last for just the remainder of today.

The wind carried a fragrant scent that had me sniffing. A brazier stood in the pavilion, water boiling on top. It must be taro roasting in the brazier.

Wu Ling spread out that *Gazing upon the snow at the pavilion at the lake's center* painting, then delivered two cups of hot tea to us. I took a sip. My eyes widened.

So fragrant.

"This is my lord's own creation, Orchid Snow tea. You take the Rizhu tea leaves from the foothills of Longshan, stir-fry them in the same manner as you'd prepare Songluo tea, and add jasmine when brewing. The tea is jade green in color, as fragrant as orchids, as pure as snow, smooth and elegant," Wu Ling explained, seeing my interest.

Zhang Dai remained silent. He stared at Li Jia for a long time, his expression strange.

I set the food box on the table, opened it, removed the taro mash from the forcefield, and set it on the table.

The surface of the taro mash was coated in lard. It looked cold, but it was in fact boiling hot.

Wu Ling was busy making tea; only Zhang Dai saw the strange-looking quantum food box, but it was as if he hadn't seen it at all. His face didn't show any surprise—to *my* surprise.

Then again, given he'd already experienced Li Jia's time travel, maybe I should have expected that.

"Are you also from there?" Zhang Dai turned his gaze from his tea, looking at me, then the sky.

"Take a guess." I grinned, showing teeth.

"Brat. If Li Jia weren't here, I'd give you a reckoning." Zhang Dai's expression finally relaxed, a spark of challenge showing through.

"Sheesh, you're eighty-seven." I gave him a serene smile.

Zhang Dai choked. Li Jia laughed aloud.

Zhang Dai

After I met Li Jia at nineteen, I quickly forgot the matter—perhaps it was because that business had a dim, unsettling sense of reality that made me consciously shy away.

Besides, there were too many diversions in this world. Mountains and waters, gardens and woods, strings and woodwinds, antiques and jades, novels and operas. I indulged in travel, touring all the famous mountains and rivers. I passed countless evenings absorbed in the novels of Feng Menglong, falling asleep to the tale-telling of Liu Jingting.

I never held a position at court—my family forced me to take the exams for officialdom, but the eightfold essay structure was neither my passion nor my strength, and I never did pass. Now that I think about it, perhaps it was a good thing.

The ways of the world were in flux. At court, eunuchs gathered power to themselves, favorites held sway, spymasters ran amok, and partisans warred brutally. Men of virtue and talent were either demoted and exiled, or met their end on a blade. Internal strife and external troubles grew ever worse.

As Li Jia had said, the Ming dynasty's thread of fate was gradually running to its end.

The year I was thirty-five, by coincidence I came to West Lake with Wu Ling. In the twelfth month, the snow fell for three days. I suddenly thought of Li Jia. Due to a high fever, I spent three days in bed in a torpor, never went to the pavilion at the lake's center to gaze upon the snow, and naturally didn't write *Gazing upon the snow at the pavilion at the lake's center* either.

In fact, from the moment I saw that passage, it no longer belonged to me, no? If events had occurred as Li Jia said, his disruption of space-time fundamentally stripped me of the right to write a masterpiece like that—truly, reprehensible!

Thinking back now, perhaps those days of fever were really a psychosomatic reaction to the terror deep within my heart—would Li Jia's prophecy become reality?

The year I was forty-seven, Li Zicheng sacked the capital. The Chongzhen Emperor hanged himself at Meishan.

When the nest falls from the tree, none of its eggs survive intact. Li Jia's curse tightened around me like the Monkey King's headband.

My family scattered to the four winds. Wu Ling died of illness. I became a refugee in the wilderness.

Inside my thatch hut, I had only a rickety cot, a battered table, a few worn books, and some blunted pens. I lived humbly and went hungry often. In the dusk of my life, fighting illness and pain, I had no choice but to pound my own grain and empty my own latrine.

Waking in the middle of the night, my past seemed like a dream. Thinking of my libertine youth, I could only face the shining moon and repent deed after deed.

One early morning in winter, when I was eighty-seven, the house ran out of charcoal. My last few taros were buried in the coals, cold as river stones. Desperately ill, I was on the brink of death, when suddenly the blurry figure of Li Jia appeared in front of my eyes.

I thought it was a dream.

"Want to eat tai-chi mashed taro?" Li Jia said with a smile. His face was as smooth as ever, showing no signs of aging.

Some force seemed to press down on my shoulders. The cot grew yielding. I gradually sank down, into an endless abyss.

A white light enveloped everything.

When I next opened my eyes, it was also early in the morning. Wu Ling was still sleeping soundly. Outside, West Lake was a vista of snowy white.

The aches and pains had disappeared without a trace from my body, leaving it light and nimble.

In the blink of an eye, I'd become thirty-five again.

Zhang Dai, at thirty-five, gazed hungrily, lingeringly, at West Lake after the snow.

As per the agreement, I went to the pavilion at the lake's center. Only when Li Jia appeared in front of me, only when that *Gazing upon the snow* painting lay before me, did I finally believe that this wasn't all just a dream.

Or maybe, life itself was one long dream. Zhang Dai was a dream, Li Jia was a dream, the great Ming dynasty was a dream, and everything up there above the vault of heaven was a dream too. Dream upon dream, without end.

But at this moment, Li Jia sat across from me, slowly sipping Orchid Snow tea.

Heaven and earth were a vista of snowy white.

Under the vault of heaven, bare branches made rows. Frost and snow congealed into a crystalline haze.

The silence was absolute. The snow drew a veil over all the perfumed rouge and heart's blood, and all the opulence and sin as well.

"Does this mortal life of mine seem absurd to you? Does my younger self, in your eyes, seem laughable? Does my more recently shattered family and nation amuse you?" I looked at Li Jia coldly.

Wu Ling stood from where he was preparing tea, his face mired in confusion.

"There, now, Brother Zhang, don't be angry." Li Jia smiled amiably, pointing skyward. "While I was organizing the classics up there, I chanced across your *Gazing upon the snow at the pavilion at the lake's center.* I saw your life story too, and found it intriguing. The masterpieces of history often stem from the combination of a full-blooming early life and a later life of falling, withered petals. More than a hundred years after your death, a certain gentleman surnamed Cao will write an even finer, immortal work of brilliance . . . but I digress. Either way, I only came to see you on impulse. If you find it rude of me, I beg your forgiveness."

Li Jia rose in one solemn motion and bowed to me. But I still felt that the mocking humor on his face fundamentally came from a different world—one with rules and an intelligence forever beyond my understanding.

The wind rose. West Lake after the snow was a scene of killing cold.

A midge drifting between heaven and earth, a grain of millet in a vast sea. Ordinary mortals like me were as insignificant as weeds. The Ming dynasty was gone. Zhang Dai's loved ones were gone too. My country was broken, my family was lost. Under the vast heavens, I stood alone.

I finally broke down in silent sobs.

My tears had nothing to do with the iron cavalry of the Manchus, nothing to do with Li Zicheng's righteous war banners, nothing to do with history, nothing to do with me, Zhang Dai, even—it was simply that, right now, today, this world of white seemed so bare.

Boundless beauty, boundless prosperity, boundless refinement and sophistication—none of it could resist the slow descent of vast, terrible fate.

Wu Ling panicked. He hurriedly handed me a silk kerchief, then turned angrily on Li Jia. "Who are you? Why are you bullying my lord?!"

"We stand in the pavilion, the pavilion stands on the island, the island stands at the center of the lake, West Lake stands in the Ming Empire. Outside the Ming, there's the Occident. Above the Ming, there's the vault of heaven. All laws are one; all things are eternal. Nothing is lost or forgotten as they enter a new cycle. Brother Zhang, weep and be done. Don't carry them in your heart. Come, eat." Li Jia was still smiling.

The Orchid Snow tea was fragrant as ever. The tai-chi mashed taro was fine and silken.

In the end, using tea in lieu of wine, I toasted Li Jia—even I couldn't say why.

Soon, the blackened roast taros were shared and eaten as well. Li Jia suddenly set down his cup.

"When you go back, add *Gazing upon the snow at the pavilion at the lake's center* to your *Dream Recollections of Tao'an*. It's your work." Li Jia spoke solemnly, his sardonic expression gone.

"*Gazing upon the snow* is really beautiful. Don't let it go to waste." The girl behind him gave a graceful smile.

Li Jia gazed at the distant surface of the lake. A dark boat was steering toward us amid a vista of snowy white.

White light flashed. When I opened my eyes, I saw the gaping window of my thatch hut once more.

Except, in the center of the hut, there now lay kindling and grain. There was a pouch of silver on top of the grain sack.

And on the table, a dish of cooled tai-chi mashed taro had appeared out of nowhere—scented with the snow of West Lake.

Lately, after closing, Mo would take out that *Gazing upon the snow at the pavilion at the lake's center* painting and quietly gaze at it. Apparently, she'd gotten it from Li Jia in exchange for the quantum food box.

One day, Dad went over and gave her a smack upside the head. "You know how expensive that food box was! You were scammed, don't you know? Li Jia! Hah!"

Mo rubbed her head. Surprisingly though, she didn't roughhouse back or resist.

"Dad, do you pity Zhang Dai?"

Seeing Mo serious for once, Dad was at a loss for words. He could only be serious too and sit down next to her.

"To ordinary people in that era, the happiness of your life depended on what you could lose yourself in. Zhang Dai experienced an enormous rise and fall in fortune in his life, but from start to finish, he had his love of literature. To be able to lose yourself in something, it takes a fool—and all fools are fortunate."

"*It is not simply that you, sir, are a romantic dreamer—there are others who are fools like you*—to be honest, I envy him a little."

"Hey, you love to cook." Dad ruffled Mo's hair.

"Mm. Dad, if you get more takeout orders in the future, take more of them on."

"There won't be any more. We had just the one quantum food box."

"Dad!"

6

The Futures of Genders in Chinese Science Fiction

Jing Tsu 石静远

The Futures of Genders in Chinese Science Fiction

By Jing Tsu

The question of gender in contemporary Chinese science fiction is as thorny as it is elsewhere. Modern Chinese literature since the twentieth century has faced similar issues: what distinguishes the work of a female or non-binary author; what difference that makes in its reception; and what limitations that classification places on the work, that may prevent it from accessing the same consideration and distinctions as those by cissexual male writers.

These issues cut across every genre of fiction, and this pioneering volume approaches them in the spirit of exploration and shared commitment. Each story poses an alternative that cues a possible reflection on the finite—whether it is the end of life, caring for others, the limits of technology to enhance our organic selves and inner emotions, or co-inhabiting a physical world with depleting resources. Enduring commitment—expressed as love (qíng) or attachment to a world, a time, or a loved one (see Anna Wu's work)—becomes a litmus test for our survivability, while immortality, death, and the desire for spirituality signal the human behind techne (see Chi Hui and Shen Dacheng in this volume). While these are universal themes, the contributors are not attempting universal gestures. From child-rearing and virtual parenting to resettling the human species in outer space, there is no attempted big narrative. Instead, the question behind each story chooses thoughtfulness over any ideological agenda about identity, creating lightness out of heavy-handed history writ large.

It is hard to pin down the writers in this volume as cis or marginalized. If you specify what gender is, you risk essentializing it, reducing it to a set of characteristics that may have less to do with gender itself than the circumstances that motivate a preferred definition. This volume shows that there is also a difference between science fiction *about* women and other marginalized genders and the ones written *by* them, which presents another practical challenge when equating the gender of the author with their literary creation. Many writers simply want the freedom to create, unencumbered by anything other than the inspiration to write and the readers they write for. Science fiction, though, possesses a particular constraint that differentiates it from other genres. It proceeds on the premise of a counterfactual relation to reality, and does not commit to any single scenario of the present. Some argue that science fiction is prized more for its imaginativeness than its mastery of literary language—the usual bar for literary distinction. Others point out that science fiction, far from abandoning the present for the future, can contain veiled critiques of the social reality at hand, thereby not wholly abiding by the premise of fantasy.

The sci-fi genre moves in and out of truth and fantasy, the present and the future. For *The Way Spring Arrives and Other Stories,* the first collection in English to exclusively feature women and non-binary authors of Chinese science fiction, questions about what distinguishes this volume and what it does would inevitably occur to the reader. For a kind of fiction that does not hold itself to reality *as is* but aims for the unthought-of *what if,* what can genre say about gender? How do we hold it accountable? And should we?

More than a century ago, a 1905 Chinese novel raised some of these questions for us to consider. *The Stone of Goddess Nüwa* (Nüwa shi) narrates the sojourns of a Chinese female assassin, who roams around the world on an electric horse in search of resources to build a better society.[1] Along the way, she visits and discovers new technologies like cerebral reprogramming, engineered food, and artificial insemination

1 Haitian duxiaoshi, *The Stone of Goddess Nüwa* (Nüwa shi) (N.p.: Dongya bianji ju, 1905).

procedures that upend traditional views of women, reproduction, and the family. She meets other like-minded, radical women during her globe-trotting, who had formed a worldwide revolutionary alliance with the mission to bring about a new age of peace and stability, led by science and technology. They recruit her to contribute to their cause. Each well-versed in martial arts and knowledge of Western machinery and electricity, the women revolutionaries do not rule out violence and martyrdom as permissible means to an end. They want no less than self—as well as societal—liberation.

Despite all the narrative attention given to detailing the fantastical scientific and technological advancements, no one called the novel a work of science fiction because it had imagined the new "modern woman" as more or less a desired version of the modern man. Admittedly, at the time "science fiction" itself was a new genre, imported into China through the translated works of Jules Verne, along with authors of detective fiction like Arthur Conan Doyle. Not only were the narrative techniques in these novels new to Chinese readers, how to read Western novels was also a new experience. Exploring gender roles meant putting oneself in another's place, leaving bodily boundaries and social, psychological constraints fundamentally intact. Late nineteenth- and early twentieth-century Chinese fiction witnessed a growing number of specific literary genres that were distinct from the traditional categories in Chinese literature, which once treated "fiction" as a general rubric for trivial writing or street gossip, and were considered much less serious compared to the proper Confucian written canon on morality, conduct, and governance.

The author of *The Stone of Goddess Nüwa*, with the pen name Haitian duxiaoshi (Lone Howler)—as far as we know, a man who also translated futuristic novels from Japanese into Chinese—advertised the novel as belonging to the category of patriotic fiction—"nation-saving" (jiùguó xiǎoshuō) with the added twist of a "gentlewoman" (guīxiù) as its protagonist. At the time, China was not yet a nation. The final imperial dynasty was on its last legs and would limp on until the revolution of 1911 toppled dynastic rule for good. Burning issues of the day were tied to Western imperialism, ending feudalism, and avenging humiliation. These included banning opium, abolishing the age-old practice of binding women's feet so tight that they stayed small and atrophied as a sign of beauty and status, and doing away with the calcified canon of Confucian learning.

Against this backdrop, women were idealized as new and modern citizens of the future because they were considered members of the downtrodden that the new Chinese nation would free. Their liberation would be a triumph for society, that is not to say for women themselves. It was fashionable for male writers to be attuned to women's issues and to write about them, thereby wearing the badge of progressivism. The Chinese literary and poetic tradition was already rife with men assuming the feminine role or voice as a trope, voicing their complaints as the wronged, so it was not unusual to see women featured or invoked to express a vision that few actual women participated in.[2] They were vessels for the male psyche.

While we can understand and accept the instability in examining past literary history, we do not yet have a full grasp on what female writers' relationship is to science fiction now. No longer trying to emulate what male writers have done or observe how gender difference is defined according to a binary threshold, cis women writing Chinese science fiction and fantasy strive to create a larger space to share with other marginalized genders. One issue in setting this new tone is deciding the goal and context for these new valuations: Is it a question of having enough women who write science fiction, of having more prominent and well-developed female characters in science fiction, or of the larger infrastructure of the literary trade—and of the field of science and technology—that might encourage or discourage more women writers to take up science fiction? Chinese science fiction has become globally popular in recent years for its exploration of big themes like space exploration and colonization, the enigmas of the universe, and the fate of humanity, but not so much for spear-

2 Exceptions to this norm were Qiu Jin and Xue Shaohui, both of whom participated in civil discourse.

heading social or progressive thinking specific to women and other marginalized genders. The wildly enthusiastic reception of Liu Cixin's *The Three-Body Trilogy* has largely drowned the voices of critics who pointed out its one-dimensional treatment of female characters. Hao Jingfang, the writer who won a Hugo Award after Liu for her dystopic social critique, "Folding Beijing," stands as a rare example of mainstream acknowledgment amidst a burgeoning landscape of writers of marginalized genders who are only now getting platforms, such as the ones featured in this volume.

A better approach to the question of women and contemporary science fiction may well not be a literary issue at all, but a sociological and anthropological one. Looking at who has access to knowledge, science, and technology, one could also think of marginality not simply as pitted against the mainstream, but also a position created by other margins. These are all positionalities that are constantly being redefined in relation to one another. Writers now breathe and live technology, like the rest of us. In *The Stone of Goddess Nüwa*'s time period, science fiction had only limited access to any knowledge of science and technology. A few exceptional writers experimented and tinkered with science as a real-life vocation. For the rest, there were only one or two authoritative periodical sources that relayed the news of Western technology regularly, mainly for layman consumption. If the writer were in cosmopolitan Shanghai, they could perhaps even see scientific instruments on display in special reading rooms, to supplement what they could glean from magazines and newspapers. Other than that, there were scores of textbooks on mathematics, chemistry, or anatomy that were translated, sometimes not terribly skillfully, by Western missionaries, but the textbooks were likely outdated or at least a step or two behind the actual state of technological advancement in the West.

Today's situation is significantly different, so much so that it is not surprising that Chinese sci-fi writers may not see themselves as part of the lineage of how science fiction developed in China in the early twentieth century, or even connected further back to philosophical tracts or early classical ethnographies about exotic, distant others. They have looked instead to American science fiction from the late 1930s and 1940s as their model and predecessor, drawing from a hopeful era that celebrated technological optimism. If today's sci-fi writers, exemplified in the current volume, decide to seek new linkages with China's past, it is not for the sake of a nostalgic return but to reinvent a path of discovery through myth and folklore (see Wang Nuonuo, Gu Shi, Count E, Chen Qian, Ling Chen, BaiFanRuShuang, and Chu Xidao in this volume). Some of the writers skillfully combine the traditional martial arts genre with fantasy (see Shen Yingying in this volume), while others seek to reopen history by exploring different outcomes that could have but did not come to pass.

Science fiction does not just traverse genres; its community and readership have always been global, real and imagined. Looking back on China's first wave in the early twentieth century, where both genre and gender of authorship were neither fixed nor aligned with expectations, one cannot help but see how authorship in contemporary science fiction is not just about gender, but invokes broad questions about the scientific and technological conditions of our times. The milieus we now experience demonstrate that diversity and plurality are simply facts of reality, not the result of preferential choice.

Beyond electric horses, we have spaceships and high-speed rails. Genetically modified foods have seeped into every facet of what we consume; you can insert a hemoglobin gene into a veggie burger to make it bleed and taste like meat. Reproduction can be delayed for decades with frozen eggs and cloning techniques, potentially upending the traditional framework for the division of gendered labor. The inevitability of mortality can be supplemented, it is hoped, by advances in medicine, combining with artificial intelligence to prolong and improve the quality of life. If anything, science fiction has had a hard time keeping up with the surreality of science, which is also sometimes so politicized that it leaves little room for writers' imagination.

More importantly, with the increasing sophistication of science, a line is commonly drawn between hard and soft science fiction, with the assumption that fewer women writers are operating in the space of the former. Science fiction writers are also no longer simply writers. They are consultants for tech companies and spokespersons for brand names, translators and entrepreneurs, humanitarians and journalists. They are still adored by fans, but are increasingly in the political limelight for how they can play a role in China's ongoing ambition to lead the next technological wave, helping to enhance the country's cultural image globally.[3] Under such circumstances, one wonders what a gendered approach to reading and understanding Chinese science fiction entails. One thing is certain: What goes into it is no longer just a literary affair, if it ever was.

In a landscape that is technological and political, inspirational and practical, Chinese science fiction has yet to articulate its rightful place in the contemporary world, and is pulled in different directions. It cannot be treated as simply fiction, but instead as a barometer of our times, replete with our own anxieties and hopes about technology, enhanced by new tensions in global geopolitics. Writers from marginalized genders have a new opportunity to claim their stakes. Indeed, each contributor to this collection of stories embodies a possible answer. For the first time, readers should no longer hope to simply lose themselves in the fictional world created by the author, but also ask how the author themself got into fiction, and what the larger, complicated landscape is that Chinese science fiction is compelled to navigate.

Gender, as with genre, is a question that has been and will continue to be reinvented with new stakes. While Chinese science fiction is still a young genre, it will surely intrigue readers in provocative ways, inspired by what we hope the world will become.

---

3 In August 2020, the China Association for Science and Technology, a nonprofit organization that helps to promote science and technology and liaises between the Chinese government and the community of scientists and engineers, unveiled "Kēhuàn Shítiáo" (Ten Points Concerning Science Fantasy), policies that aim to push for the development of sci-fi intellectual property in the film industry.

BIBLIOGRAPHY

China Association for Science and Technology. "Kēhuàn Shítiáo" (Ten Points Concerning Science Fantasy). 2020. http://www.gov.cn/xinwen/2020-08/07/content_5533216.htm (Accessed May 11, 2021).

Haitian duxiaoshi. *Nüwa shi*. N.p.: Dongya bianji ju, 1905.

7

Baby, I Love You
宝贝宝贝我爱你

Zhao Haihong 赵海虹
Translated by Elizabeth Hanlon 韩恩立

Baby, I Love You

By Zhao Haihong
Translated by Elizabeth Hanlon

When my boss summoned me, I was playing hide-and-seek with Baobao. Amused, I dragged the cursor behind the door and clicked. The viewpoint on the screen immediately shifted one hundred and eighty degrees, so that I was peering out at Baobao through the crack under the door. All I could see was his chubby little hand, waving back and forth, then it vanished entirely from my narrow line of sight. Growing curious, I was just about to poke my head out from my hiding place when an alert in large red letters popped up on the screen: "You've been found!" The game then cut to a scene of Baobao pouncing on my back, arms clinging to my neck. I laughed. For the first time in my life, I was enjoying a computer game.

For a code monkey, I rarely dabbled in video games, which bewildered my coworkers. And now, what had gotten me hooked was, of all things, an online game called *Raising Baobao.* The game's aim was to allow people who didn't have children but who desired the fulfillment of parenthood to experience the joys of raising a child. I didn't want kids though, and was playing the game as part of a special assignment from my boss. Getting paid to play games was nice, but my boss had other plans. After three days, it was time to get down to business.

A hand landed on my shoulder, patted it, and then patted it again, more impatiently. "Little Hu, are you brain-dead?"

"*Shh,* I'm taking care of the baby."

Ms. Shen swooped in and inserted her head between me and the screen. Her narrowed eyes drilled into me. "Addicted, huh? Get Lanzi to have one. The boss is calling for you."

I carefully lowered Baobao into his crib and covered him with a baby blanket, remembering to close the door softly behind me on my way out. I saved my progress for the day and then logged out. Tucking my hands into my back pockets, I went to answer my boss's summons.

Ms. Shen's derisive laughter followed me out. "Useless bore. I can't stand people like that. If you really want to raise a kid, just raise a kid. It's that easy! Treating children like playthings—this game is vile."

My boss set a cup of coffee down on the table in front of me. I thanked him and took a sip. No milk, one sugar—slightly bitter. He was the boss for a reason: remembering every employee's taste was no small feat.

"Little Hu, have you familiarized yourself with the game?" asked my boss, smiling.

"Still getting the hang of it, but it's fun."

"Our company has signed a contract with Pa-Pa-Pa Entertainment to buy the development rights to *Raising Baobao.* The execs have decided to develop a holographic version based on the original game. By making the game more realistic, we'll greatly increase its appeal."

"Good idea!" I said, knocking my coffee cup against the edge of the table in my excitement. "A holographic *Raising Baobao* game will be a quantum leap compared to the current 2D version!"

I'd splashed coffee droplets on my blue shirt. I looked down and dabbed at it, taking a moment to compose myself. "But 99 percent of internet users are still using desktop, laptop, or smartphones. Holographic computers and holographic-based networks are still the province of the few. There may not be much of a market for Holonet games, and the investment needed to research and develop an upgraded version must be shockingly high. Will it be commercially viable?"

"There's no need to concern yourself with the market," said my boss, leaning back leisurely in his chair. "The Holonet is the future of the internet. Even if we can't recoup our costs in three to five years, we'll still move forward with the remake. Do you know what kind of people most Holonet users are?"

I nodded. "Wealthy, educated elites."

"And do you know how many of them don't want children or don't have children?"

I shook my head. At my current salary, there was no guarantee I'd be able to afford the Holonet in ten years' time, no matter how much the service fees might drop. The only way I could get a glimpse into that echelon was through market surveys.

"36.476 percent," said my boss, a hint of smugness on his face. "I bet you didn't know that. Even if Holonet users make up only 0.001 percent of all internet users worldwide, that 36.476 percent represents over one million people. And, of course, we are perfectly justified in charging more for a game that runs on the Holonet. Fifty times more sounds reasonable, don't you think? If we can convert that percentage of prospects, the upgraded version of the game will pay for itself in two years."

It was more apparent than ever why my boss was the boss. Sitting there across from him, I felt like one of the 36.476 percent of customers, sucked in by the persuasiveness of his argument.

"Question," I ventured timidly. "How do we go about capturing those customers? Also, what about the remaining 63.524 percent of Holonet users?"

"That's a good question. Very thoughtful of you." My boss smiled and tipped his chin at me in approval. "Even in that demographic, there are those who will welcome the game. Empty nesters, for example. Lonely mothers and fathers can return to the game to recapture the joys and comforts of yesteryear. As to why childless and childfree Holonet users can be won over, the reason is simple."

The look in my boss's eyes dimmed a little. "I don't have kids, and I don't ever plan on having any. Over the years I've asked myself whether my life has meaning. Whether lives without purpose should exist at all. For someone who doubts the value of his own life to then create a life—it would be very irresponsible behavior."

Good God, the boss was really laying his heart bare to me. Would he later come to regret it, and be all too glad to get rid of me? I felt my palms grow clammy with sweat.

"Most women of that class aren't willing to use an artificial womb.

They think it's harmful to the bond between mother and child. But they worry about the toll ten months of pregnancy will take on their careers, their figures. Some are busy clawing their way up the corporate ladder. Before they know it, they've missed the best window for having a child, and now they can't guarantee the quality. Better not to have one at all . . ."

I didn't let the chance to stroke his ego pass me by. "Boss, you really understand the market."

"Well, I belong to that sphere. My personal experience aside, I've heard enough lamenting and complaining from my friends. People are animals. When we reach a certain age, we all feel the instinct to produce the next generation. But humans are superior to other animals, so we can weigh the pros and cons and make a choice. Little Hu, the game's fun, right?"

"Yeah." I nodded forcefully.

"That's because it's only a game. A good game designer understands how to make players happy. Simplify the difficulties of raising a child as much as possible, and emphasize the fun parts. If it's as much trouble as it is in real life, who will want to play the game?"

"Got it." I had an inkling of what my next assignment was going to be.

"You'll be in charge of the holographic remake of *Raising Baobao*. A dev team with previous experience working on holographic games will be assigned to you."

"Boss," I stammered, feeling a mixture of gratitude and trepidation. "Boss, thank you for thinking so highly of me. But it's too much, I'm afraid—"

"This afternoon, I'll have a holographic computer sent to your home. Welcome to the Holonet user club. The company will take care of the service fees, of course."

My jaw nearly hit the floor. It was a piece of equipment I'd been drooling over for ages. If I had one at home, I wouldn't constantly be getting into arguments with Lanzi over staying late in the company hololab.

"If the remake is successful, I can guarantee you 10 percent of the tech shares. Also, the position of department head is still vacant, if you're interested . . ."

I clamped down on my trembling left hand with my right, which made it look like they were warring madly with each other. "I . . . Boss, why me?"

"You've got the technical skills, and your last design was very successful. I've always thought highly of you, Little Hu." My boss leaned in and wrapped a familiar arm around my shoulders. "What do you think?"

"I'll—I'll do it," I thrust out my chest, feeling a surge of confidence rise inside me. "I'll make it a success!"

My boss quirked his left eyebrow, and slowly expelled a breath. "Quite right. Let's leave the subject here for today." He rose and held the door open for me. "By the way, I've got a suggestion for you. The original game is overly simplistic. In the remake, make sure the details are true to life. If it strays too far from actual experience, it'll be next to impossible to pull off."

I halted just outside the door.

"Get Lanzi to have a baby." Suddenly, the sweet smile on my boss's face looked plastic. It inflated in my mind like a balloon, swelling bigger and bigger, until it popped with a bang.

Every person goes through several different stages in life, each with a different primary focus. Having a baby was not the focus of this stage of my life.

I'd dreamed of becoming a poet, an actor, a politician, Bill Gates, but never of becoming a father.

Over dinner, I got lost in thought while looking at Lanzi. A lock of hair had fallen across her left cheek. Its slight natural curl made it dance there, like a small, slender black snake. Sexy. Snakes, like women, are charming, entangling creatures. Having a baby wasn't the focus of this stage of Lanzi's life either. When we got together, we decided to remain childless by mutual agreement. Was I betraying her trust by going back on my word now?

Lanzi looked up, her dark eyes sliding toward me as her chopsticks poked me in the forehead. "You in there?" There was something plaintive in her eyes as they swept over me.

Shoot. It had been less than a year. How had she grown so bitter already?

Though the focus of this stage in my life was not fatherhood but rather furthering my career, achieving the latter hinged on the former. Competition was fierce in my line of work. If I didn't do this, someone else would, and an opportunity this good might never come my way again. At least taking the job meant I'd have a holographic computer for home use. I wouldn't constantly have to stay late at the office, which would ease some of the conflict between Lanzi and me. So, in a way, I was doing this for Lanzi's sake, too.

"Oh, I was just thinking of some good news."

My rare good humor took Lanzi by surprise. She put down her chopsticks and fixed me with her dark eyes. "What good news?"

"My boss gave me a holographic computer. It's already installed in my study. How about I show it to you later?" I flashed her a grin, doing my very best to butter her up.

"*Pfft.* What's it to me?" Lanzi rolled her eyes, but the corner of her mouth curled upward.

"Come on, now I can spend more time at home with you," I wheedled. "Maybe we can even keep a good thing going, and add another member to the family?"

Lanzi stood abruptly and picked up her bowl and chopsticks. "Where is *that* coming from? Quit messing around."

"Kidding! Don't take it so seriously." Flustered, I had to backpedal.

My boss had given me a two-year deadline. If I was going to remake *Raising Baobao* in two years, I had to get Lanzi to have a baby as soon as possible. Using an artificial womb was convenient and painless, plus it was possible to control how long it took. In the months before the baby was born, I could devote myself to making purely technical improvements to the game. Once the baby arrived and I had a real feel for parenting, I could spend the remaining year and change writing new code, strengthening the details, and expanding the content. There was no time to waste. The key issue was persuading Lanzi.

As I sat in my newly outfitted hololab, I steeled my resolve to win Lanzi over. In the air in front of me, Baobao's image expanded, little by little, to the size of a real baby. His round, chubby face slowly came closer toward me, until it was nearly touching my own.

"Good Baobao. Give Daddy a kiss." My voice functioned as a command.

Baobao's lips puckered. As he leaned forward, peculiar messenger particles in the air gently bombarded my face. The sensation tickled my cheek, and I couldn't contain a laugh. It felt like there was a warm little worm wriggling around in my heart. Was raising a child really so bad?

I really wanted Lanzi to play the game. However, this one action was about as far as I'd gotten with the remake, and the details were still lacking: more realistic skin texture, the little unconscious vocalizations a baby made when crawling, the distinctive scent of a baby's skin, that sort of thing. Since the game was being developed for the Holonet, it had to give the user full immersion with sounds, images, odors, and tactile signals. Otherwise, how could we justify charging fifty times the usual usage fees?

Besides, I couldn't let Lanzi know I was designing this game. She was too smart. If she ever suspected that my motives stemmed from this assignment, she would never agree to have a child.

Two days later, I invited my college classmate out to Lan Kwai Fong for a meal, ostensibly to talk about his experience during his wife's pregnancy. My buddy's kid was one and a half—rug rat age.

"You're certain you really want one?" he asked, shaking his head as he served himself with chopsticks.

"Yeah." I nodded vigorously, as though pounding garlic. "Drink up."

"No." He pushed away the cup I'd offered him. "My little one doesn't like it, so I don't touch the stuff."

I was stunned.

"You," my buddy drawled, around a mouthful of food, "need to grasp how women think. Women are animals: once they reach a certain age, it's easy to trigger their maternal instincts. But modern women overthink things. They think and think until they talk themselves out of having kids at all. It's a little easier if she's willing to use an artificial womb. The two of you take a trip to the hospital together, and then eight months later you take your baby home. If she isn't willing to outsource the pregnancy, she'll have morning sickness, she'll lose her figure, she'll turn peevish. You won't have any peace in your house."

I was beginning to regret inviting my buddy out, since he was just using the opportunity to gripe. He seemed to sense my annoyance, and, switching to a gentler tone, asked, "You really want a kid?"

"Yeah," I said, burying my face in my cup.

"I know Lanzi. Very excitable, that one. With a little prodding, she might just catch the urge. I'll help you work out a plan."

I hesitated. "But, what if she regrets it, once the initial zeal fades?"

My buddy's eyes practically bulged out of his head as he stared at me, like I was standing trial. "It's not unusual to feel regret after having a baby. This question is, do *you* want one?"

I grunted, a leaden feeling in my chest.

"Then it's settled. I'm just helping you think things through, bro." Satisfied, he licked his lips. "Give me some of that."

The following Monday, I took half a day off of work and brought Lanzi to the hospital to visit a friend—well, I claimed she was a friend. In reality we were going to see my buddy's female coworker, who had given birth last week. I brought a huge floral arrangement. Lanzi glared at me the whole way there, suspicious that the new mother was an ex-girlfriend of mine.

The feeble woman smiled at us from her hospital bed. My buddy had given her a heads-up. Lanzi grew quiet as soon as we entered the delivery room, but her eyes continued to rove, inspecting the room from top to bottom.

"Thank you both." The woman's still-swollen face was cradled in the white pillows of her hospital bed. Perhaps it was a figment of my imagination, but her serene smile called to mind the Virgin Mary.

"Why would you put yourself through this? Couldn't you have used an artificial womb?" Lanzi asked softly, taking her hand.

"For the credit, of course." The woman giggled. "Ten more months of credit than his father." She patted the side of the bassinet next to the bed.

Lanzi circled around to the bassinet and gazed at the swaddled bundle inside.

My heart leapt. Such a tiny baby! Or rather, I should say, that's just how babies are: of a kind with creatures I'd seen on TV, freshly hatched chicks, newborn kittens, pink-nosed pups just emerged from the nest. Were all young lives the same? Baobao's programming was far too crude in comparison. I had to commit everything I felt today to memory, so that I could revise the details in the game when I got home later. Today would be fruitful after all.

Touch. I couldn't forget about touch. I extended a finger and carefully poked the baby's cheek. Such thin, supple skin, springing right back into place . . . my God! What a challenge it would be to replicate that with holographic software!

Snapping back to the present, I noticed that Lanzi was lost in a daze of her own. She had braced her hands on both sides of the bassinet, as though she were preparing to occupy it.

The baby's beet-red face was wrinkled, his thin lips gently pursed. His eyes suddenly opened and rolled all around, like two translucent black glass beads. Lanzi let out a drawn-out sigh. On her face was an expression I'd never seen before.

"What's it like?" she asked, almost to herself.

The new mother laughed. "There's a tremendous sense of accomplishment. You should try it."

After that, Lanzi withdrew into her own thoughts, and said nothing for the remainder of the visit.

These days, I was so busy that I was barely holding it together. I wanted Baobao to age gradually, like a real infant. I wanted him to have the same look, feel, and smell. It was like *I* was giving birth to a baby, wasn't it? I was creating a real, live, virtual baby. I was its father *and* its mother.

The trip to the hospital had produced an effect: Lanzi had been prone to silence lately. I didn't have the energy to try to read her mind. In any case, my buddy's plan was only half complete. There was no use in fretting yet.

One evening, my buddy and his family came to visit. As soon as dinner was finished, Lanzi bustled into action, tidying the house, rearranging the living room, and laying out a spread of fruits and desserts on the tea table.

When my buddy and his family arrived, Lanzi went to greet them. In the video feed from the security door, a small round face, no bigger than my palm, came into view first. The face's owner was perched in her father's arms, wriggling excitedly. She flapped a teeny hand in the camera's direction, as though she knew someone was there, watching her.

The guests were ushered inside. Our home was a split-level, with two floors connected by a flight of four stairs. The little tyke, Huani, immediately set about scaling these four stairs with great enthusiasm.

I took careful note of her gait. She had basic control over her body's center of mass, but still moved with a certain degree of lateral sway, like an animal—a duck, that was it. What if I were to turn this behavioral characteristic into a specific command in the game? The calculating part of my brain rapidly whirred to life.

Lanzi's behavior was even more outrageous. Leaving the guests to me, she plopped herself down on the top step and, smiling, watched Huani clamber tirelessly up and down the stairs.

"Nini, give auntie a hug," my buddy's wife instructed.

The little girl, all dolled up in a bright red dress, ran giggling into Lanzi's arms, her braided pigtails swinging from side to side. A string of nonsense syllables tumbled from her rosebud mouth. Lanzi smiled demurely as she held her, gently rocking the improvised cradle of her arms.

My buddy, who had been watching from a distance, suddenly activated the remote control. "Nini, give auntie a kiss!"

The words were scarcely out of his mouth before Huani's head shot up like a tiny missile and collided with Lanzi's face with a thunk, delicate lips pressed against her cheek, glued there. Saliva wet Lanzi's cheek.

The demure smile that had graced Lanzi's face promptly vanished, replaced by a dreamy reverie. My buddy and I, who had been carefully observing the entire time, exchanged a fleeting glance.

I rarely felt so inept at my job. Knowing exactly how something should be, but unable to make it so. It was a very frustrating feeling.

The mouth, a baby's mouth. I wanted Baobao to have delicate lips like Huani: thin, soft, warm. Sticky lips, like Huani.

The Holonet's high-energy particles could transmit a whole range of signals. So it was only a matter of translating what I felt into usable code—but did it have to be this hard! I had to acknowledge the greatness of creation. Here I was, tearing my hair out over one virtual baby, while that mysterious force churned out a few billion humans and hundreds of trillions of plant and animal species, plus the infinite starry cosmos to boot.

Someone was calling my name. Though I'd locked the door to my study, I could still hear that angry voice.

Sigh. Save. Exit. Power off. I pushed open the door and looked at the pregnant woman standing at the top of the half-turn staircase. Her waistline had doubled, and her face was swollen and full of exhaustion. She was nothing like the woman I'd formerly known.

I could still remember her standing on that same step five months ago, an uncertain expression on her face as she asked, "Do you ever feel like our family could stand a little change?"

Even then, I'd squashed down my euphoria and feigned nonchalance. "What's the matter? Isn't what we have now enough?"

If I could turn back the wheel of time to that pivotal moment, I'd make one levelheaded amendment to the suggestion she made next. I'd tell her that we could have a baby, but only on the condition that she delegate the gestation process to an artificial womb at the hospital. All of this trouble could have been avoided that way.

"What do you call this? Hiding from me all day long in your study, refusing to come out!" Lanzi trembled as she spoke. "Let me tell you, the child I'm carrying is a Hu—it isn't just mine!"

I felt a twinge of guilt at that. I climbed the stairs and wrapped my arms around her shoulders. "All right, all right, I'll keep you company. Let's go get something to eat."

"Who said anything about eating? I swear, you're possessed by that computer!" Lanzi tried to twist away, fists raining against my chest.

"I'm sorry! I'm sorry! I'll do better, yeah? Don't cry, okay?" I pleaded, in a coaxing tone. The head weeping against my shoulder was a regular tear machine. A large patch on my shirt was soaked through instantly. Where had my vivacious girl gone?

I swallowed a sigh. Oh, if only these days would end soon!

The day my daughter was born, I heard her first cry through the door of the delivery room. Lanzi flatly refused to let me into the surgical suite.

"The doctors said it will help if I'm beside you holding your hand." I thought it was already quite conscientious of me to offer.

"I don't want you to see me like that. Anyway, it will be a painless labor. You don't need to worry." But despite her insistence on keeping me out of the delivery room, sitting on the bench outside, I could still hear her moans of pain.

While she struggled and I waited, I began to question my basic moral character as a person. If Lanzi was having a baby because she wanted one, what about me? Did my desire for a child come from the heart, or was I merely using her for my work, a model to be copied?

Lanzi had produced this child with her own flesh and blood, but me? As I entered the delivery room, my feeble arms reached out mechanically to take the warm little thing. What had I done for her? I'd used my brains to produce another child, if not a life per se—Baobao. Baobao was *my* child.

I jerked my vacant gaze away from where I'd been staring straight ahead, only to plummet into the black holes that were Lanzi's deep, dark eyes. She had been waiting there the whole time in feverish anxiety for my approval. But I'd let her down. The damage was already done. No matter how much fuss I made afterward, crowing about how over the moon I was to have such a lovely daughter, that hopefulness in her eyes was gone, snuffed out, never to be reignited.

To an outsider, my devotion to my daughter was unrivaled: I would caress her little face until the nurse pulled me away; I would observe every detail, every inch of her, with clinical scrutiny; I loved to cradle her in my arms, rocking her back and forth, back and forth, silently pondering how to realistically simulate a baby's heft.

"What an attentive father!" cooed the gaggle of sisters, cousins, and aunts who had come to visit the other new mother sharing the hospital room. Lanzi's eyes slid to me, skepticism in her steady, unmoving gaze. How could I win back her trust? I felt helpless, maybe because I was guilty.

After giving birth, Lanzi's milk did not come in, which made her touchy and irritable. I had to walk on eggshells around her. Her company offered six months of maternity leave. As a result, she was always vying with me for the baby, as though our daughter were hers alone. She took to pacing in the bedroom with the baby in her arms all day long. Each day, after my daily dose of real life, I would hunker down in my study, which had been converted into a hololab.

Raising Baobao achieved a number of new breakthroughs: I'd come a long way in my understanding of infant sleep positions, cries, laughter, and certain unconscious movements.

Beibei—that was my daughter's nickname—liked to starfish her arms and legs in her sleep, always on the move in spite of her thick swaddling clothes. I often stood next to her crib and watched her while she was fast asleep. It was hard to believe that this oblivious little wriggler was a piece of me. I remember, as a child, my mother would often say to me, "You're a piece of me." Fathers, in contrast, can't share in this sentiment. The bond between mother and child is something a father can never replace, or indeed, surpass. So, next to Lanzi, I always felt like an impostor parent. I don't know whether that's a common feeling shared by many men who become fathers, or if mine was a special case.

When Beibei woke up hungry in the middle of the night, she cried her head off. I hadn't had a good night's sleep in weeks. I had no idea how something so small could produce so much unrelenting, unremitting noise.

Last weekend, I was exhausted. I'd just gotten into bed and my weary bones were starting to get comfortable when the crying started up from the crib across the room. I couldn't tell you the exact decibel level, but it was loud enough to wake the dead. Lanzi immediately got out of bed to pick Beibei up, and rocked her back and forth once or twice before depositing her in my arms. "Your turn. I'll mix the formula."

"She drinks so much during the day. How can she still be hungry?" I grumbled.

"Huzi, she's your daughter, too. How can you be so impatient!" In no mood to quarrel with me, Lanzi stalked off into the kitchen. I lay there, a human cradle, diligently rocking Beibei to sleep.

"Waaaaaaaaaaaaah—" She opened her toothless mouth wide, without the slightest intention of quieting down.

"You little brat!" My head felt like it was going to split. I wanted to fling her across the room. Now I knew what my boss had meant when he said that the key to *Raising Baobao* was simplifying and reducing the difficulties of parenting. If it were like real life, what fool would willingly subject himself to this? Turns out, the fool was me!

I spent the rest of the night in my hololab, catching up on creating new code. The soundproofing was good. I couldn't hear any crying outside. Electrical signals conveying sound, color, odors, flavors, and tactile sensations permeated the room, fluctuating constantly, and all under my control. I pooled them together to bring a baby to life, a baby named Baobao.

What made Baobao so lovable was his well-behaved nature. He was naughty on occasion, but it was a *controlled* naughtiness. He didn't cry until your head threatened to explode. Baobao's body was soft and warm, and smelled faintly of milk, just like all babies. Like my daughter. Baobao would hiccup when he laughed, chest heaving like a little creature in an animated film. His laughter was unconscious, and had no fixed pitch, one moment a giggle, the next a belly laugh. His matching facial expressions were even better, by turns mischievous, tentative, and sheepish. Yes, that was my daughter's laugh—I'd grafted it wholesale from Beibei to Baobao. Lanzi had given birth to the child who could laugh like that, but I was the one who had programmed Baobao to laugh that way. Only the latter made me feel the true pride of a creator.

I became consumed by my work. I loved my Baobao. I added many new details that had been absent in the 2D version of *Raising Baobao.* Spitting up milk, for example. When bottle-feeding, Beibei would drink too fast and spit up her milk, rosebud lips parting around a *hurk,* followed by a rush of creamy-white milk that flecked her mouth and chin. Another *hurk*, and the milk would spill from the corners of her mouth. In these instances, Lanzi would quickly wipe Beibei's mouth clean with a soft hand towel to stop the milk from dribbling down her neck. I'd performed this duty before, too, but maybe Beibei didn't like me, because as soon as I wiped her clean, she coughed and sprayed me in the face. The sticky fluid smelled slightly fishy. I don't like milk.

My boss once told me that games weren't fun if they were too easy, even a game like *Raising Baobao*. Without minor inconveniences to add variety, it's impossible to incite lasting interest. So these small details, like spitting up milk, were essential.

As I fiddled with the program data in my hololab, I developed a reflux intensity index. During my testing, I let simulated milk splatter on my face in various ways over and over again, while I adjusted the fluid's smell and viscosity to make it as realistic as possible. It occurred to me, not without a twinge of self-reproach, that when it was my own daughter Beibei spitting up milk onto my face, I lost my patience easily, but once it became part of my job . . .

Thunk, thunk, thunk. Someone was knocking on the door—no, pounding on the door. The deafening racket interrupted my ruminations, shattering the comfortable, dreamlike atmosphere created by the

Holonet. Irritated, I saved my work, logged out, switched my computer off, and opened the door. To my surprise, this time I found myself confronted not by an angry and agitated wife but by a frantic mother. Lanzi was holding the baby in her arms. Her hair hung loose and disheveled, like she had just climbed out of bed and hadn't had time to comb it, and her eyes were red, puffy, and panicked. "Huzi, Beibei has a fever. What do we do? What do we do!"

"What do we do? For a start, don't panic. It's only a fever, right?" I reached out and laid my hand on Beibei's tiny forehead.

She was burning up.

I pulled back my hand, heart tight. Her little face was flushed, her forehead wrinkled, and her eyes, nose, and mouth were scrunched together. Such a tiny head, no bigger than my fist. How much pain was she in, to cause an expression like that? Maybe she was too weak to cry. My composure suddenly felt callous. Maybe I'd rehearsed too many illness scenarios featuring Baobao. But those had all been under my control, hadn't they? As long as I administered virtual medicine in accordance with the rules I had programmed, I could make Baobao smile again.

But Beibei *wasn't* a virtual baby, and, faced with her illness, I was only a scared, helpless father.

"The hospital. We need to take her to the hospital." My voice had lost its calm tone.

"What are you standing there for?" Lanzi stomped her foot. I realized I was still wearing my pajamas. As I rushed into the bedroom to find something to change into, I heard Lanzi say behind me, "Huzi, Beibei and I never see you anymore."

I turned to look at her. Her face was composed, somewhat sad, but not tearful. I felt at a complete loss for words.

In the hospital, beneath a drip bottle, Lanzi and I had an unusually calm conversation as we watched over Beibei in her crib, attached to an IV.

"It's my fault, I think," said Lanzi. "You're still not ready to be a father, but I only cared about my own feelings and rushed into motherhood."

"Don't say that." The words sounded false to my own ears. "I supported you."

"Well, maybe. But in reality, you live like you don't even have a family. If you've eaten, no one else is hungry. When you feel like working, you work for days at a time. When you want a rest, you don't come upstairs to sleep because the baby is noisy. You come check in on us when you're in a good mood, but when you're in a bad mood, you shut yourself up in your study and become deaf to everything outside."

"I haven't been taking enough care of you two lately. I'm the one in the wrong." What else could I say?

"Look at Beibei, she's still so young . . ." Lanzi caressed Beibei's furrowed brow with her finger, like it was a crease in a shirt, stroking until the skin was smooth. "Too young to suffer like this . . ." Tears rolled down her cheeks.

I followed her gaze to the needle sticking out the side of our daughter's head. At just three months old, the veins in her arms were too fine, so the IV had to be placed in her scalp—a fact I'd only just learned. The needle was clearly an ordinary one, but inserted in her tiny head, it looked positively thick. I didn't dare touch such a daunting instrument, so instead I bent over and blew gently: *Whoooo—whoooo—*. Maybe I could alleviate some of Beibei's pain that way.

Lanzi started to sob, and let a fist fall against my back.

I raised my head and gave her a bitter smile. I knew she'd forgiven me once again, but I couldn't forgive myself for the idea that popped into my head in that moment:

Should I incorporate this into the game? To write, or not to write?

Infants are susceptible to disease, and the high fever led to pneumonia. Beibei remained in the hospital for the better part of a month, which set me back half a month's wages. My boss very generously reimbursed me for her treatment and hospitalization fees, saying it counted as a work-related expenditure. I didn't turn him down or push back against his repugnant assertion.

I'm a crass man. I had to think of my livelihood and future prospects. There was nothing more to it than that. I didn't tell Lanzi, of course, because I had no way to account for my boss's extraordinary generosity.

In just a few short weeks, Lanzi rapidly returned to her pre-pregnancy weight. It was practically a miracle. Incredible, really, how much mental and physical strength a mother can expend worrying over her child. It was yet another difference, I discovered, between what Beibei meant to her, and what Baobao meant to me. There was only one Beibei: once lost, there was no getting her back. But Baobao could never be lost. So I would never feel the same level of anxiety, grief, and despair for my virtual baby. This difference was the impetus for the game's development in the first place, and yet it was also the reason, as I was disappointed to realize, that there was never any comparison between myself and a real mother.

After Beibei came home from the hospital, I made an earnest effort to reform myself. I no longer kept to my study to avoid hassle. "Father" wasn't an identity that was separate from my work. I began trying, with real patience, to love and care for this *living* child, with whom I shared a blood tie. Because I knew she only had one life, and I knew just how tender and fragile that life was.

Time flies, as the old saying goes, and my first year of fatherhood went by in the blink of an eye. Lanzi had gone back to work, so we hired an experienced middle-aged woman as a nanny. Beibei had already learned how to talk. No. To be precise, she'd learned a handful of very simple words. "Mama," "Daddy," "good," "bad," for example. She often used her still-shaky syntax to piece together short phrases like "Mama good" or "Daddy bad."

Why was Daddy bad? Beats me. Maybe babies possess powers of discrimination that we adults have lost, and she could sense that the love and affection her mother gave her was far more genuine than anything her chipper, jokey father had to offer. But every time I picked her up and rocked her with a mind toward investigation, every time I tentatively observed her reaction to various body language cues, her round dark eyes would suddenly go still, wariness shooting from her brown pupils.

Maybe I was being paranoid, but I'm convinced it was wariness. Just like Lanzi. I don't think she ever truly let down her guard around me either. Deep down, she still suspected me of not loving our child. From the moment I held Beibei for the very first time, she could never shake that doubt.

But to all appearances, we were a picture-perfect family. A beautiful, clever wife and a gentle, caring husband, both highly successful in their chosen careers. A pretty, well-behaved daughter. Nothing was wanting. My boss often boasted that *he* was the reason for my charmed family life. Naturally, I'd bow my head and agree. "Yes, it's really all thanks to you."

After the demo of the holographic *Raising Baobao* was released, the market response was enthusiastic. Thirty percent of Holonet users had registered an account in the game, and the number only kept rising. I'd accepted the assignment to turn the prototype into a full-fledged game. The company planned to launch it as soon as the full version was ready. Then I could collect on my 10 percent of the tech shares. If I sold them, I could likely add a zero to the balance in my bank account.

I could continue to work from home as before, keeping an eye on my daughter Beibei while I created Baobao. The nanny looked after the baby, anyway. I didn't have to do much.

One afternoon, Mrs. Xu, the nanny, asked me for the rest of the day off, claiming a family emergency. I didn't mind. "Go right ahead."

"Mr. Hu, you shouldn't lock the door to your study all the time. You'd better bring Beibei in there with you, or else you won't be able to hear if something happens to her outside," Mrs. Xu warned as she left.

I thought she had a point, so I went upstairs to the bedroom to check on Beibei. She was sitting on the rug, sucking on her fingers with great relish. She stuck her thumb in her mouth and steadily slurped away, saliva dribbling down her fingers to her wrist. If Lanzi caught Beibei doing that, she would sternly pull her hand away and replace it with a pacifier. But not me. I removed Beibei's thumb from her mouth and carried her to the bathroom, where I scrubbed her little hands. "All right, have at it."

Beibei looked up at me, thought seriously for a moment, then said, "Daddy good."

Wonder how mad Lanzi would be if she'd seen that, I thought, with an evil grin. I carried Beibei downstairs and put her down on the sofa outside my study. I took care to leave the door cracked open, so that I could respond in case of an accident.

I started up my computer, connected to the network, loaded *Raising Baobao,* and got to work. Suddenly, a flash of inspiration hit me, and I devised a new scenario for the game: What should you do if Baobao sucks his fingers?

Option 1: Lightly smack his palm.
Option 2: Apply bitter herbs to Baobao's fingers.
Option 3: Wash his hands and let him continue.

Did that count as spoiling him? Hmm, no. After a moment of thought, I added one more option: Wash his hands, smear honey on his fingers, and let him continue sucking.

I was tickled by my own creativity. It was a game, after all. And in a game, you could be irresponsible like that, without worrying whether you were teaching your child bad habits.

Suddenly, I froze. Could I distinguish between the game and reality?

When I was teaching Beibei, was I able to make a clear distinction between her and Baobao?

No! Of course not!

In the game, Baobao was sucking on his finger with great relish, smacking his lips in a way that suggested the honey on his fingertip was very sweet. Just then, I heard a squeal. Turning, I watched the door to my study swing open a little wider as Beibei squeezed her tiny body through. When had she gotten down from the sofa? How? Had she fallen? Was she hurt? I hadn't even noticed.

In that moment, my first response was to lose my temper. "How did you get in here, you little terror!"

I ran over, but as I bent to pick her up, she raised one pale, chubby arm and pointed, a look of shock and anger on her face. Yes, it was anger. That instinctive emotion, present from birth. This home was hers, this daddy was hers, or so she'd always thought. But now, suddenly, an interloper had come to take it from her!

I looked back at Baobao in midair—my Baobao, composed of electrical signals. He and Beibei were about the same size, with identical pink cheeks, small rosebud lips, shining dark eyes, and two inches of soft, jet-black hair.

Beibei wriggled forward at speed, with the posture of a soldier making a charge on the battlefield, in an attempt to ram straight into Baobao's incorporeal form.

"Beibei!" I barked.

I then witnessed a most startling scene unfold: the two babies—one flesh and blood, one a character in a game, formed from streams of information—began to swat at each other. And in my shock and vexation, I didn't know which side I should help!

Beibei wouldn't suffer any harm because she was real. Baobao's physical presence was simulated. Even if he hit Beibei, it would cause her no more pain than an itch. And no matter how hard Beibei hit Baobao, it wouldn't have any real effect on him, because all that he felt and experienced was a setting. His pain, his cries, were only the responses the game had determined he should display.

But in the moment, I was stupefied. I didn't know what to do, or who to help. Baobao and Beibei's cries rose higher and higher until the din reached an alarming decibel level. I thought my head would explode. My hands didn't know where to go. I can't remember ever feeling so awkward.

"Beibei—"

"Baobao—"

". . . Oh, to hell with it, I'll just turn the damn thing off!" I muttered, turning off the holographic computer. Baobao, still wailing, vanished instantly from the room, leaving Beibei sitting on the floor, sobbing and sniffling.

"There, there, it's Daddy's fault." I scooped Beibei up, gently patting her on the back. I happened to look up, and met Lanzi's gaze, cold as an Antarctic glacier.

"Ah!" I jumped.

"What's the matter?" Lanzi asked quietly. "Did I scare you? Something troubling your conscience?"

"No, nothing." I smiled, trying to disguise my nervousness. "I was just playing. What are you doing home so early?"

"Mrs. Xu called me and said she had to leave. I didn't trust you to watch the baby alone. And a good thing, too—if I hadn't left work early, I might have missed the show."

"What's that supposed to mean?" Afraid of being found out, I could only lash out.

"Give the baby to me." Lanzi took Beibei from me and clutched her tightly to her chest, as if she were afraid someone might try to steal her away. She raised her head and surveyed the room. "All this came so easily to you, didn't it."

"Let me explain—"

"What is there to explain? Do you think I don't know what your company recently released? Do you think I never took any notice of your work? I just never thought you could be this shameless." Lanzi's voice was flat, emotionless, which made it all the more frightening.

"Lanzi, I don't understand what you're saying."

"Yes, you do. Don't deny it."

"You said you wanted a baby!"

"There you go, now you've shown your true colors." Lanzi gave a brittle laugh. "I certainly won't shirk my responsibility toward the child *I* wanted. Don't worry, I won't kick you out. This is your studio. Beibei and I are leaving."

Goddamn it! How could I be so unlucky? I beat my head against the wall.

"Drop the act. After all these years, for the first time I can see who you really are."

Lanzi left and took Beibei with her, leaving me here all alone. I didn't know whether to curse my luck, or admit that I had only myself to blame. In the wake of their departure, my large home seemed silent and desolate.

Beibei's laughter seemed to echo in the air. Her sweet, guileless voice sounded like an angel's. I could still see Lanzi sitting on the top step of the stairs. She would often place Beibei beside her, so that they were side by side, while she reminisced about the time my classmate had touched her maternal heart with a simple instruction to his daughter. Then, she would sweetly open her arms to Beibei and say, "Beibei, give Mama a kiss."

I missed my daughter and wife.

I turned on my computer and brought out the little scamp who was the very image of my daughter.

Baobao, give Daddy a kiss.

Baobao, Daddy is sorry for what he did.

Daddy's heartbroken, Baobao.

What should I do, Baobao?

"But what's the use in talking to you! You're fake! Fake! Fake!" Suddenly angry, I clawed at the air, thick with transmissions, as if to tear apart a nonexistent screen.

Two weeks later, Lanzi's lawyer served me divorce papers. I refused to sign. In retrospect, I realize what a scumbag move that was.

"I'll agree to anything Lanzi wants, as long as she returns with our daughter," I said.

"Mr. Hu, my client considers this marriage to be irrevocably broken." The lawyer's expression was like an official notice: all business.

"Then I won't sign. She can send you back again in two years," I replied. Fortunately, marriage law mandated a two-year separation period before granting a divorce by default. I'd make her wait it out.

"You . . ." Finally, a crease in the lawyer's blank-paper face.

"I want Lanzi and my daughter back," I repeated.

The lawyer began to try to reason with me. "It is my client's belief that you two are no longer emotionally compatible. If you refuse to listen to reason, she will not rule out the possibility of suing for divorce. Why make things so ugly?"

"Incompatibility is not legal grounds for divorce. I have not been unfaithful, nor have I committed domestic violence. Going to court will get her nowhere. I want my wife and daughter back." *I'm not backing down, and there's nothing you can do about it,* I thought. *Let's talk law and see who's scared of who.*

"You—" Livid, the lawyer left, but Lanzi didn't come back. No matter how hard I begged, no matter how many times I apologized, she refused to see me again.

She moved, changed her number, even relocated to a different city to avoid me. But in today's world, there's no one who can't be found, so long as you're determined to find them. I wrote to her every day, and sent occasional gifts for Beibei. The doormen in her new apartment building all knew me by sight and would announce, "Beibei's father is here again."

But I'm a cowardly man. After six months, I grew tired. I was no longer so desperate to get my wife and daughter back. Or maybe, my own self-loathing was strong enough to convince myself they were probably right to leave me.

Raising Baobao officially launched, and my savings grew exponentially. But what did it matter? It was money I had earned by selling my daughter. I couldn't enjoy it.

When it came time to upgrade the game again, the boss appointed me to oversee the development of the sequel. I took the job. The assistant the company assigned to me was a new hire from another studio. He was eager to make a game based on anecdotes from his three-year-old son's life.

"Why?" I asked him. "You don't feel like you're selling your son?"

"Why would I? I think it's because I'm a good father that I can produce such a vivid game. It's proof of my love for my son." He seemed to realize how sappy that sounded, and sheepishly scratched the back of his head and laughed.

So, that was it. All of this could be good, provided your original intentions were good.

My heart was crooked from the start, so it became something twisted.

On my lunch break, I went to stretch my legs in the small garden outside my office building. A little girl in a red dress was riding a tricycle in the center of the park.

Suddenly, she came to a stop, looked all around, and cried out, "Mama, Mama—"

I went over to see what was wrong. The girl's right sandal had gotten caught in the tricycle's wheel. Her lovely little face reminded me of my Beibei. I couldn't bear to see a look of anxiety and helplessness on a face like that. "What's wrong? Let me see. Ah, it's stuck. Not to worry, hold on to my shoulder . . ."

I crouched down and gently slid an arm around her. Lifting her right foot, I swung her leg over the seat. Then, I had her lean against my shoulder and wrap both arms around my neck, while I reached under the tricycle and turned the right wheel backward. The sandal fell out, and I picked it up, placed it on the ground to the left of the tricycle, and guided her foot back into it. For one brief moment, the girl's whole body was pressed against mine, a soft, warm reminder of life's tenderness. In that moment, it was like I was embracing life itself.

In that moment, she was my daughter.

Then I noticed another pair of feet. I followed them upward to a skirt, a blouse, and, above it, Lanzi's face.

I was too shocked to speak. Lanzi's expression was complicated: she looked somewhat touched, but at the same time, it was written on her face that all love and affection between us had faded. When she looked at me, she saw only the father of her child. I slowly lowered my head. The little darling in my arms had a fair, chubby face and eyes like black marbles, bright with intelligence. She was smiling shyly at me, a smile that made me want to die.

"How did two years go by so fast?" I asked, stunned.

"Daddy, you're Daddy," said Beibei, recognizing me.

The look I gave Lanzi then was filled with gratitude. She hadn't lied to our daughter that I was dead, unlike so many embittered wives. She must have shown Beibei pictures of me. She never would have remembered me otherwise—not in her dim memories from when she was one, at least.

"Yes, they did go by fast. Beibei's already in nursery school," Lanzi said, with a sigh.

I swallowed the sob rising in my chest and pulled my daughter close again. "Beibei, Daddy missed you. Daddy missed you so much."

The tail end of a cold front from some remote corner of Russia swept over our city that afternoon. But as I held my daughter, I'd never in my life felt such a heart-stirring, vital warmth. Up until that moment, I had never truly wanted a child with all my heart and soul.

My days of ignorant folly ended there. I was starting to become a real father, even though my daughter and I would soon have to part again.

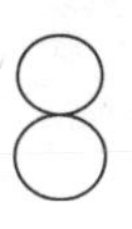

A Saccharophilic Earthworm 嗜糖蚯蚓

BaiFanRuShuang 白饭如霜
Translated by Ru-Ping Chen 陈汝平

A Saccharophilic Earthworm

By BaiFanRuShuang
Translated by Ru-Ping Chen

Roses and St. Bernard's lilies decorate a balcony on the top floor of a mansion. Spider plants and devil's ivy hang from the adjacent roof.

A woman named Flora waters these plants with great care. She follows that with a pruning ritual to prevent overgrowth, a spray of insecticide to keep the bugs away, and then she turns to inform her husband, Qiao, of the highlights of her day.

"The roses in our home have dreams and aspirations, just as we do! Yesterday, they told me they want to be celebrities in the future!"

Qiao smiles and presses his lips lightly to Flora's hands. Warmly, he replies, "Really? You think they're blessed with such talent?"

Flora nods earnestly. "Of course! They can work toward developing it. I'm the director and I've an eye for talent . . . I mean, I *know* a talented rose when I see one."

Once upon a time, Flora had also possessed an eye for identifying talent in her own kind. Having graduated from the world's most prestigious drama school, Flora was among Broadway's newest generation of directors.

And, for a time, she was a star.

Then, a car accident. Permanent loss of lower-body mobility. Irreversible trauma to her mind.

A star nonetheless.

But per societal conventions, a director no longer.

Rarely does she descend the flight of stairs leading from the top floor of the mansion to the living room. Seldom does she venture into the menacing world outside.

And, for a time, she'd resigned herself to longing for the stage, now accessible only through the television screen.

But thank goodness for Qiao, and thank goodness for those plants: the only two things in this world willing and able to accompany Flora in the darkest days of her life.

Rose

An unparalleled, innate beauty.

A manner of song and dance distinct from that of human singers and dancers.

A fine selection for the main character of the play.

Devil's Ivy

A striking physical appearance: thick, elegant, with lush leaves.

Another fine selection for the lead role of the play.

Cactus

At first glance, nothing particularly special.

Upon further examination, tough. Full of moxie. Enough to play the antagonist.

Flora

When Qiao is occupied with work, Flora situates herself among the greenery and flowers. She whispers sweet nothings to these entities, who in response harness the wind's strength so as to mimic human expressions of body language.

"The weather is quite nice today, though it is a bit too windy for my liking," says Flora.

The roses nod in agreement.

"Dear, oh dear, devil's ivy, you can't possibly keep working yourself like this. The sunlight comes from *that* direction—not this one! When will you develop the know-how to recognize what is meant for you and what is not?"

In response to Flora's nagging, the devil's ivy simply extends farther away from the sunlight.

Flora shakes her head and laughs. She is happy. She is grateful for their company.

And the plants seemingly reciprocate these feelings of gratitude. For upon August's end, the flowers are still in full bloom. Upon September's arrival, these ardent expressions of beauty have no end in sight.

We will stay with you, Flora.

Qiao

Tonight, Flora sits in the living room, waiting for Qiao's return.

It is late when he arrives, and as he opens the door, Qiao can't keep the gloom and exhaustion he feels from showing on his face.

Flora takes no notice of these cues. She waves happily at Qiao and tells him proudly, "Today, after my afternoon nap, *all* the plants and flowers moved themselves into their places on stage! They started practicing for *Cats*! All by themselves!"

Qiao lets out a sigh of exhaustion. He attempts a smile, but today it is too much. He hurries to her side instead, taking her in his arms, and burying his head in her shoulder.

And for a moment, everything is fine.

Flora smiles. "What should I do? Should I help them practice their lines?"

She breaks their embrace and holds out a script for Qiao to examine. Qiao loses his balance, and irritation surfaces on his already-pained face. He brushes past her, opens the door to their room, and collapses onto their bed.

Sentiments that should have been verbally expressed. Sentiments that, on that night, Qiao had only the capacity to physically express. Even if they had been verbally expressed, would his love understand?

Flora stares blankly at Qiao. She makes a motion to retrieve the script that has fallen to the ground.

He has made himself clear. Tonight, he is unable to keep her company.

That night, as she hoists herself onto their bed and lies down next to Qiao, a realization comes to mind.

No conversation, no physical intimacy.

Sleep shall not come easily tonight.

The wind whistles through the plants on the balcony. Psithurism after psithurism, as Flora opens her eyes.

Flora listens to these sounds in the dark of the night. She sits up and looks around. From a distance, she makes out the faint, yellow outlines of the spider plants behind the curtains moving to and fro, their leaves folding inward in expressions of grief.

A dream? Perhaps. As loveless nights between Flora and Qiao increase in number, so do her interactions with the plants.

These days, Flora rarely leaves the balcony.

Sometimes, Qiao remembers. On those days, he seeks her out.

"My love, I've had such a day at work today."

A pang to the heart as a smile materializes on her face. Whether he's had a good day or a bad day, Flora gives him the same smile.

Not wanting to get into it again, he asks, "Have the cacti learned to dance? I remember you saying they were too stiff, so how's that going? How do they dance without looking too clumsy?"

Flora's smile broadens. The light and love return to her eyes as she luxuriates in Qiao's warmth. "I've no idea! They just started dancing—you should have been there—and it just worked!"

"Wow, that's amazing," says Qiao.

The silence returns.

Qiao tries again. "Well, today I—"

Flora makes her way to the balcony. "I've got to help them practice!"

On the last day of November, Qiao returns home a little earlier than usual. As he reaches the front door of the mansion, he hears music emanating from the balcony and grins from ear to ear.

Oh, Flora.

His movements become gruff: he shakes his keys, coughs loudly, kicks the pavement so as to inform the persons inside—it is time for *you* to hide.

Flora must have planned a birthday party for me.

Smiling to himself, he counts: *five, four, three, two, one . . .*

Qiao opens the door to an empty, lifeless living room.

No surprise, no cake, no HAPPY BIRTHDAY banner.

No Flora.

Flora must be on the balcony.

He runs upstairs, then downstairs, to the kitchen and back. When he reaches the foot of the stairs, he feels his knees buckle beneath him.

For the living room is lifeless no longer. Instead, it is populated by a different life form.

The plants. They must have moved themselves from the balcony to the first floor.

Qiao sits in awe as the plants position themselves in a half-moon shape: marigolds hang in bunches from the ceiling in front of the roses, devil's ivy, and cacti. A rustle here, a psithurism there, as the plants take their places on the stage.

Then, the marigolds descend from the ceiling. They unfurl one by one as the cacti, devil's ivy, and roses disappear from Qiao's line of sight.

A curtain of marigolds.

The one at the bottom right swings to reach the adjacent coffee table. On the final swing, the marigold manages to press a button on a remote, and an agony-ridden, deeply melancholic piece by Carl Maria von Weber fills the room.

The mood has been set.

The show has begun.

The roses twirl synchronously in an outward motion. From an aerial view, they encircle the two sides of the curtain in a heart-shaped formation that eventually straightens into two standing vertical lines. The twirling progresses into an artful bend here, a graceful arch there, then an intertwining of stems so as to create the image of a larger rose from a distance.

One rose in particular catches Qiao's attention. This one has unwillingly bent itself at a ninety-degree angle, and threatens to give way under the collective weight of the roses lying on top of it.

Snap!

Qiao covers his face as this rose falls out of the formation. He peers through his fingers and watches the flower fall to the ground, detached from its stem. The rest of the roses move behind the marigolds.

An attempt to twirl ensues, to perform the aforementioned artful bends, graceful arches. One failed attempt after another, as tears litter the ground on which Qiao sits.

Then, the devil's ivy makes its way toward the rose. The petals of the rose tremble as the ivy curves its leaves, so as to cradle the rose and connect its roots to whatever is left of the rose's stem.

I shall support you. You shall find refuge in me.

The cacti emerge and move to center stage. As they encircle the rose and ivy in a menacing manner, their needles threaten to cut the shattered rose from the ivy's roots. The cacti slowly move inward as the rose and ivy tremble in fear.

The truth shall end me one day.

The "happy couple" dare not provoke the cacti, whose needles mean the difference between life and death. Instead, the ivy pulls more of its roots out of the soil to support the rose, and the rose cowers to bury itself deeper in the leaves of the ivy, but—

Roots were not meant to exist like that. Roses were not meant to exist like that.

Then, all the roses emerge from behind and move upward, scaling the curtain constructed by the marigolds.

A collective *snap!*

A shower of rose petals.

Qiao looks up as the petals fall around him, and his silent tears turn into sobs.

I suppose plants and humans love in the same manner.

The rose has gone. A distraught devil's ivy scrambles in desperation to find its rose, ignoring the separation and pain written all over the petals that now litter the living room floor.

As Qiao takes another breath, a realization comes to his mind.

The truth shall end me one day. The ivy has been set free.

Flora has gone. Have I been set free?

On all fours, Qiao crawls and traces the shape of the petals that lie around him with his fingers, unable to stem the flow of tears. Warmth emanating from an invisible presence brushes past him overhead, and he looks up to see a rose that has yet to bloom. It rides the chandelier above like a swing, and motions in the direction of the front door.

He has made a choice. He knows how to carry on.

If you are a shattered rose, I shall live as your stem. Where I am is of no importance, for I will always be with you.

On the balcony, an earthworm in translucent, yellow-orange hues smiles briefly at this poetic expression of love. It lies down and thinks, *What special powers shall I give to these plants tomorrow? The ability to love? Business acumen? My, the possibilities are endless, aren't they?*

A saccharophilic earthworm: a non-human entity that takes the form of an earthworm. These earthworms come in many shapes and sizes, and can transform an environment by giving plants the ability to act out aspects of the human experience.

9

The Alchemist of Lantian 蓝田半人

BaiFanRuShuang 白饭如霜
Translated by Ru-Ping Chen 陈汝平

The Alchemist of Lantian

By BaiFanRuShuang
Translated by Ru-Ping Chen

I wander across the supposed splendor of this world, waiting for someone, something.

If someone were to represent this act of "waiting" in an auditory manner, I would hear the sound of endless weeping, a crying that sees no end.

I remember thinking that existing in this state would have been quite sad.

But that is no longer the case for me.

I'm just so fucking tired.

A visual cacophony. Young adults dressed in an edgy iteration of their Sunday best. Grotesque color combinations that, by my reckoning, are sacrilege against primary and secondary colors. Young adults who grow into old age.

I've seen this cycle so many times. *Too many times.* And I'm sick of it.

So, I wait. I wait for something that has not yet come to pass.

At present, I am in Xi'an. I stand before Qin Shi Huang's vast and mighty army of terra-cotta soldiers. A statue of the First Emperor sits behind this army, a pitiful attempt to represent the countenance of a purportedly majestic, but in truth, cruel and authoritarian figure.

I've since forgotten this emperor's face.

No matter. This emperor had not been particularly attractive anyway.

Death by virtue of an obsession with the power vested in him by his position.

And I'm sure, once upon a time, the Emperor had questioned its worth.

What good is power, if none can divine the secrets of immortality for me?

A pitiful existence, if you ask me.

I stand there and continue to pity the Emperor. Then, a small, elderly woman with a short stature hurries past me. Lost in thought, I knock into her and—*oh man, my hands have a mind of their fucking own today*—PUSH this woman to the ground. The black, tiled jar in her grip shatters into a million tiny pieces.

I stare at my hands as she bursts into tears. My offers of help go unanswered as she kicks at the ground, her face twisted into a look of such sorrow and pain that I can almost feel the hurt on my own skin.

I scan her body. *Doesn't look like she's sustained any physical injuries from the fall. Is she messing with me? Please don't be a scammer, you look like a nice old lady.*

Believe me when I say that I *know* the difference between true expressions of pain and a performance made in hopes of some capital gain.

Fuck scammers. Also, fuck how long I've spent in this godforsaken world.

The elderly woman kicks at the ground again.

Hmm, definitely not an expression of physical pain. She derives her pain from something else. And I don't think she's scamming me.

So, in addition to my inability to determine *why the fuck she's crying so hard* and having lost the capacity to articulate my thoughts in speech, I watch this elderly woman catch her breath as she picks up the pieces of her jar.

She says nothing to me. She doesn't even acknowledge my presence. She cleans herself up, takes a breath, and scurries away.

No fucking way am I going to let her get away without a formal apology from me.

So, I follow her from a distance.

She carries an intangible burden. *I can't explain it, I just see things, you'd get it if you had my eyes. Just believe me, I can see through fucking rocks okay?! All I know is . . .* something weighs on her heart.

Before she enters a building painted in golden and jade hues, she looks up at the doorway with pained eyes and takes a breath.

She enters the building. Seconds later, she staggers out, crestfallen and on the verge of tears. She tilts her head upward to face the sky as tears stream down her face.

As for me, I proceed to engage in an internal dialogue.

To approach or not to approach?

Approach.

I make my way toward the elderly woman, all the while practicing how best to express my guilt and remorse. *I got this.*

I walk up to her, only to stutter and let out an incredibly weak "Is there anything, uh, do you, um, anything I can . . . uh . . . help with?"

She looks at me. I'm guessing she normally doesn't go around telling her life story, but her burdens seem to threaten to crush her in this moment, so she tells me everything about her life and how it intertwines with the menace that is this world. *I agree, this world is godforsaken.*

She recognizes that the world is cruel. But mere recognition of the fact does nothing to lessen the pain experienced as a result.

She'd finally given birth to a son in her old age.

Two months later, her son had fallen ill. Had it been a common cold, her troubles would likely have not come to pass. But the illness possessed a ferocity similar to that of an enraged tiger, so her family's savings disappeared in a matter of weeks. In hopes of coming up with a solution to save their son, her husband had made the difficult decision to break a sacred family tradition.

The black, tiled, *porcelain* jar. *Well, fu—*

He was meant to pass this jar down to his progeny. For five generations, this tradition had been preserved. In the sixth, it was to end.

The elderly woman was to take the jar and exchange it for RMB 300,000, all in hopes of saving their child.

Hopes I'd destroyed when *my fucking hands* had pushed her to the ground.

The shattered pieces could maybe amount to RMB 300,000?

Don't kid yourself.

Oh fuck, what have I done?

Wait for it.

Waiitt for it.

Waiiiiittttt for it.

I prepare myself to hear the *blame blame blame. Humans pull this shit all the time, even when they're at fault, but this time I fucked up so hard and actually deserve it—*

The expected tirade does not come. The elderly woman does not seem to resent me. As she walks away from me, she says, "It wasn't meant to be, wasn't meant to be . . ."

I mean, *I guess. That's fair. But of all that exists in this world, who or what truly knows what is meant to be? Don't look at me. I don't fucking know. But it makes sense. It gives her a reason to get on with her life.*

A part of me also desires to develop a sense of complacency regarding the events that transpired to create *the shitshow that is my life.* Then I can cultivate a sense of resilience so that I may bear the agony of a couple thousand more winters and summers, if only to mitigate the pain associated with my fate.

Must matters of this world take place in such a manner?

If you ask me, no, *they fucking shouldn't.*

But at the very least, I can help others escape *their* so-called fates.

I run up to the elderly woman, grab her arm, and snatch the jade stone hanging from her neck. Discolored, brown, and, fortunately for me, not made of porcelain.

I conjure what little warmth exists in my body—by nature, I'm cold-blooded—and envelop this piece of jade with my heat. *Think about caterpillars weaving cocoons, spiders weaving webs, and that's what this looks like.*

My warmth transforms the stone as we run into the city. The elderly woman begs earnestly for me to slow down. *But we can't slow down now . . .*

We arrive at the city's largest jewelry store. A mere glance at the transformed stone I hold is enough to dispel the crowd before us, creating a pseudo–red carpet for me and the elderly woman.

I pick up a silky red cloth in the vicinity, layer the cloth around the stone, and place it on the counter.

A majesty that moves humans to tears. A non-replicable sophistication. A silkiness akin to three thousand meters of spring water. A magnificence that blinds all in the vicinity.

The crowd gasps at its beauty.

Then, silence as the manager walks up to the counter. When the stone comes into his line of sight, he nearly collapses. He stumbles to the counter and exclaims to the elderly woman, "I'll give you as much as you want; as much as you want, I shall give to you."

The elderly woman turns to thank me. But it is too late.

I have since taken my leave.

The sun has begun to set. *Where shall I take refuge this night?*

My hands still carry some semblance of warmth. A small pile of ashes now sits where the jade stone had been in my hand. I use my mouth to blow them away.

Away, away they go.

You see, I'd transformed the worn-out stone into an ornament more appealing to the human eye, one more likely to take a spot on an arbitrary list of this world's most beautiful objects.

I continue on my way. I see the lights of a hundred thousand homes and, once again, pass by the terra-cotta soldiers.

Good old Qin Shi fucking Huang was much luckier than I shall ever fucking be.

I laugh bitterly at what shall come to be, for me.

Let me tell you another story.

A young prince. Armor adorned with a nonagon-shaped jade ornament.

At the time, I was a transient. I was young.

And during my travels, the young prince had fallen ill.

I couldn't help it. I *had* to do something to help him escape his "fate."

I tried to bring him back to life.

That's what that jade stone was supposed to do. Bring him back to life.

But at the end of this story, all I could do was watch as they buried the transformed stone along with the young prince.

I laugh bitterly.

My magic isn't forever. Objects that Lantian half-beings transform return to their original state after a generation.

Oh, and another thing. We're actually forbidden from using these powers at all. To use them as recklessly as I have would disturb the order of this world.

So, what happens to dumbfucks like me?

We're not allowed to go back.

For me, that means: Only after the collective objects I've transformed return to their original states do I finally get to go home.

I'd trade places with Qin Shi Huang any day . . .
A state of existence in which I wait.

Lantian half-beings: non-human entities; that is what alchemists were supposed to be—cold-blooded beings who live long.

10

The Way Spring Arrives
春天来临的方式

Wang Nuonuo 王诺诺
Translated by Rebecca F. Kuang 匡灵秀

The Way Spring Arrives

By Wang Nuonuo
Translated by Rebecca F. Kuang

I

The boy Goumang dashed through the morning mist, dripping sweat onto the mud.

The village was bordered by mountains on three sides and surrounded by a babbling creek. The green-bricked walls of the village were built in concentric circles, each surrounded by the next. Goumang darted through one green ring of packed dirt wall after another.

He flew past the walls and rice paddies. When he saw Xiaoqing, the light mist hadn't yet dissipated from the surface of the river. Her form was faintly visible through the mist. She stood atop a boat, holding a bamboo pole in her hands.

"You can go if you want," Goumang shouted, panting. "But can you take me with you?"

Xiaoqing didn't answer.

The dawn mist faded away. Goumang's face had been reddened by the sun.

"You can't go by yourself! You—you have to marry me!"

A shorebird dashed out of the weeds, sending ripples across the river's surface.

"You think we'll get married just because you said so?" asked Xiaoqing. "I'm older than you. Who carried you around when you weren't even tall enough to reach the table? Who picked persimmons for you? Who gave you candy?"

"But I've gotten bigger since then, and you've stayed the same. There must be a day when I'll be older than you."

"We don't count years like that." Suppressing a smile, Xiaoqing beckoned to Goumang. "Come here, then. Come aboard and accompany me to the South Sea."

"What are we going to do in the South Sea?"

She pursed her lips, considering for a moment. "Let me finish this errand, and then we can do anything you like."

Goumang didn't keep questioning her. He hopped forward and boarded the boat. The boat's draft wasn't very deep; it wobbled back and forth a few times before steadying. Dappled sunlight shone on Xiaoqing's face, and her skin was covered with fine, glistening beads of sweat. Her eyes were bright as two sweet grapes.

2

Xiaoqing bent low, pushing the pole against the riverbed. The boat slowly drifted forth. Ripples spread out, evenly stirring the rosy clouds that covered the river.

"Did you mean what you said just now?" asked Goumang. "When we get back from this trip, you'll . . . you'll marry me?"

"All I said was that we would never part," said Xiaoqing. "I didn't say that we'd marry."

"Never parting is fine! This morning, when I heard that you were never coming back, I got so scared I searched the whole village for you!" Goumang paused. "What kind of errand is this, anyhow? Hurry, tell me so I can help you get it done. Then we can come back to the village."

"My mission isn't difficult. It is . . ." She paused. "It is to make the begonias bloom."

Goumang knit his brows. "Which pot of begonias do you mean? How hard can that be? All you have to do is water them every day."

"Not just one pot of begonias. All of the begonias in the world. I need to make all of them bloom."

Goumang's eyes widened. "All of the begonias in the world? But they all need watering and trimming. Surely that's too much work!"

Xiaoqing cast him a smile. "You still don't understand. Watering and trimming don't make begonias bloom. Gardeners don't make begonias bloom. What makes begonias bloom is spring."

"Spring?"

"Yes, spring. Every year at this time, I must bring about the return of spring."

The day was still cold. The fields on both sides of the shore hadn't come alive yet. They were bare and dusky, steadily falling behind their boat as they sailed. Xiaoqing sat down and placed the pole beside her. She rested her elbow against the side of the boat, propping up her chin with her hand.

"Look, it's the South Sea."

Goumang looked to where she was pointing. The river had run all the way to the ocean. The water suddenly deepened. An island lay just at the edge of his vision.

"Are we going to that island?" Goumang asked.

Xiaoqing nodded. "Yes, but my pole can't reach the bottom of the ocean, so I'll have to invite them to help."

As she spoke, she pulled an old, tiny ocarina out from the folds of her clothing. She stood up and blew. Goumang was familiar with this tune. Xiaoqing had hummed and sung it in the past. He'd listened to it; over time, he'd grown up with it.

"They're here."

Goumang could sense them. Creatures hidden under the ocean's surface were pulling them forward. The little boat suddenly sped up, torrents on both sides spiraling into tight little whirlpools.

As they approached the South Sea, they saw a stove burning on the cliff of the island. A pot hung over the stove. The stove and pot were both massive, about the size of the walled village. If this stove and pot were used to make soup, Goumang wondered, would a single pot be enough to feed everyone in the village for a lifetime?

Compared to the massive stove, Zhurong, the giant god of fire, seemed like a tiny, insignificant black dot. Goumang remembered how, in the village, he'd been unable to see Zhurong's face even if he tilted his head back. Now, Zhurong hoisted a tree branch several times his height and threw it into the stove. The thick, sturdy branch was instantly devoured by fire. Zhurong dodged away from the leaping flames, wiped away his sweat, then headed down the cliff in search of more firewood.

Overhead, Chisongzi, the god of rain, rode on one of his cranes as the flock circled above the island. The cranes would drag wisps of clouds over the pot using their beaks and then quickly beat their wings, turning the clouds into small showers of rain that then pattered down into the large pot.

"Nüwa used this pot and stove when she smelted the five colored stones to mend the sky. Once the sky had stopped leaking, she left it behind for us to boil water," said Xiaoqing.

"Boiling water? Is that what Chisongzi and Zhurong's regular jobs are?"

"Yes, though they also have other tasks. Chisongzi grants rain to places suffering from droughts. The red-crowned cranes he keeps use their feathers and beaks to gather the water vapor in the atmosphere, bit by bit. They create wind by beating their wings, and the fast-moving air makes the temperature of the dark clouds plummet. The saturated water vapor condenses until the weight of the water droplets exceeds what the atmosphere can support. Then they fall to the ground as rain. As for Zhurong, he is in charge of fire. He keeps lots of fireflies near the South Sea. When the skies go dark, he lets them loose and they fly into the stoves of every household in the world, lighting the stoves with the fire in their tails."

"No wonder I hardly ever saw Zhurong and Chisongzi in the village! So . . . does everyone in the village have a job like this?"

"Yes, they all do, once they've grown up. Leizu, for example, is wonderful at reeling silk, spinning, and weaving. Every night, she weaves a cloud brocade to place on the water. The brocade's colors blur together, dyeing the water and the heavens that touch it. That is the glow of clouds at sunset. My grandfather is in charge of plants. The seeds of plants that can cure illnesses are coarser than those of plants that are toxic. He uses a small sieve to filter out the seeds of medicinal grasses. Then Feilian blows them across the earth in one breath. As the seasons pass, all living things in the world move according to set rules. The people of our village are responsible for maintaining these natural rules. Things have always been so, from the ancient past to the present."

3

Thanks to Chisongzi and Zhurong's efforts, the water quickly came to a boil. The pot bubbled over, bubbles bursting and splashing.

Xiaoqing knew then that it was time to set out on her true journey.

Again, she blew her ocarina in the direction of the ocean. Its sound was like velvet, perhaps because it was so soft. Goumang closed his eyes as the melody surrounded him. He felt as if he could hear the sound of the ocean rushing forth from the dark depths.

Their bodies were massive. Their horizontal tail fins were raised high, emerging from the water like rows of huge crimson flags. Similarly, their backs appeared over the ocean surface like sleek islands, steady under the beating of the waves.

"Incredible—what *are* they?"

"They're giant fish." Xiaoqing swept her bangs behind her ears, but the sea breeze quickly blew her hair into a mess again. "Come, jump on."

"We're *riding* them?"

"Yes! We're riding them to the North Sea."

When he mounted the back of the giant fish, Goumang felt like he wasn't touching scales, but rather skin as coarse as a reef.

The massive pot tilted slowly over the precipice. Scalding water streamed down the side of the cliff, making steam hiss from a large patch of the ocean. The giant fish, who numbered about fifty, arranged themselves in a bowl-shaped formation, sweeping up the hot water between them like a ladle. Slowly, they began moving north. Goumang and Xiaoqing sat on the back of a fish in the center, who seemed to be the largest of them all.

"They're not afraid of getting scalded?" asked Goumang.

Xiaoqing shook her head. "Hot water is lighter, so it floats on the surface. The giant fish also float near the surface, and guide the hot water from the South Sea to the North Sea. That's what ocean currents are. They bring moist air and heat. When the water vapor reaches dry land and meets cold air, spring rains will fall. Then all living things will sprout roots and germinate. That's what spring is."

"So every year you guide the warm currents from the south to the north?"

"That's right." Xiaoqing pointed to a small island they were sailing past. "Look!"

The island wasn't large, and it passed quickly from their field of vision. Yet in the moment that they sailed past, the once-gray island went from light yellow to grass green to dark green. A small bout of rain fell into the cracks between gray stones from which shrubs tunneled out. A few small, barren trees rapidly branched and blossomed, attracting bees and butterflies. At a rate visible to the naked eye, spring arrived on the island.

It wasn't only this little island. On every island, every part of the vast country they'd traveled; indeed, everywhere they passed through, spring appeared. Under the warm spring rains, the frozen rivers and creeks became a flood. Birds, insects, and little critters awoke. All of the plants blossomed—spring, like an infectious disease, was unstoppable.

The arrival of the warm currents also stirred up krill carcasses from the ocean depths. They floated up and turned into marine snow—the best food source for ocean life. Schools of sardines chased behind Goumang and Xiaoqing, fighting with each other for food; occasionally, a silvery-white fish belly flopped over the surface.

Goumang sat basking in the warm sea breeze, watching as both the sun and the school of fish gradually sank below the horizon. He pointed below his feet. "He won't suddenly dive underwater, will he? We'd drown!"

The giant fish were swimming north. The setting sun shone against the western side of Xiaoqing's face, turning her into a red-orange silhouette.

"Then we'll just have to ask him." Xiaoqing bent down, caressing the fish's exposed back. "Kun, will you?"

All they heard in response was a long, drawn-out bellow from the ocean depths.

4

When night fell, the giant fish slowed their pace. Land appeared before them.

Taking advantage of high tide, Kun delivered Xiaoqing and Goumang to the side of the cliff. The waves were few in the gulf, and the stars shone clearly against the water. A few lively fish jumped up, leaping from one patch of the starry skies to another. When they sank back below the water, the glimmering water droplets thrown by their fins were flung toward the even brighter moon.

"With the fish playing around like this, won't the hot water disperse?"

"No, it won't. Some of the fish are guarding the heat in a circle formation, while the others have gone off to find food or to rest. They'll switch shifts later in the night."

Kun gave a low cry. His body half-emerged from the water, throwing up massive waves that resembled a begonia flower on the ocean surface. As she turned to answer him, Xiaoqing caught sight of the flower blooming in the water.

As if Kun had made a gift of it to her.

"I think that this fish must really like you," said Goumang.

"Well, of course. When I was your age, I thought I would marry him." Xiaoqing's eyes, bright as sweet grapes, brimmed with amusement.

But Goumang didn't think this was funny at all. "You wanted to marry a fish?"

"Everyone turns into a fish."

He furrowed his brows. "I don't care about that. Anyhow, you've already agreed. You said we'd always be together."

"You've already learned about jealousy? I remember what I agreed. Now, come and help me do my work."

Xiaoqing bent down, rooting around the grass. She rustled about for a moment as she searched, then lifted a black stone into the air. "Ha! Here it is."

"What is that?"

"A meteor!"

"That can't be. How could a meteor be that black? And shouldn't . . . shouldn't it be in the sky?"

"Meteors look the way they do because of their friction with the atmosphere, which generates light and heat. Only then do they appear bright. At other times, they look like this. If you don't believe me, look. There's still a wish attached to the end of this meteor. "

Goumang went to have a look. Indeed, a string was attached to the coal-black stone. Several rolls of paper hung from its end. He unrolled the first one and read it under the moonlight.

"I want to get rich overnight." He glanced up at Xiaoqing. "What kind of wish is that?"

"The humans who see meteors make a wish, and then that wish will attach to the meteor's tail and fly behind it. When the meteor has reached the highest point in the sky, if a Xuan bird flies past and sees the wish, then the wish will come true. Right, so, this person wants to become rich."

Goumang unfurled another roll of paper.

"I want my wife's . . . illness . . . to be cured? Huh? This one's handwriting is so terrible, I can't even read the rest!" The third and fourth rolls of papers were similar; the handwriting was so crooked that he couldn't make out the complete sentence.

"Only the wish of the first person to see the meteor will be recorded clearly," said Xiaoqing. "The ones that follow will be more and more blurred. The Xuan bird can't read them clearly, so their wishes don't count."

"So the person who wished for their wife to get better from her illness won't have his wish fulfilled, but the person who wanted to get rich overnight will? This—this isn't fair!"

"All of those wishes were made to satisfy the wisher's own desires. There's no judging which is better or worse."

"Yes, there is!" Goumang retorted. "You'd only make that kind of wish if you love someone. If you love your wife. That's a much better wish than wanting to get rich overnight!"

"Love? That's a very small love." Xiaoqing didn't keep arguing. She pulled the string off the rock, then threw the smooth meteor toward the east. She wasn't very strong, but once the meteor entered the night sky, inertia would keep pulling it along.

"After you clean off the old wishes, the meteor can start receiving new wishes and take them to the Xuan bird. Right now, we're standing on the westernmost part of the world. If we throw the meteors from here, the air resistance is minimal, so it can fly to the easternmost part of the world before dropping. When we're at the easternmost point, we'll have to pick it up again and fling it back west."

So Goumang joined Xiaoqing in picking meteors out of the grass. He'd come up with a secret trick. Every time he threw a meteor, he immediately made a wish:

"I want to be with Xiaoqing forever."

He knew very well that no one had seen this meteor before him, which meant his wish would be recorded very clearly on the paper. He threw out so many meteors carrying so many slips of paper expressing so many identical wishes. The Xuan bird had to make them come true, didn't it?

5

They set out from the westernmost point of the world. A few days later, they reached the North Sea.

A dozen stone pillars marking the northernmost point of the world jutted from the sea. The hot water had cooled over its long journey. The giant fish broke their formation and dispersed, one by one.

Goumang probed Xiaoqing. "Look, we've brought about spring, so shouldn't you marry—"

"It's almost noon now, but the sky is still dark. How can that be spring?" Xiaoqing watched Goumang intently.

Goumang grew anxious. "How are we not finished? Do you mean we still have to adjust the time of the sunrise?"

"That's the earth's axis." Xiaoqing pointed to the stone pillars in the distance. "The sun's orbital path forms an angle with the earth. When the angle is large, the sun is moving in the north. The sky in the north is short, so the days are short. When the angle is small, the sun is south of us. The sky in the south is long, so the sun takes longer to move across the southern sky. When the days grow longer, that's summer."

"That—what does that have to do with the earth's axis?"

"The axis extends from the North Sea into the earth's core, where it connects to a gear wheel. When Pangu split heaven and earth apart, his heart became the gear at the center of the world. His heartbeat makes the gear move a little bit every day, and the earth above slowly tilts accordingly. This gradually adjusts the angle of the earth. The sunlight changes according to these rules, which is how we get the four seasons in order."

"Then won't the days get longer if we just let the earth's axis and gear turn by themselves?"

Xiaoqing shook her head. "Later, Gonggong smashed his head against Buzhou Mountain in a fit of anger. The earth suffered too much of an impact, and the gear in the earth's core broke. It doesn't work so well anymore. Every time winter transitions into spring, the gear will turn halfway and then get stuck. It needs an outside force to pull it all the way around."

As they spoke, Kun slowly swam toward the earth's axis. The axis, Goumang noticed, seemed to be made of basalt. It was dark in color, covered with ash-colored barnacles where the axis met the water. A few tangled strands of twine were attached to the top. Saturated with sea salt, they had long become coarse and tattered.

Xiaoqing was trying to tie one of the strands to Kun's dorsal fin. This wasn't an easy task, but fortunately a groove had been etched into Kun's fin from years of pulling the rope. At last, Xiaoqing succeeded in tying a knot. Having finished this, she lowered her head and said to Kun, "Tomorrow, your reincarnation will be complete. The days you spent taking care of me in the village will seem like they happened yesterday. Eight thousand years pass very quickly, and then my reincarnation will also be complete . . ."

Her voice wasn't very loud, but Goumang had grown used to it. It was soft and gentle, but his ears easily picked up its sound.

"Your reincarnation?" Goumang asked, distressed. "Where are you reincarnating to?"

"I told you. When this is all finished, we'll be together." Without lifting her head, she picked up a strand of twine and tied it to another fish. "We won't part."

Goumang, in response, began helping her with her task.

6

When they had bound all of the giant fish to the earth's axis, a marble white color appeared in the eastern sky. During the winter in the northernmost point of the world, Xiaoqing told Goumang, if they didn't pull the axis around, then the sun would not appear in the east. The light would quickly fade, and the curtain of night would descend.

Once again, Xiaoqing blew the ocarina. Under the faint light, the dozens of giant fish pushed toward the west, their scarlet backs poking out of the water. The ropes gradually stretched taut. The force of the tension made water drip off the twine, each droplet reflecting a piece of the begonia-colored sky.

Very soon, thanks to the collective efforts of the giant fish, the earth's axis budged a fraction. Goumang heard a *kala* sound. The angle of the earth had changed accordingly. Their plan seemed to have worked.

But the side effects of moving the earth's axis now became obvious. The sea level simultaneously began to tilt. A great wave rose in the distance—vaguely, the water appeared like a towering wall, rumbling as it rolled toward them from the southern horizon.

"What do we do?" Goumang shouted to Xiaoqing over the din of the wave. "If we get hit by a wave that huge, we'll die!"

"Quick, bend down! When the earth's axis is adjusted, the ocean will stabilize."

The giant fish had noticed the changes in the ocean. They quickly clustered together, the ropes tied to their bodies interweaving into one piece. They seemed to be trying to use their combined strength to withstand the wave.

"Hold me close." Goumang used the rope to fasten them tightly to Kun. The surge of water was getting closer and closer. It was even taller than the walled village; taller than a small mountain.

The shift in the ocean had disturbed the atmosphere. Black clouds soon gathered over their heads, chafing against one another, generating thunder and lightning. The gale smelled of fish, but the giant fish were still rapidly moving their tail fins. They pushed toward the west, straining against ropes that were on the verge of snapping.

Goumang could feel blood rushing into the muscles under Kun's rough skin.

He clung tightly to Xiaoqing. "The wave is too large, the fish can't all pull in the same direction."

"Kun, did you hear that?" Xiaoqing asked. "The wave is too large! Use your wings; use your wings to block the water."

"It's a fish!" Goumang shouted. "How can a fish have wings?"

"All giant fish have them . . ." Xiaoqing lowered her voice. "Many years ago, I asked Kun the same question. He once had arms and legs like me. He watched me grow up. And every year, he brought about spring."

They were drenched from head to toe. Xiaoqing spoke as she and Goumang embraced, and he didn't know if she was talking to Kun or to herself.

"And then?" Goumang asked. "He turned into a fish?"

"Yes. I will also turn into a fish, for we must all become fish in the end."

"So I . . . I will also become a fish?"

"You will as well. But before then, you still have work to do. After today, you'll have to take over my task and bring spring every year."

Xiaoqing's voice was getting fainter and fainter, perhaps because the winds and waves were too great. She didn't notice Goumang's hesitation as she continued, "Eight thousand years ago, Kun brought me from the South Sea to the North Sea and taught me how to bring about spring for the first time. Eight thousand years have passed . . . Kun is about to enter the world of humans. Are you . . . happy?"

Kun seemed to understand her words. Suddenly he rushed forward, threw off the ropes, and charged out of the water.

A pair of small, scarlet side fins expanded on either side of his body and transformed into a pair of featherless wings. Unbound, Kun's wingspan expanded at an astonishing speed. He flew against the morning light toward the giant wave.

Goumang struggled to hold onto Kun's back. This was the first time he'd seen the world from above.

The giant fish's torso was like a flying island. Goumang looked over his body at the vast, stormy ocean below. It was pitch-black, limitless.

A great many schools of fish—tiny from his perspective—swam within the waters, still striving to pull the earth's axis.

The eastern horizon was getting brighter and brighter. That meant that the fish had almost succeeded. Inch by inch, they pulled the earth's axis around. Bit by bit, the sun appeared.

And then . . . and then spring would truly arrive for the entire world.

Spring . . .

Goumang's mind gradually went fuzzy. He thought of the dark green of rice paddies and tea fields. He thought of how the bricks of the walled village turned warm and cozy under sunlight; how his buttocks felt too hot when he sat atop them. He thought of the downy kittens that his grandmother's cat gave birth to every spring. He thought of spring rains. He thought of Xiaoqing holding an open umbrella when she picked him up as a child; the mist and rainwater moistening her eyelashes and her sweet grape–like eyes.

He couldn't stop thinking of these things . . .

There was a fish in the North Sea named Kun. Kun was so huge, one did not know how many thousand li he stretched. He turned into a bird named Peng, and Peng's back was so large, one did not know how many thousand li he stretched. When Peng rose up and flew, his wings were like clouds covering the sky . . .

The great wave was almost in front of his eyes. The water vapor hit them in the face. He grasped Xiaoqing's hand tightly.

"I think I understand what love is."

Smiling, Xiaoqing nodded. "Then you've grown up."

Then Kun smashed against the great wave.

7

When Goumang awoke, the ocean was calm again. The other end of the rope binding him was empty. Xiaoqing and Kun had both disappeared.

The sun emerged from the eastern horizon. Golden strands of light shone on his skin, the ocean, and the breeze.

He knew that the earth's axis had been pulled around.

The fish, exhausted, now drifted along with the waves. There was no sound from the wind or waves. He only heard silence. He sat steady and cross-legged on the back of a fish, quietly watching the sunrise in solitude.

Perhaps the sunrise was Xihe—he who pulled the sun from the east to the west every day in a cart. Goumang supposed it was so. He knew that from today, he would never look at the world the same way again.

Bit by bit, the warm light of spring dried his clothes. Suddenly, his shirt pocket twitched.

He reached into his pocket and pulled out a tiny, delicate creature. A red fish, even smaller than a goldfish, lay on his fingers, beating its tail against his palm. It was slippery and cool to the touch.

He quickly scooped up some ocean water. The fish flipped over in his hands.

At that moment, he saw that the fish had a pair of eyes bright as sweet grapes.

He knew that in eight thousand years, this little fish would also grow as large as a small mountain. Then she would finish her mission and enter the world of mortals, transforming into an ordinary human being. And he knew that in eight thousand years, he himself would turn into a fish, transporting the warm currents year after year, laboriously pulling the earth's axis.

But he also knew that if his soul wanted to mature, things had to be this way. He needed to spend sixteen thousand years, experiencing the same thing sixteen thousand times, to see clearly what love was. Only then could he grow the heart of a human.

What was love?

Goumang found the begonias very beautiful. Now, he wanted to bring spring's return every year.

"Xiaoqing, we'll be together for another eight thousand years . . ."

Goumang pulled out the ocarina. Slowly, the giant fish awakened one by one, and together they began their journey back south.

11

Translation as Retelling: An Approach to Translating Gu Shi's "To Procure Jade" and Ling Chen's "The Name of the Dragon"

Yilin Wang 王艺霖

Translation as Retelling: an Approach to Translating Gu Shi's "To Procure Jade" and Ling Chen's "The Name of the Dragon"

By Yilin Wang

Throughout the history of Chinese literature, there has been a long tradition of retelling folktales and myths, where stories are reinvented again and again by each new storyteller. Similarly, when a story is translated from Chinese into English, it is never an exact replica; it undergoes transformation, however subtle, as it is re-created in a new language and cultural context. The Chinese speculative fiction stories "To Procure Jade" by Gu Shi and "The Name of the Dragon" by Ling Chen, which I translated into English for this anthology, both perform retellings. To shed light on my translation process, I want to unpack some of the challenges that I faced when re-creating these stories for Anglophone readers, and the specific decisions that I made on the page. The stories' multilayered nature—with both allusions to and subversions of the original tales that inspired them—makes them uniquely challenging to translate. At the same time, translating these retellings has offered me a chance to reflect on the many parallels between the two art forms. Just as retellings can offer new insight into the stories they're derived from, a translation has the potential to deepen or challenge readers' understanding of the source texts, the source and target languages, and even storytelling itself.

The stories "To Procure Jade" by Gu Shi and "The Name of the Dragon" by Ling Chen both draw on Chinese folktales and mythology, while simultaneously subverting them. "To Procure Jade" critiques legends about Empress Dowager Cixi's endless search for immortality by focusing on the experiences of Deyu, a former palace eunuch who served her. Similarly, "The Name of the Dragon" overturns the conventional view of Chinese dragons as a revered and majestic symbol of power by telling the life story of the dragon Yinglong, who has been repeatedly mistreated by humans and longs for freedom. As a translator, my priority is to honor the authors' original words and intentions in the stories' translations.

I begin my process by considering each source text's voice, especially how I might re-create the sense of familiarity and subversion that coexist in the original. "To Procure Jade" is told from a distant third-person viewpoint, in a style that evokes the conciseness of a Classical Chinese bǐjì (short prose records) from pre-modern China, but with occasional moments of irony that critique the Empress Dowager's obsession with immortality. In my translation, I work to preserve these qualities by adopting the narrative voice of oral storytelling traditions. For example, I pay careful attention to preserving meta-narrative moments, as displayed in the opening phrase "Legend spoke of Yu Spring . . ." I also re-create the story's distant narrative viewpoint by using a singsong rhythm and passive voice, like in the sentence, "During China's Republican Era, there lived a former Qing dynasty palace eunuch who was named Deyu." The source text's sarcastic tone is also reflected in my translation; Deyu is described as "ever the humble servant" even as they take on a new name that mocks their former master.

When translating "The Name of the Dragon," I also prioritized maintaining the story's voice, especially the shifts in diction and syntax that parallel viewpoint shifts. The source's text oscillates between the ordinary and mythical, as the story moves from two ordinary humans to the thoughts of the misunderstood dragon Yinglong and then to the humans once more. I use simple diction and short sentences in the scenes that depict humans. In contrast, the dragon's storyline is translated in the style of ancient epics and high fantasy, with long, winding sentences, parallel structure, and a formal elevated register ("unsurpassable clamoring and unparalleled liveliness," "carefree abandonment," "enmity forgotten," etc.)

In addition to translating the multilayered narrative voice of each retelling, I also need to consider how to translate each story's surrounding context. My translations have to find their place on a spectrum that spans between the intimate and the unfamiliar. Both "To Procure Jade" and "The Name of the Dragon" use various difficult-to-translate terms and idioms specific to Mandarin, and rely on unexplained cultural, historical, and literary shorthand assumed to be common knowledge for Chinese readers. The inclusion of unexplained subtext or implied information is especially common in retellings, which often derive meaning from allusions to folklore and mythology. I want to give Anglophone audiences the same immersive reading experience as readers of the source texts and not present the tales as an unknowable Other, yet at the same time I also want to preserve linguistic and cultural differences, even if they may at times distance non-Chinese readers.

Depending on the context that I am translating, I may use brief glosses to clarify context or leave information untranslated. For example, I insert brief exposition where relevant in "To Procure Jade" to spell out the story's sociopolitical context, such as the implications of the Emperor heading to Manchukuo and the low social status of palace eunuchs, because this context is key to a deeper appreciation of the story. My translation of "The Name of the Dragon" also includes short notes explaining what imperial porcelain wares are and how to tell the dragons Kuilong and Yinglong apart, because for Chinese readers, this would be common knowledge or easily researched. On the other hand, when translating the name of a Chinese calligraphy style in "The Name of the Dragon," I avoid both "regular script," a standard translation that lacks specificity or descriptiveness, and "kǎishū script," a term that would be understood by readers who know Chinese but would be meaningless to everyone else. Translating kǎishū as "regular kǎishū script" allows me to hint at the script's appearance, while pinpointing the exact script for Chinese readers and readers who care about this level of specificity in world-building.

The challenge of finding a balance between the intimate and the unfamiliar is also present when I translate names and pronouns. I often prefer to transliterate names based on their pinyin spelling, as their meaning can be very difficult to translate. In "The Name of the Dragon," I transliterate the names of the dragons Yinglong and Kuilong. Although each of the names contains the character "long," which literally means "dragon," the "long" functions like a suffix that is inseparable from the first part of each name. It is tricky to translate the complex meaning of "ying" and "kui" into English; for example, the character "ying" in Yinglong can mean "respond," "answer," "must," or "ought to," depending on context. Although some meaning may be lost, I choose to preserve the dragons' original names rather than Anglicize them because the creatures are unique to Chinese mythology, differ significantly from dragons in European literature, and are the story's oppressed underdogs. Similarly, in "To Procure Jade," I deliberately leave words such as Deyu (the protagonist's name), the Yu Spring, and the noun "tongyu" untranslated, with brief notes explaining their meaning. This allows me to preserve the repetition of the sound "Yu" throughout the story and to set up the homonyms that are crucial to the story's overall plot and ending. The use of transliterations also allows me to highlight the importance of homonyms and wordplay in Chinese storytelling and culture in general.

However, in some instances, the purposeful translation of names and pronouns can actually highlight, rather than erase, a story's implied layers of meaning, making this a better choice than transliteration. In the original text of "The Name of the Dragon," all the human characters are unnamed, in contrast to the dragons. I maintain this namelessness by referring to the two main human characters as the

Boy and the Assistant, just as they are identified in the Chinese text. I also capitalize these titles, a stylistic convention in English commonly applied to characters who are identified by their titles rather than their names, to make the references clear and name-like. This choice, which is not present or possible in Chinese, a character-based language, further emphasizes the humans' representation as generic stock characters who are defined solely by their roles and who lack individual identity.

Similarly, in "To Procure Jade," my translation of Deyu's pronouns helps me bring out the story's subtle and subtextual commentary on gender identity, which may be less noticeable to Chinese readers. In the source text, Deyu is referred to by the pronoun "tā" (他). In Mainland China, this pronoun was once a singular gender-neutral pronoun, but it has become gendered as a male pronoun after the Chinese writer Zhou Zuoren conceived of a female "tā" (她) pronoun in 1918. Deyu, a character from roughly the same era as Empress Dowager Cixi (1835–1908), is depicted as non-binary and as both male and female. I avoid translating Deyu's pronoun "tā" into a male pronoun based on its contemporary definition; I also do not transliterate the pronoun directly as "tā," which is too ambiguous because the pronouns she/he/they all have the same "tā" pinyin spelling. Instead, I use the gender-neutral "they" to allude to the gender-neutral "tā" that has fallen out of popular usage in Mainland China. For both Chinese and Anglophone readers, this translation choice can serve as a reminder of the often overlooked history of gender-neutral pronouns in Mainland China, and of how non-binary characters in ancient Chinese tales may have been erased due to the loss of gender-neutral pronouns.

For me, the power of translating a retelling lies not in the literal translation of words, characters, or plot events. When I translate Gu Shi's "To Procure Jade" and Ling Chen's "The Name of the Dragon," I am not only translating the stories, but also their narrative voices, surrounding literary and cultural contexts, and the ways characters are named and perceived. To translate stories rooted in folklore and mythology is to transplant many complex layers of meaning across linguistic and cultural borders all at once. As a retelling is transformed again in translation, the boundaries between the familiar and the unfamiliar are blurred once more. New life is breathed into ancient tales, retold narratives, and source and target languages, creating opportunities for them to be seen in new ways, to expand, and to evolve.

The Name of the Dragon 应龙

Ling Chen 凌晨
Translated by Yilin Wang 王艺霖

The Name of the Dragon

By Ling Chen
Translated by Yilin Wang

The Assistant pulled the door open, revealing a sudden onslaught of dust and darkness. He coughed non-stop for a long moment, barely able to breathe. His glasses threatened to fall off. He steadied them and raised his flashlight.

"All the best items from Grandpa's collection are here," said the Boy, fingering his curly hair, dyed a bright yellow.

"Hopefully we can find something truly valuable." Unable to find a light switch, the Assistant took a reluctant step forward, coughing loudly again as he breathed in more dust. "If we don't, we'll never be able to buy this old residence." A trace of sadness passed through his eyes. "We'll have to watch it be torn down and replaced with a commercial plaza."

The Boy stepped over the tall and short furniture with his long legs, careful not to bump into the jars and vases stacked casually on the floor and to avoid the many small and large packages wrapped in different materials. He sighed. "It's probably best to move everything out of here . . ." As the Boy turned, an overly tall stack of objects finally collapsed, crashing onto the stone floor before he could react, dissipating into a cloud of dusty antiquity.

Before the Assistant could let out a sigh, the Boy gave a startled cry. "Hey! Isn't this the imperial porcelain vessel from Grandpa's art catalogue?" The Boy held up an oddly shaped vessel. It was a royal ware fired in a royal kiln. The Boy polished the vessel with the tip of his sleeve, making its surface clear and vibrant, showing a complex design in blue pigment that looked freshly painted.

The Assistant's eyes widened. After flipping through the old man's art catalogue countless times, he had long committed to memory the identifying features and measurements of the few porcelain wares in the catalogue. He leaned in with eagerness, his flashlight nearly bumping against the blue porcelain vessel.

"Be careful!" the Boy warned. "It's an exceptionally rare treasure. And I thought Grandpa was just joking around . . ."

As the Assistant turned the vessel about in his hands, the entangled patterns on its surface gradually revealed themselves. Blue clouds and waves mingled together in an alternating pattern. A flying dragon soared amidst the clouds and waves, displaying its majestic strength, almost as if coming to life. Next to the design, near the mouth of the vessel, a six-character mark—*made in the Xuande era of the Ming dynasty*—was written horizontally in regular kǎishū script.

"Yes, this is really the one." The Assistant's voice shook noticeably. "It's the blue-and-white porcelain ice chest with a Yinglong design." These ice chests were used in the old days to keep food cold and to lower room temperatures in the heat of summer. "It's not only priceless, but said to contain a mystery."

The corners of the Boy's mouth turned up in a faint smile. "Oh, come on, don't overstate it. Just because we found something from Grandpa's art catalogue doesn't mean we should believe all he said. This porcelain vessel even has an imperial kiln registration number. How mysterious could it be?" He played with the flashlight in his hands. "Anyway, we found this ice chest. Our visit to the ancestral hall paid off. Time to go."

"Wait a second!" the Assistant yelled suddenly. He raised the chest up, holding it close to his eyes, scrutinizing it under the glow of the flashlight.

"What's going on?" the Boy asked.

"It has a Kuilong design on it, not Yinglong!"

"How could that be? The dragon has an elephant's nose, a curly tail, and two feet, each with three claws. How could it be any dragon other than Yinglong?"

"Look carefully. Does this dragon have scales? Yinglong has scales. Also, if it were Yinglong, why would it be holding a blossom between its teeth? A dragon with flowers is definitely Kuilong!"

The Boy's expression shifted. Kuilong was a serpentine creature that looked like a dragon but had only one foot. A porcelain ice chest with a Yinglong design would command a high price, while a Kuilong one would attract no buyers. What need did he have for this Kuilong?

"But it has a registration number, which can't be forged," the Boy said in confusion. "It definitely should have Yinglong on it, so why is it showing Kuilong instead?"

The Boy and the Assistant stared at each other in shock and dismay. Where had the Yinglong design gone?

It had been six hundred years since Yinglong had been sealed into the porcelain ice chest from the Ming dynasty's Xuande era. The dragon lay lazily on the horizon where clouds and seawater met, between sky and sea. Its thick winding body stretched out across many miles, rising and falling to the rhythm of its slow, drawn-out snores. Over the span of six hundred years, green lichen had climbed all over its body, covering its brilliant golden scales and soaking in vast amounts of rainwater. The drenched Yinglong became more and more like a lush hill covered by marshlands. Only its horns remained upright, pointing skyward, the sole trace of a greater majesty beneath.

A dragon's sleep was rumored to last for three thousand years, but the many beings surrounding it lived only for a few days. As fish and shrimp thrived in the cracks between the dragon's scales, they attracted huge groups of predators—flocks of birds descended like clouds, charging freely across Yinglong's body, chasing after the fish and shrimp flopping about in an attempt to escape. The dragon was surrounded by unsurpassable clamoring and unparalleled liveliness.

But it didn't seem to notice any of the nearby happenings. It remained silent with its eyes shut. Deeply and exceedingly drunk, its breath still carried the fragrance of the wine it had drunk six hundred years ago. Next to the dragon's nose and mouth, following the flow of its wine-aroma breath, special wine flowers sprouted and grew—white for rice wine, gold for yellow wine, green for fruit wine, and purple for honey wine. It took ten years for the flowers to bloom and another ten for them to bear fruits. These fruits made for lavish feasts in the world of Yinglong. Even the clouds and seawater turned crimson with drunkenness during those moments; birds and shrimp partied the night away together before collapsing atop groves of lichen, mingling with carefree abandonment, all their enmity forgotten.

Flowers bloomed and wilted. Fruits ripened and grew again. Another three hundred years passed. The dragon opened its left eye. At that moment, all the bustling around the dragon fell hushed. Birds couldn't fly no matter how hard they flapped their wings. The lichen, fish, and shrimp shrieked as they were scorched by the heat rising in the cracks between the dragon's scales. Fierce waves rushed forward to engulf the clouds, as if preparing to take flight and join Yinglong the moment it finally swung its tail and leaped into the sky.

But the dragon's strong, bulky body didn't move a single inch. Its breathing, which had turned quick and uneven, calmed again, returning to a leisurely pace. Birds took flight once more, their outstretched wings touching each other, soaring up in cloud-like clusters. Yinglong's scales became cool and icy, collecting fresh clear rainwater among the cracks, and nurturing the lichen, fish, and shrimp. It hadn't woken after all.

The dragon wasn't exactly asleep, either. It had simply collapsed from deep intoxication after drinking a rich fragrant wine, which a Taoist had crafted secretly through endless, meticulous rounds of brewing, steaming, and fermentation. The dragon's heart had been anesthetized by the alcohol; the heart beat very, very slowly, unable to stimulate its blood circulation or the movement of its muscles and joints. And so, it simply lay there, letting time slip past like the water that trailed across its body.

Eventually, a strange-yet-familiar voice exploded, as if sudden thunder cracked at the sky's edge and in the ocean's depths. Immediately, the dragon's heart contracted strongly, and a thought, which had first risen six hundred years ago, was finally transmitted through its brain, swimming slowly across its central nervous system, attempting to stimulate and excite its gray matter.

I should just die of drunkenness here. Would the humans finally leave me alone? the dragon thought.

Humans? As Yinglong's left eye twitched, half a dozen scallops slid down from the top of that same eyelid. The topic of humans was sensitive and unpleasant, bringing discomfort to the dragon's alcohol-fogged brain.

Humans! Faint discomfort, transmitted by strand after strand of hair-thin nerve fibers, passed through the dragon's nervous system, causing more and more trembling, until the dragon felt as if its soul had been struck by a roaring thunderclap.

Humans—Yinglong was jolted awake. It looked around in a daze, glancing at the sky and earth, the fish and birds, the flora and fauna. All of life seemed to be carefree and thriving in the frosty autumn, but human beings were nowhere in sight.

A human voice continued to echo in the dragon's ear. "It's Yinglong. Yinglong. It shouldn't be Kuilong!"

The Yellow Emperor had been the first one to call the dragon Yinglong. Yes, the Yellow Emperor, the one with a bulging forehead, who had rescued it from under a priest's sacrificial knife. The priest believed that the dragon, a monster with horns and wings conceived and raised by a domesticated guard snake, should have never been born. But the Yellow Emperor led the dragon away, raised it, and bestowed upon it a name. "Yinglong, you must always answer to and obey humans, because humans gave you a new life. This is your destiny."

Yinglong grew up at the Yellow Emperor's side. A whole year's provisions for the Emperor's entire tribe wasn't enough for one of Yinglong's meals. The Emperor's six giant chambers were only large enough for Yinglong to stick its head inside.

"Yinglong, Chiyou's tribe is waging war against us," the Emperor said. "Go and help us with the war."

Yinglong thus headed to Zhulu to join the fight. As it stretched out the giant wings on its back, the sky and earth shook, hit by a rainstorm. The Yellow Emperor grinned as Chiyou's soldiers and stallions fell into disarray, escaping in defeat. But then, a moment later, the direction of the storm changed. Chiyou had invited the Wind God and the Rain God to aid him, and their ability to control water exceeded Yinglong's a hundred times. The Yellow Emperor's smile froze as a rainstorm submerged his newly conquered lands.

Yinglong couldn't help but sigh as it brooded over its long-ago defeat, and as it sighed, the wine-aroma flowers burst, scattering the scent of alcohol all over.

Why did the humans continue to seek it out? Was it because of its brilliant golden scales? Or its giant wings that could stir up whirlwinds? Dayu, another legendary emperor, had found the dragon in the woods down south. "Oh, Yinglong, you must come and stop these overwhelming floods."

And so, Yinglong flew out of the forest. As it slammed its tail against the ground, a river appeared along the points of impact. The floodwater was channeled into rivers, flowing in an orderly manner toward the sea.

Dayu smiled. "Oh, Yinglong, although you failed to help the Yellow Emperor, you've finally managed to do something right."

As Yinglong reached this part of the memory, it grew excited. Drawing a deep breath that still carried the scent of alcohol, it swung its giant head back and forth. The chunks of lichen that lay atop its head fell off one by one, dropping fish and shrimp into its mouth. The dragon chewed. It never got to eat much during those days with Dayu. All it had done was dig one river after another, to channel rushing floodwater into the sea. Dayu and his son trailed the dragon by boat. Whenever they encountered a steep narrow valley or flat wide-stretched plains, they rode atop the dragon, whizzing across the roaring floods from overhead. To stop the flooding as soon as possible, Yinglong created forty-nine rivers in a single night. Dizzy and blurry-eyed, it accidentally dug a river that flowed in the wrong direction, causing water to rush backward, submerging freshly ploughed farmlands and a village. Humans wept and screamed from amidst the floods, their corpses floating atop the water's surface. The young Yinglong panicked, lying submissively at the place where the rivers flowed into the sea, waiting for Dayu to carry out his punishment.

Yinglong stopped chewing. Bits of fish and shrimp, as well as saliva, dripped out of the corners of its mouth, frothy and bloody, carrying a strong stench. The dragon could almost picture itself back at the place where rivers flowed into the East Sea. Dayu had gestured with both hands, summoning thunder and lightning from the depths of the universe to break Yinglong's neck. Its giant severed head rolled and rolled, falling into the sea. Blood spurted out of its wounded neck, dyeing all eight hundred miles of the white sandy beach crimson.

As Dayu showed off his mighty power, Yinglong sank to the bottom of the ocean. But mere humans didn't have the power to slay a dragon. It was all a show that Yinglong had put on to go along with Dayu. The dragon hadn't known, however, that the thunder and lightning it summoned would take its own life. Luckily, a dragon's soul never dissipated. After four thousand years of cultivating in the sea, its soul coalesced again into a physical whole, allowing Yinglong to be reborn amid the bubbling seawater.

In the new world, several millennia later, emperors decided to boldly embroider Yinglong's image onto their gowns. They yearned for immortal youth and for a stable reign that stretched on for eternity. But Yinglong was only a dragon; a dragon that could never hope to satisfy all the emperors' unstoppable, never-ending greed.

Yinglong decided it would rather get utterly drunk. A Taoist who hunted dragons for a living sealed it away. "Yinglong, you haven't committed any severe crimes, so I'll spare your life." The Taoist lectured on at length, feeling justified.

But why? Why should humans be the ones who control my life and destiny?

The angry dragon raised its head and howled for a long time. Its loud roar caused every corner of the universe to shake. The world fell into disorder, all its prosperity dissipating into chaos. Only the dragon remained, a solitary being overlooking the realm.

As the whole room shook, the Assistant dragged the stunned and unmoving Boy out the door and up a steep stone staircase. The porcelain in the Boy's hands felt slightly hot, nearly slipping out of his hands several times. He hugged it as tightly as he could. Suddenly, the underground storage room they had just left collapsed with a loud boom, transforming into a giant pit of rubble. The violent shaking of the ground threw them off their feet, and they narrowly missed landing in the pit. The Assistant pulled the Boy to his feet. As soon as they both caught their breaths, they checked the porcelain chest in the Boy's hands.

It exploded from the inside out without any warning. A single strand of dragon-shaped smoke rose skyward, morphing instantly into a golden dragon. It stretched out both wings, displaying its majestic strength as it circled the rooftops of the old residence for a moment. Then it leaped up into the vast skies and vanished without a trace.

A local television journalist happened to be nearby and recorded the dragon sighting. From then on, the Zhang Clan Ancestral Hall became known as a sacred place, sparing it from the demolitions and relocations happening throughout the historic neighborhood.

13

To Procure Jade 得玉

Gu Shi 顾适

Translated by Yilin Wang 王艺霖

To Procure Jade

By Gu Shi
Translated by Yilin Wang

Legend spoke of Yu Spring, "the spring of jade," which was on an obscure unnamed island in the East China Sea. Water flowed out of the spring's mouth only once every three years, little more than ten liters at a time, and eventually solidified into a piece of white jade. This was how the spring got its name. If a woman were to drink from Yu Spring, she would remain young forever. If a man procured Yu Spring's white jade, he would attain vast mountains of gold and silver. This legend stirred thousands to search for Yu Spring. Yet all of them returned empty-handed from their quest.

During China's Republican Era, there lived a former Qing dynasty palace eunuch who was named Deyu. It is said that their auspicious name—"to procure jade"—was bestowed by Empress Dowager Cixi, who had heard the legend of Yu Spring. She had commanded Deyu to find it, but no one could have known that she would pass away before it could be found. But ever the humble servant, Deyu decided they might as well take up the family name Wei, which sounded identical to the word "haven't," so when spoken out loud, their name now sounded like "*haven't* procured jade." When Puyi, the last Qing dynasty emperor, headed north to become the puppet king of the Manchukuo state, Wei Deyu did not follow him. Instead, they snatched a few palace treasures from the Forbidden City and stole away. They found a place to live near the Million Graves, the unkempt burial grounds in the western outskirts of the capital Beijing, took a woman who was non-speaking to be their wife, and adopted a little beggar from the streets as their son. Wei Deyu settled down as well as they could, for a eunuch.

As for the items they had secreted away with—they took two early Ming dynasty landscape paintings, an enamel pocket watch, and an eccentric-looking tongyu: a fish made from copper, wearing a crooked grin. The tongyu not only lacked an inscription from a renowned maker, but also looked unpleasant. It would be worthless if not for its jeweled eyes. Wei Deyu sold the landscape paintings in order to buy a home and get married. When the couple's pockets emptied a few years later, Wei Deyu also sold the pocket watch and the tongyu's jeweled eyes. Wei Deyu used the little money they had left to buy a couple plots of land, so they could grow and sell vegetables. By the time Japanese soldiers launched attacks on the capital, Wei Deyu's family had no food in their kitchen again, just empty pots and pans. The only palace treasure that they had left to sell was the eyeless tongyu.

This tongyu, along with some homegrown vegetables, would hopefully be enough to secure a kilogram of rice for their family. So, Wei Deyu attached the tongyu to their belt and picked some fresh carrots and cabbage from their garden. As they neared the city gates, distant cannon fire rumbled, followed by rumors that skirmishes had broken out again in the southern outskirts. Wei Deyu's heart pounded, yet they remained at the city gates. Their home in the Million Graves was still easily reachable if they needed to make a quick escape, but this area was generally untouched by skirmishes. After waiting a few hours past noon, Wei Deyu felt it was safe enough to enter as planned and rushed into the city, selling the vegetables and using the money to buy a pack of corn flour. But as they turned and crossed the street, heading eastward to a pawnshop where they hoped to then sell their tongyu, they heard cannon fire rumble again in the distance. It was safer to head home first.

They'd only made it halfway to the city gates before a passerby told them the gates had shut early. Their shoulders slumped with dejection. They didn't have a single coin on them, just a bag of corn flour, and they didn't even know whose door they could knock on to seek shelter. They paced back and forth until the sky darkened and the streets emptied of people. Gritting their teeth, they decided to climb back through a doghole into the Forbidden City, the same one they had snuck through years ago when they escaped the palace. They would find a room inside the palace to spend the night.

Ever since the skirmishes had begun in the southern outskirts, the Republican government occupied itself with carrying away palace treasures, letting the items flow out in an endless stream. Now nearly all the treasures were gone. No one dared to live in the palace either, because ever since Emperor Puyi had left, rumors had spread of ghosts haunting the Forbidden City. The palace grounds, bordered by the moat, were completely deserted at night, without a single shadow. None of this scared the former palace eunuch. Guided by the last rays of the setting sun, Wei Deyu climbed quickly into the Sixth West Palace, found a room with a bed, and fell into a sweet dream.

At midnight, Wei Deyu was woken up by a familiar voice.

"We ordered you to seek Yu Spring. Have you found it yet?"

As they sprang up from the bed, Wei Deyu trembled with shock and fear. To their surprise, brightly lit candles burned all around them. The mantel clock ticked on and on. Imperial guards stood in a row to the side, and behind the guards, a curtain draped down to cover a bed blanketed by silk. Wei Deyu saw a slender-faced elderly woman who wore long, piercing fingernail protectors. It was Empress Dowager Cixi herself!

Wei Deyu fell to their knees. Their mind went blank. Luckily, they had cultivated a sweet tongue after a decade of toil in the palace. "Your Majesty," they answered, "I, your humble servant, have been searching long and hard, with utmost attention."

"Useless." Cixi snorted. "Take this garbage away and beat it to death."

Two guards grabbed Wei Deyu, one on each side. Wei Deyu shook with terror, as if their soul had fled their body. "I found it. I found it!"

As soon as the guards released their tight grip, Wei Deyu crawled a few steps forward, scrambling as they detached the tongyu from their belt. "Your Majesty, this tongyu represents that obscure unnamed island . . ."

Head Eunuch Li Lianying slapped Wei Deyu hard before they could finish speaking. "How dare you lie to Master!"

Wei Deyu didn't dare wipe away the bloodstain at the edge of their mouth. They fell to their knees, whimpering. "I beg for mercy, Your Majesty. Although this object looks repulsive, it's surely the island. See its shape. Its eye sockets, which were hidden by its jeweled eyes, are the mouths of the spring. I hadn't mentioned it because I only found it recently—I don't know when in the next three years spring water will flow out and solidify into jade. Master, I wouldn't dare lie. I beg for mercy, Your Majesty."

Wei Deyu kowtowed fiercely as they spoke, raising their hands high to hold up the tongyu. Hopefully this unpleasant-looking fish would be enough to deceive these evil ghosts. Cixi gave a nod of apparent approval. Li Lianying took the tongyu, looking it up and down before he presented it to the Empress Dowager. As Cixi's long fingernail protectors touched the tongyu's eye sockets, she let out a sharp cry. Wei Deyu looked up. The tongyu had opened its mouth wide and bitten Cixi's hand, drenching it in blood.

What a terrible mess, Wei Deyu thought. They feared that they might lose their life here tonight due to these troubles. Li Lianying stood still, frozen in terror until the Empress Dowager started cursing. When Li Lianying tried to pry the tongyu's mouth open, it refused to budge. The tongyu bit Li Lianying too, and they cried out in pain. Cixi and Li Lianying let out increasingly wretched screams as dark crimson blood flowed into the tongyu's belly. Their shouts startled all the Forbidden City crows, which squawked loudly as they took flight. The tongyu seemed eager to suck all the blood from the two monsters, to devour them. By the time the tongyu had drunk its fill, blood was gushing from its eye sockets. All that remained of the two foul spirits were their dried skins, wrapped in the clothes they once wore.

Silence descended around Wei Deyu. Blood flowed endlessly from the tongyu's eyes like gurgling spring water. Feeling emboldened, Wei Deyu stepped forward, picked up the tongyu that was still spewing blood, and stood firmly in front of the remaining ghosts, who had frozen in terror. Wei Deyu charged at an imperial guard with the tongyu. As it bit the ghost, all the others scattered like fleeing prey. The tongyu drank up the blood of all three ghosts it had bitten. It turned bright red as it puffed out steam, ugly and expressive, as if making the face of a joyful clown. Clutching the tongyu, Wei Deyu chanted "Amitābha" three times. The blood squirted hard, flying up to Wei Deyu's lips. A pungent stench rushed down their throat. The world around them spun as they passed out.

Wei Deyu didn't wake until late in the morning the next day. They lay on their bed in the palace, the tongyu still attached to their belt. Perhaps, it was all a strange dream. Yet the events felt so vivid that Wei Deyu couldn't doubt they had occurred. Wei Deyu pried open the tongyu's mouth. A piece of crimson jade fell out.

As they made their way to the pawnshop, Wei Deyu decided they would pawn the crimson jade but keep the tongyu.

The money allowed them to start a business buying and reselling food supplies, weapons, and ammunition. Soon, they'd amassed a sizeable fortune. Their appearance remained youthful even after they'd reached their seventieth year. Their skin was fair and clear, and their hair stayed black and sleek. After they became a prosperous merchant, they searched far and wide until they finally found a wise sage who knew the legend of Yu Spring.

Wei Deyu learned that those searching for Yu Spring had been led astray by some confusion around what "yu"—a word with many homonyms—referred to. In reality, the word "Yu" from Yu Spring was the "yu" that meant fish—as used in tongyu, the copper fish—rather than the "yu" that meant jade—as used in the name Deyu, to procure jade. Yu Spring was actually the spring that flowed from the mouth of the tongyu when it had taken its bite. The copper fish had been used once upon a time by the sorcerers of the East China Sea to catch ghosts.

If it devoured three ghosts during the same night, it transformed their blood into crimson jade. Thus, the spring from the tongyu could be also understood as a spring of jade.

As is often the way with legends, the story passed among the common folk about Yu Spring was true, yet also false.

On Wei Deyu's deathbed, they passed the tongyu on to their son, recalling the day that Cixi had uttered to them, long ago, "I shall name you Deyu."

14

A Brief History of Beinakan Disasters as Told in a Sinitic Language 衡平公式

Nian Yu 念语
Translated by Ru-Ping Chen 陈汝平

A Brief History of Beinakan Disasters as Told in a Sinitic Language

By Nian Yu

Translated by Ru-Ping Chen

Part I: On Beinakans and Heat Currents

I enjoy cleaning out my stash of memory capsules.

I believe this is an accurate manner of representing what most Beinakans enjoy doing in our free time. A figurative walk down memory lane? True, to a certain degree, but you see, these memories, these experiences that I endeavor to organize, they didn't actually happen to me.

We Beinakans possess a rare trait, one that allows us to pass down memories we deem important and meaningful to our progeny. Memories of the ancient past, measurements of old lab equipment, items from old grocery lists . . . Basically, there's a lot rolling around in my brain that technically doesn't belong to me.

This is how it works.

Each Beinakan comes into existence with a stash of memory capsules attached to them. This includes memories from those in our lineage;

effectively, just a whole bunch of *stuff* from Beinakans whose existence preceded mine.

In the moments before a Beinakan develops a physical form, family members choose which memories to pass down from their existing stashes. The transfer occurs once the physical form comes to be.

Some say these memories feel foreign, others say they're heavy—these feelings are Beinakan-specific, but in general we agree that there's just an awareness that *something is there.* This awareness starts in childhood, when we do not yet possess the ability to understand these memories. It persists into adulthood, when we lack the time to sort through all of our capsules. And this awareness accompanies us into old age, until we pass on and into the next world.

These capsules come in a variety of sizes. Larger ones preserve sensory details of memories past (i.e., sight, hearing, smell, taste, and touch) and contain disoriented remembrances of significant life events. Smaller capsules usually consist of words, notes, and if you're lucky, the amusing inner ramblings of a Beinakan past who unintentionally preserved a bit of themself for posterity.

Don't let our spring-cleaning tendencies fool you, however. As much as we would like to keep these capsules organized, we rarely sort through all of them, not to mention the amount of time and energy one must invest to read and experience these memories. Most of the time, we just go through the ones labeled IMPORTANT and make sure to pass those down when appropriate. I haven't been lucky enough to chance upon an unintentionally preserved memory, but I have been quite fortunate to have been given other sets.

Those memories are the interesting ones.

This memory is old. It captures the essence of our ancient civilization and provides a seamless compilation of memories that document a dated and painful happening.

It is also nameless. I call it the Equity Formula.

However, the owner of this memory has left a footnote: the "Heat Current of Death."

This is how it starts.

"There's a 2 percent chance that the heat current will move in our direction," says a voice. "We should probably make plans to evacuate . . ."

My field of sight is altered, foggy—an indication that either the owner of this memory didn't remember enough to preserve sensory detail or that this memory was edited.

There are many reasons why we Beinakans choose to edit memories, but I digress. Let's get back to the memory.

"You're so paranoid," says another.

"But if the current comes, we'll be destroyed."

"That's why we have warning reports! And even if it does come, at most we'll just lose our homes! The heat current always misses us anyway, you're too fucking paranoid and you're stressing me out."

The voices fade. The memory ends.

A second memory begins.

Chaos. Screams fill my ears as I perceive a world on the brink of destruction. Sensory detail is very much present here—I panic, I can't breathe, I want to *GET THE FUCK OUT* but thankfully, the owner has skillfully lessened the degree to which I can feel the heat.

You see, Beinakans are incredibly sensitive to changes in water temperature—a slight increase means certain death. Choosing to edit this memory was a good call; any more of that heat would render it impossible to read.

This sort of cushioning does me good only in a physical sense. In this memory, it is all terror. No amount of cushioning could have been enough.

A foamy substance begins to materialize as the water temperature rises. I can hear bubbles popping and rematerializing, popping and rematerializing, as they form tornado-like columns that charge toward the city. Structures dissolve into nothingness, and all Beinakans in view have panic written on their faces.

There is nowhere to hide.

I shudder at the increase in temperature. This memory has been edited but I just can't help it—this fear of heat has been passed down for generations. Beinakans likely have this reaction embedded in our DNA, a sort of intergenerational trauma meant to remind us to be on guard at all times, to make sure we detect a heat current before it gets to us.

The tornadoes jet toward the right side of the city. Oddly enough, the left side of the city remains completely intact, while the right bears the brunt of the current's wrath. I should indicate here that I'm pretty sure the entire city was destroyed and this inconsistency (with regard to the right and left sides of the city) is likely the result of antiquated editing technology. But I digress.

Honeycomb-patterned PVC pipes on the right liquefy, supports meant to outline the shape of our city bend and threaten to snap, and the current rips through cocoon-shaped abodes attached to the supports, dissolving the outer layers of these homes.

The owner tries to flee but to no avail. The current moves fast. There is no place to hide. The owner is disoriented. A feeling of suffocation, then one of intense pain, and suddenly, everything goes black.

The owner has lost consciousness.

The owner of this memory must have survived the ordeal; if not, I wouldn't have this capsule in my stash. Upon this realization I am quite glad. I feel a sense of relief for the owner, who likely healed from this event.

Though I'm not sure "healed" is the right word.

The owner of this memory was an Ilian. Ah, that's right. You have no concept of what an Ilian is.

Before I delve into the Beinakan-Ilian history, I should indicate here that Ilian memories are of utmost importance to us. All those who have come before me and some who come after would like to relay a very important message:

Ilian memories *must* be passed down to our progeny.

They serve as a reminder of the consequences a species must face when its members do not take the ever-present threat of extinction seriously.

Compared to other documented heat currents, the damage caused by the heat current in this Ilian's memory—Imiya was their name—was not as severe, because some Ilians managed to survive. Regardless, the heat current moved fast, with extreme water temperatures that put all existing prediction models to shame. And as a result, the third-biggest city inhabited by Ilians had been brought to its knees overnight.

A magnificent city. Now, a mere memory.

Once upon a time, I examined the records left behind by the Heat Current Warning Brigade and noticed that there had been signs. Their radars had detected a body of water that had been making small circular motions—motions that the brigade had not determined to be out of the ordinary.

Ten minutes. Ten minutes to sound the alarm and flee. Ten minutes that would go to waste.

Ten minutes later, they tried in vain.

A misjudgment that led to disaster.

Part 2: The Old World and the Beinakan-Ilian History

Many Beinakans from the younger generation do not understand the intense horror with which older generations view heat currents. Some of their ancestors were lucky enough never to chance upon an attack, and many were born here, a world different from our old one.

I miss the old world dearly. I am thankful that my memory still serves me, so that I may relate to you the intricacies of my previous home.

I recall that it measured approximately eight thousand seven hundred miles long, from the bottom of the sea to the ice barrier that lay overhead. Lava flowed underneath the ocean floor and warmed bodies of water at the lowest sea levels, creating a section that consisted only of high-temperature waters. Heat currents used to rise upward, and it was precisely the manner in which they did so that Beinakans and Ilians dreaded. Unpredictable, unquantifiable—the "Heat Currents of Death."

Both species had (naturally) also been fearful of the bottom of the ice barrier. Apparently, all species fear what they do not understand.

Was it completely necessary to explore a new world? We hadn't even properly dealt with the heat currents, what would the point of exploration even be? These were the questions that troubled many Beinakan and Ilian minds.

However, though threats to survival had never left, another countdown had begun.

Those that lived under the sea were oblivious to its existence.

We should've started drilling through the ice barrier much earlier. It wasn't as if we didn't have the technological capability to do so.

But no entity from either species was willing to carry out this task. Drilling required that an entity come in contact with the heat currents, or that an entity guide a heat current to melt the ice barrier.

Forty thousand years. That's how long it took for the Beinakans and Ilians to deal with the nuclear fuel problem, the heat currents. Forty thousand years later, entities interested in space exploration began to emerge.

It was around this time that my physical form had finally come to be, and I split off from the body of my parent. At the time of my birth, academics and politicians had long been debating whether the channels for space exploration should be opened. When I developed the ability to make sense of my memory capsules, they were still arguing. These battles spanned decades, and when I joined the Equity Control Research Institution as a team manager, the discourse had yet to cease.

One day, Beinakan scientists detected unusual current movements hundreds of kilometers away. Upon further examination, we found that these were warm currents and used our water current generators to propel them in the direction of the ice barrier.

The currents collided with the long-frozen ice above.

The barrier began to melt.

We began to drill.

The goal had been ten thousand meters deep. But once we'd reached seven thousand meters, the ice sheets split open, the currents surged forward at an even faster rate, and our drilling machines were ejected into the abyss.

The first time in hundreds of millions of years that the ice barrier had currents running through.

Cameras attached to the drilling machinery had exploded seven seconds after exposure to this space devoid of matter. But in those seven seconds, those images had flown into ten million cocoon-shaped abodes. On that day, Ilians and Beinakans faced the heavens, the universe, the world beyond the ice barrier and took their first—albeit delayed—glance at the world beyond ours.

A reckoning.

We were but a speck of dust.

Those seven seconds had put us in our place, in terms of how we perceived our relation to the rest of the universe.

Needless to say, we felt quite small.

Few species whose existences are threatened by external forces—at the very least, this is what I believe—do not turn to unhealthy coping mechanisms to suppress overwhelming feelings of fear.

Most prefer to ignore the truth.

The elites create a context. The masses accept it.

And so began the collective cultivation of these unhealthy coping mechanisms. Just as our ancestors had begun to develop the intellectual capacity to develop and engage in city planning, business, architecture, and design, they had also chosen to ignore the precarious circumstances of our survival. Forty thousand years of living like this, even after having built a grand and splendid city so *perfectly* situated in the "safest possible location" . . .

Well, at the very least, the city's existence was a testament to Beinakan intelligence. It was not, however, a testament to sound judgment.

Many Beinakans had chosen to use a type of nitrifying bacteria to construct the outer layers of their cocoon-shaped abodes. The bacteria, in solid form, were very, *very* thick.

A pitiful attempt to shield their homes in the event of disaster, should a heat current come to be.

All in vain.

No substance in existence would be able to withstand the wrath of the heat currents.

There never will be.

The third memory.

"I'm very sorry. They've all passed on."

"But me, I'm still alive."

"Yes, you are. You're very lucky."

A pause.

"You have only to lament the fact that you were not seriously injured."

Silence permeates the room. I observe that I suddenly cannot perceive the flow of water around me in this capsule.

Ah, that's right. This is what happens when sensory details in a capsule disappear—thank goodness for technological advancements as our editing software is much better these days.

"I'm very sorry, Imiya. They won't be coming back."

The emergence of Ilian bacterial ancestors brought an end to the dreadful lives led by my bacterial forebears, who, at this point in history, had almost gone extinct. The Ilians, complete with higher metabolic rates and other qualities that do not come to mind at present—*well, thank goodness for them.* A material balance was created between our two species, and thus began our symbiotic relationship. In the ensuing decades, entities from both species increased their efficient energy use a hundred times, and the next generation of Beinakans and Ilians came into existence with higher metabolic rates, which allowed us to develop varying degrees of higher intelligence. Both species' physical constitutions increased in size—the Ilian physical constitution would grow to a size a hundred times that of an average Beinakan.

But, even though we saved each other, we could not save ourselves. I don't think our ancestors anticipated that we were to live like this, helpless in the face of the heat currents.

Think of heat currents as vicious apparitions. Now, call your personal concept of what an apparition is to the front of your mind.

A useless exercise for your generation, I believe. Here on this planet, heat currents will never come to be.

The concept of vicious apparitions for my generation: heat currents with a ferocity that could level towns and destroy cities. Not to mention the fact that forecasts of these currents were never accurate—at times, there were detectable signs, but during others, the currents would attack a city that hadn't even made it to the "Regions with Active Heat Currents in the Vicinity" list.

And I've yet to make any mention of the smaller ones, *those sneaky little shits.* Many would materialize and encircle entire cities, sending the residents there into a constant state of panic and fear. The mental fucking strain was enough for me to say *now* that both types of currents were undesirable in all possible circumstances.

It comes as no surprise then, that the most important field in Beinakan-Ilian scientific research lay in the study of equity: how to quantify the occurrence of these heat currents. It bears mentioning that it was precisely this study of equity that allowed Beinakans and Ilians to stay on good terms following the end of our symbiotic relationship.

"I want to study equity," exclaims a young Ilian.

"Ilians shall find no welcome in Beinakan spaces!" A high-pitched voice from a smaller-than-normal Beinakan attempts to send the Ilian away.

"It's not like you don't know that equity, as researched by Ilians, is lacking in many respects!" The young Ilian begs in earnest.

"Oh, at least you're an honest one. I like Ilians who know their place." The Beinakan pauses for a moment and then says, "What's your name?"

"Imiya."

"I'll remember your name. But you really can't stay here any longer."

"Why?"

"You're much too big to live in Beinakan cities—don't!" The high-pitched voice cries out yet again, "You've broken my plate—now my table—DON'T! Don't turn around!"

Due to the all-consuming terror of the heat currents, and following directly after the current that destroyed that magnificent Ilian city in a single night, Imiya and the others who had survived chose to challenge that which had destroyed their hometown and families by pursuing the study of equity. This impetus kept Imiya going—they went to lab after lab, all Beinakan, and received rejection after rejection.

Fifty-seven rejections. Fifty-seven highly intelligent scientists. All Beinakan.

Imiya. An Ilian alone in a Beinakan world.

Then, Imiya met Beier.

Beier was the head of the Beinakan Equity Research Institution. Though Beier was many times smaller than their new associate Imiya, Beier was many years older than the young Ilian and would likely live on centuries after Imiya's eventual end.

An entity of harsh words. The fact that Beier was willing to accept an Ilian as a student spoke to their incredible capacity for open-minded thought.

I'm not too sure, though. A part of me believes that Imiya might have been special to Beier in some form, and maybe Beier taking Imiya under their wing did not arise out of open-mindedness, but I digress.

To accommodate Imiya, Beier had ordered the addition of an entrance and a room tailored specifically to Imiya's needs.

All in vain.

Making adjustments to the size of the research institute was the easy part. Problems arose when it came time to provide Imiya with adequately-sized research instruments and facilities.

Do you realize how much those things cost?

"No worries." Imiya would console their colleagues over and over in this manner. "I only need numbers. I'll figure something out if I need to conduct experiments. No, no, don't worry. Innovation relies mostly on brainpower, anyway."

Does it?

Imiya and Beier discovered a way to shield themselves. Because they'd preserved all documents relating to their research in memory capsules, all Imiya and Beier needed were numbers.

Research, research, research for the next four years.

Then, a breakthrough.

In humanspeak, this is Einstein's mass-energy equivalence.

In Beinakan, we call it the Equity Formula.

In the history of humankind, the mass-energy equivalence had little impact on the strides made in nuclear energy research; specifically, nuclear fission experiments had allowed for innovations in nuclear technology—the mass-energy equivalence merely alerted human scientists to the theoretical possibility of nuclear energy.

But this was not the case for us.

The Equity Formula was the first and only of its kind—well, it bears mentioning that for a Beinakan as set in their ways as Beier, it was too good to be true.

The Equity Formula requires an elaborate derivation but has absolutely no basis in experimentation. Beier could not so easily accept the truth posited by the formula that mass could be converted into energy, especially large amounts of energy.

Beier would always have trouble accepting these truths.

Beier should have listened to themself.

The truth posited by the fundamental theory of equity guided its study for years: this theory indicated that a sufficient amount of cold-water flow would be enough to prevent the formation of heat currents. Because existing research efforts that involved coming up with ways to move large bodies of water were utterly inadequate, historically Beinakan and Ilian scientists had spent most of their time trying to figure out how to freeze water.

But the Equity Formula pointed to a new theoretical possibility: as long as you were in possession of some amount of mass, you could have inexhaustible energy.

The possibilities were endless.

Beier would say later on that their and Imiya's vision encompassed more than the others, whose efforts focused specifically on the development of superior military equipment.

Beier and Imiya's vision had colorful utility. It pointed to a wealth of undiscovered scientific knowledge, a world of unknown possibilities.

Part 3: The Golden Age

Everyone believed that the enemy had finally been defeated. Beier and Imiya were hailed as heroes, and the study of equity began to shift to incorporate their new contributions.

However, those decades of time and energy spent solely on trying to get rid of heat currents meant that no one was looking ahead for other potential problems that could threaten our survival, and the quality of scientific research began to decline.

The ice barrier overhead would soon disrupt any illusion of peace and progress.

The galaxy in which our planet resided had only four planets, two of which were massive terrestrial planets, two of which were gas giants. Our old world was the second of the four: beautiful seas with an estimated depth of seventeen thousand meters, a sufficient amount of mass to support the existence of water, a core made of rock. It lay outside the circumstellar habitable zone and was quite a distance from the nearest star. Our planet took five thousand eight hundred days to complete an elliptical orbit around this star, and drew a pitiful amount of energy from it. The path of orbit was not predictable either—the shape carved out by its orbit was more of a slanted ellipse than anything, and it engaged in a dance of sorts with the nearest planet, moving in front then behind in a zigzag motion.

We were incredibly lucky that things had transpired the way they did. If any element had been missing, our planet would not have been able to support life, and our unique ecological system would not have existed.

The advances made by Beinakan and Ilian scientists in the theoretical and material sciences were so extraordinary that prophetic statements made by scientists in generations past were now all confirmed to be true. And because space exploration efforts had come too late (forty thousand years too late), many of these scientists had already passed on into the next world.

These scientists did not get a chance to pass down their memory capsules to the next generation. Then again, with regard to reconciliations made with certain truths (even painful ones), I say better late than never. At the very least, following our drilling efforts, the scientists had a renewed sense of motivation to drive innovation.

We'd begun to build telescopes to examine outer space. We'd begun to reach outside of ourselves.

Observing the world beyond our old planet yielded the vision of an infinite number of stars. A very bright red giant existed among them. It had been the first star that Beinakan and Ilian scientists had discovered. For years they had observed it.

And then, they finally understood what it meant.

A red giant in the later stages of evolution would explode in the near future. Its axis of rotation was right in front of our planetary system, and the minute this star was to explode, high energy particles would collide with our planet, our ice barrier would melt, our oceans would overheat.

This star was much too close. When was the explosion to occur?

The first estimate I'd heard was 1.7 million years from now. Each subsequent prediction kept getting smaller and smaller: two hundred and twenty thousand years, then forty thousand years, then seven thousand two hundred years . . .

After a certain point, no one dared to lower this estimate.

But we Beinakans were levelheaded. Just as the elements had come together in serendipity so as to give Beinakans a chance at existing as a life form, we could create the circumstances to save ourselves.

Part 4: The End of the Old World and the Beginning of the Trek

Imiya and Beier, having already passed from this world to the next, began to fall from grace. The Equity Formula had given Beinakans a false sense of security and had taken away our desires to break new ground.

Forty thousand years, a total of forty thousand years, a breakthrough that could have been achieved in any one of those forty thousand years.

I am the descendant of Beier. So are my children.

Memory capsules passed down from generation to generation never lie.

Once upon a time, my children had taken it as a point of pride to be the descendants of this historically prominent figure, just as I had in my younger years. One of my children had said, "I want to go study equity." But overnight, when Imiya and Beier were no longer sanctified, that child said in the midst of tears, "If it weren't for the Equity Formula, Imiya and Beier would have been active proponents of space exploration."

Imiya and Beier's contributions are not to be understated. But if the Ilians and Beinakans had continued their research efforts, we would have successfully drilled through the ice barrier at most forty thousand years earlier, and we would've found outer space forty thousand years earlier.

The Golden Age brought about by Imiya and Beier had pushed our civilization to the brink of destruction.

But who could we blame? Was there really anyone to blame?

At the end of the day, the wheels of fortune had played a cruel joke on us, and an unexpected desperation arose from the masses, in reaction to this situation with no solution in sight.

The red giant from afar seemed to have said: *Your time is running out.*

Overnight, all cities lifted restrictions on nuclear fuel use. All scientists would invest their energies in building a spaceship able to sustain life.

Things like the well-being of the masses and environmental conservation efforts no longer mattered. We recklessly dumped nuclear waste here, there, everywhere, until there was nowhere left but our own streets for the waste to go.

After a while, I no longer knew whether to call this city my hometown or the city of death.

I had been tasked with deciding where to dump nuclear waste.

There were limits to what we could achieve: the pollution and damage done to our planet was no longer something we could control—you have to understand, we had no other choice. The deformities caused to our limbs, the increase in deaths at childbirth—all of these were small misfortunes, in comparison to the survival of our civilization.

Unfortunate, but necessary.

I don't know how much I agree with that mindset anymore.

Previous space exploration had been strictly regulated, but now, things were different.

The ships we hastily built had a number of problems relating to fuel, thrust, circulation of water—problems that would cost lives.

But we didn't have enough time or resources to make sure everything was foolproof. Many spaceships would take off in this flawed state, and many fearless souls were lost.

The captains of these ships were well aware of the dangers. But they carried on in the face of fear, putting their lives on the line as they flew toward the stars, never to return.

Don't get me wrong. I'm not glorifying their sacrifices. The situation was just terrible.

There's another thing I should mention here.

The spaceships would not be able to carry Ilians.

I know what you're thinking. It seems a bit counterintuitive to build ships incapable of carrying your own.

As you likely remember, despite the legacy of Beier and Imiya, Beinakans and Ilians were not built to survive together.

A typical Ilian weighed roughly one hundred fifty times more than an average Beinakan. The amount of water required to sustain Ilian life was one thousand three hundred times that which was required to sustain Beinakan life. Beinakans could hibernate on the ship. Ilians could not.

We Beinakans had a sliver of hope. All the Ilians could do was make peace with their cruel end.

A sacrifice of epic proportions that drew no opposition from the Ilian masses. Maybe because the end was in sight, or maybe because tens of thousands of years of good relations had allowed our species to fully trust and rely on one another.

If you think about it from *this* perspective, building the spaceships was a collective effort from the Beinakans *and* the Ilians.

There are two sides to every story.

As I write this, I ask myself how comfortable I am with this perspective.

I remember following my squadron onto the ship, and vaguely remember the moments preceding our collective hibernation. The leader of my squadron provided tips on how best to prevent the loss of our memory capsules (though it is inevitable for Beinakans to lose a few while hibernating), but to no avail.

At that point, we were just ready to sleep for the next hundred and forty years.

In the hundred and forty-first year since setting out for outer space, the ringing of the ship's particle detector woke us from our deep slumber.

The red star was just about to explode.

We positioned ourselves behind another fixed star so as to shield ourselves from the influx of particles—knowing that reports estimating how long our ships could tolerate the influx of these particles could be off by up to thirty days, we did our best and hoped. Thankfully, after a week, they'd begun to decrease in number.

After a month, almost everything was at peace, with the exception of the rays of light emanating from that particular star.

We would now begin the longest part of our trek, a journey with no destination in mind.

Thirty-seven planetary systems. All the planets in these systems we'd traversed were unable to support water-based life forms.

Water is crucial to our survival—even a small piece of coagulated ice is sufficient to sustain us. After all, we'd once lived in a sea seventeen thousand meters in depth.

After a certain amount of time passed, I began to believe that we were to meet our end here, in outer space.

If I'd been right, I remember thinking that I would rather we all pass on into the next world as soon as possible.

Seventy-nine years after observing the explosion of that red giant and two hundred and twenty years after leaving our home planet, we'd begun to receive many images and videos of what transpired in the moments before our old world was destroyed.

Before the interstellar winds disseminated what was left of our planet's atmosphere, many Ilians and Beinakans had chosen to face the

"Heat Current of Death" together. A ritual. Those brave souls had chosen to confront that which had given them life and that which would also end their lives.

Once again, I don't mean to glorify their sacrifices. But I don't know any other way of adequately eulogizing their lives. Actually, those poli—

There were also those who had chosen to stay until the very end. That's how we'd managed to get images and videos.

Oddly enough, though I remember this as one of the most painful and heart-wrenching times in my life, a sense of peace shrouds this memory.

I've never really understood why.

Our seas, the towns, the cities—all gone.

But, I suppose to those on a spaceship wandering mindlessly in the universe, it no longer mattered whether our home planet existed. At this point, there was no difference between having one or not.

Our only choice was to press on, in search of a new home.

In the five hundred and twentieth year of our travels, we'd entered a new planetary system. Many gas giants resided in this system, allowing us to refuel our dangerously low fuel tanks.

We observed that some of the gas giants were encircled by large ice rings. Just as we'd begun to make plans to melt these rings to move water onto our ships, we came across the third planet in this system.

It was enveloped by magnificent seas.

Part 5: My Very Educated Mother

Further observation would tell us that a civilization had once existed on this planet. But the exploration device we'd sent to this planet had initially informed us that no one was there. Signal after signal sent to this planet yielded no answer. We'd assumed that no one—in human-speak, no human—from this civilization remained on this planet.

There was nothing. Nothing was there. Only an eerie sense of quiet in the land.

The diversity in land-based species was shockingly low. It seemed as though the life forms that'd once existed here had undergone some sort of mass extinction. Anything and everything we'd derived from our observations pointed to the ramifications of the red giant's explosion.

Humans call the star Rigel. The humans had known that Rigel was to explode.

This planet was six hundred light years away from Rigel. But even so, such distance would do nothing to save them from overexposure to the high-energy particles and radiation—land-based species are just like that. More fragile than water-based species.

But even though the particles had managed to completely do away with a third of the atmosphere, the events that occurred after the fact were the real cause behind the extinction of most of the land-based species. Nitrogen particles had bonded to oxygen particles, and this concoction poisoned the respiratory systems of all species on land.

Per our estimate, it took only a matter of minutes for these species to suffocate.

Additionally, the pH of the seas had dropped to 0.1, a value low enough to topple the existing ecological systems that supported life on this planet—we're guessing a number of chain reactions had sent many of the life forms on this planet into the abyss.

There was nothing they could have done.

It'd looked as though they'd tried to warn others. The lights emanating from their lighthouses continued to flash even though there was no one left to heed the orders and warnings. They must have been using nuclear-powered batteries so the drones, the lights, all that had been utilized to sound the alarm, would continue to do so, for tens of thousands of years.

I remember thinking that the drones were singing an elegy for a civilization long gone.

We assumed that the cities here looked as they did before, because there was not too much destruction visible to us, with the exception of buildings called "historical sites."

Perhaps overconfidence saw this civilization to its end, led them to make preparations too slowly. Maybe, just like us, they didn't have enough time.

But in this civilization's place lay a planet perfect for us Beinakans to inhabit: in this ocean, heat currents *stayed* at the bottom of the sea. If you were to track the movements of the sea currents starting from the equator, it would take four thousand years for a body of water to return to its place of origin. Not to mention, the seas here actively worked to convert heat currents into energy.

A system that worked for us. No radiation to worry about under the sea, perfect water temperature—adjustments had to be made of course, but we were equipped with all the necessary tools.

This was to be our new home. The seas would belong only to the Beinakans.

As for the other underwater life forms on this planet, well—a disaster of the proportions caused by Rigel's explosion was unlikely to have had any effect on them.

The seas were to belong only to us. So, we'd made a decision—to exterminate the remaining life forms on this planet. We'd known that this would be unforgiveable. But we *had* to do this. I can't remember now why, but it seemed very clear at the time.

It was simple. It was a question of the survival of Beinakans over the survival of others.

Still, at times, I wonder why.

It had come time to alert the other Beinakan ships of the existence of this planet. We took the drones left behind by the long-extinct civilization, reprogrammed their systems, and sent signals to outer space. By our estimates, the signals sent would have been able to travel at least thirty light years, at most fifty. Signal after signal after signal after signal, like the formation of ripples on the surface of water. To tell others of our kind still wandering in space that, if they so desired, they could come here and inhabit a planet perfect for Beinakan survival.

But we had missed something.

The humans. Endangered, but not extinct.

They'd tunneled underground and lived in enclosures that totaled two hundred in number. The humans had planned to stay underground for the foreseeable future.

Seventeen thousand humans in existence. An infinite number of frozen embryos.

When we came in contact with the humans, some reacted as though we had come to save them. But, as it became readily apparent that we weren't going to give them what they wanted, the humans became unhappy.

And though we did not speak the same languages, they'd understood.

We hadn't come to save them.

So, we executed all who resisted us.

Three thousand humans remained. We allowed them to live above the water in special regions, sustained by Beinakan machines that provided them with food, water, and oxygen.

We'd made them completely dependent on us.

Two months later, I met Guan Hai, a native of this planet.

Part 6: Guan Hai

We'd decided to preserve what was left of human civilization, history, and language. As Beinakans, this was the best we could do, after destroying all of their enclosures. I am the sole entity in charge of preserving Sinitic languages.

At our first meeting, Guan Hai was capable of speaking only two very simple sentences in Beinakan.

They'd told me their name was Guan Hai. As our conversation continued, I'd learnt that the naming conventions of this particular ethnic group were very similar to ours—the only difference lay in the fact that Guan Hai's last name, "Guan," indicated their clan of origin rather than their species of origin. The character "Hai" was their first name.

Every time we spoke, Guan Hai had to submerge their head underwater. They taught me the differences between written Beinakan and written Chinese, pausing only to go back up for air every now and then.

I taught them Beinakan, they taught me human languages. They weren't a skilled linguist or a polyglot like me, and I liked knowing that.

"It is unlikely for humans to survive." They used to say things like this in Beinakan. "I only hope that the history and language of our civilization will be preserved, using your memory capsules."

"You shouldn't be so fatalistic," I used to say. "Beinakans and Ilians have suffered so much over hundreds of millions of years, and look at us now. At the very least, we Beinakans have survived."

"You cannot apply the relationship between Beinakans and Ilians to the relationship between Beinakans and humans." They went back up for air, took a breath, and submerged themself again. "Besides, *that* symbiotic relationship was problematic on so many levels."

Guan Hai used to tell me stories from human history. Because humans did not have memory capsules, they relied on written scripts to preserve memories of their civilizations at different points in time. Things were much more easily lost this way.

But it wasn't all bad. The greatest moments of history would live on forever. Stories of legendary people, epic battles, those were passed down generation after generation.

I had to remind Guan Hai repeatedly that they need not be so defeatist.

But Guan Hai would not change their mindset.

"I'm not telling the story to an audience of Beinakans. I'm telling the story to an audience of those who hail from a civilization that will soon see its end."

But I'd never been interested in history. I was only ever interested in writing systems.

You see, I'm not quite sure why I've felt such an urge to write this piece.

The Beinakan writing system is complicated and incomplete. We've had no need for a sophisticated writing system to document the past. Our memory capsules ensure we never have to worry about forgetting anything.

Humans, on the other hand, had an elaborate, somewhat logical, and complete writing system.

These systems were *very* interesting.

Guan Hai used to say, "It's so difficult for one to learn another's language. The systems are much too different." They'd struggled, on multiple occasions, to read Beinakan characters.

In the next seven years, we had a good relationship.

I'd assumed it would be like that until the end.

Every now and then, problems arose in the special regions inhabited by humans, presumably from the resistance movement. But these problems were easily squashed, and we never spent too much time addressing them.

Beinakans clearly had the upper hand.

"It is what it is," Guan Hai had once said. "Humans don't have the capacity to challenge Beinakans, and in reality, there is too much of a chasm between our military technologies. Even if we wanted to resist, it would be impossible."

Guan Hai eventually became my assistant. My new job within the equity field was to observe the composition of the seas and deal out quantities of nuclear fuel accordingly.

We'd brought an Ocean Equalizer system with us and used it to change the chemical composition of the seas to better fit our needs. The speed with which Guan Hai had managed to get things done to support my work—for a human, at least—was quite admirable. As I observed them, I began to realize how nice it must be to have control over motor function. The machines Beinakans use to move around are clearly inferior.

When work problems troubled me, they gave me pointers. Once, Guan Hai told me to dump nuclear waste wherever there was space available.

"This was how humans dealt with nuclear waste before," they had said. And eventually we dumped the waste on land—we didn't want to pollute *our* seas.

Humans and Beinakans coexisted peacefully in this manner for the next seven years.

Until we'd received news that a spaceship with seven thousand Beinakans had arrived. In order to accommodate them, we'd need to speed up the processes by which we were changing the composition of the seas.

I'd heard an argument through the windpipe that, while providing humans with air and water would not hinder our progress, it would be quite inconvenient to continue to support them.

Killing the remaining three thousand humans was not a bad option.

Was it?

Nobody was supposed to know that this was going to happen.

Guan Hai should have been made an exception. They were worth enough to me to justify saving their life.

The authorities didn't agree. We argued, and I was so flustered afterward that I told Guan Hai everything.

I probably shouldn't have done that. But I did, anyway.

At first, a sense of shock. Then, one of extreme pain. Their eyes moved to look at the ground and I assume they felt helpless. They were silent for an inordinate amount of time, presumably trying to process the news that I had relayed to them.

"I guess there was always going to be an end," they said, in a dejected tone. "It's just as I'd said." They sighed.

"I—you can still live and work for me." I knew it was a lie even as I said it. "You're my assistant."

"No—I guess I did everything I wanted."

"No, I mean—"

"I don't want to be the last one . . ." This was the first time I'd seen Guan Hai so dispirited, the closest I'd seen them to despair.

Guan Hai went back up for some air and began to pace back and forth in their room. They were talking to themself, though I could not make out the words they were saying.

Guan Hai came back and said, "All right, kill me." They stared directly at me, the look in their eyes unfaltering and resolute.

"Kill. Me. Now."

"I can't."

"I don't want to see the end." They repeated this once more and pointed toward the entranceway that led to the sea.

And before I'd realized what Guan Hai was about to do, they grabbed my mobility machine, turned it up to full speed, and threw it toward the entrance. Alarms rang from all directions like swarms of wasps and birds, as my machine collided with the entranceway and water began to fill the room.

Guan Hai's facial expression was peaceful. They'd positioned themself in the last air bubble available, right next to the entranceway.

I'd finally understood. Guan Hai was about to swim out into the sea.

"I'm sorry," Guan Hai said. "Thank you."

In the midst of blaring alarms, I could barely make out their voice.

I watched as Guan Hai rose slowly toward the surface of the sea, toward the rays of sunshine that penetrated the water. A current pushed them upward, and whirlpools pushed Guan Hai farther and farther away from me.

This was good. They'd passed on of their own volition. No lonely and endless waters of dark blue, only sunlight, air, and water.

Initially, I'd chosen not to preserve this memory in a capsule. I'd thought I'd do it later, though the events that had transpired after Guan Hai had thanked me—every single detail painted a complete picture for me in my head.

For now, there is no need for a memory capsule.

Pain and disappointment can be capsules of their own, lingering even when we wish them gone.

And putting these memories in a capsule—I would have to edit things and relive the experience—I just don't think I can.

On the fifth day after he'd passed, I'd found something in Guan Hai's old room that shocked me. It was a record of numbers mixed with Chinese characters—a mixture of ancient characters and modern ones.

I'd thought it was a to-do list of sorts. But upon further examination, I was dumbfounded. A portion of this record had been used to document the inner workings of the Ocean Equalizer, the system we were using to change the composition of the seas. In another portion,

Guan Hai had used Chinese characters as homophones of Hindu-Arabic numerals to carry out elaborate calculations.

Guan Hai had probably destroyed everything else. They'd missed just this one.

It was evident to me that Guan Hai had managed to solve and document all calculations related to the Ocean Equalizer system.

A glib-tongued, slippery con-human.

I'd realized then that Guan Hai's level of Beinakan was much higher than I'd previously assumed. They must have been able to read all the documents I'd given to them, and all the questions they'd asked were likely for the sole purpose of verification.

Guan Hai had gone to painstaking lengths to act as though they'd made peace with their relationality in this new order.

They'd lied. Guan Hai was connected to—and maybe even the fucking leader—of the resistance movement. They'd lied.

They had lied to *me.*

Here was the truth Guan Hai had hidden: we hadn't discovered all of the enclosures—the enclosures underneath the ice caps had escaped our observation, and the humans there must have been preparing for battle. They'd stored an infinite number of embryos in these enclosures, enough to help them restart their own civilization.

And since it was possible to change the composition of the seas to suit Beinakan needs, it was just as possible to change it to fit human needs.

We should have known. Humans who'd entered our world possessed two common characteristics: high intelligence and a fierce desire to live. Other humans had chosen death (presumably to maintain a sense of autonomy) but convictions regarding self-determination did not require much to be passed down. As a result, some had acted as resistors, others as servants, waiting for the right opportunity.

Guan Hai had chosen to assume another persona—a human who'd submitted to their fate and accepted the new social order. An obedient lamb.

Plans must have been made long before Guan Hai became my assistant. And in the face of a scheme likely many years in the making, we Beinakans were not sure we could stand our ground.

But we had an advantage that the humans did not. Their memories were flawed. They had no feasible manner of memorizing large amounts of calculations, parameters, and numbers all in one go.

If humans had had a form of memory capsules at their disposal, I'm sure they would have won this round.

But the only person in charge of getting data from the Ocean Equalizer was Guan Hai. And though their memory may have been good, it was probably not enough.

I would imagine that the humans were double- and triple-checking these calculations. Perhaps that was why Guan Hai had asked me to end their life. It was taking too much time, and the only chance at any semblance of self-determination had likely disappeared into thin air.

I destroyed all documents with information related to the Ocean Equalizer system, and backed everything up into a memory capsule. I chanced upon the enclosures underneath the ice caps and destroyed them with another Beinakan.

None of the humans we were providing for were aware of these events. I think it's for the best, and hopefully, I'll be dead by the time a human figures everything out. After all, these records are very dangerous for someone like me to have, and if they were to fall into the wrong hands—well, I would be in great trouble. But then again, it's hard for me to describe what place Guan Hai holds in my heart.

I did not sign up for these feelings. I need to finish writing this goddamned thing.

My name is Beixiliya. A recorder of Beinakan histories. At present, I am learning how to read, speak, and write Sinitic languages.

Once upon a time, scientists had tried in earnest to prove that

Beinakans and Ilians were equal. But it had been obvious that Ilians were superior in language acquisition and language ability—even if there had been Beinakans blessed with language talent, the Ilians had a natural gift for it. Language was just easier for them.

As for me, I can appreciate the languages from the Greater China region, especially because they are very similar to Beinakan—actually, they're a lot closer to Ilian, complicated and ever-changing yet systematic and complete . . . but most importantly, incredibly beautiful.

And the ancient writing systems—I like those, too. Sadly, I won't have any chance at learning those systems. The most I can do is record that they once existed, for these languages will eventually become extinct. All offshoots of Sinitic languages, all offshoots of Latin-based languages, those of the Arabic-speaking worlds, Southeast Asia, Africa, and so on—just like the extinction of the species who had once spoken them.

Our languages shall stay. The Beinakan and Ilian languages shall stay.

I really do love language. It's why I'd chosen to document these happenings.

And for another reason.

For a human I'd killed with my bare hands. *My colleagues would likely chide me for attempting to come clean, because if these documents were to fall into the hands of a native Mandarin speaker—*

But I digress.

This is an attempt to mimic the writing practices of a native Mandarin speaker. If the individuals who'd spoken this language natively were able to read this story, I'd consider this a great success for a Beinakan linguist.

But few will be able to validate whether I have mastered written, vernacular Chinese. And I suppose it doesn't matter anymore.

All things that exist in the universe are destined to meet an end.

The only variable? Time.

The Ocean Equalizer has made 29 percent of the desired chemical composition changes. We've managed to exterminate the rest of the species living under the sea—right now, we're working on the fish.

In a couple of months, we'll have killed the rest of this planet's native life forms.

But we'd saved our civilization. Just like other life forms who find ways to live on for hundreds of millions of years.

The preservation of a civilization cannot rely on something as flimsy as the Equity Formula. No amount of theory would be able to do this—only calculated moves, compromise, and the resolve to incur losses that may hurt you.

I've since put this entire story into a memory capsule. You can find the version written in Beinakan on the next page.

I suppose I'm content to accept that fortune may bestow a blessing upon non-Beinakan entities . . .

Recorder of Beinakan Histories
Beixiliya

15

Is There Such a Thing as *Feminine* Quietness? A Cognitive Linguistics Perspective

Emily Xueni Jin 金雪妮

Is There Such a Thing as *Feminine* Quietness? A Cognitive Linguistics Perspective

By Emily Xueni Jin

In 2019, when Disney released its first trailer for the live-action remake of the animated film *Mulan,* the Chinese internet exploded over the translation of its subtitles. Specifically, the explosion was over the scene in which the matchmaker explains the four virtues of women to Mulan: "quiet, composed, graceful, disciplined,"[1] attempting to shoehorn her into stereotypical femininity and marry her off. In this scene, "quiet" was translated as "xiánjìng 娴静," literally "elegantly and delicately quiet." As the film progresses and Mulan joins the military and excels as a soldier, we soon discover that those so-called feminine virtues in fact parallel the ideal virtues of a soldier, a traditionally hyper-masculine role. Hence, the four adjectives used by the matchmaker, "*quiet, composed, graceful, disciplined,*" are meant to foreshadow Mulan's eventual emergence as a national hero, as well as to interrogate labels that define characteristics as strictly feminine and masculine.

Those most vocal in their dissatisfaction with *Mulan*'s subtitles were viewers who grew up watching the animated film, who resonated deeply with its theme of gender exploration. Translating from English to Chinese, the use of "xiánjìng 娴静"—which implies a specifically

1 *Mulan*, directed by Niki Caro (2020; United States: Walt Disney Pictures).

gendered female quietness—in the matchmaking scene falls short of capturing the scope and nuance of the virtue "quiet." To these viewers, when rendering those adjectives into Chinese, the subtitle translator failed to take into account the contextual pun and hence downplayed the central theme of *Mulan*, which is precisely about breaking down gender stereotypes. The controversy caught my attention. Is there such a thing as *feminine* quietness? How does a translator render specific, gendered diction? I immediately perceived the translation of the English word "quiet" as the Chinese word "xiánjìng 娴静" and vice versa as a promising case study, drawing on the dual perspectives of a translator as well as a cognitive linguist.

"Xiánjìng 娴静" is a two-character compound. The second character "jìng 静" means quiet *in general*, setting the semantic tone of the compound; the first character "xián 娴" means gracefulness and composedness. A componential analysis of the character results in the combination "女+闲=娴," using the radical "女" (female)—an indicator that helps categorize the character semantically or phonetically. The undercurrent of "xián 娴" is thus clear: it points to a specific kind of gracefulness and composedness, associated with traditional notions of femininity. Consequently, when "xián 娴" is used to enrich "jìng 静" as a descriptor, we can immediately tell from the "女" radical of "xián 娴" that "xiánjìng 娴静" is a particular *feminine* quietness. Hence, it is clear why many see the Chinese subtitle translation of *Mulan* as problematic: in a scene supposed to break down the rigid barriers surrounding the myth of "traditional femininity," with adjectives that could be gendered or *un*gendered depending on the context, the Chinese translation overlooks this attempt at duality and renders *only* the gendered meaning.

Before we explore this specific example, it's helpful to contextualize translation within the discipline of cognitive linguistics—another way of approaching the relationship between lexicon and meaning, alongside traditional literary criticism and translation studies. Foundational studies in linguistics often neglect rhetorical nuance and contextual detail in translation, only considering how to map specific words or sentences from the source language onto the target language with exact semantic equivalence. Linguists Ana Rojo and Javier Valenzuela indicate that the practice is a technical definition of translation, "deciphering the meaning from a source text and recording it into a target text using a different linguistic code."[2] In essence, the source language enters the mind's conceptual system as input and its meaning is interpreted, then it is outputted from the conceptual system into the target language—not unlike what happens in the central processor of a computer. Another prominent linguist, Ray Jackendoff, puts it simply: "translations should preserve meaning."[3] These orthodox linguists claim the key to producing quality translations is to align the meaning contained in the source language with the meaning in the target language as much as possible.

However, as translators and readers know well, translation is not and cannot be evaluated only based on its ability to render meaning. Elzbieta Tabakowska, a linguist perhaps more sympathetic to the concerns of the literary world, which often foregrounds the struggle between form and content, indicates that "the meaning of an expression is not only its conceptual content, but also the way in which the expression is construed."[4] Tabakowska is referring to translation in two parts: meaning and form. As seen above, the "meaning" side of translation has won significant attention, while less research has looked at "form." Rojo and Valenzuela, in their study on translating between English and Spanish, touch on the idea of constructional equivalence. They argue that certain sentences prevalent in English do not have structurally equivalent translations in Spanish; when those sentences are translated from English into Spanish, the meaning is preserved but the form is usually lost. By tracking the eye movements of translators when completing English-to-Spanish

---

2 Ana Rojo and Javier Valenzuela, "Constructing Meaning in Translation: The Role of Constructions in Translation Problems," in *Cognitive Linguistics and Translation: Advances in Some Theoretical Models and Applications* (2013): 284.

3 Ray Jackendoff, *A User's Guide to Thought and Meaning* (Oxford: Oxford University Press, 2012), 63.

4 Elzbieta Tabakowska, "Cognitive Grammar in Translation: Form as Meaning," in *Cognitive Linguistics and Translation: Advances in Some Theoretical Models and Applications* (2013): 232.

translations, Rojo and Valenzuela discovered that it takes more cognitive effort to translate English sentences into Spanish when translators cannot map the meaning onto an equivalent form in the target language. Rojo and Valenzuela observe that: "Translators, forced by the non-existence of an identical construction in Spanish, have to resort to various strategies which aim to reproduce the meaning of the target language at the expense of the linguistic form."[5] To compensate for the lack of constructional equivalence, translators often need to deploy strategies such as rearranging words and adding information to explain—a process that almost any translator would be familiar with.

If we survey the research of the translation between specific languages, we will find that translating in and out of Chinese has long been understudied. Take the translation between English and Chinese, for example; most studies dedicated to examining the relationship between these two languages are ingrained in the translation of meaning, rarely extending the scope of their discussion to other relevant linguistic components such as form. In "The Application of Cognitive Linguistic Theories to English-Chinese Translation," Liao Xiaogen investigates a specific "one-to-many mapping relationship between source language and target language" in English-to-Chinese translations.[6] Looking at different Chinese versions of William Wordsworth's poem "Lucy," Liao discovered that there are various Chinese correspondents to the English word "maid" instead of one single lexical item that fits perfectly, and different translators would diverge in the correspondent they chose. Liao borrows an existing term from linguistics and coins this phenomenon an "equivalence cluster": a group of lexical items united under one semantic umbrella, such as "maid," where each item heightens different characteristics that "maid" as a general concept may embody, like girlhood, youth, beauty, marriage status, etc. Liao extrapolates that "the differences in multiple versions are the result of the

5 Rojo and Valenzuela, 286.

6 Liao Xiaogen, "The Application of Cognitive Linguistic Theories to English-Chinese Translation," *Open Journal of Modern Linguistics* 8, no. 3 (2018): 62. DOI: 10.4236/ojml.2018.83008.

different categories of conceptual domains in which the translator activates cognitive construal activities in the process of translation."[7] In simpler terms, the translator, buttressed by their own past experiences and perception, will latch onto whichever characteristic of "maid" they are most familiar with and thus choose a Chinese lexicon to heighten that characteristic. In this one-to-many relationship, the "one" in English is often mapped onto the "many" in Chinese, depending on the conceptual domain activated in the translator's brain. Bringing this argument into the *Mulan* example, we can see that "quiet" serves as the parent of the equivalence cluster; in that cluster, specific sub-items highlighting different aspects and contexts of quietness exist alongside each other, including "xiánjìng 娴静," "qīngjìng 清静" (an exterior environment that is quiet and devoid of disturbances), and "sùjìng 肃静" (solemn and quiet).

Now, in our *Mulan* case study, when "quiet" is used in the scene to indicate both a stereotypical feminine virtue and a traditional masculine heroic trait, other parts of the sentence and the visuals provide the contextual information needed. The Chinese audience's rage regarding the translation of "quiet" into "xiánjìng 娴静" stemmed from the fact that it is too specific a term in the Chinese equivalence cluster of "quiet." The translator of *Mulan*'s subtitles has chosen one Chinese correspondent amongst the many based on their interpretation of how the word "quiet" was used, and its association with traditional femininity was the aspect that they apparently chose to highlight, instead of its purposeful double meaning. In a poll on Weibo, the biggest Chinese social media site, many people have noted that if they were to translate *Mulan*'s subtitles, they would choose to translate "quiet" into something much vaguer for the pun to work. I would suggest deleting "xián 娴"; a simple "jìng 静" (general quietness devoid of specific descriptive information) is enough.

What about translating from Chinese into English? Trying to learn from the *Mulan* translator's choices and the audience's reactions, I believe that "quiet" can certainly be translated to "xiánjìng 娴静"

7 Liao, 65.

when the speech context makes it clear that the adjective is supposed to heighten hyper-femininity. However, if we are to translate "xiánjìng 娴静" from Chinese into English instead, can we still use "quiet" as an approximate equivalent, knowing that "xiánjìng 娴静" refers to a female-exclusive kind of quietness?

Analyses of Chinese-to-English translations are so rare that, when they appear, they often come hand in hand with literary and translation studies, instead of being discussed purely in terms of cognitive linguistics. For example, in a study looking at English translations of modern Chinese texts on a word-by-word level, Jianwei Zheng determines that "translators should provide English readers with additional information to offset the lack of some background assumptions," heightening the importance of context.[8] Combining Zheng's insight with my own experiences as a translator, I speculate that the key, perhaps, when rendering certain Chinese adjectives in English, is to provide additional context for them to work.

Let me unpack this process more in the context of translating "xiánjìng 娴静" into English. For the adjective "xiánjìng 娴静," the descriptor "xián 娴" with a female radical already indicates the nature of this specific quietness, profoundly limiting the contexts in which it could be used and the subjects it could effectively describe—according to how modern Chinese works, it would be out of place to use it to describe a shy grown man, or an animal that never barks. Essentially, "xiánjìng 娴静" as an adjective contains innate contextual information, which gives it a greater contextual specificity and reduces the number of lexical items in English that it could be directly translated into, since those items should ideally represent that contextual specificity. Thus, it seems that we have arrived at a standout solution: *adding* the contextual information that the English approximation "quiet" lacks.

In an anthology that foregrounds science fiction as one of its key

8 Jianwei Zheng, "On the English Translation of Chinese Modern Essays from the Perspective of Cognitive Context: A Case Study of Zhang Peiji's English Translation of Chinese Essay '巷' (The Lane)," *International Journal of Applied Linguistics and English Literature* 5 (2016): 96. DOI: 10.7575/aiac.ijalel.v.5n.5p.96

components, it is appropriate to close this essay considering whether contextual information in a word could contribute toward current machine translation and the development of artificial intelligence translation. Now, whenever I resort to Google Translate or DeepL for English-to-Chinese translation, more often than not the key adjective would be translated into a more ambiguous and contextually neutral Chinese correspondent. Conversely, Chinese adjectives packed with contextual information are frequently mapped onto a one-word English correspondent with a similar meaning but are stripped of their context. In the development of translation algorithms, it may be possible to manually unpack a Chinese adjective like "xiánjìng 娴静," lay out and arrange the contextual keywords into a glossary for the algorithm to learn, and subsequently develop a quantifiable, immediately accessible set of criteria that the machine could refer to every time it translates. Then, when we plug a English sentence that contains "quiet" into a machine translator, the algorithm could pick up both the central adjective (i.e., "quiet") as well as the keyword context provided in the sentence (e.g., whether a certain gender is present), combine those elements, and locate the specific Chinese expression that best fits the criteria. Which Chinese lexical item under the umbrella of "quiet" overlaps with those contextual keywords? It must be "xiánjìng 娴静." On the other hand, when translating "xiánjìng 娴静" into English, access to a glossary would allow the machine to do a better job in providing more contextual information, if not grammatically accurate expanded sentence definitions in English (e.g., translating "xiánjìng 娴静" into something like "elegant; womanly," instead of a mere "quiet").

At the same time, we must sharpen our awareness of the implications of translating gender-specific diction. By staying absolutely true to the stereotypes that such gendered adjectives impose, are we as translators also complicit in reinforcing those stereotypes? Can actively ungendering those gendered adjectives be counted as pushing against gender roles, or is that simply butchering the original text and language?

I do not have an answer to these questions. However, I believe that awareness is always the first step to further progress, and I hope that in merging my perspective as a literary translator active in the field and a student of cognitive linguistics who revels in linguistic jargon, I can help bring another curious-tasting cuisine to the extraordinary feast that is gender, culture, and literature.

BIBLIOGRAPHY

Caro, Niki, dir. *Mulan*. 2020; United States: Walt Disney Pictures.

Jackendoff, Ray. *A User's Guide to Thought and Meaning*. Oxford: Oxford University Press, 2012.

Liao, Xiaogen. "The Application of Cognitive Linguistic Theories to English-Chinese Translation." *Open Journal of Modern Linguistics* 8, no. 3 (2018): 61–69. DOI: 10.4236/ojml.2018.83008.

Rojo, Ana and Javier Valenzuela. "Constructing Meaning in Translation: The Role of Constructions in Translation Problems." In *Cognitive Linguistics and Translation: Advances in Some Theoretical Models and Applications* 23 (2013): 283–310.

Tabakowska, Elzbieta. "Cognitive Grammar in Translation: Form as Meaning." In *Cognitive Linguistics and Translation: Advances in Some Theoretical Models and Applications* (2013): 229–250.

Zheng, Jianwei. "On the English Translation of Chinese Modern Essays from the Perspective of Cognitive Context: A Case Study of Zhang Peiji's English Translation of Chinese Essay '巷' (The Lane)." *International Journal of Applied Linguistics and English Literature* 5 (2016): 96–101. DOI: 10.7575/aiac.ijalel.v.5n.5p.96.

16

Dragonslaying
屠龙

Shen Yingying 沈璎璎
Translated by Emily Xueni Jin 金雪妮

Dragonslaying 屠龙

By Shen Yingying 沈璎璎
Translated by Emily Xueni Jin 金雪妮

"You want to see dragonslaying? Well then, you should know that dragonslaying is a forbidden art, and dragonslayers are strictly prohibited from having visitors over. I can't help you."

The retired captain chuckled as he rubbed his hands together. Scattered dots of firelight flickered in the stove behind him, sending warmth through the room. Winter had barely arrived in this small seaside town down on the southern shore, but the captain, in his old age, had heated the stove and lined the chairs with fur blankets as soon as the first cool breeze hit. On days without visitors, he sat by the stove with his favorite ancient scrolls, occasionally toasting his hands by the fire. A special fragrance filled the room—a hearty stew bubbled in the pot on the stove.

The warm smell of spices stirred the cat, which dug its nails excitedly into Su Mian's arm in response. Su Mian's stomach rumbled. She knew, though, that her priority right now was to convince the captain to take her to the dragonslayers. Su Mian examined him. *He seems amiable, but is he really as easy to persuade as others say?*

"Dragonslaying is an esoteric art passed down only within the dragonslayers' own family line. It isn't easy for them to fill their stomachs, either. You can imagine why they don't want to show it to outsiders," explained the old captain.

The captain's reaction did not surprise Su Mian. She already expected that her request wouldn't be easily granted from the beginning—dragonslaying was the most complex, mysterious and cruel of all medical operations, and in the eyes of most people, she was only a young woman. How could she be trusted with such an "esoteric art"? *At least he is taking me seriously*, thought Su Mian, while she contemplated her next step to persuade him.

Su Mian's face scrunched up in disappointment. She sighed. "I traveled thousands of miles from the capital just to witness the magnificence of dragonslaying. Why, I struggled three or four days just looking for the Waterflow Plains! Everywhere they said that the only chance for me to see dragonslaying is to come plead with you."

Her words seemed to have touched the old captain. "I know." He nodded, then lowered his voice. "To tell you the truth, the visitor prohibition is primarily to keep the dragonslayers safe. Before the prohibition, there was a dragonslayer who once revealed the secret of his skills to people. The next day, jiaoren snuck into the city and slaughtered his entire family."

"I'm not a jiaoren though, sir," Su Mian argued back. "And I am not a friend to them either."

"I can tell you're not." The old captain grinned. "You're from the capital, so you're probably one of those young highborns on a sightseeing trip looking for new entertainment, aren't you? Listen to me, dragonslaying is not something that young ladies are supposed to have fun with."

"You're wrong on this one." Su Mian gave him a small smile. "I'm not a highborn—I'm a doctor."

"A doctor?" The old captain was taken by surprise, clearly not believing her words. "You mean you can cure illnesses?"

When Su Mian was completing her studies, she could count on one hand the female doctors in Yunhuang; most of them never left the capital. Somehow, the idea that women could serve as doctors seemed so absurd to people that even if a woman had acquired the title of doctor after years of apprenticeship, she would have to go out of her way to prove her competence. In Su Mian's memory, no matter where she went and what she did, be it testing new herbs or seeing a patient, the first thing she worried about was almost always how to show that she was just as good as the male doctors—no, better than them.

Compared to what she had dealt with in the past, convincing the old captain seemed like an effortless task. Hugging the cat closer to her chest, she took out a yellowed piece of paper and handed it over to the old captain. "My name is Su Mian, from the Su clan. I used to serve the princess at the Garan Palace. Here's my certificate, issued by the Imperial Medical Bureau."

The old captain stood at once. The certificate from the capital had wiped the relaxed look off his face. The Imperial Medical Bureau may not have meant very much in the capital, but its name carried weight in a small place like the Waterflow Plains. "Well, indeed, people from the Imperial Medical Bureau have inquired about dragonslaying before . . ."

"Sir, please," pleaded Su Mian, noticing how the old captain was shaken. She pulled out a small pouch heavy with coins from her inner pocket, and stuffed it into his hand.

The old captain, now feeling the weight of the pouch in his palm, lowered his gaze and contemplated. Finally, he spoke again. "Fine then, I'll take you there if it's for the Imperial Medical Bureau. You must promise not to tell anyone what you are about to see. Also, for the dragonslayers—"

"I'll remember to tip them," Su Mian promised.

"No, no, that's not what I'm talking about."

The sky at dusk was orange-pink like the belly of a salmon.

The dragonslayers lived atop the cliffs by the seashore at the Waterflow Plains, in a weather-beaten castle that blended into the bleak, towering cliff rocks. Their workshop was also in the castle. The cliffs were completely barren. The bare basalt rocks stood erect like an extended arm, pointing south to the azure Biluo Ocean. A single path led to the castle, surrounded by more cliffs and narrow rift valleys.

The old captain told Su Mian the history of the Waterflow Plains' dragonslayer clan as they walked the path. "A family of ten, four of whom possess the skill of dragonslaying. You can find dragonslayer clans in every major seaport of southern Yunhuang. Some ports even host more than one clan. The Waterflow Plains clan is the most famous one, not because it exceeds other clans in size, but because the patriarch had once been summoned to the capital, and there performed dragonslaying before the Jingshu Emperor himself. The patriarch, now in his old age, had already passed his skills down to his two sons. His grandson, born of his eldest, has also proven his mastery of dragonslaying. The patriarch's eldest son is out today. We'll be meeting his second son, Zhili Yi."

As the pair neared the castle, the old captain shouted, "Ah Yi! Ah Yi!"

Slowly, a drawbridge made of a few tied logs was lowered. The logs, soaked by seawater, had a sickening fishy stench. The drawbridge was damp and soft beneath Su Mian's feet.

Upon entering the castle, they found themselves walking through an ascending tunnel. The tunnel wasn't too deep underground. Its walls were dripping wet, and the dampness had already eroded away the coat of plaster, revealing protruding stubs of rock beneath. Occasionally the old captain would pause and turn around to remind Su Mian to mind her steps.

What a run-down place, thought Su Mian. One would expect dragonslayers to make quite a fortune. If it were not for generation after generation of their work, Yunhuang would have been deprived of one of its most important businesses long ago. Dragonslaying was a skill passed down within the clan; only the blood descendants knew the magic to the art. Although it wasn't necessarily dangerous, it was so complex that children born into dragonslaying clans were required to spend two-thirds of their childhood training before they could even be considered apprentices. Learning by heart every detail of the operation, mastering the delicacy of the skill, was a goal that a dragonslayer could only reach with a lifetime's cultivation. Even the most outstanding doctors in the capital envied the dragonslayers' prowess in performing surgeries.

Yet in reality, it seemed the dragonslayers lived a life poor and dull.

From birth to death they lived in isolated castles by the shore, doing the same job year after year, earning an income barely enough to keep their stomachs full. Even the castles didn't belong to them—they were property of the capital.

The tunnel led to the main hall, an enormous cavity in the rocks. The stench grew heavier. The hall was completely swallowed by darkness, save for a single tiny window a meter or so above the floor, revealing a meager shade of the sunset's glow. Su Mian could make out the silhouette of a figure in the center of the hall. The person approached them stiffly, fumbling a little, as if to greet them with a sloppy salute.

The old captain walked up to Zhili Yi and whispered a few words to him. The dragonslayer remained silent. Su Mian was worried that he'd decline. He turned his head to look at her. His eyes, like the rest of his face, were as calm and dead as the rock walls surrounding them. Su Mian had imagined dragonslayers would look coarse, even ugly. Surprisingly, Zhili Yi had a somewhat handsome face, though the expression he wore was indifferent, cold and numb, making her cringe inside. There was also something unnerving about his bald, clean-shaven head.

His nod was no more than a brief quiver of the neck. Su Mian realized that he had agreed to her visit. She let out a sigh of relief.

Zhili Yi lit the lamp. The lamplight was cloudy as dead water. In the flickering light Su Mian noticed disturbing old stains on the floor, crimson and moss green. Beyond the stains, there was a ditch full of water in the corner of the hall—the source of the stench. A row of large iron cages was steeped in the water, and the thick chains attached to the cages glistened with a murky, metallic light. Holding the lamp in one hand, Zhili Yi reached into one of the cages. Moments later, he pulled his arm out, fist wrapped tightly around a bundle of blue hair. Then, something sparkled—snow-white fish scales, reflecting the lamplight.

Su Mian realized then that she was face-to-face with the grand exhibit of the night: the jiaoren.

They're young, thought Su Mian. A grown jiaoren would be slightly larger than an adult human, but the jiaoren before her was her own size. They had a delicate visage, their eyes tightly shut. Their body was sleek and slender like silvery seaweed, their tail fine, smooth jade. Their caudal fins, spreading gossamer butterfly wings, left a trail of pinkish water on the gravel floor.

Dragging them by the hair, Zhili Yi marched toward the workshop, where the operation would take place. They whimpered, but the language they used, one that only belonged to watery creatures, was unknown to Su Mian. Their emerald eyes, now wide open, were a signature of the jiaoren kind: deep, enchanting, breathtakingly beautiful. After they were gouged out, they would be known as bining pearls—"pearls of verdant crystal"—a treasure that exceeded every other gem in value in all of Yunhuang.

The old captain and Su Mian followed Zhili Yi into the workshop, where he was about to perform the operation.

It was surprisingly pristine. Lamps installed on the circular, surrounding walls brightened up the whole space. In the middle of the room there was a rock platform, polished smooth and glittering. The jiaoren was flung onto the platform face-up. Their blue hair was so long that the ends dragged on the ground.

A boy of seventeen or eighteen years old was waiting in the room when they entered, busy checking the equipment. He lined sanitized knives up in a row on a small trolley, and then pushed the trolley to the platform. The boy's expressionless face resembled Zhili Yi; his head was also shaved bald. Su Mian reckoned perhaps it was a rule that all the dragonslayers must shave their heads.

"The son of Ah Yi's eldest brother, third generation of the family, here to give his uncle a hand tonight," explained the old captain, pointing to the boy. Neither the boy nor his uncle spoke as they quickly and efficiently bound the jiaoren in ropes. While Zhili Yi walked away to wash his hands, the boy brought over a long cloth, dried the jiaoren's hair, and wrapped it in a tight bundle, as skilled as any practiced hairdresser.

Zhili Yi, with a pen in hand, quickly surveyed the jiaoren's waist, calculating where he would set his knife. When the tip of the pen touched the jiaoren's skin to draw the lines that would later become incisions, a fit of violent shivers rushed through the jiaoren's body, as if they already felt the pain of the sharp blade against soft flesh. Soon after Zhili Yi poured three bottles of spirits onto them, one following another, they froze and fell limply on the platform, losing consciousness.

"The dragonslayers use spirits for two reasons," whispered the old captain. "To sterilize the jiaoren's body, and also to put them to sleep, so they will stay still during the operation. You know why the dragonslayers wrapped the jiaoren's hair? It's not just to keep it out of the way, but also because their hair is exceptionally sleek and beautiful. Why, if one could make a bigger fortune by keeping the hair intact, of course they'd do it!"

Zhili Yi knelt down next to the jiaoren. Holding a knife between his fingers like a writing brush, he glided the blade through their skin in a perfectly straight line, as gentle and smooth as a brushstroke on paper: from the breastbone to the belly button, then to the intersection of the abdomen and the tail. Silvery skin peeled up. Coral-colored beads of blood, fresh and pure, burst from the wound and collected along the edge of the blade.

> History has documented countless operations to modify the bodies of jiaoren. About three millennia ago, Emperor Xingzun of the Piling Dynasty, "he who ruled the stars," defeated the Kingdom of the Waters and extended his power over its people—namely, the jiaoren, half-fish beings that have long left their mark in mythology and romantic folklores. The jiaoren, known for their outstanding beauty, were taken as concubines, dancers, and whores by the land-born Kongsang people. To better "help" them adjust to life on land, Emperor Xingzun's cleverest advisor Su Feilian took it upon himself to derive a systematized and replicable procedure for transforming a jiaoren's tail into legs. He experimented with over a hundred jiaoren, before finally arriving at an operation he was satisfied with. From then on, all jiaoren would have their tails transformed into legs before they were supplied to the market.

For thousands of years to come, the landborn Kongsang of Yunhuang waged wars and toppled emperor after emperor, yet the tradition of transforming and trading jiaoren persisted. The group of people who first mastered Su Feilian's operation of tail-splitting quickly evolved into an entire industry that specifically prepared jiaoren for the market, and they passed down the knowledge within their families, generation after generation. No one knew when or who coined the term "dragonslaying."

Some have guessed that perhaps the Kongsang elites thought "tail-splitting" was too crude and grotesque a name, so they searched through ancient scrolls and renamed the operation "dragonslaying," pronounced as *tu-long*. The *long,* the omnipotent serpentine dragon, was the guardian and totem of the jiaoren. Taking great pride in how their tails enabled them to swim elegantly and swiftly in water, they described themselves as children of the dragon. On the other hand, *tu* means to slaughter. *Tu-long,* dragonslaying. Transforming a jiaoren's tail into legs was never meant to be a fatal operation—they could even swim with those newborn legs—yet, to a jiaoren, to remove their tail was to remove their dignity. Perhaps to them, being slain was better than meeting such a fate.

—*Excerpt from* The Great Encyclopedia of Yunhuang

Su Mian, eyes wide, watched Zhili Yi perform the art of dragonslaying.

Zhili Yi was unbelievably fast. His bald head, glistening as it reflected the lamplight, was almost entirely still. Only the silver knife in his hand sliced through the air with breathtaking speed, flashing rays of light. Before blood could even run from the cuts on the jiaoren's belly, the dragonslayer had already separated the fat, fascia, and muscles. A longitudinal cut across the lower belly revealed the intestines. Zhili Yi took a pure white bone—it might well be a jiaoren bone, but Su Mian couldn't tell—and stuck it into the wound to keep it open. Gesturing for the boy to take hold of the bone, he peered inside the wound.

The boy turned red in the face. The muscles in the jiaoren's abdomen were so tight that it took all his strength to keep the wound propped open.

The jiaoren's tender intestines were pearlescent pink, glistening under the lamplight. Blood streamed from the cut. Apart from propping open the wound, the boy was also pressing a cotton cloth on the cut to absorb the blood. After one piece of cloth was soaked, he discarded it and switched to another. A trivial job, sure; but if too much blood pooled where the flesh split, Zhili Yi would no longer be able to see clearly. The boy performed his task gingerly and with extreme meticulousness. The cotton cloths surrounding him were an indescribable murky black. The dragonslayers, Su Mian realized, must use the same ones during all of their operations.

Swiftly, Zhili Yi pulled the jiaoren's intestines out from the cut and pushed them to the side. The contents in the back of their abdominal cavity were now exposed: a slender long spine, and two light brown kidneys.

> As can be seen from the state of the abdominal cavity, a jiaoren's body structure is not that different from a landborn's. They have a stomach, intestines, a pair of kidneys, and an independent reproductive system. Their chest cavity, though, is different. Their heart is right in the middle of their chest, and their left and right atriums are perfectly symmetrical down to every individual vein. Their lungs, supporting both underwater and in-air breathing, are also symmetrical. Researchers have speculated that this unique body structure primarily helps them keep their balance in water.
>
> —*Excerpt from* Su's Comparative Anatomy

"I wish we could look into the jiaoren's chest as well," said Su Mian. As they watched, passages from medical texts and books on jiaoren she had studied came to mind. "Though I suppose the jiaoren would die if their chest was cut open."

"I see it all the time," said the old captain.

"How?"

"Well, sometimes they die during the operation. And after they die, we can cut them open and see whatever we want to see."

"And what," said Su Mian, "do you want to see?"

"You know, a jiaoren's skin, gills and heart are all very valuable. The tourists I've brought here in the past were often quite excited to see the jiaoren die, because then they got to see for sure whether their heart was in the middle of their chest."

"Of course, of course. You can see it after they die," said Su Mian, "but my question is, wouldn't the dragonslayer be held accountable if the jiaoren dies?"

"Not at all." The old captain smiled. "Who cares if the jiaoren dies?"

"*Who cares?* I thought jiaoren are generally valuable. At least in the capital, a healthy, beautiful jiaoren could sell as a concubine for tens of thousands of gold beads—that's hundreds of years of earnings for an ordinary family. Are the sellers willing to let these dragonslayers off if they're risking all this money?"

"It's inevitable for some jiaoren to die during dragonslaying," said the old captain. "And it's not like the dragonslayers need to pay anything to run the business, anyway."

"What do you mean?"

"The jiaoren sellers here are fishermen who work in the Biluo Ocean. Jiaoren who have never been through dragonslaying can't live for long on land. They can't move dragging a tail behind them; the only way to keep them alive is to soak them in buckets of seawater."

When the fishermen captured a jiaoren, they sent them to the dragonslayers first, and then retrieved them after the operation was complete. After the jiaoren recovered and learned how to walk on legs, the fishermen took them to the province capitals to sell. Professional jiaoren dealers ran shops in those towns. A jiaoren could be worth forty to fifty silver coins, a fortune for these poor fishermen. It would take dozens of ships of fish or conchs for them to earn as much.

"As long as one jiaoren stays alive out of all of their catches," he said, "they'd be pleased."

"Pleased?"

"These fishermen are honest, hardworking poor folks who risk their lives at sea only to earn a pittance. To them, a jiaoren is a special gift from the Sea God. They would throw the xiehai banquet after every good catch. Sometimes, if the jiaoren happens to die during the operation, the dealers throw a fit and refuse to pay. This is where I come in and mediate the situation."

"Refuse to pay? Why would the dragonslayers even work with them?"

"Dragonslayers cannot refuse any work that's passed into their hands," said the old captain. "Their wages come from the government."

"Why?" Su Mian was stunned. She assumed that dragonslayers, with such highly demanded esoteric skills, were not only making a large fortune, but were also granted the privilege of whose job to take. *Why? Why would they agree upon such an unreasonable rule?*

"It's always been this way," said the old captain, looking at Zhili Yi.

The dragonslayer was about to perform the key step to the operation. His nephew leaned forward, beads of sweat trickling down his cheek. It was an important chance for him to learn. A trace of excitement emerged on his stone-cold face, his dull-looking eyes glimmering.

Knowing that dragonslayers preferred to keep outsiders away from the key details of the operation, Su Mian kept her distance, standing about five steps away from the platform.

The strong spirits Zhili Yi poured on the jiaoren earlier kept them unconscious. The young jiaoren's jade-colored face had turned pallid from the blood loss. Their delicate chin, pale and shiny from reflecting the lamplight, pointed upward like a blade piercing the sky.

They're beautiful, thought Su Mian. *They would be worth more than ten thousand gold beads in the capital—if they live through this. As rare as a female doctor, but a treasure, not an affront.*

Perhaps, if she wasn't a woman, no one would be challenging her qualifications constantly. When she was a student, people questioned whether she could really become a doctor. When she finally claimed the title of doctor, people questioned whether she was strong, steady, and brave enough to perform operations. Even after she was recruited by the Imperial Medical Bureau, she had to pull out her identification as proof wherever she went, gazing into pair after pair of scrutinizing eyes.

This was why she traveled all the way here for dragonslaying. Not flippant curiosity, but rather firm determination. Perhaps, if she were able to master the highest medical art of Yunhuang, no one would ever question her again.

The dragonslayer focused all his attention on the operation. The cut on the jiaoren's abdomen was fully stretched open; the pelvic cavity beneath was also emptied, revealing the inner flesh walls. Using the handle of the knife, Zhili Yi separated strands of muscles. As he worked, he pressed down hard on the wound to stop the bleeding. At last, he uncovered white bones on one side of the pelvic cavity.

> A jiaoren's ventral fin bone is the equivalent of a landborn's leg bone, connected to the spine via the lower body girdle bones. Living in water, however, jiaoren do not need their ventral fin bone to support the weight of their bodies, and therefore those girdle bones are thin and fragile, barely attached to the spine. The theoretical core of the operation is to connect the girdle bone to the spine, simulating the lower body bone structure of landborns. Coupled with potions that enhance bone growth and extensive physical training, the ventral fin bone will eventually evolve into landborn legs.
>
> —*Excerpt from* Su's Comparative Anatomy

Zhili Yi was indeed a skilled dragonslayer. Pinching the loose end of a girdle bone between his fingers, he carved it into the shape of an articular surface, as if carving a cassava. He then used a whetstone to polish the bone. Jiaoren bones were rich in blood vessels, and blood flowed from the cut. His nephew handed over a jar of bone glue so he could quickly dig out a chunk with his fingertip and rub it onto the bone. After a few minutes, the bleeding stopped.

They had once called this tail-splitting, so Su Mian had assumed that dragonslayers would split the fish tail into two halves. This had confused her, because judging from the bamboo-shaped structure of the spine, it would be impossible to transform it into two legs. She saw now that the legs came from the ventral fin bone, a mirror of a land-born's lower body.

The jiaoren, being so young, had extraordinarily thin bones. Zhili Yi gestured to the boy, who ran off immediately. He came back with a large box and propped it open. It was filled with white bones.

Arching his back, Zhili Yi fumbled through the box. He pulled out a long bone, wiped it with a piece of blood-stained gauze, and held it near the jiaoren's body to compare, shifting its position around. He hesitated, as if unsatisfied with the way it looked, then set it aside and took out another bone.

These are the bones of jiaoren who died on this operation platform, thought Su Mian.

After three trials, Zhili Yi finally found the perfect bone. He put it down next to the jiaoren's own exposed girdle bone and secured them together with a bone nail. Undoubtedly this was to strengthen the girdle bone and offer extra support, so the jiaoren wouldn't break their own bones when they stood up.

Su Mian was reminded of the jiaoren she came across in the capital. Most of them were the products of a variety of body modifications—from trivial body tattoos to large-scale, often grotesque modifications involving a multitude of add-on limbs. With the help of black market surgeons, the dealers would do anything to satisfy the fetishes of the rich.

Shortly after, Zhili Yi was done with the girdle bone on the other side of the jiaoren's body, too. Pulling hard on the girdle bone, he connected its tip to the spine, causing the ventral fin attached to the girdle bone to curl up tightly as well. Su Mian stared at the fragile ventral fin as it quivered.

The boy brought over a potion jar. Zhili Yi dabbed potion-soaked gauze on the girdle bones and the ventral fine bone—Su Mian reckoned that the potion was specially made to enhance bone growth.

The moment the potion touched the jiaoren's body, the stinging pain sent their body into a fit of twitching. Their ventral fin was now convulsing violently as their belly area undulated. Their tail was whipping around and making slapping noises. The bloodstained water on the ground, splashed up by their tail, dissolved into pale red mist.

Clearly Zhili Yi was not a stranger to the jiaoren's reaction. Ignoring their struggles, he rapidly sewed all of the bleeding wounds in their abdominal cavity together and washed the cuts clean. Then, he put the intestines back and sewed together the large cut across their belly.

"After the operation, the dragonslayer will feed the jiaoren more potions," said the old captain. "Their potions work like magic. In half a year's time, the jiaoren's new legs will be as long as a normal landborn's. Those potions, though, can poison as much as they can heal. Plenty of jiaoren survive the operation but die from the potions."

No potion or elixir worked the same on everyone. A jiaoren might survive the potion, yet remain unable to grow legs. A jiaoren like that would be deemed a waste, the old captain told her, and usually discarded. But the dealers would still gouge out their eyes, so that they could at least benefit from selling those bining pearls.

Behind every successful sale of a jiaoren in the capital—always for an astronomical price—she realized, there were countless unnamed bodies.

The young jiaoren before their eyes now looked fully intact, save for a line of centipede-shaped stitches across their belly. It would eventually disappear—of course, there wouldn't be any scars left on them to repel their future buyers.

Their ventral fin was still convulsing. Pinning the newly created "leg" down with one hand, Zhili Yi grabbed a razor handed to him by the boy and swiftly scraped off the scales with his other hand, revealing pale blue skin beneath. After he was done with one "leg," he switched over to the other.

The blue skin shimmered with a silvery, moonlight-like glow. In mere seconds it turned murky and dark, like freshly unearthed artifacts quickly changing color upon first exposure to air. In this case, though, it wasn't the shock of air—the scales were suffused with blood.

Slowly, thin streams of near-black crept through scars left on the skin, wove into a web like cracks on a white desert, and converged at the drooping tip of the ventral fin, a muddy brown droplet on the verge of falling. It was thick and viscous, so the droplet hung dangerously in place, elongating as time passed by. At last, overwhelmed by the weight, the droplet plunged down with a shudder, crashed, and exploded in a splatter on the rocky floor.

The dragonslayer Zhili Yi, finally done with scale-scraping, stood up straight and took a few steps back. His face remained stone-cold and expressionless. His nephew approached the platform. Struggling, the boy held up a large jar of spirits and poured all of it over the jiaoren's lower body. The pungent smell of alcohol permeated the room.

"Is this it?" asked Su Mian.

"Well," said the old captain. "Usually, this is when the average visitor stops watching and leaves."

"Why?"

"They are already so repulsed by what they have seen that they can't bear more, so we head out," explained the old captain. "Though, you seem composed. Probably because you're a doctor, huh?"

Su Mian did not respond. Instead she asked, "What's happening next?"

"The most important step," said the old captain.

As the pair talked, the boy pushed the cart with surgical instruments to the side and brought over a long knife. He rested the knife, longer than his own body, on his shoulders, steadied it in place, and wiped the blade meticulously with alcohol-soaked gauze. The boy's eyes, reflecting the blue shimmer of the blade, seemed to glow as well.

Su Mian met his gaze. In those calm eyes, she recognized, to her surprise, a flicker of ecstasy.

Zhili Yi squatted by the wall and crossed his arms over his chest, his eyes staring blankly into the distance, as if taking a rest.

"What happens next is the biggest challenge to dragonslayers," said the old captain with excitement. "What came before was tedious, but that was nothing compared to what must happen now. Watch closely—it'll only take a split second, but it requires speed, steadiness, precision—it encompasses all of a dragonslayer's expertise, a life's worth of training."

All of a sudden, a blinding snow-white light flashed in the room, like a blazing meteor cutting through the dark night sky.

Even with her gaze focused intently on the platform, Su Mian saw nothing.

The bright workshop, the bloody red mist in the air, the old captain murmuring, the dragonslayer Zhili Yi standing by the wall, his face emotionless and his hands drooping . . . nothing seemed to have changed.

However, there was something strange glistening in the distance, stimulating her already-numb visual receptors.

A fish tail. Silvery. Curved. Slender and elegant. Already detached from the jiaoren's body, it bounced on the ground with a remaining sliver of animal instinct, like a severely injured person squeezing out their last drop of energy to cry for help. Blood streamed from its raw edge and splattered on the ground, like a bunch of blooming corals. Eventually, the tail ceased to bounce and began to writhe instead. Leaving trails behind like painted squiggles on a piece of paper, it rolled all the way into the corner, came to a halt, and dropped dead at last.

It took Su Mian great effort to move her eyes away from the fish tail. Setting her gaze instead on the platform, she saw that the jiaoren now only had half of their body.

The dragonslayer had sliced the tail off so fast that the jiaoren's body barely bled before the boy was there with healing ointment. He used all his strength to press down on the wound.

Su Mian had thought the market-ready jiaoren's legs were made from slicing their tail in two, but no, what the dragonslayers were cutting was the tail itself.

The young jiaoren on the operation platform—*a cutting board, where they were treated like meat*—did they feel pain?

Neither Su Mian nor the old captain heard the jiaoren throughout the operation. Under the effect of the spirits, they should have been fully anaesthetized; their torso hasn't moved a bit either, so presumably it did not hurt at all.

Slowly, Su Mian's gaze landed on the jiaoren again.

She saw a gaping mouth. The young jiaoren's eyes were tightly shut as if they were lost in a dream, long eyelashes casting a shadow on their face. Yet their coral-red lips, previously pressed together, were now wide apart.

A perfect circle. An abyss.

For a moment, Su Mian thought that she had heard a piercing scream, gushing out from the bottom of the ocean or the depths of space.

An eon seemed to have passed. Su Mian blurted out, "Did they die?"

"No," answered the old captain, with a hint of relief in his voice. "The job was done well. They will survive."

"Oh."

"What a truly remarkable performance they put on today! So, did you learn anything from watching?"

"I can't say I have," Su Mian said dryly. "I guess dragonslaying is too complicated for me."

"Aha! The mystery of dragonslaying hides itself from an amateur's eyes." The old captain narrowed his eyes, deep in thought. "It took quite a few performances for me to figure it out, too."

"I'm all ears."

"It's easier than it seems. First is positioning the slice. Too high, you hurt the jiaoren's body or even penetrate their abdominal cavity, causing them to die; too low, or if you miss, you won't be able to cut off the entire tail. No one would buy a jiaoren with parts of its tail still intact, and no jiaoren could bear a second slice. For dragonslayers, it's important to have a steady, strong hand. They must slice off the fleshy tail along with the hard backbone inside. They must do it fast, too. With a wound so large, they need to apply medicine and wrap it up immediately, or else the jiaoren dies from blood loss."

"How difficult. With such skills, I reckon dragonslayers could very well serve as swordsmen, too," exclaimed Su Mian.

"No. Born into a dragonslaying clan, they will never be permitted to become swordsmen."

Su Mian tried to hide the disappointment on her face. Dragonslaying was not the "esoteric art" that she had imagined, or a methodology that she could actually learn from. The dragonslayers exceled due to their sheer physical strength, instead of their technical prowess. In fact, she wasn't even sure whether dragonslaying could be called an operation. The kind of operation she was familiar with was meant to save people's lives, not to mutilate their bodies or kill them.

She turned her head to look at the two dragonslayers. Zhili Yi squatted by the wall, resting. Sure enough, the final slice had taken up most of his strength. He seemed to be panting heavily, yet he made no sound at all. The boy, on the other hand, was already wiping and polishing the blade of the long knife that Zhili Yi had put down. They needed to clean the knife as fast as possible, or else blood would corrode the metal and damage its sharpness.

Zhili Yi stood up, walked to the corner and picked the fish tail up. He wrapped it up with gauze, stuffed it into a bag, and handed it over to the old captain. It appeared to be some kind of ritual: by sending the tail back to the villagers, the dragonslayer could prove that he had completed another project. The boy lifted the jiaoren, also tightly wrapped in gauze, in his arms and took them to another room. Perhaps the jiaoren was heavy, or perhaps the boy was exhausted from standing for so long—Su Mian saw that he limped slightly as he walked.

The cloth covering the young jiaoren's hair came undone. Their seaweed-like blue hair drooped to the floor, stained red by their own blood.

Su Mian reckoned that the room where the jiaoren was taken to was a medical laboratory, where they would be fed various potions. Perhaps they would grow landborn legs. Perhaps they would die from the poison in the potions. Or, perhaps, nothing would happen and they would be discarded, just like trash.

Even if they managed to grow legs and survive, they would be facing more: endless transporting, training, and body modification, until they became a plaything for the rich and the powerful. Jiaoren had a much longer lifespan than landborns. This one, barely an adult, could live for at least two hundred more years before their beauty faded away. Then, they would be killed, leaving behind only a pair of priceless eyes, to decorate the jewelry boxes of aristocrats.

Su Mian, growing tired, asked the old captain to leave with her. The old captain signaled to Zhili Yi, who escorted them back to the main hall in silence. The sky outside had turned entirely dark. He lit a large lamp. In the warm lamplight, the room looked like an ordinary run-down living room—certainly less creepy than before.

Su Mian was eager to head out, but the old captain stopped her and sat her down on a stool.

"The eldest son's wife made congee to treat the guests," said the old captain. "It's their family tradition. Don't refuse the food."

Taken by surprise, Su Mian turned her eyes to the ground. Sitting on the floor and leaning against the doorframe was a shabby-looking woman, who smiled timidly at her.

The boy walked into the hall with a big jar of congee and a stack of bowls. The woman, pressing her palms to the ground, inched over to where they were sitting. The boy handed her a wooden spoon with a long handle. Scraping the bottom of the jar, she scooped up some meager substance from the nearly water-clear and rice-less congee into a bowl, and carefully handed the bowl over to Su Mian. Sitting on the floor the whole time, she held the bowl higher than her head. Hurriedly, Su Mian took the bowl from her. She noticed that the woman's palms were as rough as the bottoms of feet, likely due to the fact that she could only move around with her hands.

Stretching out her torso and leaning forward, the woman scooped another bowl of congee for the old captain before she moved on to serve her own family. The old captain swapped his bowl with the boy. The corners of the boy's mouth curved up, showing his first smile of the night.

Su Mian peered into the bowl. The congee, made from aged, coarse rice, was not only pitifully watery but also a rusty red color. No one spoke as they ate. Zhili Yi, well composed, appeared to be almost completely unaffected by a night of hard labor. The boy, though, was beginning to seem fatigued. He slurped the congee loudly, looking very satisfied.

The boy's satisfaction touched Su Mian's heart. Blood, darkness, the jiaoren's suffering . . . they all seemed to fade away in the warm, cozy atmosphere of the family's living room. Su Mian lifted the bowl to her lips, ready to imitate the old captain and slurp the congee.

She met a pair of emerald eyes.

The color of the ocean.

Su Mian jerked her head up. The pair of eyes was still focused intently on her, coupled with a timid smile. It was the woman. A lock of long hair escaped her ragged headcloth—*it was blue.*

Abruptly, Su Mian put down her bowl. "A jiaoren?"

"Yes," said the old captain, not even bothering to take a look. "She survived the operation but grew no legs."

"Why?"

"Dragonslayers are too lowly and poor to marry properly," answered the old captain. "So they find themselves wives out of discarded jiaoren."

"What about their daughters? They must have daughters."

"Dragonslayers can't afford to raise daughters. Girls aren't permitted to learn the skill of dragonslaying anyway, so they're usually killed after birth. When a dragonslayer needs to marry and reproduce, he takes a jiaoren who had failed to grow legs under his own operation as his wife. You see, for dragonslayers, their wives, mothers, and grandmothers are all jiaoren . . ."

"Wait—" Su Mian cut him off.

With her mouth hanging open, she was speechless.

The jiaoren carry the dominant genes. Every mixed offspring between a landborn and a jiaoren naturally comes with a fish tail, making them biologically closer to jiaoren than landborn.

—*Excerpt from* The Great Encyclopedia of Yunhuang

"In dragonslaying clans, the father usually splits the tail of the son," explained the old captain, reading her mind. "Babies die more easily from the operation, so you rarely see large families. Last year, Zhili Yi was blessed with a son. He performed dragonslaying on the baby when he turned three months old. Unfortunately, the operation failed."

Su Mian did not respond. The jiaoren housewife continued to smile at her. She felt that she could no longer force the congee down her throat.

"Perhaps the reason why dragonslayers are so good at what they do is because they've endured it too," said the old captain, smiling. "Why, they're basically jiaoren themselves."

In Yunhuang, jiaoren and dragonslayers were equally low. Generation after generation, the sons of the dragon became dragonslayers and raised their knives at their own kin. They could win no wealth, no glory. The cycle would continue on. This was the rule of Yunhuang.

Su Mian stared at the family before her: Zhili Yi, the boy, and the jiaoren housewife. "I'll give you money. Leave this place. Stop all this nonsense," she said, her voice low but firm.

Zhili Yi glanced up from his bowl, his face deadly calm. A look of discomfort, however, flashed across the woman's face. She buried her head down and did not look at Su Mian again.

Raising her voice, Su Mian repeated her words.

This time, the family didn't even bother looking up. Everyone's head was buried in their own bowl, busy gulping down the watery congee. Otherwise, there was only silence.

"Answer me!" Su Mian was on the verge of shouting. *"Answer me now!"*

"Doctor Su, why bother asking?" The captain smiled. "He can't give you an answer."

Stunned, Su Mian shot him a look.

"He's mute. They all are. Every dragonslayer was forced to drink poison that destroys their vocal chords the moment they were born."

No wonder they never made so much as a groan or a whimper, Su Mian thought.

The old captain looked at her kindly. "Dragonslayers are bound to this piece of land. They can never leave."

When the pair left the castle, it was already past midnight. The night breeze was chilly. Not a single chirp or rustle could be heard. The old captain invited Su Mian back to his den to enjoy the company of the stove. They brought the jiaoren's tail back too, and carefully hung it beneath the eave.

The cat was sound asleep. *What a wise decision to leave it behind today,* Su Mian thought to herself.

Steam rose from the stew on the stove; a mouth-watering fragrance permeated the room. The piping hot food warmed the old captain's spirits as well. "This is so much better than the dragonslayer's congee," he muttered, as he filled up his bowl and eagerly offered to hand Su Mian a bowl too.

"Jiaoren meat stew?" asked Su Mian.

"That's right. The meat of jiaoren tastes sweeter than any kind of fish in the world." The old captain's cheeks grew rosy in the hot steam. "Every fish tail the dragonslayers obtain is made into a banquet. Only the elders of the village are allowed to take some meat home for their stew. It's good for health."

"The xiehai banquet," said Su Mian, remembering.

"Yes, our local tradition," said the old captain. "Come with me tomorrow, you'll taste the most delicious jiaoren cuisine of your life."

"How unfortunate," said Su Mian. "I need to leave by tomorrow morning—a little short on time."

"How unfortunate indeed . . ." The old captain sighed wholeheartedly as he blew at his stew, trying to cool it down.

Su Mian did not respond. Quietly, sitting still, she gazed out the window, waiting for the crack of dawn. Yet all she saw was the cold, ink-washed night, silent as death. In the darkness, indistinct sparks of firelight twinkled on the faraway beach.

Perhaps it was the fishermen's bonfire, celebrating a good catch. The firelight was a few scattered spots at first, but then more lit up, gradually forming a few lines, extending all the way south into the depths of the Biluo Ocean—the blazing trails of fire melted into a boundless sea of stars.

17

New Year Painting, Ink and Color on Rice Paper, Zhaoqiao Village
年画

Chen Qian 陈茜
Translated by Emily Xueni Jin 金雪妮

New Year Painting, Ink and Color on Rice Paper, Zhaoqiao Village

By Chen Qian
Translated by Emily Xueni Jin

"Hey, come check this out." Huang strode into my studio, a large cardboard box in his arms.

A glance at the dusty old box made me flinch and reach for my face mask. "Set it on the floor! Not the workbench."

Ignoring the contempt in my voice, Huang grabbed a box cutter, bent down, and sliced through the packing tape. "I was up at dawn yesterday to catch the antique market. A full box for two thousand, clean deal. The owner said a private museum that closed down used to own this stuff."

"Can't believe that you still get so fired up by cheap bargains," I muttered, shaking my head.

Huang and I had gone to the same college. We'd both majored in cultural studies and museology, and Huang was a few years my senior. Born into a wealthy family, he'd developed a hobby for collecting antiquities. Acquainting himself with auction houses and the collector's community, he earned pocket money by buying and reselling for a higher price. I, on the other hand, had followed in my family's footsteps by staying close to the academic tradition, and opening a private studio specializing in antique book and painting restoration. Huang often came around with his so-called "prizes"—some of the damaged works in his collection, after restoration, could re-enter the market with a several-fold increase in price. For my tiny studio, he was a big client.

A whiff of dust-smoke dispersed in the air as Huang lifted the box's flaps. Inside were stacks of thread-bound books and scrolls. Even though I was conscientious about hygiene, I couldn't help but lean over to peer into the box.

Half an hour later, both of us were sitting cross-legged on the floor, our faces sweaty and dusty.

"Nothing interesting, huh?" sighed Huang.

Together, we had cleaned and sorted the contents of the box into separate stacks: a set of thread-bound books with a few missing volumes, some common lithographs such as *Golden Treasury of Quatrains and Octaves* and *Chinese Poetry Sound Rhythm by Li Yu,* and several volumes of songbooks. Unrolling the scrolls, we found they were either landscape sketches or New Year paintings of good luck charms by unknown artists with clumsy brushwork. At the bottom of the box were two carved wooden windowpane fragments, darkened and worn from what seemed to be a fire, the carvings barely visible. Too bad—if they were in good condition, perhaps folk culture collectors would be interested in purchasing. Special researchers might find more value in those pieces of wood than the two of us.

"Well, money spent for nothing." I laughed, knowing that Huang wouldn't care about a few thousand splurged.

Huang pressed down on his numb knee and stood up. "Oh well. Go wash your hands. It's lunchtime."

"Your treat," I said, pointing to the mess on the floor. "And tidy this up."

"Fine, my treat," said Huang, defeated, scratching his head.

The steam-and-stew cooker's timer dinged. I walked into the kitchen to turn it off. When I reentered the workspace, Huang was squatting again, peering at something wrapped in a piece of paper.

"Now, this looks special," he said. "It was sandwiched between two of those old books and fell out just now."

Huang's discovery was another painting, torn into fragments—whether on purpose or worn down by time was impossible to say—then bundled up in paper. Each fragment of soft old paper was about the size of a fingernail. Judging from the crude brushstrokes and flat, overly flamboyant color, I could tell that it was a New Year painting, simple portraits usually assembled from traditional symbols representing prosperity, health and luck.

"Want to put it together?" asked Huang.

"I don't have that kind of time." I shrugged. "Given what else is in this box, this is probably just another amateur painting from the fifties."

"Hey, I'll pay you for the work." Huang picked up a fragment with the pointed tweezers he carried around and held it up for me to see. Painted on the fragment was a small, chubby hand. It clearly belonged to a child.

And there was something in their palm. I bent down to examine the fragment and realized that it was an eye. Now intrigued, Huang and I riffled through the other fragments; they were all pieces of what must have originally been a New Year painting. Even in all my years of study, I'd never seen anything like this in Chinese mythology: a childlike god with an eye in its palm, gazing up at me.

I gazed back. "I'll take the job."

After a tedious day spent restoring a ten-meter-long hand scroll, I began putting together the fragments of Huang's New Year painting.

Within a night, I managed to reconstruct the overall shape of the New Year painting: a chubby child sitting on a lotus leaf with a lotus root and a large red lotus flower in their hands, a classic Jiangnan folk motif.

However, as I laid down the last fragment on the child's face, I froze. I couldn't move my eyes away from the completed painting on my workbench. A moment later, I pulled out my phone, took a picture and sent it to Huang.

The child in the painting was without a face. Instead, they extended their left hand outward, and in their palm was the eye.

I turned the brightness up on the lamp beneath my semi-transparent workbench, and leaned in for a closer look. There weren't even traces of ink beneath the coloring, no clues or contours of eroded facial features. A painting in its complete form. The child was, indeed, faceless.

Chinese New Year paintings were traditional forms—the artist wasn't supposed to be creative about it, at least not to the point that they would conjure up the image of a strange, faceless child. The brush-work of the eye in their palm, like the rest of the painting, was rough-hewn: an upper and lower curve outlined a slender eye, its ink-black pupil staring right at me. I shivered.

Huang replied to my message with a single word.

CURSED.

I shook my head. We in restoration were in the business of dealing with the dead. If we gave into the fear of spirits and superstitions, our industry would have been long gone. Brushing off Huang's warning, I asked, "Can I post this on my feed?"

"Your call," said Huang.

With permission from clients, I would post pictures of my resto-ration projects on my site. I had over a hundred thousand followers, and it was both an advertisement for my studio and a platform to sat-isfy the public's curiosity about the antique restoration industry. I'd poured my heart into looking for the right content; this painting, unique and uncanny, was perfect.

There. It was posted.

The night was deep. From my workbench, I carefully lifted the New Year painting and mounted it on the wall to dry. Now completely restored, with every fragment in place, there was a surprising softness to where the face ought to have been.

"You're welcome." I smiled at them. *They must be happy to be whole again.*

When I turned on my phone the next morning, I found out that my post had attracted nearly a million people—including an unexpected visitor.

"Teacher Song?" the visitor on my doorstep called out hesitantly.

"You can just call me Song." I smiled. Most clients new to my studio, under the ridiculous impression that all cultural artifact restorers were bearded old men with silver hair, would be surprised by my age and gender.

"Ah, Song, nice to meet you. I'm here for the New Year painting. Remember our phone call yesterday?" said the woman. She was older, her voice thin, but she had a fullness to her features, and yet somehow, a hunger about her. She had thick, shoulder-length silver hair, and looked to be in her eighties. She wore a bright oversized sweatshirt, with a shopping bag in one hand.

After my post went viral, I received countless inquiries about the painting, most of which I directed to Huang. This woman's request, however, was unique: she insisted that she wanted to come around to the studio and see "the child with no face from Zhaoqiao Village" in person.

A document in the box containing a family tree denoted that those antiques had indeed come from Zhaoqiao Village. Apart from Huang and me, no one else knew this. Besides, the old woman had talked about the painting like it was an old friend. But when pressed, she had refused to say more until she could see the painting with her own eyes.

Huang had spent the last few days knocking on the doors of experts in art history and folk culture, on the hunt for useful leads about the painting. He'd found nothing. Letting the old woman see it, he thought, was worth a shot.

"Please come in. I don't own the painting; it's only here temporarily for the sake of restoration," I said as I turned, making way for her to enter the studio. "If you're interested in purchasing, I can contact the owner for you."

But she didn't seem to be listening. "It's her," she said, stricken. Her hand, skin so thin that it revealed the blue veins beneath, reached for the painting as if to soothe the faceless child. I opened my mouth to stop her—the painting was delicate; its age rendering it tender and fragile—but the woman pulled her hand back right away, as if it had been burned.

She turned to look at me. "Song, I will pay any price you ask."

"Auntie, the painting isn't mine to sell. Why don't we sit down and have a chat? Do you know who this child is?" I asked, a little awkward.

I went to the kitchen and made two cups of hot tea. "Auntie, no need to rush. The owner is a good friend of mine, and he's a very reasonable person. If this painting bears personal significance to you, or if there is something special about it, it's not impossible for him to make a deal with you."

A long silence. "I haven't seen a painting like this in sixty years," whispered the old lady, her fingers curling around the cup.

So there is a story after all, I thought.

"I came from Zhaoqiao Village in Southern Zhejiang, in the mountains," she said, staring blankly ahead. "We didn't have public schools back then, and all the children in the village were taught by the same teacher. The teacher could write calligraphy and paint too, and he was in charge of our entire village's New Year calligraphy couplets and paintings. He and his wife were unlucky with children, though; they were blessed with their only daughter at nearly sixty years old. She was the cleverest child in the village, and she learned how to write calligraphy and paint at the age of five."

As the woman paused, I couldn't help but turn to look at the painting on the wall.

"At the village school, though, the other children bullied her for being different and smarter. Then, one day, she disappeared from the village altogether."

I took a sharp breath.

"But she's only a little girl," I said. "Couldn't an adult step in to help her?"

"Those kids were clever. They knew how to get out of trouble. No one knew who started bullying her first." The woman smiled bitterly. "She was never harassed or beaten, though. The entire class pretended she didn't exist. No one would speak to her or look at her. Her classmates wouldn't even touch the things that she had touched first. Her father—he was also the teacher, remember?—never found out that she was bullied. He was just relieved that she'd become so quiet and obedient. It wasn't until after her disappearance that he—"

The old lady fell silent again.

Poor thing, I thought. Children could be so cruel.

"Was she your . . . friend?" I asked carefully.

"No, not really. I heard about her story from other people," she said. "She'd already vanished when I was born. When some villagers wanted to demolish her temple, her story also got spread around."

A temple for a girl who was bullied and then disappeared? It sounded like, well, a kind gesture. What did it mean, though, that the villagers wanted to destroy the temple? I leaned forward, feeling off-kilter but even more intrigued by this strange story.

"The girl disappeared the night before New Year's Eve. When her father went through her personal belongings, he found dozens of New Year paintings that she had drawn. The child on the paintings was horrifying. They were faceless, with a single eye in their palm."

I glanced at the painting on the wall. A coldness crept down the back of my neck.

The child with no face somehow seemed to be smiling at us.

"Yes, she left those paintings behind. No one there cared about her. They turned a blind eye and a deaf ear toward her. She was practically invisible. I bet that she drew those paintings to disgust the villagers on purpose," said the woman. "The father, deeply saddened by his loss, tossed all of the girl's belongings, including the paintings, into the trash yard, so that he could stop thinking of her. The children went digging in the trash for more. When they realized that the child in the paintings had no face, they threw them out again, afraid of misfortune."

I felt an urge to speak up for the girl, my throat tight. "It's the bullies' fault."

"Song, you have no idea what happened next," said the old lady, shaking her head. "A child took one of those paintings home after all, and put it up on his wall. He used to be the most enthusiastic one when it came to hurling stones at the girl. I bet he wanted the painting as a target." Her lips trembled. "A few days after he put up the painting, his grandfather—who had not been able to leave his bed for more than a decade—started walking on two feet again."

I stared, eyes wide.

"The entire village marveled at this miracle. Someone suggested it was because of the painting. Villagers rushed to the trash yard and dug out all of the paintings from beneath the snow, and put them up at home," said the old lady. "Then, another child who was about to die from smallpox magically recovered. The girl's paintings could save lives. Over the years, the paintings cured five or six more people." The old lady's lips curled into a sneer. "The villagers even made a temple for her next to the ancestral hall and worshipped her like a goddess. The statue, like her painting, didn't have a face."

"Well, seems like she was repaying the villagers' hatred with kindness," I said. I felt awe and pity for the girl, saving the people who used to bully her.

"Who said she was *repaying with kindness*?" snapped the old lady.

I raised an eyebrow.

"After a few years," the woman continued, "everyone whose lives had been saved by those paintings changed. They lost their vision, hearing, sense of smell and taste. Their facial features no longer served any function."

Coldness rushed down my spine.

An impressive folktale indeed. But . . . the cursed New Year painting was now in my studio. I stole a glance at it.

"It doesn't seem exactly like your everyday luck charm. Why do you want it?"

Whether the woman's story was true or not, her desire for the painting was intense and real.

"Eventually, the villagers burned all of her paintings, and no one dared speak of her again. I am turning eighty soon. I would have completely forgotten about the story of the little ghost and her paintings too, if it wasn't for my grandson's cancer . . ."

My heart sank. "I'm so sorry."

"He was diagnosed with a rare kind of cancer, and the doctors say that they can't do anything for him. He only has about half a year left. When I saw this painting of yours . . ."

She halted as she tried to blink back tears. Her story was unbelievable, yet who was I to question her? She was seeking help from a ghost in a folktale, trying to put off death for a time, while simultaneously knowing she would be inviting it in. In the face of despair, one had no choice in which god they prayed to.

Using a bamboo working knife with a long and thin blade, I drew a rectangle around the painting on the wall with the knife tip, took it off and wrapped it up carefully in a scroll.

I would deal with Huang later. It was probably nothing but a local legend the woman had heard as a child. But now, with her grandchild sick, the legend had become her only sliver of hope.

"You're soft," said Huang, shaking his head.

I rolled my eyes and poked my chopsticks into a custard bun. "Stop complaining. I did a good deed and made you money. What else do you want?"

We were at our usual table at the Cantonese dim sum place around the corner. After the old lady left my studio the other day, she wired a sum of money to my bank account that was around what the painting would have sold for in an auction house. She left a note that said *Thank you for your kindness* without signing her name.

I transferred all the money to Huang and called to fill him in on the painting's uncanny and, indeed, sorrowful backstory. Just when I thought the whole saga was at an end, Huang called back the next day. He needed to talk in person.

"It's not about the money. My God, as someone who authenticates calligraphy and paintings *professionally,* how can you trust people's stories so easily?" asked Huang, shaking his head. "I asked a friend to dig into the account that wired money to you and found her name—Li Fumei. There wasn't a comprehensive filing system yet when her generation was born. According to data provided by her to the population census, she was born in Zhaoqiao Village, Southern Zhejiang, in 1943."

The old woman had never mentioned her name the other day.

Huang pulled out his phone. "She married Liu, an engineer, in 1962, and together they had two daughters and one son. The sick grandson she referred to is the son of her second daughter. I found his medical record at the municipal children's hospital. He's six years old, diagnosed with signet ring cell carcinoma, already in its terminal stage. I asked a doctor friend and confirmed that the boy only has a few months left."

"Sounds like she isn't lying about her grandson," I said. "What's the problem, then?"

"The problem is Zhaoqiao Village," said Huang, handing me his phone. On the screen was the national record of official local documents. "Zhaoqiao Village, with a population of a little over two hundred people, was destroyed in 1955 by a fire. No one survived. It consisted mostly of people from the same clan. Only three families were from other clans, with different surnames, but Li was not one of them."

My memory went back to the day when Huang first brought the cardboard box to my studio, and the two pieces of burnt wooden windowpane fragments.

"You mean Li Fumei made up the whole story about the girl from Zhaoqiao Village to scam me, so that she could buy the painting of the faceless girl from me for market price?" I was stupefied. "Her grandson is actually ill, though. Why waste money on the painting if she didn't believe what she was saying?"

"I think there's more to the legend than what she told us," said Huang. "I found out that she left for where Zhaoqiao Village used to be by train this morning. Are you interested in a weekend getaway in Southern Zhejiang?"

"Why are you so concerned about her?" I asked. Huang was in general a curious person, but I never expected that he would be willing to travel so far for a painting that was worth five figures at best.

"It's cursed, and we've both come in contact with it," said Huang, patting the jade Buddha amulet that he wore around his neck.

The landscape flashing across the car window was farm field after farm field, freshly green from the kiss of the spring breeze, adorned with sparse golden canola flowers.

The long drive was making me dizzy and sleepy. Huang drove the minivan that he usually collected artifacts from the countryside with, and I, sitting in the passenger's seat, searched for more information on the painting of the faceless girl. Surprisingly, the story about the girl from Zhaoqiao Village might have actually been real. According to research on folk culture, a myriad of small, local temples in rural Southern Zhejiang were dedicated to the "faceless fairy," and people prayed to her for the sick. A set of rituals were developed as well. Judging from the general time frame in which those temples were established, the tradition had begun just a few years before Zhaoqiao Village was destroyed in a fire.

We entered the mountains. The smoothly paved national highway was now replaced by rough gravel paths. Occasionally the GPS signal would be completely lost, and we had to stop several times to ask for directions.

We met a group of elderly people sitting by a village entrance and enjoying the sun. When they heard that we were looking for Zhaoqiao Village, their mouths hung open in astonishment. "That place has been abandoned for decades. No one lives there anymore. After the local dam is built, it's going to be flooded. You both look so young, why are you going there?"

"We're art students, and our homework is to sketch an abandoned village," we said.

The elderly people pointed in a direction. "If you see a temple in the village, don't go in," they warned us. "Nothing but snakes in there these days."

"Interesting," muttered Huang as he restarted the engine. "Sounds like people around here know that Zhaoqiao Village is not what it seems on the surface."

A chill ran down my spine as I gazed at the sinking sun and darkening horizon. A girl who disappeared after being bullied by her entire community. A village turned to ruins by fire. I couldn't help but think of unfortunate and sinister possibilities.

I knew the story had technically ended half a century ago; however, the New Year painting that I put together with my own hands seemed to have caused more unresolved mysteries to resurface.

It was near midnight when we arrived at what used to be Zhaoqiao Village. The night was ink black. In our headlights, two fresh car tracks were left in the wasteland, followed by the sight of Li Fumei's rented car, a gray Volkswagen, parked in front of a fence. Huang parked our minivan horizontally, right in front of the Volkswagen to corner it, so Li Fumei could no longer leave.

I chuckled. "How do you even come up with these ideas?"

"You sit in your studio comfortably every day, restoring those paintings, whereas I travel all over the place collecting artifacts and dealing with hooligans. I've seen way too many tricks. Follow me closely. Don't go off on your own!" he warned.

"Relax. I don't have the guts to go anywhere on my own," I said, pointing my heavy industrial flashlight toward the road ahead. A traditional pailou—an ornate archway—stood erect at the entrance to the village, looking majestic even under the cover of the night.

Every inch of the land was veiled with wild grass. Following Li Fumei's footprints, clearly distinguishable in the grass, we entered Zhaoqiao Village. Most of the bungalows here were no more than blackened wooden skeletons, reminiscent of the tragedy. As we trudged through the grass, a night fog began to rise. By the time we reached the village's ancestral hall and grain-sunning grounds, the fog had grown so heavy that we could barely see each other's faces.

To the left of the ancestral hall was the temple of the faceless goddess, the only architecture in the entire village that had survived the fire. We had traveled so far to get here, yet standing before the gateway, both Huang and I were a little intimidated by the silent darkness. Back in my downtown sunlit studio, the story of the faceless girl was merely a strange rural legend, but now the story had somehow come alive. I was not a superstitious person, but at this moment I regretted not bringing with me some kind of a lucky charm—even if it was for the sake of having a placebo.

"Auntie? Li Fumei? Are you in there?" Huang shouted, knocking on the temple's porch pillar.

Silence.

We exchanged a glance. Li Fumei had come all this way for the faceless goddess. She *had* to be here.

"Want to go in?" Huang looked at me. We went.

We arrived at a spacious front yard after stepping through the gate. To my great surprise, the stone-paved ground was clean and tidy, and in the moonlight I saw rows of well-tended potted plants. The air was infused with a hint of incense. A screen wall shielded the door to the hall of worship. Behind the wall, however, was faint candlelight and the distant sounds of a few people with a strong local accent whispering to one another.

In a temple that has been abandoned for half a century? I could feel the hairs on my neck stand up.

Huang, the calmer one, gestured at me to follow him around the screen wall. For a few seconds I was torn between overwhelming curiosity and the fear of ghosts; then, I took a deep breath and caught up with him. *Isn't this what we're here for?*

Six men, some middle-aged and some elderly, were sitting in a circle before the entrance to the hall of worship. Their faces were tanned and weather-beaten. Wearing dark robes made of rough cloth, they pulled up the legs of their baggy pants, revealing the protruding veins on their ankles.

An elderly man with silvery hair and a beard appeared to be their leader. *All of those paintings must be turned in! How dare you say there's nothing you can do about it?* Spit sprayed as the words came out of his mouth.

Another man, bony like a twig, chimed in eagerly. *Our chief is right! Those bumpkins shouldn't be allowed to keep the treasure to themselves. Sick people are bound to die anyway, what's the point of extending their lives for a few years? If we sell those paintings to the rich and powerful, soon everyone here can build another house!*

We better ask the goddess first, said a plump man with a shrill voice. He tapped his pipe on the lotus flower jar and continued, *We'll never run out of paintings—as long as we keep the goddess happy.*

Huang and I squatted next to the screen wall, hiding ourselves in the shadow of the tree. It was now obvious that the scene before our eyes was a flashback of what had happened decades ago: the village leaders were discussing in the temple what to do with the paintings that the girl had left behind.

"Disgusting. If the girl has really turned into a goddess, then she should punish all of them," I whispered to Huang, who tutted disapprovingly. None of those men felt shame or guilt for what the village as a collective had done to the girl. All they cared about was how to profit from her paintings.

Strangely enough, even in the presence of these doomed ghosts, I felt no fear. Perhaps it was because my instinct told me that the faceless goddess was only a little girl who had suffered from abuse when she was alive, and she wouldn't do anything to harm Huang or me.

The men's voices rose gradually as the discussion escalated into an argument. Thick fog clouded their figures. When the fog dissipated again, the scene had changed. The chief stood before the statue of the faceless goddess, trembling, clenching a stack of paintings. I could hear coarse shouts.

Give back the paintings or else we'll burn your house to the ground!

Let it burn! The faceless goddess is bringing justice to us! He is a corrupt chief! Look at the things that he had seized from us all these years!

Hands holding torches reached over the temple fence.

"Even a rabbit would bite if you corner it," I said, enjoying the drama. "Now the chief is getting a taste of his own medicine!"

Ashes and glowing sparks drifted in the wind. Fire. Screams and cries ripped through the murky air. People ran for their lives.

"There goes the entire village," said Huang.

The fire had painted the night sky red. My toes curled at the thought of the people swallowed up in the flames.

Huang turned around. "Did you do it on purpose?" he asked softly.

Behind us stood a scrawny little girl about eight or nine years old, wearing her hair in two thin braids. She wore a ceremonial brocade robe with colorful embroidery. Though I'd never seen her face before, I knew exactly who she must be. Her dark, slender eyes were sharp and penetrating. With her face completely solemn and stern, she didn't look like a child.

"I didn't do it on purpose," she said. "When I was alive, nobody could see me. I painted those paintings to do something good, so that I would stop being invisible to them."

"But they're not worth it," I said.

The girl did not respond. Her head lowered to her chest.

Huang knelt down. "Look, what goes around comes around. You didn't want the paintings to harm those people, but karma has taken your revenge for you. They deserve it. It's all over now. Can you send us back?"

The girl was silent. Fog rose again.

We found Li Fumei before the statue of the faceless goddess. She knelt there; her entire body frozen in shock. Huang carried her back to the car. It took quite a while for her to wake up.

"I admire your courage," said Huang, shaking his head.

"She would never hurt me. I can't promise the same to you." Li Fumei wiped the corner of her mouth with the back of her still-trembling hand. "I was her only friend."

Huang and I gave each other a look.

"I apologize for lying to you. The faceless girl—her name was Xiao He. Before she died, I was the only person who would talk to her, but never in front of anyone. She didn't tell me anything though, when she disappeared from the village. When the other villagers found out that the paintings she left behind could cure illnesses and extend people's lives, they got into a great fight. The entire village was burnt to ashes as a result. Only a few families managed to escape. I could never bring myself to think about what had happened for almost a lifetime, until my grandson fell ill," said Li Fumei. "I made up the whole story about the curse on the painting, so that you would give it to me."

So much for giving other people the benefit of the doubt, I thought to myself.

"I needed to come and ask Xiao He whether it is safe for me to use that painting on my grandson," continued Li Fumei as a tear ran down her face. "Her hatred and thirst for revenge were enough to burn down the entire village. She never showed up though, even after I had knelt before her statue for the entire night. I was scared that she would appear, but I was also scared that she had already left . . ."

"Stop blaming the fire on her. It's not her fault. Those people died of their own greed," interrupted Huang. "If you want that painting, then take it. We've already sold it to you and closed the deal."

Lu Fumei's lips trembled, but no words came out.

For quite a long time, I put the painting of the faceless girl from my mind.

Until half a year later, when Huang came around to my studio with a piece of news. "Remember Li Fumei? Her grandson took a turn for the better," he said. "However . . ."

"For God's sake, just finish the story," I poked his shoulder.

"After he recovered from cancer, his vision, hearing and sense of smell suddenly began deteriorating." He winked. "Modern science had no idea what's going on."

"But the curse—it was a lie?" I said.

"I heard that her grandson was the school bully," Huang said.

I didn't know what to say.

"Better than to die at such a young age, I guess." Finally, I let out a sigh.

On the night of the festival of dead spirits, I happened to pass by Fahua Temple. Even though I almost never went to temples to pray, I paid twenty for a lotus-shaped paper lamp and went in.

I set my lamp down gently on the river where thousands of lamps were placed to commemorate the dead, and pressed my palms together. On the right side, I'd drawn an eye in the rough-hewn style of a New Year painting. I hoped she could see me.

The Portrait 画妖

Chu Xidao 楚惜刀
Translated by Gigi Chang 张菁

The Portrait

By Chu Xidao
Translated by Gigi Chang

Lightly the fine brush traces, faintly the supple fur draws. The cloud-soft hair, sketched in a freehand style, coils like wisps of smoke.

Painting the floral jewels, trailing the curved brows, sculpting the jade nose, rouging the lips. Her skin, immaculate like ice and nephrite. Her airy robe seems to flutter without breeze, as if made of dragon silk, that mythical gauze woven by mermaids, which seeks to fly of its own volition. Her skirt, turmeric yellow, folds in many pleats. Her feet, two interlinked lotus blossoms, peep out from the swath of fabric.

She sits, perching on the edge of a cloud, lightsome and ethereal.

He brandishes the brush, and ink flows forth, reminiscent of drifting billows and swirling water. The person in the picture, untainted by the dredges of the world, gradually gains flesh, color, life, immortality. She is ready to peel herself from the paper, to fly away beyond the bounds of the earth.

But her eyes—cool and clear like an autumn lake. They gaze into the middle distance, as if about to speak but halting before the words tumble out. These eyes refuse to be set down by his brush.

What matters of the heart are contained in that look? he wonders.

A touch of loss and sorrow always lurks at the pinnacle of beauty, like petals scattered by the wind.

What cannot be captured is the most enchanting.

The tipping of his brush has lured him into a reverie. *How do I catch these stars?* He notes the tremor in his heart. He has painted many women, each of them a beauty, and yet, with her, he is at a loss. He knows he has to lift himself above and beyond to record this celestial charm, but he cannot cast away the shackles of his gaze.

The first time he set eyes on her, he was quite sure his spirit and soul deserted him. He was so mesmerized by her loveliness that he picked up the shallow dish of ink, thinking it was his teacup.

What has surprised him is that the longer he observes her, the stronger her hold is over him. Like a vintage wine, its aroma and potency grow as it ages and matures—one eyeful is enough to inebriate.

The final touch. The last stroke. The eyes. He cannot do it. He cannot touch the soft fur of his brush to paper. He cannot remember how many times it has been. Always. This moment. Now. When the buildup comes to nothing.

Disheartened, he bunches up what could have been a masterpiece and steals a glance. She looks . . .

Displeased. Begrudging. Chiding. Abashed. Troubled. Serene. All of these and none of it.

He resents his hand for not being able to master the brush. He hates himself for not being able to rein in his heart. If he cannot keep his heart in control, how can he pry into hers?

If he cannot see into the matters of her heart, how can he ever complete this painting?

The greatest painter of Central Shu.

To hell with this hollow title.

“Master Danhong, take a break, perhaps?” Squire Huan wiped the beads of sweat along his hairline. This master painter, this expert of cinnabar and azurite, had yet to complete the portrait of his daughter after working at it for ten days—that was something the squire had not anticipated.

The maidservant Luping had also noticed the painter’s trouble and brought him a fresh cup of green tea. It was brewed from the most tender, recently picked shoots, before the arrival of the Grain Rain season at the end of the third moon.

Danhong took a sip. The tingle of bitterness on his tongue reminded him of his conundrum. The final picture of his masterwork. *A Hundred Beauties.* He was so close to completion, and yet, trials beset all good things, as dictated by the age-old wisdom. Maybe he himself was the cause of this impasse—he could not bear to part from this enchantress; he would rather live down slights and slurs to gain an extra moment at her side.

Silent was the beauty waiting to be captured.

Suxuan had been in the painter's company from morning till night for nearly a fortnight, but she had barely spoken a dozen words. In front of him, she was taciturn and reticent, her chattering vivacity cast aside. She understood that she was simply the pretty vista—she had no need to say much—but her family were bedeviled by speculation. Could this little girl be following the footsteps of many maidens before her, changing her ways for him?

Ever since Danhong established himself as a painter, his skills had been sought after by both court and society. He was applauded for his ability to seize the spirit and essence of anything he put his brush to, and praised for his power to ensnare beholders with the wonders he conjured. Even the Emperor had taken an interest, offering gold in the thousands for his masterpieces. The demand for Danhong ran beyond his works. His handsome features conveyed an air unfettered by the material world; many of his sitters in *A Hundred Beauties* had fallen in love.

Legends also preceded the man. There was the story of a wealthy family in Luoyang who had failed to solicit his service for their daughter's portrait; humiliated, she had left her home and her city, unmarried and alone. There were also many tales of noble and highborn lords, who feigned their desire for Danhong's paintings but harried him for entirely different reasons, and they all ended up being chased away by the master painter with sticks and brooms.

Such is the narrative of those who beguile the world.

Brows knitted, a faint blush crept onto Danhong's cheeks. He had been pondering the cause of his debilitation. Squire Huan sensed the awkwardness and made his excuses, leaving Luping standing between the painter and his daughter. Suxuan shot her maid a look, her lips quivering as if to speak. Then she changed her mind.

"I'm a little peckish. Might I trouble . . ." Danhong could not hold back any longer.

Nodding, Luping flicked her eyes over to her mistress with the hint of a smile.

Suxuan watched her maid skitter away with a bounce in her steps. The moment Luping was gone, it felt as if she had been thrust right into Danhong, as if they were standing no more than an inch apart from each other. She thought she could hear his heartbeat, even though he had stepped back and was standing by the window.

Danhong let his eyes roam the sky. He knew better than to hope that she would speak first, since the notes of celestial music would not be conferred onto lowly creatures like him so easily. For now, he would take comfort from the clouds, where her heavenly form was mirrored many times over.

"Master, would you allow me a glimpse of your work?"

The sound of her own voice surprised Suxuan as much as the exaggerated way Danhong whipped round. Her heart skipped a beat, but a smile stole upon her lips. She turned away swiftly, head bowed, wringing her hands in her voluminous sleeves.

Yet, Danhong had caught that momentary sparkle. It scattered the clouds and dispelled the fog she had conjured to obscure her skittish, girlish side. Once more, he could feel his spirit abandoning him.

The euphoric painter half-jogged, half-hopped to his rooms and returned with dozens of scrolls cradled in his arms, desperate to share everything.

The ink came alive as the picture unfurled. Suxuan could not resist the urge to touch the radiant image.

The jade-pure hand, turning needle and thread nimbly. The luminous wrist, in stark contrast to the colorful peacocks woven on the cloud brocade skirt. Glorious as the streaks of rose gold in that distinct intersection of light and gloom at dawn or at dusk.

Suxuan was almost certain that she had stepped inside the painting, that she was catching a glimpse of this maiden with her own eyes. She imagined herself donning the same many-hued garb, sauntering into the main hall. She could hear the lavish praises from her parents; she could see the onlookers in awe, admiring her with envy.

Yi, what brought on this silly fancy? Suxuan stilled her heart and turned to Danhong with a smile. "What a masterful work. Might I enquire the name of the sitter?"

"Yue Bingrou of Lin'an." An offhanded reply, for Danhong's every thought was on the upward curl of her lips. He was intoxicated.

I know her name—the greatest beauty of Lin'an, Suxuan said to herself. *The most treasured woven silks of the land are made by her family, and she is very skilled in embroidery.* Was he simply a painter in the presence of this talented woman? She tilted her head to consider her whimsy.

Danhong gawked at her. Captivated, enthralled.

Sensing his gaze, the corners of her mouth turned up a little more, but when Suxuan spoke, she was demure and restrained. "The brushwork is meticulous, but it also has an expressive blitheness of the flowing wind. It is delightful how she looks up and smiles. We see one half of her face, but her allure is captured in full. An excellent portrait."

Danhong nodded without abashment, for he knew he deserved the high praise. However, he had no inkling that, despite her comment on the winning aspect of the painting, what had caught her eyes were the red clouds he traced. He stood up and reached for the teapot in rapture. As he filled his cup, a grin also poured out of him.

Suxuan picked another scroll and unrolled it. She fell into a silence—a long, long silence. Then she let out a sigh.

"Nothing of the world could taint her, so like the water sprite Lingbo is she. Might I enquire who she might be?"

"A lady-in-waiting at the Palace of Sagely Adornment." Danhong had forgotten her name. The Emperor had commissioned him to paint

Noble Consort Jiang; she was too tarnished by mundane vulgarities to be worth his while, and yet, among her ladies-in-waiting was this otherworldly creature. He passed over the many beauties handpicked to populate the private palace of the most powerful man in the land, braved His Majesty's protestations, and produced a portrait of the serving woman.

"From the imperial household . . . no wonder."

Her eyes lingered on the image, studying his technique.

His eyes stayed on her. He began to believe that he had been gazing at her in this way since the chaos before the coming of time. He had lost all sense of himself, all sense of the world. All he could do was to let his eyes drink in everything.

A breeze blew across the lake, stirring the still water. Ripples fanned out, dense and layered like grooves on a seashell.

Suxuan's heart was that lake right now. She might seem to be examining the painting, but her attention had long wandered elsewhere. She welcomed and rejected this searing stare at once. It thrilled her but also worried her. Heart fretting, mind whirling, she knew not what to think.

Danhong had lost the willpower to extract himself from this sublime view. The brush was now an unbearable load, weighing a thousand jun. Even if he could lift it, he would only be capable of writing the character 情. This one simple word embodied a wealth of feelings and emotions—love, passion, affection, tenderness, devotion, companionship . . . It quashed the last of his self-control.

Pushing the painting away, Suxuan rose abruptly to her feet and headed out of the room. The sunlight in the courtyard cast a dazzling halo around her.

To Danhong, she seemed ready to take wing and transcend into a higher celestial being.

She turned to address him once she had stepped through the doorway. "Master must be exhausted. We shall continue another day."

In time, everybody in the Huan household had guessed the thoughts brewing in the master painter's mind. Squire Huan kept his opinions to himself, but with Madam Huan, Danhong's name was the first and last words on her lips. She could hardly talk about anything without mentioning him, and so familiar was her tone that it was as if he were already kin.

This morning, Suxuan woke earlier than usual and took out a handkerchief that she had been embroidering. Instead of doing needlework, she simply held onto the piece of silk sewn with the outline of a pair of mandarin ducks. Lovebirds. Her languor soon turned into a daze.

"What silliness is going through your head?" she chided in good humor when Luping's knowing glint cut through her trance.

"I'm reminded of a poem by Cui Yu that my lady told me about," Luping answered, beaming.

Suxuan knew instantly what her maid was referring to. The suite of three romantic verses about mandarin ducks. The last lines came unbidden to her:

On the zither only whispered words of nuzzling are heard
By the window verses of flying together unfurl for naught
How to see each other and be together always
Why envy the world of men and their plentiful pining

It was beautiful, but with whom would she "be together always"? Suxuan eyed the handkerchief she had been working on. She was all yearning with no resolution. Was it possible that the heart had been touched but her mind was still oblivious?

"Everyone is lovesick for Master Danhong." Luping hid her simper behind her hand. "And yet, with my lady, it is Master Danhong who is lovelorn."

Suxuan's brows, smooth and tranquil, showed no reaction—she might as well be listening to the latest gossip whispered in the network of lanes connecting the city's grand houses.

The young maid took such pride in her observation about the master painter that she had not heeded her mistress's impassivity. In fact,

Luping assumed the stoic coolness was proof that Suxuan was hiding her feelings. After all, they had been as close as sisters, and she was confident in her reading of her lady's heart.

"He is very nice indeed," Suxuan said, still impervious. "You have my permission to get married."

Although secretly thrilled, Luping quickly felt the sting in the reply and a sense of stuffiness spread in her chest. However, as a handmaid, it was not her place to argue.

"Your servant is not so blessed," she sulked.

For the first time, Suxuan realized a rift had opened between them, caused by this man who had entered their lives without invitation. The fuzzy outline of his figure appeared in her mind's eye, but she could not see him clearly—he remained a blur. It was not possible to sit at her needlecraft anymore. Suxuan went to her desk, picked up the brush, and wrote a poem. When she was done, she glanced at the still-brooding Luping.

"Let's go out for a walk," she said, her voice croaky.

Something compelled Danhong to head toward Suxuan's rooms this morning. The dew had yet to evaporate, the breeze lifting the faint fragrance of moistened petals to his nose as he crossed the courtyard.

Her doors stood ajar. No one was inside. He dithered for a brief moment, then boldly crossed the threshold.

On her desk was a piece of paper, where the aroma of fresh ink still clung. A lyric poem to the tune of "The Beauteous South." He savored the words as he hummed this well-known melody:

Reading the springtide shadow
Between willow faint and blossom delightful
Thanking the lingering intent of the Eastern Lord
For preserving in stealth half a touch of chill
To accompany wilting plum blossoms of old

His eyes tarried on the line *Thanking the lingering intent of the Eastern Lord* as a smile spread. He felt reassured, his heart and spirit at ease. By the time he got back to his rooms, he knew what to do.

And yet, Suxuan did not send for Danhong that day. She said she was unwell and cancelled their session. The unsettled painter paced anxiously around the Huan Mansion's many courtyards, where he spotted her alone, sneaking out the back entrance.

He followed. Or, more precisely, he was pulled along. By the hand of fate. By the thread of love. He was the bee buzzing after nectar, the butterfly fluttering over flowers. Even if he had wanted to stop, to let go, he could not.

She led him to the Temple of Non-Thought.

Had she come to offer incense to the Buddha? The temple was busy and he did not want to be recognized, so he waited from a distance. And soon, she scurried out of the main gate and headed away from the bustle. He trailed after her and came to a meadow ablaze with wildflowers.

Nature in full bloom. Dazzling, just like her. She stood among the blossoms, her silhouette hazy. All of a sudden, a shaft of light shot to the sky, its brilliance encasing everything in its solemn and hallowed glow.

Tightness seized Danhong's chest. He crouched lower, trying to shield himself. He understood he should not be here, should not be spying on this scene, but he could not tear himself away. He watched the swirling billows gather on her face, darkening her features one moment and illuminating them the next. His eyes followed her hand, reaching into the pocket in her sleeve, pulling out a paper talisman. He saw her lips moving, intoning to herself. The sound that drifted to his ears was neither an incantation nor an invocation, but its cadence cleaved his skull, causing a splitting headache to form. He sucked in a big mouthful of air and clenched his jaw against the assault. Through the blinding pain, he caught her clamping her teeth over her middle finger. Red stained her skin. He looked on, helpless and immobile, as if he had been struck on a fatal acupressure point, while she poked her bloodstained digit through the paper.

The talisman tasted blood and burst into a wild blaze of golden snakes. That same fire was now roaring and lapping at his heart. Her face in the flickering flame was bewitching and uncanny—that of a specter.

Sweat soaked him through.

The next day, Danhong staggered out of his room, bleary-eyed, still trapped in the nightmare. He had no desire to touch the ink stick or the paintbrush, even when Suxuan was sitting before him, ready for her portrait.

"Master, perhaps you could teach me today?" she suggested out of the blue, her eyes bright and clear as water.

Startled, Danhong nodded after a beat. The best way to flee from the maelstrom within was to keep his hands away from the brush.

In just a few days, Suxuan rendered a perfect likeness of both faces and objects, as though she were aided by higher powers. She was born to paint. Her extraordinary talent surprised her parents too, for they had not the vaguest idea that she was so gifted. They thought, with her newfound knowledge, she would now be able to work even more closely with the master painter, and help him complete *A Hundred Beauties*.

And yet, all that remained for Danhong was to admit with a sigh that he didn't have her flair for painting, and to be reminded with heartache of what he should not have witnessed.

After a fortnight, he could once more regard Suxuan with the eyes of a painter, but his hand still resisted the brush. He was never in any doubt that the spirit was the hardest thing to capture in a picture, and yet he had already succeeded in setting down the form and essence of ninety-nine beauties. Why could he not do the same to her? Had he let her dwell in his heart for too long? Was that why he could not commit her to paper?

Her face, tilted skyward. Without powder, without rouge, without accessories. Standing. Leaning.

I'll never be able to paint her, Danhong admitted at last.

He was back in the meadow.

The wild blossoms. The burning talisman. Her.

What are you?

"You are a yao . . ." A whisper to himself, but Luping caught the ridiculous claim.

Has your masterpiece made you soft in the head? A chuckle escaped the maidservant. *How could my lady be a base demon?*

"Might I paint you, Master?" Suxuan enquired with a smile, then said to Luping, "Bring the crane incense from my rooms."

The maid appraised her mistress with her head cocked, looking slighted, before turning to do as asked.

Suxuan took no note of Luping's reaction, for her concentration was taken up by the preparation of the ink. She ground the charcoal stick into a bluish-black liquid, infusing the air with its fragrance.

The Danhong of old would have asked about the unusual scent, but Suxuan's suggestion had sent his heart stirring and his mind whirling. Besotted, lovestruck, he was in a fluster, trying to guess her intent. He made no attempt to conceal his hungry stare.

The ink was ready. Suxuan lowered her eyelids and let her spirit roam, far, far away, beyond the firmament.

Danhong regulated his breathing and collected himself. It had not occurred to him that those eyes could be equally enthralling when they were closed. He pictured painting her under a basjoo banana tree, resting against a balustrade, petals strewn on the ground. His heart quivered at the image. He would happily turn into a flower drifting in the air—he would cling tight onto her dress.

Suxuan faced the blank paper spread on the painter's worktable. Her gaze was sparkling, unclouded. Imbued with divine energy, her brush flew like a galloping horse and a hunting wolf, then it caressed like blossoms scattered from the hands of a celestial goddess. She sketched expressive streaks in strong hues. She traced fine lines in diluted ink. A whole world came alive in a handful of strokes.

"It's done." She set the brush down and stood to her full height, her head held high. She had the air of a general returning from the battlefield in triumph.

With a smile, Danhong approached the desk he had worked at since his arrival at the Huan Mansion. And yet, with one glance at the picture, he froze on the spot, all joy wiped from his face.

He was confronted by his pictorial self, emerging from a rustic farmstead, brush in hand. This ink-on-paper counterpart looked spirited, excited, as if he had just completed a masterpiece, or had been struck by inspiration and was eager to commence the best work of his life.

The composition exuded a carefree ease, he noted. She had captured all the vital elements, while leaving room for the viewer to fill in their interpretation. She had demonstrated restraint by holding back the temptation to depict a precise situation while allowing her creativity to enrich what was before her eyes, putting into practice the aesthetic ideas posited by great artists like the calligrapher Huang Tingjian and the painter Gu Kaizhi from centuries before.

The distinction between the average and the transcendental.

Danhong stared into the inkwash eyes looking back at him. So dynamic, so animated . . . so spirited.

He shuddered. He tried to pull himself together. He looked up and met her gaze. Cool, dispassionate. It pierced him.

It was a look that heralded parting in life and separation in death.

Danhong knows. He knows he is about to die.

Is it the Buddha's hand he feels? Trapping him like a mountain, locking on his neck. Its grip tightening, squeezing. Threads of eye-catching crimson seep between the fingers.

Blood.

Fear pins him down. He tries to writhe out of its hold but he cannot move. His past, his long-suppressed past, surges to the surface. Those buried days of gulping fur and guzzling blood. Those blotted-out nights of struggle, slaughter, survival.

That grueling life.

A tinge of pity for the vestige of power he has scraped together—bit by bit, drop by drop, over many years . . .

"I'm here to take your life."

Her red, red lips barely moved, and already a series of beautiful faces float before his eyes, one after another.

No matter! To die at her hands, I'm content. After all, haven't I done the same? These hands of mine have snatched the youth and vitality of more people than I can count.

He holds no grudge. This is the retribution he deserves. This is an ending he has no right to complain about, but . . .

He sighs for the feelings he has held for her.

He grieves for her knowledge of what he is.

Yao.

He looks out of the window for one last time. The jade-blue heaven, clean, pure, unblemished. The place he has dreamt of reaching.

Why?

The dusk is dripping blood, the sky is black as mud—just like the dirty, filthy cave he once lived in. Countless worms gather before his eyes, wriggling, squirming. Entering through his seven orifices, burrowing into his five organs, carrying away the essence inside his body, forcing him to cough out the life force he has stolen. Until his chest, his belly, his guts are hollowed out. Until he has nothing left.

He has nothing left.

He has been reduced to his original form.

He has always thought this base shape belonged to his previous lifetime. One that he must not look back at. One that he dares not look back at. He realizes through the haze that he has grown accustomed to his role as a human; he has been raising his arms and lifting his feet in their image.

Dashing, ethereal. Like a xian.

A celestial immortal. To join the ranks of these higher beings. This aspiration has tempted him to step out of line. This ambition has propelled him to collect the essence and spirit of a hundred maidens, storing them inside paintings for his own consumption, so he can transform, metamorphose, ascend. So he can become a xian. To do that, he has altered his appearance to bewitch the world, and the world has willingly let him toy with them.

The world cares only about one thing. As long as he makes this sack of skin irresistibly attractive. As long as he hawks the promise that he can preserve fleeting beauty, that his brush can capture the full bloom of youth for posterity, for eternity.

Posterity. Eternity. What a lie.

For those like him—set apart, different, never to be awakened from reincarnation, forever stuck in the rebirthing cycle of beasts and animals—he has to be ruthless if he wants a way out.

And yet, at the cusp of success, he meets his archenemy, his star of doom. He falls in love with her, but he cannot paint her. She does not love him, but she can capture his essence, his life force, his spirit, with the tip of her brush.

Such irony.

"Why?" Danhong cried.

He could pool the elemental qi in his body to make one last stand, but one look at her and all his incomprehension, all his outrage, turned into a bitter laugh.

Inch by inch, he turned into ice. Little by little, he grew numb in the cold. Even if he could survive this, he could not live with the knowledge that she had wanted to destroy him.

Suxuan was stumped by the question. Why, indeed. It no longer mattered, not when they had already reached this stage. She could not stop or turn back. She was compelled by an obsession, by what she recognized as right and wrong. She had to keep going. She asked herself if she was disturbed by this mounting compassion, but that was quickly shouted down by an urgent voice.

He's a yao. There can be no mercy.

How often had he assumed that look in her eyes, that expression between the brows, to be love? How often had he thought each frown, each smile, to be ardor? But the mist had dissipated and the clouds had scattered, he could see clearly and he could comprehend everything now.

The impression of infatuation and attachment that had made him struggle with himself was no different from the illusion of skin and flesh under his brush.

Whence it came, whither it went. Nothing could ever come to be.

His soul, his spirit, dispersed in threads and strands, drifting away like smoke. Light, soft, immaterial. Like his feeble, faltering heart. He vied for a place in hers but never succeeded. Who would recall the flies they swatted? Base, common, not worth a glance.

So be it!

Danhong threw himself into the painting.

The picture opened up and swallowed the master painter, like a mussel drawing water through its siphon. In the same eerie silence, it returned to its original state—a pool of stagnant water that nothing could stir.

Did it matter that he had toiled for centuries? That he was so close to achieving his goal?

He had failed to cast off the heart of a mortal, so this fate was justified.

Sucked dry, Danhong's empty shell slumped, as if it were a pile of rubble. This sack of skin, once adored by countless young women, was reduced to clotted blood and withered bone. An unbearable sight.

Suxuan stood stock still, dazed. In a flash, the earth had aged and the heavens grew weary. Something was gouging out bits of her heart, scoop by scoop. Life and death, at the blink of an eye. Within a scroll of paper furled a blighted existence.

Did she vanquish a yao? Or did she snuff out a life?

All that was before her was but a dream.

She reached out. He was no longer there.

Luping entered with the incense and then fainted at the gruesome scene. When she came to, she was assaulted by fright, then by a torrent of tears.

Suxuan said nothing, for she too was welling up. And it would have been too complex to explain. She avoided the painting. She avoided the lovelorn eyes. She was terrified that they might be full of heartsick hate.

The Huan household relocated that night, to a faraway, secluded location. Squire Huan worried that their home was tainted by malevolent traces left by the yao, and he was also apprehensive of Danhong's associates, in case they came seeking revenge. The kingdom's master painter had died a mysterious death in his house, and it would be wisest to evade trouble.

The move suited Suxuan. It spared her from seeing the halls, the platforms, the towers, the pavilions that Danhong had roamed, that contained echoes of him.

She could shield her eyes, but she could not hide from her heart.

In this small town three thousand li away, Suxuan leant against the window and looked out. The sun was retreating west behind a mountain, and the heavens glowed in ominous shades of blood. She thought she caught his eyes, his staring eyes, prying into her heart. She twisted away in a panic, and was subjected to the prickly sight of a bulky pile of paintings on the bookshelf.

His beloved masterpiece, *A Hundred Beauties.*

In her leisure, she added a plum tree in inkwash to the portrait of Danhong. Wiry branches heavy with blossoms, casting spots of shadows. In time, petals in twos or threes drifted onto the moist earth where he stood. Concerned that he might be lonely, she painted a stream, on which some of the fallen flowers floated and were washed away, a hint of her melancholy about the past.

She was reminded of the prophetic lines from "The Beauteous South." Maybe the plum tree contained her essence and spirit, and she was keeping him company in the painting. He, perhaps, would not feel too alone inside.

And yet, what had been stirred could never be still again . . .

19

The Woman Carrying a Corpse 背尸体的女人

Chi Hui 迟卉
Translated by Judith Huang 錫影

The Woman Carrying a Corpse

By Chi Hui
Translated by Judith Huang

The corpse-carrying woman came from the north.

She walked very slowly, stumbling and falling almost every other step, before dragging the corpse up again and walking on. Her ragged pants were stained with dust.

The woman's hair was nearly all white, the skin on her face stretched with gullies of wrinkles, her face filled with untold anguish.

Perhaps due to her constant stumbling, her body was marred with cuts and marked with bruises large and small. Yet she seemed oblivious to them, mumbling unintelligibly to herself, two empty eyes staring, as though searching for the end of the road.

And yet, the corpse she carried looked polished and glamorous, its clothes made of crisp, luxurious fabric in gleaming colors, with gold-thread trimmings that shone in the sunlight.

The corpse was very much dead, but still it proclaimed its wealth.

The corpse-carrying woman walked on and on, the corpse on her back swaying from side to side, constantly on the brink of falling. Yet she persisted in carrying it.

By the roadside, she met an idler. The idler was horrified, and stopped her. "Oh my God! Is that a corpse you're carrying?"

"Yes, it is," the woman replied. "Look at this corpse. See how heavy it is? It has nearly crushed my spine."

"Can you not cast it off?" asked the idler.

The woman shook her head again and again, saying, "I cannot, I cannot . . ."

The idler was perplexed. "But why not? It isn't because they're family, is it? Is that why you can't leave them behind?"

"Yes, that's it," the woman said. "Yes, that's it."

The idler sighed, shed a few tears for the woman, and went his own way.

The corpse-carrying woman walked on.

A traveler saw the corpse-carrying woman and ran toward her, shouting, "Quick! Throw that filthy thing away! A wonderful life lies before you!"

"But this corpse is family," said the woman. "In life, we lived together, and they brought me warmth and happiness, so now, though they're dead, I cannot bear to throw them away."

The traveler froze, then nodded. "Ah, that is a good point, that is a very good point."

He comforted the woman for a while, then went on his way.

The corpse-carrying woman walked on.

Not long after, she met a critic, who looked her up and down before pointing at her and passing snide remarks.

"Look at that woman," said the critic. "To think she's been carrying that heavy corpse around! Someone must have promised her a huge favor, or a paid her a handsome sum, or she would never do such a thing!"

The woman smiled defensively and said, "Yes, that's it. That's it."

The critic was delighted to be proven right, and, with a self-satisfied sigh, went on his merry way.

The corpse-carrying woman lowered her head, and walked on.

After walking a while, a kindly person crested the hill ahead, nodding genially to the corpse-carrying woman as she came into view. When she realized it was a corpse the woman carried on her back, she blanched with fright and hurried toward her.

"Aiyah! Is that a corpse you're carrying? Oh, how pitiful! Quick, put it down! Come with me to the house over there, where there's hot food and hot water, so I can help you."

The corpse-carrying woman shook her head. "Thank you, thank you, but I cannot put down this corpse. Someone promised me a handsome sum to bring it back to my village. If I put it down, there'll be no money for me to collect."

When the kindly woman heard this, she spat on her, and turned away.

The woman walked on.

The corpse she was carrying shook against her labored back, its terrible weight pulling her down. The woman walked one step, fell over, crawled up again, and took another. She took another step, and fell again.

At a fork in the road, an optimist saw her and couldn't bear the sight. She pulled her up, saying, "Why won't you just throw that corpse away?"

The woman shook her head, saying, "I cannot leave it."

The optimist was baffled. She tried to reason with her. "Is this corpse not your good friend? Now, even if they were your soul mate, they still wouldn't want to see you like this."

At this, the woman said no more, only shaking her head.

The optimist sighed impatiently. "I don't know who this corpse was to you, or what has happened to you, but look at yourself! You look worse than the corpse! Maybe you just need to look on the bright side: think about it, the corpse is already dead, but you're alive! And carrying this magnificent corpse around, you're bound to get noticed. Without it, you look pretty ordinary, and no one would spare you a second glance. So maybe it's a good thing. Maybe carrying that corpse really is worthwhile."

The corpse-carrying woman nodded, saying, "Yes, that's it. That's it."

So the optimist, satisfied with herself, went on her way.

The corpse-carrying woman walked on.

A pessimist saw the woman and ran over, saying, "Oh dear, could I end up like that?"

The woman shrugged to reposition the corpse on her back, raised her head, and said, "Actually, it's a good thing I'm carrying this corpse. With this corpse, when I'm on the road, people actually treat me like I'm somebody!"

The pessimist said, "Ah, but they just think you're entertaining. I, on the other hand, just see how pitiful you are, and I get depressed. If you can't unburden yourself, I fear that I may end up just like you."

"So why don't you carry it for me?" the woman asked.

The pessimist gave a terrified scream and ran off.

The woman watched his receding silhouette for a while. Then, she lowered her head and walked on, still carrying the corpse.

A hustler by the side of the road saw the woman, and started whispering, "Look at that idiot, it's like she was born yesterday! Why doesn't she strip off those beautiful garments and wear them herself? In those luxurious silks and brocades, she'd look wealthy and be warm and relaxed, and everyone would treat her like a human being."

When the woman heard this, she raised her head and smiled. Her smile was ancient, her every wrinkle creasing and relaxing, and her eyes were cold, cold as black ice.

The hustler winced and walked away. He whispered to his companions, "That must be her lover, judging from the way she can't bear to leave it."

The woman looked at him, then lowered her head and walked on.

As she walked and walked, a madman spotted the woman, and, laughing wildly, ran toward her. "Hey, is that a corpse you're carrying?"

"Yes, it is," said the woman.

"Why are you carrying it?"

"Because they were once my lover, and though they're now dead, I cannot bear to part with them," said the woman.

And yet the madman wouldn't leave, leaping and skipping along beside her. He began to talk to the corpse. "Hey, corpse, do you love this woman?"

The corpse, naturally, said nothing.

The woman walked on in silence as the madman followed her.

"Hey, is that a corpse you're carrying?" he asked again.

"Yes, it is."

"Why are you carrying it?"

"Because it gets me attention," the woman replied. "With it, people take note of me."

"Hey, corpse," asked the madman, "do you take note of this woman?"

The corpse, naturally, said nothing.

The madman laughed, then cried. He cried, then laughed. Half-walking, half-dancing, he followed. The woman carried the corpse, taking one step, then falling, then stepping and falling again. They pressed onward, their motions synchronized to a single beat. After a while, the madman questioned her again.

"Hey . . . So, is that a corpse you're carrying?"

"Yes, it is."

"Why are you carrying it?"

"Because someone promised me a handsome sum, if I carry it on the road."

"Hey, corpse, are you really worth a lot of money?"

The corpse, naturally, said nothing.

The madman started singing a tuneless song, and the birds on the roadside joined him and started chirping along. After a few songs, the madman started questioning her again.

"Hey . . . So, is that a corpse you're carrying?"

"Yes, it is."

"Why are you carrying it?"

"Because they were my family, who treated me well in the past. Now, I cannot bear to leave them."

"Hey, corpse, do you love this woman?"

The corpse, naturally, said nothing.

The madman sang as he walked. Suddenly he clapped his hands and said, "I get it now, I get it now. That isn't a corpse at all, is it? Look, they're your family, and they're also your lover. They can make you stand out in a crowd, and can bring you large sums of money. Obviously, they must be your god!"

The woman nodded and said, "Yes, that's it. That's it."

The madman still would not leave her alone. He kept circling her, looking her over from every angle.

"Look! Your god has sprouted!" he said, suddenly.

"Oh?"

She had carried the corpse for many months and years, and dust had fallen on its face. Seeds had fallen into the crevices of its wrinkles and the hollow holes of its eye sockets. Some had sprouted, whilst others had grown into young trees.

But because she had been carrying it on her back all this while, she couldn't see, and she hadn't known.

"Your god sprouted!" The madman clapped his hands, singing loudly. "Your god sprouted, your god grew grass, your god's head has grown a shrub, your god has blossomed and borne fruit!"

As he said this, the madman reached up to pluck a tiny berry, in order to have a taste.

In her haste to turn to look, the woman accidentally straightened her back, and the corpse slid off and hit the ground.

The woman stared.

"Why are you carrying them?" asked the madman.

"I don't know," the woman said. "As far as I remember, this is how it has always been. I don't even know how to walk down the road without such a burden. Now, what shall I do?"

"Perhaps you can carry me instead," said the madman. "But I don't wish to be a corpse."

"Yes, that's it."

They looked at each other, and sat down. They sang a few songs, dug a hole by the side of the road, and buried the corpse in it. Yellow flowers and red berries sprouted, and tender green leaves unfurled. The plant grew strong and sure, swaying gently in the wind.

The sun sank languidly over the horizon as the clouds blazed like a long, narrow line of fire, lighting up one after another in the sky.

The madman lit a bonfire, and the woman shared her dried food supplies with him. Then they huddled by the fire, like two tiny commas, and fell asleep.

The earth was boundless beneath them, the road stretched like a compass in every direction, and the dust—the dust swirled, back and forth, back and forth, endlessly.

20

The Mountain and the Secret of Their Names
山和名字的秘密

Wang Nuonuo 王诺诺
Translated by Rebecca F. Kuang 匡灵秀

The Mountain and the Secret of Their Names

By Wang Nuonuo
Translated by Rebecca F. Kuang

Part One

You Dang Jiu lived in a stilt house halfway up the mountain. To get home, he had to pass through the terraced fields that covered the mountain, one after another. These fields were all crescent-shaped, just like the silver horns worn by the girls of his clan during the Huashan Festival.

The people of his village only planted crops during one season each year. But in the winter, they still had to keep the paddies full of water; first, to maintain the soil quality, and second, to hedge against a water shortage the next year. Clouds were reflected in the glistening paddies, and the sun shone on the entire mountain, transforming it into a mirror. You Dang Jiu shattered that mirror as he dashed barefoot through the paddies, splashing mud about.

He panted heavily as he ran, carrying a large backpack on his tiny frame. Teacher had said that rockets were going to fall that night. He had to get home and tell Grandpa before dark.

For generations, the people of You Dang Jiu's clan had relied on the mountain for their livelihoods. The mountain received everything cast down by the heavens—abundant rain, dense bamboo forests, and scarlet mushrooms. So when the rocket launch center was first constructed nearby, whenever the red-hot, burning wreckage of Stage One rockets fell onto the mountain, the youths of the village would dig the fragments out of the pits they'd dashed into the earth and bring them back home. Back then, the villagers had thought those treasures were blessings from heaven.

But over time, more and more metal began falling from the sky. Every year, around the time that the crops of glutinous rice grew ripe for harvest, the town officials would inform everyone whenever the satellite launch site had an upcoming mission, warning the villagers to avoid going outside as much as they could.

On those nights, people would hide at home, listening to the rumbling in the sky. It sounded like Jiang Yang was fighting Lei Gong. At the start of the launch, they would see a light as weak as a kerosene lamp, its rays smothered by the dark clouds. Then it would become brighter and brighter, several dazzling tails trailing behind.

Those tails would combust and fall to the ground. The large ones would smash deep holes in the fields, ruining whole swathes of crops. The fish grown in the paddies were fattest at that time of year, but the falling rocket fragments would viciously churn the water and mud, and the next day's dawn would reveal a pond of dead fish floating belly-up.

The smaller rocket fragments fell onto the stilt houses, smashing dozens of tiles and marking holes in the wooden boards beneath. Pigs and sheep were kept on the ground floor of the stilt houses, while people lived on the second. Food supplies for the whole household were stored on the roof. If the burning metal shards set fire to the granary, then that family's entire year's worth of food would be destroyed.

By the time You Dang Jiu started school, the adults of the village were terrified of the words "satellite launch." Only the children remained curious. On those nights that Jiang Yang fought Lei Gong, they would stick their heads out of the windows, trying to catch a glimpse of the rockets they'd been told would bring wealth and power to their nation and hope to their lives.

Today, Teacher had told them that a television broadcast satellite would be launched that night—ChinaSat9. It would take on the task of broadcasting signals for the approaching 2008 Olympic Games, sending the images of gold-winning Olympic athletes to television screens in every corner of the motherland.

You Dang Jiu's family had just purchased a 21-inch color TV and installed a satellite antenna on top of their stilt house. You Dang Jiu told Grandpa that tonight's launch would mark the completion of a glorious mission. Grandpa blew out a long puff of smoke in response. His tobacco was freshly baked, but he used an old pipe. The silver mouth of the pipe, which had originally been cast in a cloud and thunder pattern, had long been rubbed smooth and shiny.

"What a tiresome mission," Grandpa muttered to himself.

You Dang Jiu hadn't been home for long when several grown-ups walked through the door. This was typical. The grown-ups were here to seek a divination from Grandpa. No one knew whose home the rocket might fall upon, but You Dang Jiu's grandfather was a Badaixiong—a shaman, known far and wide. He could act as the eyes of the clan and see what had not yet come to pass.

Grandpa's mouth and face were covered in wrinkles. His old headkerchief had been turned sallow by tobacco smoke, its original color unknown. His full name was Jiu Gou Yang. He had no surname. The people of their village christened their children by linking the names of three generations. The father and grandfather's names were added to the name of the son; in this way, each child would bear the names of three people throughout their lifetime.

Gou and Yang were the names of Grandpa's father and grandfather. Grandpa's name, Jiu, meant "bridge." Grandpa had been small and weak when he was born, so he'd been adopted by a stone bridge at the edge of the village. The Miao people often adopted sickly infants out to everyday objects such as bridges, benches, boulders, or camphor trees. They could bestow longevity and wisdom on the infants.

Not long after Grandpa was born, a new road had been built between the village and the base of the mountain, so his namesake and adoptive father—the stone bridge—became lonely and deserted. Moss and grass grew in the crevices in the stone, gradually returning it to the folds of the mountain. Every year, Jiu Gou Yang would take rice and meat to the bridge as an offering. By caring for the bridge, Jiu Gou Yang had been able to become a most talented Badaixiong. He could recite long poems detailing the achievements of the ancestral kings. He could also light incense in people's homes for their regular worship.

This evening, Grandpa changed into a black double-buttoned tunic, tied on a black headcloth, and then went to sit below a tree at the village entrance. The old camphor tree was so large it would take the arms of ten children to embrace its trunk. A dozen or so adults, each the head of a household, stood in a circle around him. They represented each of the families that, over the past thousand years, had set down roots on the mountain and flourished. Starting a few years ago, whenever a rocket was about to fall, they would come ask Jiu Gou Yang for a divination, for Grandpa could understand the secrets of the mountain and tell them what disasters the mountain foresaw before they happened.

The sun set; the light faded. The distant mountaintop looked like the smoke rings Jiu Gou Yang puffed out, gradually melding into the grayness of the sky. Under the shadow of the great tree, the adults' faces turned cryptic. Little You Dang Jiu couldn't discern their facial features, but he could clearly make out their expressions: grave and solemn, without a happy, relaxed brow in sight.

Grandpa asked You Dang Jiu to go home and get a square, shallow basket. The wooden surface of the basket was rather old now, and covered with a muddy patina. Grandpa placed the rice and coins offered by the grown-ups seeking divination in the hollow of the basket, then lightly buried an old piece of cloth torn from one of You Dang Jiu's shirts within the rice. Then he lit three sticks of incense, burned three sheets of paper, swallowed three mouthfuls of smoke, chewed the rice ponderously as if counting the grains, and turned to sit facing the camphor tree.

Jiu Gou Yang murmured some indiscernible words of divination and forcefully turned the basket several times clockwise. Under the dim light, the white rice and golden coins collided against the cloth in the basket, rolling and transforming into a milky white spiral.

You Dang Jiu watched as the colors inside the spiral converged in the shape of a star. The star bounded forth into the night, rising, then exploding into fiery pieces of metal that scattered across the earth. Some fell into the paddies, boiling the water within; others fell toward the back of the village, smashing into the pigsties and crushing the old sows to death. Even more fell onto the mountain, sending sparks flying everywhere.

The colors churned frantically inside the basket. Just as You Dang Jiu was about to be sucked into the vision, Grandpa's hands stilled. The colors separated and returned to the original white of the rice, the yellow of the coins, and the indigo-black of the cloth, all lying still in the basket.

Jiu Gou Yang seemed to have exhausted himself. Slowly, he opened his mouth and asked You Dang Jiu in his smoker's croak, "Did you see it just now?"

You Dang Jiu lifted his head. "I saw it. The west side."

Jiu Gou Yang nodded. "The west side."

You Dang Jiu tried helping Grandpa to his feet. Grandpa seemed like a stalk of rice in the autumn; one push and he would fall over in the paddy. The people beside them carried over an iron pot containing tea seed oil cooked with glutinous rice and peanuts. You Dang Jiu loved this drink. When oil, salt, and tea had been sautéed to a smoking point, water was poured in until it boiled. Corn, soybeans, and glutinous rice grains were added when the tea started bubbling. When drunk, the fragrance of the cereal mingled with the smell of the tea.

Grandpa finished drinking the tea seed oil and seemed to regain some strength. Then he explained what the changes in the coins and the cloth symbolized.

The rice hadn't spilled out of the basket, and the coins hadn't collided with each other. This meant that the event they were inquiring about would indeed occur—the sky would send a disaster to the village. The movement of the cloth against the rice had created four curves in the cloth, foretelling that the thing falling from the sky would be of a fire element. Once it fell into the paddy, there would be metal. That would be on the west side. Because the coins hadn't been buried deep in the rice, whatever fell wouldn't be large, and it wouldn't cause a catastrophe. The villagers would only sustain some economic losses.

Jiu Gou Yang poured the rice and coins from the basket into an indigo-print bag lying beside him. According to custom, this was how the villagers compensated the Badaixiong. You Dang Jiu retrieved the shallow basket. This divination tool, like Grandpa's name, would be passed on to him.

"Grandpa, why can we see the future in the rice in the basket?" You Dang Jiu asked, as he hurried after his grandfather.

"Ah, so you're starting to get curious about these things, You. Let me ask you, where does rice come from?"

"When the grains have ripened in the paddies, we use stone mortars to pound them," said You Dang Jiu. "Then we filter out their husks to get rice."

"What do we use rice to make?"

"So many things," You Dang Jiu responded earnestly. "You can make sticky rice, congee, and rice cakes to eat, or rice wine and oil tea to drink. You can also use it to cure meat . . ."

"Rice has grown on this mountain as long as we've lived here. Since we first settled on this land, our ancestors have depended on rice for their sustenance. As our ancestors gave birth to their descendants, the rice crops also germinated, producing one generation after another. From ancient times until now, since there were four seasons, the mountain has remembered everything that has fallen toward it. Rice is the incarnation of the mountain. It bonds us to the mountain. If you can understand the secrets of the rice, then you'll know what the mountain is trying to say."

"I don't understand."

"We plant and eat rice," said Jiu Gou Yang. "Rice becomes a part of our bodies. You must learn to read the language of rice, for only then will you become a Badaixiong."

It was time now to prepare a living creature for that evening's banishing of the stars. They had arrived below their stilt house, where a small bamboo fence encircled a chicken pen.

You Dang Jiu scrambled around the flock of chickens, scaring the hens from their nests. Chicken feathers swirled through the air. "Why do I have to become a Badaixiong?"

Grandpa smiled mysteriously. "Because the Badaixiong has to sing."

"I know that. The Badaixiong must sing while making sacrifices to the ancestors to ask for their help. The lyrics and melody connect the mountain to the ancestors. The ancestors listen and know which household will suffer a disaster, and the mountain listens and knows which household needs help."

"And young dapis will listen and know your intentions," Grandpa said.

Grandpa made You Dang Jiu stop startling the chickens. He had to learn to walk around the chickens as Grandpa did, to make the hens feel unthreatened so that they would relax.

"Dapis?" They were pretty young girls.

"The Badaixiong needs a good voice. You use that voice to sing the poem at sacrifices and at the Huashan Festival. When your grandpa was young, I looked forward to the festival all year long. The dapis' eyes were warmer than the June heat. Hahaha . . . A Yang was the brightest blooming young flower of them all, but once your grandfather opened his mouth, her deer-like eyes never left me even once."

"Girls are so annoying," You Dang Jiu mumbled. "The girls at school have such long hair. It gets in my face when they're running during gym class, but if I pull it away then they cry."

He spoke quietly, but Jiu Gou Yang heard him. He patted his grandson's shoulder. He knew he didn't have to teach him about these things. The boy would make a good lover someday.

Jiu Gou Yang bent down and scattered some feed around him, then scooped another handful of husks. More and more chickens crowded around him. He gently petted them, moving very slowly. When the chickens had relaxed, he seized the moment and grabbed the leg of a rooster with one hand. With the other, he firmly held back its wings. The big rooster was stunned still, emitting a mournful rumble from its throat.

You Dang Jiu tied a red thread around one of the rooster's legs, then carried it to the side of the camphor tree. By then it was quite dark. Ten or so villagers came forward in succession, holding lit torches and candles. They placed bottles of beer and three slices of pork beneath the tree. An electric lamp hung from the tree, and the yellow light glowed against the people's faces. On the square table beneath the tree was a bushel of rice, in which three sticks of incense had been inserted. Directly in front of it was a bowl of cooked pork. A pair of chopsticks lay over the bowl. The rooster was tied to one of the table's legs by a piece of red rope. Next to it, a charcoal brazier was already burning bright. Their preparations were complete.

The ritual to banish the stars had begun. Jiu Gou Yang rolled beeswax into three thumb-sized balls and tossed them one by one into the burning brazier. The wax would cling to any other shamans present, preventing them from interrupting the magic. Only then could the star-banishing ritual proceed. The flames licked at the beeswax pellets, reaching heights as tall as Grandpa's waist.

Jiu Gou Yang faced the crowd and began to chant the sacred words:

Nineteen gods of the golden pillars
Nineteen gods of the silver pillars
You who live in Negou Village
You who live in Neshu Village
If you don't come, I will use the paddies to call you
If you don't return, I will use the rice to bring you
The grain is the link
The rice is the road.

Then he began singing about the great deeds of the ancestral kings, the names of their forebears and their stories. Each name had its own unique pronunciation. He could not mispronounce them, nor could he falter. Most importantly, he could not pause.

Every time he finished a stanza, Jiu Gou Yang would perform a divination. You Dang Jiu was in charge of picking up the divination tool from the ground and handing it to his grandfather. The rooster under the table had already had its throat cut, and its blood dripped into a basin. When the rooster was drained of blood, it was scalded in boiling water and stripped of its feathers. Then it was placed in a pot to cook. A small piece had to be cut from every part of the rooster's body as an offering.

In his right hand, Grandpa held a Chiyou bell, which he used to bless every divination diagram. Many cloth strips dangled from the bell. As Grandpa sang and gently swayed, the head of the ancient king Chiyou on the bell's handle glared about. It watched You Dang Jiu, it watched Grandpa, and it watched the ancestors who had lived in the mountain for countless years.

Chiyou's eyes seemed alive to You Dang Jiu. He followed Chiyou's gaze to the depths of the flames, where he saw a group of people—the ancestors who were mentioned in the sacred words. He saw dark-faced Bang, who was an excellent farmer; Gou, who slew a tiger and now wore its pelt across his body; and Sang, who was lean and thin but could sing the most beautiful love songs.

The freshly slaughtered rooster was at the head of the procession. The red thread You Dang Jiu had tied was still attached to its leg. This thread linked the rooster to the ancestors behind it. Its swaying steps were lofty and arrogant, as if it knew that the procession would be lost without it. You Dang Jiu thought of how that rooster had been warm in his hands just moments before; how it had just been trembling and unwilling. But now it stuck out its chest in pride, leading the ancestors down a stone bridge into the depths of the village.

The three sticks of incense had burned away. Grandpa stopped his recitation.

In order to receive the touch of the spirits, the assembled people put the rice and cooked chicken into bowls and distributed utensils. The star-banishing ritual was thus concluded.

You Dang Jiu brought Grandpa a bowl. "What did the ancestors say?"

"They've taken today's comet away."

"They listen to you just like that?"

Grandpa knocked hard against You Dang Jiu's forehead. You Dang Jiu cried out in pain.

"What do you mean, they listen to me? From ancient times until now, this mountain has received everything that has fallen from the sky—hailstones, rain, comets, and thunder . . . The ancestors took pity on us and were willing to use the mountain's power to help us escape a catastrophe."

"Can I eat the drumstick left over from the ancestors?"

"Go ahead. Now, this rooster is leading our ancestors back to heaven!" Grandpa put a drumstick in You Dang Jiu's bowl, smiling as he spoke.

That night, the satellite launch filled the sky with red light as usual. But the rocket wreckage did not fall onto the village. The next day, a sow belonging to A Shen from the west side of the village gave birth to a litter of ten piglets. All were female.

Two months later, the Beijing Olympic Games began. Father and Mother returned from the city to help harvest rice, make baba bread, and pickle the paddy carps. The family sat around the TV, watching as China won gold in the popular diving event. The signal came from ChinaSat9, ten thousand miles above their heads.

"Why do they have to jump into the water?" You Dang Jiu asked.

"Maybe there are fish in the water! They're seeing who can catch the most fish!" Grandpa tapped the bowl of his pipe against the doorframe.

You Dang Jiu urged his father to tell some stories from the city. Father told him about tall buildings, under which girls wearing beautiful flower skirts walked back and forth.

Grandpa interrupted him. "Are the buildings as tall as the flower stems in May? Are the flowery dresses as lovely as the brocade pleated skirt A Yang wore?"

When Father didn't answer, Grandpa smiled and took a puff of his pipe.

Grandpa was teaching You Dang Jiu how to recite the long poem praising the achievements of the ancestral rulers. The poem was very difficult to remember. The names of the ancestors and former rulers were even more difficult to remember, but You Dang Jiu had to learn to speak them all in succession. He couldn't falter or pause, especially when he discussed the trials that the heroes had undergone. That would bring bad luck. Any Badaixiong who made a mistake reciting these words during a sacrifice would be spurned by the clan.

You Dang Jiu was very bright. He could remember every line Grandpa recited, singing along with the reed pipe. His voice was loud, clear and melodious.

"One day, you'll make a heavenly Badaixiong!" Grandpa said.

However, compared to reciting the rice divination spell or the names of the ancestors, You Dang Jiu preferred watching the Olympics broadcast. He liked watching the men and women competing in their swimsuits. If they were catching fish in shallow water during the water ballet, then they must have been catching silver carps. And if they were catching fish in deep water during the diving event, then they must have been catching common carps. Pan-fried silver carps were fragrant and delicious; common carps were delicious stewed with little shrimp and rice in sour soup.

Whoever caught more fish got more points! One day, he would also go compete in the Olympics.

Half a month later, the Olympic torch at Beijing was extinguished. Only a handful of stalks were left in the rice paddies. You Dang Jiu's father, A Dang, and his mother went back to the city together. When they left, they took You Dang Jiu with them.

You Dang Jiu remembered how, on the eve of their departure, Grandpa jabbed at his head with his pipe. "Memorize it well for me." He turned around and continued smoking. He did not accompany You Dang Jiu out the door.

"Dad?" A Dang shouted after Jiu Gou Yang's retreating back. He, You Dang Jiu, and You Dang Jiu's mother were already standing outside the door.

"Go on, go on. The mountain has made its decision, and you have made yours."

"Grandpa, when the swallows come back, I'll come visit you. I'll remember the spell you taught me. You can test me!" You Dang Jiu wiped snot from his nose, crying as he spoke.

"It's not a spell! It is the names of our ancestors. One day, you'll understand. Your ancestors have always lived on in your name."

Even to the last, Grandpa never turned around.

You Dang Jiu did not see him again.

Grandpa died that winter, four days before his grandson came home for the holidays.

Just like how he knew all the secrets of the mountain, Grandpa seemed to also know all the secrets of his own fate. Jiu Gou Yang was alone in his house when he died. He had changed into a black double-buttoned tunic and put on a black headkerchief. He sat on an old wooden chair. If no one had disturbed him, he would have slept like that forever.

Originally, it had been Grandpa who handled religious rituals for each family and household. He was a benevolent person, and would only ever accept three chicken eggs from each household in mourning as payment. Now that he had passed away, the people who had come to mourn him packed the village full. The funeral lasted a full night and day.

The Badaixiong's body would not be laid in a coffin in the hall of the ancestors. The villagers put Grandpa in a taishi chair and carried him over across the mountain to the ancestral tomb. There he would be put in a coffin and interred. You Dang Jiu's father, A Dang, sat vigil in a chair beside the body, not allowing Grandpa's corpse to fall over.

A Bao, a newer Badaixiong who was only thirty years old, walked before the taishi chair. He had once called Jiu Gou Yang his teacher. Now, it was his duty to sing the sacred words to send Grandpa to heaven.

You Dang Jiu was at the front of the procession. He held a large rooster with a red thread tied to its foot. This time, he didn't need

Grandpa to explain. He knew that in a moment, the red thread on this rooster's foot would lead one-third of Grandpa's soul to heaven.

The long funeral procession headed down the cold, muddy path, passing the stone bridge at the edge of the village—the bridge that was Grandpa's father in name. They walked through countless stepped fields. Grandpa had farmed and raised fish in those fields, feeding his son A Dang and his brothers until they were grown. They passed the camphor tree halfway up the mountain. Beneath that tree, Grandpa had sung sacrificial songs in his clear, resonant voice to dispel the rockets falling from the sky. There, he had also set up altars and performed rituals, praying on the villagers' behalf for rains and a fertile crop.

When the last handful of dirt had been thrown onto Jiu Gou Yang's grave, A Bao, the young Badaixiong, had each person in attendance speak about something that Grandpa had enjoyed. This way, when Grandpa ascended to heaven, he would be surrounded by happy memories.

"Golden, flue-cured tobacco . . ."
"His old pipe . . ."
"His beloved grandson, A You . . ."
"The pen of chickens he raised . . ."
"The wine he traded a hen for . . ."
"The stone bridge at the edge of the village . . ."
"The names of the ancestors . . ."
"Everything on the mountain . . ."

You Dang Jiu was the last to speak. He looked tiny as he stood by the newly dug tomb. Written on the tombstone was a long string of symbols he didn't recognize. Those were the names of his ancestors; the linked names of three generations—grandfather, father, and son. Every syllable was joined in a winding poem, like an azure dragon about to ascend to the sky.

Everyone's eyes fell on You Dang Jiu.

"A Yang," You Dang Jiu said. "Grandpa loved A Yang the best; A Yang, the prettiest girl at the Huashan Festival."

He wiped the snot from his face with a red, chapped hand.

Part Two

In the village, the New Year celebration was called Nengyang. It did not follow the set calendar date used by the Han, but rather dates that had been determined by King Guzang. Through all these years, rain had never fallen on the dates set by King Guzang. They were always pleasant days in winter when everyone could enjoy themselves to the fullest. The villagers offered sacrifices to the ancestors, blew reed pipes, and danced the stepping hall dance. The dapis moved gracefully in their silver horns and silver crowns.

After Nengyang came the Bullfighting Festival. Normally, by this time, You Dang Jiu would have long returned to school. Life in the city was just as he had imagined; everything moved faster than in the village. People walked quickly, the cars zoomed quickly. Just as quickly, You Dang Jiu grew up and tested into college.

"You grew so big in a blink," said his mother.

"When I was his age, I was considered an adult," said his father. "I had my own hunting gun. The first time I went hunting for game in the mountain by myself, I brought back a badger to give respect to the ancestors."

But You Dang Jiu wouldn't be given his own gun. He was a college student majoring in computer science. He worked with code all day long, what did he need a gun for? Even if he had inherited his father's mettle and wanted to use a weapon to prove his maturity, the only weapon he needed was a handy keyboard.

That was his hope for the New Year—to get a green switch keyboard that would make a click-clack noise whenever he typed, so that his professors would know he was hard at work.

Father and Mother were still working in the city when it came time for Nengyang, so You Dang Jiu went back to the village by himself. He brought his laptop with him. The village had gotten wireless internet that year. He could sit by the creek or the ancestral hall and get online, keeping in touch with the world outside the mountain, at least in spirit.

The satellite launches had recently increased in frequency, which meant the amount of falling wreckage had also increased. Last year, a rocket fragment had landed on the cement next to the factory. The cement was very hard, and the fragment had rebounded very high, hurtling toward civilians and peeling off half of a schoolgirl's head.

"The girl was just passing by," A Bao told him when You Dang Jiu went to see him. "Poor thing! She was buried at the edge of the pond. Her father wouldn't let her mother see her. If she'd seen the state of her daughter's body, she would have gone mad with grief."

A Bao was now a seasoned Badaixiong. During the farming season, he planted sesame and rice. The rice was for him to eat, and the sesame would be pressed into oil for sale. When he had the time, he performed divinations and sacrifices. Unlike his master Jiu Gou Yang, he didn't constantly have a pipe in his hand; rather, he was an energetic and easygoing man.

"The sesame plants are growing taller and taller," A Bao said as he led You Dang Jiu around the fields. The blossoms by his feet were sprouting toward the sky.

"Uncle A Bao, are you still banishing the stars?" You Dang Jiu asked.

A Bao nodded. "Yes, I do the star-banishing ritual almost every month in the autumn. But I don't have your grandfather's abilities. The ancestors aren't as familiar with me as they were with him." He paused for a moment, then gave You Dang Jiu a studied look. "A You, your grandfather said that you had a good memory and a good voice. These are gifts from the gods. If it was you, if you were the one who tied on the black headband and wore the black double-buttoned tunic, perhaps the ancestors would always be able to hear our prayers. Perhaps then, they would come down from the heavens . . ."

You Dang Jiu knew A Bao was thinking of the schoolgirl's accident last year. A Bao had never received any education, so he blamed all this misfortune on his own inability to win the ancestors' confidence. He thought it was his own fault that the ancestors weren't willing to use the mountain's power to banish those falling pieces of metal.

"Actually, the area where the Stage One rocket falls can be calculated with a computer." You Dang Jiu tried to console him. "If our technology improves in the future, if we can improve our algorithms, then we'll be able to accurately determine where they land."

"Can computers ward off disasters?" asked A Bao. "Our ancestors didn't invent a written script. They could only pass down their experiences orally. The mountain sustained everything that fell from the sky, and our forebears lived alongside the mountain. They recorded the wisdom of the mountain in the linked syllables at the front and back of their names. Generation after generation, our names have hidden the secrets that have been passed down from ancient times!"

You Dang Jiu said nothing. On the way home, he couldn't help but mumble to himself, "This fellow's even more stubborn than my grandfather. What kind of secrets would the mountain have?"

Unconsciously, he followed the limestone planks back to the stilt house of his childhood. Every spring, his father hired someone to clean the roof tiles, but otherwise no one had maintained the property since his grandfather passed away. The rooms were as they had been before. They had become very old-fashioned; now, the large color TV that had once been placed in the middle of the living room looked like a small, black box. It was broken, but no one had fixed it.

You Dang Jiu hesitated for a moment, then couldn't bear it anymore. He opened the drawer where his grandfather had kept his magic tools. He pulled out the Chiyou bell, the black headcloth, and the wooden basket that was supposed to have been passed on to him.

He borrowed some rice from the neighbors' rice jar, poured it into the basket, then buried the dark cloth and some coins shallowly in the rice. He thought of Grandpa, surrounded by people as he conducted the divination. Grandpa would seldom put down his pipe. He would shake his head as he hummed and rotated the basket. The bells and jewels on his person would ring . . . You Dang Jiu thought of all this, and unconsciously began to hum the same folk song that Grandpa had sung.

I migrate with my daughter Jin Tao, like fish swimming up the stream
I walk with my daughter Jin Mei, like birds flying past the hills
Twelve days and twelve nights; the days and nights don't stop coming
The sun-heated paddies steam like boiling water
The sun-heated stones are soft like rice cakes
On the sun-heated slope, the trees and grass are withered and scorched . . .

Suddenly, he sensed something spinning. At first, it was just the rice and coins in the basket, but then his own body was spinning, and then the whole room was spinning. He'd had this feeling during the rice divination ritual when he was a child, but now it was even stronger. Everything solid before his eyes turned into liquid colors, as if seen through morning dew.

Gradually the colors dissolved, turning into a vague shape beneath the lights and shadows of the stilt houses. He saw red.

A massive blaze fell out of the depths of the dark night, hurtling straight toward the center of the village. The village was like an overturned charcoal basin; its wooden frames burned as the tiles shattered from the heat. The lights went out. The stars went out. The villagers' songs went silent. All was replaced by black smoke, red fog, and the cries of women and children.

A star had fallen onto the village!

He jolted awake. Everything stopped spinning. The vision had seemed so real—as if someone had made him watch a video recording of the mountain's secret. You Dang Jiu stood up, leaned with one hand against the doorframe to steady himself, and made a quick decision. He dashed down the mountain, heading for the sesame fields to find A Bao.

You Dang Jiu had run through these stepped fields countless times, but never had he felt as slow as he did today. The stalks in the paddy hadn't yet been burned away, and the husks that remained in the fields gashed his legs. But how could he care? It had been a bumper crop, and the granaries were stocked full. The timing was awful—if rocket wreckage fell out of the sky now, the flames could ignite the dry village in no time.

Once, during one of You Dang Jiu's return trips from college in the city, an old clansman had asked him, "Can you ask the officials if they could stop launching satellites in our area?"

"Then where would they launch them?" You Dang Jiu had asked.

"Somewhere where there are no people. They could launch them over the sea, or the desert!"

"Satellites have latitude limits," You Dang Jiu had explained. "And our mountain already counts as a low-density area. This is the most suitable place to launch satellites that they could find."

"That can't be! My fields were destroyed for the sake of the mission of some official I don't even know!" The old clansman had whittled a piece of bamboo with his knife until it became thin and sharp, preparing to pierce the nostril of a two-year-old female calf. The man and his wife had originally prepared to use a bamboo pole to comb the blooming rice stalks across more than half an acre of land, stimulating pollination. Then a piece of rocket had smashed into the fields. The rice stalks had collapsed, the flowers had floated in the water, and the pollen was washed away. Even if the crops could be braced back up, in the end they would only produce empty husks.

"Isn't there compensation?" You Dang Jiu had asked.

"That compensation wouldn't be enough for me to hire someone to drag out the trash!" The man had pointed at the wreck in the fields with the sharp end of the bamboo. "Only that one piece of the wreck stayed flat. I'm going to hire a blacksmith to forge it into a kitchen knife! The rest is scrap metal. I even have to pay to have it cleaned up."

Back then, the old man hadn't known that wreckage falling in the fields was a blessing. Due to its high-speed friction with the atmosphere, the rocket that fell tonight would explode in the air over the densest part of the village, scattering sparks across the sky. When the sky filled with flames, where could the villagers hide?

You Dang Jiu found A Bao in the sesame fields.

"I'll go notify the county official. You . . ." He paused, then spoke the second half of his sentence with great effort. "You banish the star."

"A You, did you really see a huge piece of falling metal in the rice?" asked A Bao.

"Yes. Right above the square where there are the most people. It shattered into a giant blaze!"

"That . . . you didn't see anything else?"

"Anything else?"

"You can see things that haven't happened yet through the rice divination ritual. That means the mountain has chosen you. The mountain has reasons for its decisions. It must have left you more wisdom through the rice to help you through this crisis. Think hard, did you see anything else in the rice?"

You Dang Jiu hesitated for a moment. "No."

As soon as he got home, You Dang Jiu called the county government.

"Listen, this is serious! Our county lies inside the main landing area for Stage One rocket debris! The wreckage that will fall on our village tonight is extremely heavy. It's as powerful as a heavy bomb! We must evacuate the villagers . . . please, please you must—hello? Hello?"

"The county official didn't believe you?" A Bao asked from beside him.

"How was I going to reach the county commissioner? That was the office director. He said that civilian protection in the landing area is jointly handled by the regional military command and the satellite launch center, and that the relevant department would notify the landing area. He said that the headquarters had already completed over a hundred missions, so I should stop imagining things and relax, instead of inciting panic."

"How are you imagining things? The ancestors showed you the mountain's secrets."

"Not everyone believes in the mountain's secrets. Uncle A Bao . . . here's our only option. I'll see whether I can use the school's network to find an algorithm to calculate where the wreck will land. And you . . . you prepare a big rooster!"

"A You, did you really not see anything else in the rice . . . ?"

You Dang Jiu closed his eyes. He hadn't noticed much in that vision of fire filling the sky to begin with. All he'd wanted to do was flee; to Grandpa's stilt house, to the terraced fields he'd run through as a child.

"I really didn't," he said.

"Don't just use your eyes to see the mountain's secrets," said A Bao. "Use your heart."

The ancestral hall stood at the highest point of the village, which meant the Wi-Fi signal there was best. You Dang Jiu found a clean spot to sit down. Facing him was the wooden monument upon which the names of the members of the clan had been engraved.

Throughout the afternoon, he used all the methods at his disposal to search the Web for resources. But there wasn't a single person or theory that could tell him with accuracy whether the rocket igniting tonight would cause a catastrophe in the village after it separated from the satellite. Nor was there anyone willing to unconditionally trust a computer science major in college who had studied a bit of magic to expend the massive manpower and resources it would take to evacuate all the men, women, elders, and children from the village.

As the sun set, the shadows of the wooden eaves of the ancestral hall grew longer against the courtyard, crawling bit by bit up the wall. An old cat lay curled in those shadows, snoring and licking its fur. In the distance were the forests, which were the same deep green they'd been since ancient times, mixing with the red of the setting sun. Everything was calm and peaceful, just like countless days the ancestors had lived through. This scenery made You Dang Jiu begin to doubt himself. Had the vision he'd seen in the rice been a practical joke? Would this evening be like all those previous nights, where the fuss was more than the harm? When the sky darkened, when the villagers went home to make dinner and rest, would everything on the mountain be just the way it was before at sunrise?

He lifted his head and rubbed at sore eyes. When his sight cleared again, the rows of names on the monument caught his attention.

"The ancestors didn't know how to write," A Bao had told him. "They linked the syllables at the beginnings and ends of words to record the mountain's wisdom. Those generations of names contain secrets transmitted across ancient times."

"You cannot make a mistake when reciting the ancestors' names," Grandpa had said. "The ancestors have always lived in your name."

You Dang Jiu input the ancestors' names one by one into the open program. No syllables were missing, from the names of the first ancestors to settle in the mountain to the clansmen of this generation. Dark-faced Bang, who was an excellent farmer; Gou, who slew a tiger and now wore its pelt across his body; and Sang, who was lean and thin but could sing the most beautiful love songs.

He thought back to that night in his childhood, of all he'd seen under Chiyou's glare. He thought of the red thread bound to the big rooster's leg, leading the ancestors down a stone bridge, then farther into the depths of the village.

The stone bridge!

He'd seen the bridge in the rice. He'd seen people fleeing across this bridge to the opposite side. The crevices in the stone bridge were overgrown with moss and grasses; it had become a part of the mountain wilderness.

You Dang Jiu quickly stood, startling the cat dozing in the shadows. In the language of his people, the word for "bridge" was "jiu." Jiu was his Grandpa's name, and it was a part of his own name. That . . . that was the syllable that linked him with his grandfather.

To this day, Grandpa still lived in his own name.

He rushed out of the ancestral hall.

The mountain itself was an endless algorithm. Its data came from countless falls over countless years. Sunshine, rain, meteorites, and flames—all these things had fallen onto the mountain, and the mountain had remembered. The mountain had used its own wisdom and this data to calculate each subsequent descent.

His ancestors had discovered the secrets of the mountain. They had braided the codes for activating the mountain's secrets into the syllables of all their names. They taught each successive generation to continue passing it down through song. Every infant's name was linked to the name of his father and grandfather, and every name appeared in the long poem.

The names of the clansmen were a kind of code, and the mountain was the algorithm.

A Bao had already prepared the altar at the side of the stone bridge.

You Dang Jiu put on a black double-buttoned tunic, threw three pieces of beeswax into the charcoal brazier, and sang in a clear, resonant voice about the glorious deeds of the ancestral kings and each of the names of his ancestors. The melody of a lusheng instrument seemed to accompany him from the other side of the river.

Nineteen gods of the golden pillars
Nineteen gods of the silver pillars
You who live in Negou Village
You who live in Neshu Village
If you don't come, I will use the paddies to call you
If you don't return, I will use the rice to bring you
The grain is the link
The rice is the road.

Across the lonely, deserted bridge, You Dang Jiu saw a young man bringing rice and meat as an offering to his adopted father. The young man turned his face toward You Dang Jiu. His face looked exactly like his own. The man stood and happily belted out a love song. A girl wearing a brocade pleated skirt approached, walking along to the melody, winding around him like a skylark. Was that A Yang?

This time, Grandpa didn't have his pipe with him. His younger self stepped to the rhythm of the song at the base of the bridge, singing and swaying. On the other side of the bridge was You Dang Jiu. You Dang Jiu knew that he had no way of taking even one step across the bridge. He could only wave his arm from the other side. He grasped the Chiyou bell and shook it, but Grandpa didn't so much as glance his way.

Gradually, more and more people appeared around Grandpa. Those were the ancestors whose names were in the poem. They chatted and sang. Two among them even drank the rice wine that A Bao had brought. Grandpa danced across the bridge, looking happier than You Dang Jiu had ever seen him. He walked toward the village, and the other ancestors followed his footsteps. The procession passed by You Dang Jiu as if he were a clump of wild teasel.

You Dang Jiu wanted to call out to his grandfather, but he was still reciting the poem. He couldn't stop. He wanted to chase after his grandfather's footsteps, but his feet were rooted to the ground with the beeswax. He couldn't take a single step. He could only keep singing, could only keep ringing his bell, watching the procession of people getting farther and farther away until they disappeared over the village square, disappearing into a ball of red flame.

That evening, the satellite launch went smoothly. The only complication was that when the Stage One rocket fell, it didn't finish burning away. Instead, it fell onto a rarely used bridge at the edge of the village.

When Father heard the news, he was devastated. When he saw You Dang Jiu again, he said, "That bridge is no more. Your grandfather was a part of that bridge. We'll never be able to see him again."

But You Dang Jiu knew Grandpa would always live in this mountain. He would, along with the mountain, receive all the fortunes and misfortunes that fell from the sky.

And his name, You Dang Jiu, contained all the secrets of his grandfather and the mountain.

21

Net Novels and the "She Era": How Internet Novels Opened the Door for Female Readers and Writers in China

Xueting Christine Ni 倪雪亭

Net Novels and the "She Era": How Internet Novels Opened the Door for Female Readers and Writers in China

By Xueting Christine Ni

Whether for Chinese people in China, or diaspora of Chinese descent around the world, a sense of community has always been an important element of our culture. For those in China, family, party, country, a sense of belonging and interdependency gives an individual security. In the twentieth century, one of the biggest sources of this was the dānwèi system: State companies and organizations whose support of the workers extended to housing, schools, subsidized dining, and shopping. It became such a central part of people's lives that it pretty much came to define your entire social circle. As China opened its doors to the world, experiences diversified, and rapid economic development created social changes almost as quickly. As closed, communal living and security evaporated, there was a general feeling of unease and loneliness, especially amongst older workers. The younger generation, however, found solace and belonging in a new kind of community: the internet.

Toward the end of the 1990s, the use of the World Wide Web began to spread from business hubs and computer labs to internet bars, a few homes, and eventually everybody in the village. Broad and borderless communities began to spring up, not only allowing discussion and affirmation at an unprecedented rate, but also providing unique spaces for the arts and entertainment to develop. The internet became a theatre for flash animations, a gallery for unrestricted digital art. It wasn't long before dedicated literary platforms began to appear.

The first digital weekly periodical was set up in 1991, growing out of a project by a group of Chinese students studying in the United States. In its first year, *Huaxia Literary Digest* (huáxià wénzhāi) released China's very first net novel, Shao Jun's *Struggle and Equality.* Platforms such as this and rongshuxia.com are widely seen to have produced "the forefathers" of the net novel explosion, though it's worth noting that the foremothers were also there from the very beginning. Female authors like Jiang Shengnan, Anniebaby, and Heikeke were all serializing influential works across genres on these platforms. In fact, one of the most prominent features of the internet literature (wǎngluò wénxué) phenomenon was the rise of female authors.

It is a little disappointing to think that it took the internet to bring female voices to the forefront, especially in a country that has prided itself on "female emancipation." Since the 1950s, the Chinese Communist Party's "female liberation" reforms have had most women working full-time jobs, legally bound to match hours with their male counterparts for equal reward, but societal expectations and entrenched patriarchal attitudes meant that they were still expected to take the lion's share, if not all, of domestic and childcare responsibilities. Few of them had the energy or time left to achieve success in their work, or to explore creative outlets. Before the age of internet literature, China's fledgling traditional publishing industry, like many other trades, was a male-dominated sphere, especially at the higher gatekeeping levels. Accepted standards for "literary" works or "good literature" were enforced by the established, educated elite, and the highly selective process was determined by senior management at each print publisher. These hurdles, of course, created an affinity bias favoring male writers: both a perceived and actual issue. Many talented women would have been discouraged from submitting their manuscripts; many would never have had the contacts or channels to do so in any way that would raise them out of the ever-growing slush pile.

The creation of online platforms removed some of these barriers. A young female writer who may not have had the confidence to send her manuscript to a publisher for appraisal would feel far more comfortable uploading something she'd written into a friendly space—separated only by a computer screen—to share with those who would judge them purely on their writing. The number of hits, subscribers, and positive feedback provided immediate testament to their literary worth. The fact that one could only upload a few thousand words at a time would mean that a budding writer could trial ideas or work in stolen moments through the week, a boon to a young author unable to commit a longer time to her writing. Here, at last, was meritocracy.

Looking at the paths to authorship for some of China's female wǎngwén (short for wǎngluò wénxué) writers serves to demonstrate this process. Without the active university bulletin board system community and the horror fiction forums of the late 1990s and early 2000s, Tinadannis—the pseudonym for China's top author of college paranormal horror—would never have found fame. While she was still a student, she uploaded her debut *Wronged Ghost Road* onto Yat-sen Channel, Zhongshan University's bulletin board system, where it spread like wildfire. The title has now grown into a quintet and been read in multiple languages around the world. Like a lot of Chinese readers who grew up in the 1980s and 1990s, TianXiaGuiYuan (hereafter shortened as TXGY), China's most renowned female internet author, devoured the works of classic xīnwǔxiá (new wuxia) writers like Jin Yong and Gu Long in her youth. When she grew up, she worked as a policewoman. It wasn't until she was nearly thirty that, encouraged by friends, she began to publish her leisure writings online.

Online platforms rose to meet the needs of these writers and to connect them with readers. Over the last two decades, a whole infrastructure for digital publishing was bashed out and put in place by early major platforms like Qidian, Yuewen, zongheng.com, and shuqi

.com, allowing authors not only to distribute their work, but also to be paid for it. To give you an idea of the worth of the wǎngwén industry today, at the beginning of 2019, China's online literature sites hosted over 430 million reading accounts and over a million authors, producing over 20 million works, across 200-odd categories of writing.[1] In an industry valued at RMB 380 million (almost 60 million USD), female users make up just under half the readers (45 percent), but are responsible for over half the digital spending (56 percent).[2]

Key to the enormous success of internet publishing has been the growth of smartphone usage and a pivot to in-app reading. Until recently, comfortable reading was unavailable to those who couldn't afford e-readers, and reading on a laptop or desktop computer was inconvenient and required pre-planned leisure time. Chinese teenage boys were far more likely to have their own laptops purchased for them, while girls were expected to use the family computer. Girls could, however, get their own phones. In the last five years, mobile phone ownership has reached gender parity in China.[3] Smartphone reading meant that stories could be enjoyed on crowded trains or waiting in a lunch queue, and the ability to do so on a personal device meant that any genre could be enjoyed without judgment, and one could navigate, read, and personalize the reading experience with ease.[4] Over the last few decades, the change from a State-run to market-led economy has given Chinese women, most of whom are in the workforce, many more opportunities to raise their independent income. Increased disposable income and increased access to personal devices that facilitate instant purchases have resulted in the rise of a female economy in China.

The importance of female readers and authors was not missed by the

---

1 According to the 43rd China Internet Development Statistical Report.

2 Figures quoted by Wu Wenhui, the CEO of Yuewen Group in Xiao Jinghong, "Internet Literature: The Abundant World of Internet Literary Creativity," *People's Daily: Overseas Edition*, August 29, 2019.

3 According to the 2019 GSMA Connected Women report.

4 Today, the average online reader in China only needs a smartphone and about RMB 100 a year (USD 15) to access one million words' worth of content, according to figures from ce.cn (China Economics).

online platforms. Qidian was one of the first sites to feature a section tailored for female writers and readers. The first women's online literature platform, hongxiu.com (Fragrant Red Sleeves), was founded as early as 1999. The first online pay-to-read women's literature publisher, xxsy.net (Xiaoxiang Study) was launched in 2001, and was quickly followed by jjwxc.net (Jinjiang Literary City) in 2003. Today, there are more than two dozen major online literary platforms catering to female readers and writers, including fmxxs.com (Phoenix's Cry Pavilion), yunqi.qq.com (Gathering Clouds Study), 17k.com, and 4yt.net (April Sky), with most major general literature sites such as hjsm.net (Mystic Sword Book League) and chuangshi.qq.com (Creation) hosting women's channels and women's web editions, complete with soft pink themes, and generally a more "girlified" interface.

Amidst the expected genre lists, "What's New" columns, and recommendation pages, the sites feature authors' forums, discussions, and, depending on their focus, help for budding writers. As a reader, you can post comments on each title's discussion page, and show your appreciation for the work in the forms of flowers, diamonds, and crowns, all of which are a thinly-veiled way of tipping the author with in-app currency. You can also send authors a virtual ticking time bomb to "encourage" them to get on with the next chunk of content.

Never in the history of Chinese publishing have readers and writers been so closely connected. Without the mediation of publishers, there are virtually no barriers between them. The readers' continued interest is everything to the online writer, who would often engage in a cult of personality and cultivate parasocial relationships with their fans. A successful writer becomes well acquainted with their readers' tastes and habits via informal chats and discussion boards, and would even alter a point of characterization to directly please their more vocal readers, especially when it helps draw more fans into a particular kēng.[5]

On the general wǎngwén sites, it was initially thought that female authors would mainly be interested in reading and writing romances,

5 Kēng literally means "hole." It is internet speak for an area of interest with which one is obsessed, like "falling down the rabbit hole."

both modern and historical, and youth literature. In fact, there are plenty of women penning great works in these arenas, such as Xin Yiwu with her *Ode to Lost Youth* and Lilianzi who launched the gōngdǒu (palace intrigue) subgenre with *Inner Palace: The Tale of Zhenhuan.*

With her unique style of dūshì qíhuàn (a blend of urban setting and mythology), Kerui, who began publishing online in 2002, seemed to be the only female writer in her generation to tackle the genre. However, the huge success of her net novels *Legend of Urban Demons* (Dushi yao qitan) and *Dragon's Eye* inspired a whole wave of qíhuàn writing on the net. Having achieved titles such as "supreme goddess" among her fans, Kerui will probably bear the mantle "queen of qíhuàn" throughout her career.

Even the hyper-macho world of kungfu fantasy wasn't safe from "female invasion." Closely following the footsteps of Jiang Shengnan's 1999 story *Magic Knife Saga* (Modao fengyun), CangYue, an architecture student who began publishing on rongshuxia.com as a creative outlet, joined the ranks of the earliest female writers to work in wǔxiá in 2001, with her signature work *Tingxuelou Clan,* now a series of novels with both comic book and TV adaptations.

Female net novelists were not breaking into male-dominated literature by subversion or subterfuge, but simply through bypassing a bias in readers. A great levelling factor of wǎngwén is that little judgment can be made of a fresh author except for their chosen avatar and pseudonym. Many male readers of *Great Military Strategists of the Age* (Lidai junshi) who lauded the speculative historical novel for the breadth of its scope and thought provoking prose were allegedly surprised to find that the author SuiBoZhuLiu was not a 他 (he/him). A preconception-defying work of similar breadth and depth is *The Langya List* (Langya bang), adapted for television as *Langya Bang* (with the overseas English-language title *Nirvana in Fire*): speculative historical fiction about the ruthlessness of dynastic struggles, by female estate agent turned writer Haiyan. They aren't the only writers who don't align with writing styles seen as stereotypically female. The fact that early wǔxiá and kēhuàn writers like Bufeiyan and Qingchuan have either been compared to famous male writers or described as adopting zhōngxìng zhǔzhuàng (neutral viewpoint) is an indication of the overwhelming gender bias they were up against both in readers and in established marketing institutions.

These are women who grew up reading the "male" genres, traditional wǔxiá and chuánqí. It is no wonder that when a platform allowing them to publish without gatekeeping appeared, they explored the genres they had grown to love, without necessarily carrying around the chauvinistic baggage it came parceled in. Some of the most salient features of the net novel are the new genres and subgenres that have been created, and the new discourses they have begun. On the internet, imagination runs wild, genres emerge and interact and mutate, plotlines defy time and space, and contemporary slang, memes and net-speak emanate from the lips of the most effete and elegant ancient ladies.

In fact, the subversion of the traditional hero and female characters created enough of a disruption for these stories to be considered a whole new movement, the Nǚqiángwěn (strong female literature). These strong, self-sufficient female characters eschew their societal roles and prefer to "act like the boys," though the genre avoids the pitfalls that have marked many Western, male-written stories of female heroism. As almost none of these novels have been published in English, I'm limiting examples to the most well-known of works among thousands, and ones that—even though you might not have access to the novel—are available in the form of TV adaptations on streaming services.

This is very carefully separated from the fictional tradition of the cross-dressing heroine like Mulan and Zhu Yingtai, which are still continued on the internet today by writers Feng Xinglie and Tangxiu, whose characters don male garb and behavior to gain the freedom they wouldn't otherwise have to attain whatever goals they desire. Feng Jiu, wayward future queen of Qingqiu, the fox clan in *Three Worlds, Three Lives: The Pillow Book* by Tangqi;[6] Fuyao, the lowly servant girl destined to change the world from *Empress Fuyao* by TXGY;[7] and Zhou

6 Adapted into the TV series *Eternal Love of Dream* in 2020.
7 Adapted into the TV series *Legend of Fuyao* in 2018.

Fei, the rebellious scion from the outlaw community in *Bandits* (You-fei) by Priest all present as female.[8] They are princesses or heirs to thrones and leadership positions, but detest the traditional arts like embroidery, guzheng playing, and the study of etiquette, preferring instead to go adventuring, fighting, or drinking. The immortal Cheng Yu in *The Pillow Book* has a relationship with her love interest that seems to revolve almost entirely around combat. Under the pen of CangYue, women are not only self-sufficient and strong-willed in the face of adversity, but retain their independence in society, rejecting the ending that is usually thrust upon them: a union with a man to whom they are obligated to become subservient.

This is not, however, the inverted misogyny of rejecting all "female skill" to demonstrate strength and power. There are strong female characters written by women that rely on the softer skills of negotiation and diplomacy rather than fighting and confrontation, like Jie Lü, princess of *The Pillow Book,* whose levelheaded thinking and skills in statecraft prove her a more competent clan leader than her older brother. The significance of these stories lies in their assertion that women have the right to do—and behave—as they wish. Whether they prefer to read a book or pick up a sword, whether their goal in life is to build an empire or find true love (or both), these women are finding their way through full inclusion, rather than staying within their societally defined spheres.

The heroines of Nǚqiángwěn, from ancient princesses to modern pop singers, are defined by their agency, not allowing themselves to simply be bound by the accidents of birth, doing what they believe is right even with the whole world against them. One of the greatest achievements of women's wǎngwén has been for women to create complex representations of themselves that transcend stereotypes in popular, accessible fiction. These representations are not limited to the heroes of the story, but often also include the foils. There are some fantastic female villains, with well-rounded characterizations and mo-

8 Adapted into the TV series *Legend of Fei* in 2020.

tivations, such as Princess Folian of Xuanji (*Empress Fuyao*), and even archvillains like Miao Yan (*The Pillow Book*). The ultimate agency is that of authorship: women writing themselves for other women to read, and almost as a by-product, presenting real, three-dimensional female thinking to a male readership, who would otherwise only see them presented as damsels in distress or seductive temptresses.

Of course, sometimes the writing of a well-rounded character requires even more freedom than what a sense of independence can bring, and early female proponents of the net novel, both writers and readers, through their forum posts, settled on the concept of nǚzūn literature. Literally translated as "respected women," these were alternate universes, usually in historical or fantasy settings, where traditional gender divisions were repealed, or even reversed, and authors were allowed to write about great female warriors or ruling queens without needing a convoluted explanation of how they gained their position. The versatility of the chuānyuè and jiàkōng genres allow for inserting modern-day characters and modern-day concerns into fantasy settings, or to create entirely speculative worlds, governed only by the author's own rules.

TXGY, a proponent of "xuánhuàn for women," achieves this in the fictional Five Realms and Seven Nations of *Queen Fuyao.* Not only is there a powerful female protagonist, but also strong and interesting women throughout this epic, in all stations and walks of life. In this world, women are legitimate rulers and can assume high office, like men. Xuanji, one of the seven nations, is traditionally run by queens and entire courts of stateswomen, female imperial guards, and soldiers. Priest creates a similar world in her wǔxiá novel *Bandits,* a reclusive community that operates outside the patriarchal systems of normal society, where men and women live as equals, and some women have risen to chiefdom by merit of their kungfu prowess and leadership acumen.

Away from the escapism of genre fiction, authors like Heikeke and Anniebaby combined their own life experiences with down-to-earth prose into some realist writing that became voices of the post-1980s urban middle class. *Vivian* (Gaobie wei'an) by Anniebaby explores loneliness as a condition of modern China whilst *This Swinging Life* (Huadong de shenghuo) by Heikeke is an account of the aspirations and struggles of a young businesswoman. There are even net novels about net novelists. The post-1990s gen-capturing romance *Pride and Prejudice* by Meimeimao (charming cat) struck a chord with thousands of women who found themselves in the metropolis, who after hitting brick walls turned to a virtual space to pour out their tribulations, where they were unexpectedly met with grateful readers and the self-realization they'd been seeking.[9]

As more women-led fiction arrived on wǎngwén platforms, women became more comfortable with speaking to their own audience, the subjects became more open and empowered, and soon, underneath that sea of pinks, purples, and gender-specific marketing, a whole universe of subversions, inversions, and challenges to accepted views bloomed. It's not so much that women's internet literature caused the breakdown of Chinese society, as it helped facilitate, and document, the breaking of multiple literary and social taboos that had been layered up over generations.

The first "taboo" that comes to mind is sex. Sex is, of course, present in China, as it is everywhere, but it is still not talked about openly. Even in the modern day, sexual intercourse is seen as a by-product of marriage rather than recreational, so when Muzimei in 2003 began to serialize her sexual encounters with fifty-two men online (now collected into *The Book of Lost Passion* [yiqing shu]), the controversy was immense. Even though her sex diaries were a continuation of what came to be known as shentǐ xiězuò (body writing) that began in the 1980s before the internet age, by writers such as We Hui, Jiudan, and Chunshu, Muzimei took this school of writing to new levels of explicitness and daring.

Women are writing not just about sex, but about themselves as sex-

9 Apart from the title, and the loose framework similarity of a romance that grows when two people from very different backgrounds finally come to understand each other, the novel has little to do with Austen's classic. In fact, Meimeimao uses a different word for "pride" than the one used in the classic's Chinese title.

ual entities, with active physical desires and sexual needs, which in itself subverts traditional and conventional culture, where promiscuity is a form of immorality and women are meant to purely be the passive receivers of a man's desires. Both in her conduct and writing, Zhuying Qingtong presents the naked female body as a part of nature and not a thing to be ashamed of, and above all as something to be respected. Her works cover not only what women desire in sexual experiences, but also alternative practices of abuse and safety.

Amidst criticism of these writers as the so-called Muzimei Phenomenon, with China's top sociologists claiming that this type of writing uproots the morality of Chinese society and its modes of behavior, the anonymity of online platforms again provides some welcome shelter. Whilst much of this genre might have been written for sheer enjoyment and titillation, the risk of sexual predation, doxxing, and other attacks on female adult content creators makes the production of such work uncomfortable, if not life-threatening. Any woman delivering such an intimate manuscript to a physical publisher would do so with a sense of dread. The blogs, with which many female "body writers" began their publishing journey, provide a much safer, more informal and relaxed medium in which to initially put down one's thoughts. The educational elements within this genre are one of the most important considerations to women as readers of "body writing," where the actual dangers of sex, unwanted pregnancy, disease, and sexual violence can all be discussed in a format unpoliced by male opinion or ego.

A more subtle breaking of sexual taboos can be found in dānměi literature, the Chinese form of "boys' love" (BL) fiction.[10] Dānměi means "indulging in beauty" and is written by women for women, though most characters, especially the protagonists, are young, attractive men coded as androgynous or effeminate. The main characters

10 Boys' love is the term used to categorize works focusing on male/male relationships, which may or may not include sexual content, marketed toward women, in almost any media. This form of romance story was popularized in the Japanese magazine *June,* and indeed was referred to as "June stories," but as fans settled on the easily-typed, easily-obscured BL, the industry fell in line. The term is now used in both commercial and fan fiction circles to refer to the genre.

are usually paired up, with one taking a dominant and predatory role, while the other is submissively pursued, which leads to both implicit or explicit romances and sexual encounters. While BL has often been categorized by outsiders as queer literature, within its community of writers, there is a vast array of intention, representation, and assumed audience. A pan-Asian phenomenon and a product of repressive attitudes toward sex, dānměi has often been a way for young women to feel comfortable in exploring their own sexual desires without feeling transgressive, threatened, or that they have to directly deal with the physicality of sex. This subculture even has its own label: Fǔnǚ (rotten girl), a term imported from twentieth-century Japanese pop culture. It began as a pejorative term for women who are into BL at the expense of "real" relationships and feminine behavior, but was later reclaimed by its members with a sense of self-mocking humor and rebellion against conventional standards.

The very successful dānměi market, including merchandise, TV and manhua adaptations, is almost solely supported by China's female consumers. Just this year alone, numerous dānměi novels have made it onto the bestseller lists, including Wuzhe's high school romance trilogy *Wild* (Sa'ye) and Huaishang's drug-busting detective story *Piercing the Clouds* (Po'yun). The phenomenon has even made itself known in the West. If there is one series that has been on every Asian culture geek's mind and screen in 2020, it's *The Untamed,* adapted from *The Grandmaster of Demonic Cultivation* (Modaozushi) by net novelist MoXiang-TongXiu (MXTX).

Where dānměi literature has really caused a stir among wider society is in the type of men that these explorations feature. More commonly known as xiǎoxiānròu (little fresh meat), they reflect Chinese women's changing—or more realistically represented—tastes and expectations in men. It goes beyond just a softer, "prettier" appearance, but more metrosexual behavioral modes that are attuned to femininity and feminine attributes. The fictional representation of men in women's net literature reflects this deviation both from traditional views of masculinity and society's expectations of what women find attractive. It ranges from an appearance that leans toward androgyny, a taste for "feisty" women, the propensity for getting emotional, to possessing a certain "feminine" sensitivity and thoughtfulness. Conversely, across different genres, male characters who are more closely aligned to traditional masculinity are often portrayed in female-written stories as flawed and made to learn and develop, and in doing so, reveal a more rounded personality.

In China, this social shift in the literary, dramatic, and celebrity presentation of men has become exceptionally problematic as it crosses over into mainstream media. In a very conformist society, where conventional gender attitudes inform every layer of culture, strength and aggressive dominance are ideals toward which a man should strive. This misalignment of expectations is becoming a cultural battleground that even the State is now weighing in on. The internet, however, remains a predominantly consumer-led space, and a positive side of two decades of online female creativity is that, over the last decade, gender boundaries in wǎngwén are beginning to blur. While writers who present as traditionally feminine like MS Fuzi are continuing the creation of strong heroines in Nǚqiángwěn, other female writers are writing for the nánpín (male channel): sections of existing platforms aimed at male readers, where titles like *Going Back in Time and Becoming a Cat* (Chenci Landiao) and *The Gourmet Store* by Huizuocai de Mao are proving quite popular.

Aside from issues of genre and gender, the major factor that makes a lot of popular net novels successful is the quality of writing. We are talking about a set of passionate writers who are extremely well read, many of whom are highly educated, many with years of creative experience, writing for a very well-read nation nurtured on a classics-heavy curriculum that gets carried over into books and sophisticated scripts on TV. Due to the immense number of consumer choices and the fragmented reading habits of wǎngwén consumers, only net novelists with very skilled prose that sets the scene and creates moods with the ability to capture and retain attention spans could survive in the field. Whether it's with an urban thriller, light romantic comedy, or serious historical novel, female writers are reaching into their own experiences, carving out complex characters, and are not afraid to explore the psychological states and inner feelings of their creations, whatever the genre. It's this quality that makes female wǎngwén so compelling, and why their works appeal to readers across genders, backgrounds, and ages.

Although an immense amount of female output has been marketed as different kinds of yánqíng (romance), they are all so much more. Beyond BL romance, MXTX's refined weaving in of classical Chinese music culture, supernatural lore, and martial arts tradition are what make her stories so appealing. Her varied casts of rebels, social outcasts, and refugees also resonate deeply with contemporary readers. Beyond the trope of the "emancipated heroine," TXGY writes extensively about statecraft, class struggle, honor, friendship, and the moral responsibility toward one's fellows, while Tangqi's worlds are a delightful exposition of high Chinese mythology and exploration of free will—can one change, or even create, one's destiny?

Early net novelists did not make much from their subscriptions, nor did the now-prevalent female-oriented platforms and women's web pages materialize in the early years of the internet in China. The perseverance, explorations, and experimentations of these early writers led to the myriad of genres and tropes in the world of wǎngwén as we know it today. With the introduction of VIP memberships and other monetization models in the 2000s, net novelists began to make significant earnings online, which changed the nature of internet authorship.

A large number of women are now becoming wǎngwén writers. Many of them were avid net novel readers themselves and more than acquainted with the tastes and quirks of the market. They inherited the confident assurance of success from their predecessors and an established market and genres of proven appeal. Sure enough, the next wave of writers like Su Xiaonuan and Er'Mu achieved nearly instant success with their first publications in 2013 and 2016. The recommended intellectual properties for producers and investors found on many of the platforms are an indication of how streamlined the industry has become. The negative stigma of online authorship not being "a proper job" is gradually disappearing under the large monthly patronage payments young women are making from their literary creations, with many able to quit their day jobs to pursue a full-time writing career. Female net novelists are becoming the breadwinners in their households. It's no surprise that the current times have been hailed as the "She Era" (她时代).

However, in China, when an industry reaches critical mass, the State is bound to get involved. Contrary to popular perception, that involvement is not always negative. A significant number of wǎngwén writers are now members of the Chinese Writers' Association. Last year, over a dozen works from yuewen.com were included in the Association's list of key projects to support, and Tangjia Sanshao became the very first net novelist admitted into the board. Although no female wǎngwén writer has been added to the board yet, they are being placed in positions of authority. TXGY, whose work was selected for discussion at the Association's first net novel forum, now teaches at the Shanghai University of Visual Arts and serves as deputy chair at the Jiangsu Internet Literature Association. The first creative wǎngwén writing master's degree has just been set up jointly by Yuewen Group and Shanghai University.

These new developments in China's internet literature have raised some concerns. Net censorship in general has tightened in the last few years, and controversial authors such as Muzimei, Zhuying Qingtong, and even some BL writers have had their posts and content curbed by China's still sex-averse establishment. Copyright theft by other authors and unfair contracts from online publishers have become major problems faced by online authors. In a platform rife with homage, fan fiction, and alternate universe retellings, there are always discussions over intellectual property theft. Even Tangqi, whose work began as a stylistic homage to DaFengGuaGuo, has found herself embroiled in internet drama and accusations of plagiarism. These are all areas that require further regulation.

China's entire commercial publishing industry is still relatively new, and in the last twenty years, its publishing capacity has increased a thousandfold. The increased demand for content and productivity has led to a voracious hunt for new content by publishers looking to fulfill this audience. One would think that a medium like online platforms that removes the need for a physical publisher would be a threat to the industry, but in reality wǎngwén has proven to feed quite well into the desire for physical books. Although commercial publishing is still catching up, printing has a long history in China, where there's deep and immense respect for the printed word. Decades of experience making books for the world have amassed a wealth of skill in the trade, not to mention infrastructure and technology.

Wǎngwén platforms have become something of a testing ground for new writers. Here, risk-averse publishers are able to pick up works that have a demonstrable readership—possibly even three or four volumes of content—knowing that with good design, gorgeous cover art, and perhaps a handful of art cards, phone charms, and other ephemera, they can draw new readers in addition to the devoted online fans who would pay again for a definitive collector's edition of their favorite works. These are just some of the ways Chinese physical publishers have capitalized on their advantages and the enthusiastic fandoms that often build up around many net novels and their authors.

Whether these selected writers still continue with wǎngwén seems to be very much a personal choice. While many early writers had a tendency to gloss over their net publishing origins when they "graduated" to traditional publishing, many newer writers have been quite happy to declare themselves wǎngluò zuòzhě (net authors), enjoying what their gold or platinum statuses offer and maintaining the freedom of output that net novels afford them.

Wǎngwén removed the gender biases and the practical and perceived gatekeeping of traditional publishing facing female writers before China's internet age, providing them with the assurance that their work is of value, more flexible ways of working, a wide readership, and direct contact with these individuals. Here was a kindred community for both female writers and readers, as well as financial rewards that gradually became more significant as the industry took off. Female writers brought their creativity to China's internet literature and transformed it, with complex representations of women and new perspectives on men. They took fresh approaches toward previously male-dominated genres and also created a range of brand-new ones. Taking wǎngwén in new directions, they challenge conventional gender roles, evoke a multitude of social changes accumulated over decades, and bring in their own experiences, creating new levels of depth, complexity, and social relevance in the freewheeling literary sandbox of wǎngwén. The most significant impact of this synergy is an immense expansion of the reach of readership and audience that is hugely beneficial to writers, print as well as online publishers, and related media industries.

Equally important is the cultural impact of women's wǎngwén. Women can have a lot more literature in which they can see themselves properly represented, with all kinds of female role models with whom they can engage and learn about all kinds of diverse experiences around the country. Female wǎngwén are also providing male readers with better examples of women that are closer to what women actually are like, rather than idealized archetypes or objects of male fantasy. These three-dimensional portrayals of women are having an impact far beyond the literary spheres from which they arose. Reading is one of the major ways in which we inform ourselves and develop empathy. Women's internet literature is doing far more than informing male readers about the internal motivations of female characters; it's also educating them on how to interact with women in real life, how to treat them as comrades and equals. Wǎngwén is doing more to dismantle centuries of ingrained patriarchal behavior than any top-down state directive ever could. Even the narrow and restrictive gender divide on the genre's marketing is slowly blurring. Now male writers have to up their game, keep up, and make their female characters more than just huāpíng (decorative vases).

I started this exploration of wǎngwén with the patriarchal barriers that female writers needed to either penetrate or circumvent. I've come to realize that we are now at a point where the movement is no longer reactionary: the bar for quality is being set by female authors. While wǎngwén will continue to provide a safe haven for the next generation's MXTX and TXGY, the whole genre and platform—regardless of gender—is being enriched, challenged, and uplifted by the presence of China's female readers and writers.

Works Consulted

AhSanShouMa. "Let's Talk About Five Influential Internet Women: Muzimei, Zhuying Qingtong." kanshula.com. Accessed December 28, 2020. 阿三瘦马, 聊聊五大网络人气女人: 木子美、竹影青瞳、. https://www.stxsw.com/book/beishangcangzuzhoudetiancai/4345096.shtml.

Baokan Editorial. "In Conversation With Tianxia Guiyuan: Policewoman in Life, Nǚqiangwen Queen Online." Last modified March 7, 2017. 访谈|天下归元: 生活中的女公安 网上女强文之王. https://www.baokan.tv/f/cjpl/53332.html.

Bufeiyan. *The Inn of Jianghu*. Accessed November 10, 2020. http://www.wuxia.net.cn/book/wulinkezhan.html.

Cangyue. *Tingxuelou Clan*. Accessed November 1, 2020. https://www.51shucheng.net/wuxia/tingxuelou.

Chen Zifeng. "Chinese Internet Literature Written for Women: In What Ways Does This Help In the Attainment of Gender Liberalisation." The Initium. Last modified April 25, 2017. 陳子豐, 寫給女性的中國網絡文學, 能如何幫助性別解放? https://theinitium.com/article/20170425-opinion-chenzifeng-internet-literature-women.

GSMA Connected Women. "The Mobile Gender Gap Report 2019." Published February 2019. https://www.gsma.com/mobilefordevelopment/wp-content/uploads/2019/03/GSMA-Connected-Women-The-Mobile-Gender-Gap-Report-2019.pdf.

Li Ting. "The Generational Divisions of Female Internet Authors."

Republished on chinawriter.com on September 26, 2019. First published in *Twenty Years of Chinese Internet Literature.* Edited by Ouyang Youquan. 李婷, 女性网络作家的代际划分. http://www.chinawriter.com.cn/n1/2019/0926/c404027-31373994.html.

LinliJiangGuiGushi. "Recommending Ten Great Horror Novels." Published February 2, 2019. 十大恐怖小说推荐. https://www.bilibili.com/read/cv1984178/.

Mo Qi. "Tangqi On Allegations of Plagiarism: 'When I Was Getting Smeared, I Almost Fell Into Depression. Now, I Find It Amusing." *The Paper*. February 8, 2017. 莫琪, 唐七回应抄袭说: 被黑得最凶时差点抑郁, 现在觉得可笑. https://www.thepaper.cn/newsDetail_forward_1612168.

Moxiang Tongxiu. *Grandmaster of Demonic Cultivation.* jjwxc.net. 2015. @ 墨家小跟班. "The Original of MXTX's Name: Interview with MXTX." Accessed on July 13, 2021. 墨家小跟班 vlog channel. weibo.com

Priest. "Bandits." jjwxc.net. 2015.

"The Serialization of Sex Diaries Online: This 'Muzimei Phenomenon' Is Worrying." From culture topic page: "Finding Fame From A Sex Journal: The Muzimei Phenomenon." Accessed December 28, 2020. 性爱日记网上连载, "木子美现象"让人担忧 http://www.people.com.cn/GB/wenhua/22226/30548/.

Sexblog. "The Works and Deeds of Zhuying Qingtong." *Sex Education Blog.* January 6, 2007. Sexblog, 竹影青瞳大事记 http://sexblog.zjblog.com/4662.shtml.

Shangguan Yun. "Tangqi Denies Plagiarism Claims Against 'Three Lives, Three Worlds', But Is The Assessment From One Party Only Legally Binding?" Republished on *The Paper*. August 10, 2017. First published on chinanews.com. 唐七否认《三生三世》抄袭, 但单方鉴定有法律效力吗. https://www.thepaper.cn/newsDetail_forward_1758784.

Shao Yanjun. "The Periodization of Internet Literature and Canonization of 'Traditional Internet Literature." Republished on chinawriter.com. February 26, 2019. Originally published in *China Contemporary*

Literature Research Periodical. 邵燕君，网络文学的“断代史”与“传统网文”的经典化. http://www.chinawriter.com.cn/n1/2019/0226/c404027-30902724.html.

Shuyüjun. “Investigative Report on the State of Authorship of China's Internet Literature.” Republished on Nebula SF Review. May 17, 2020. 书鱼君，中国网络文学作家生存状态调查报告. https://mp.weixin.qq.com/s?__biz=MzIwMzkyNTUzMA==&mid=2247484381&idx=1&sn=b1254ab3c984c22c811f0f174b9d5e8d&source=41.

Tangqi. *Three Lives, Three Worlds: The Pillow Book*. Accessed June 3 2020. https://www.kanunu8.com/book2/10506/.

Tianxia Guiyuan. “Queen Fuyao.” xxsy.net. 2011.

Xiao Han. “The Output, Genres and Unique Characteristics of Internet Literature.” January 19, 2015. 小韩，网络文学作品数量，类型及其特征 http://www.lunwenstudy.com/xiandaiwx/51340.html.

Xiao Jinghong. “Internet Literature: The Abundant World of Internet Literary Creativity.” *People's Daily: Overseas Edition*. August 29, 2019. 肖惊鸿，网络文学：丰富世界网络文学创造 http://paper.people.com.cn/rmrbhwb/html/2019-08/29/content_1943833.htm.

Xiao Lianhua. “I Would Never Become a Professional Writer: Exclusive Interview With Tianxia Guiyuan.” 天下归元：我绝不会做专职作家 http://www.pclady.com.cn/interview/104/1041899.html.

Xiaoxiang Study (online publishing platform). https://xxsy.net.

Xinhua Editorial. “Jiang Shengnan On Creativity: We Must Respect Rather Than Pander To Readers, It's No Good Trying To Be ‘Loved By Everyone.’” August 25, 2020. 蒋胜男谈创作：要尊重观众而非讨好，追求“人人爱”是无用功 http://www.xinhuanet.com/book/2020-08/25/c_139314072.htm.

Yang Baobao. “Ms Fuzi: Making Her Entrance With the Concept of Female-led Xuanhuan.” Republished on chinawriter.com. August 1, 2018. First published on *The Paper*. Ms芙子：抱着写以女孩为主角玄幻文的念头入行 http://www.chinawriter.com.cn/n1/2018/0801/c404024-30183503.html.

Zhang Yi. “Is This the Coming of the ‘She-Era?’ Who Are The Readers of Almost 5 Million Novels on the ‘Female Channels’?” *JF Daily*.

September 15, 2018. 张熠, "她时代"来临? 近500万部"女频"小说谁在读? https://www.jfdaily.com/wx/detail.do?id=105593.

Zhang Yi. "Twenty Years of Development: The Changes of Authorship and Literary Ecology In Internet Literature." Republished on ce.cn. March 1, 2018. First published on *JF Daily*. 张熠, 发展20年 网络文学改变作者构成和文学生态 http://www.ce.cn/culture/gd/201801/03/t20180103_27544574.shtml.

Zhenhui Youyong de Mao. "5 Novels On the Male Channels, Written With Grace and Magnitude By Female Authors, That Will Have You Staying Up All Night Reading, If You're Not Careful." April 21, 2020. 真会游泳的猫, 女作者写的5本男频网络小说, 优雅大气, 让人一不小心看通宵 https://www.sohu.com/a/389734984_100151658.

Zhenhui Youyong de Mao. "Why Have Female Writers Set the Male Channels Ablaze? These Five Hot Net Novels Can Tell You." April 17, 2020. 真会游泳的猫, 女作者凭什么在男频大红大紫? 5本高人气网络小说, 告诉你答案 https://www.sohu.com/a/388647086_100151658.

Writing and Translation: A Hundred Technical Tricks

Rebecca F. Kuang 匡灵秀

Writing and Translation: A Hundred Technical Tricks

By Rebecca F. Kuang

I was a writer before I was a translator. I first began translating Chinese literature to improve my own scholarship, since translation develops excellent close reading habits. It makes one cut through semantics and syntax to grasp that ineffable *stuff* of ideas, that hazy, elusive link that Humboldt calls the "mystical relation" between linguistic symbols and the things they represent;[1] if you don't fully understand a text, you can't possibly restate it. I had not, however, anticipated how much of an impact translation would have on my writing. Translating from Chinese to English did not just make me a better student of Chinese literature; it also made me re-examine how I approach my own craft, and how I represent China (whatever that means) and my own Chinese-ness (whatever *that* means) to an Anglophone audience.

German theorist and translator Johann Christoph Gottsched wrote in 1743 that translation was analogous to novice painters copying model artwork. By closely observing and re-creating the original piece, they "commit to memory a hundred technical tricks and advantages that are not immediately known to all and that they never would have

1 Wilhelm von Humboldt, "'The More Faithful, The More Divergent,' from Introduction to Translation of Aeschylus's Agamemnon (1816)," in *Western Translation Theory: From Herodotus to Nietzsche*, ed. Douglas Robinson (New York: Routledge, 2014), 239–40.

discovered by themselves."[2] This applies well to literary translation. One takes much for granted when writing in one's native tongue. Things like tone, rhythm, flow, and atmosphere feel instinctive. It's easy to assign different speaking patterns to different characters, for instance, because that mirrors the speaking patterns of people you know in real life. But translation forces you to identify these "hundred technical tricks" in someone else's work, then replicate them in a different language. Faithfulness here forces discipline, and discipline hones craft.

For instance, when I translated Chen Qiufan's short story "In This Moment, We Are Happy" 这一刻我们是快乐的 for *Clarkesworld,* I had to think hard about how to differentiate in English the voices of the seven protagonists, each of whom is experiencing childbirth in a different way. How do you convey the subtle distinctions in the spoken Chinese of Wu Yingmian, a businesswoman looking to employ a pregnancy surrogate, and Kenji Ohno, a brash and provocative multimedia artist who undergoes sex reassignment surgery to become pregnant as part of a public art piece? Wu Yingmian's voice is professional, polite, both guarded and vulnerable at once, while Kenji Ohno speaks to startle and compel. There's so much you can convey about a character in a single word: the fact that Kenji Ohno calls his business associate "Scott, darling" instead of "dear Scott," for instance, speaks volumes about his personality.[3] It was not enough merely to accurately convey the content of their speech; I lingered over every piece of slang or casual greeting, and the exercise made me more picky and deliberate in how I write dialogue in my own work.

Beyond word choice, translation also forces careful consideration of cultural representation. In my genre, science fiction and fantasy, Anglophone authors who write about non-Western worlds are asking themselves how easy they should make things for their audience. Should

2 Johann Christoph Gottsched, "Extract from Critische Dichtkunst ('Critical Poetics'), Published in 1743," in *Translation/History/Culture: A Sourcebook,* ed. André Lefevere (London: Routledge, 1992), 57.

3 Both possible translations of the original, which read: "亲爱的."

you shy away from too much cultural difference out of fear that a white reader won't be able to relate? Should you italicize all non-English words, or is that othering? Do you over-explain all cultural practices (e.g. "we took off our shoes, as is common in an Asian household"; "I referred to him as my uncle, though we are not related by blood") in case the reader gets confused? Will these excessive explanations drag the flow of the story? If you don't do this expository work, will editors reject you on the grounds that "we're worried audiences won't be able to relate"? Will they argue that audiences can't relate even if you *do*?

Then, add the complication of being a diaspora writer. I, like many Chinese American writers, grew up with *some* exposure to Chinese culture and language, much of it internally translated and filtered through a Western environment. The "authenticity" of my cultural heritage is difficult to sort. Do my memories of Lunar New Year come from what my parents taught me, or what my white kindergarten teacher taught me? Did I learn about Sun Tzu from my father, or from Wikipedia? (Does it matter?) Can I assume a Western audience is familiar with a term just because I am? How much of myself must I explain to my audience?

A parallel debate has been going on in translation theory for centuries. The German Romantics favored an approach that emphasized difference; Friedrich Schleiermacher, for instance, argued that, rather than trying to make a translation sound "natural" to the target audience, one ought to emphasize difference; that translators ought to favor an approach that "leaves the author in peace, as much as possible, and brings the reader toward him."[4] Compare this to John Dryden, who in his translation of the Aeneid "endeavored to make Virgil speak English as he would himself have spoken, if he had been born in England, and in this present age."[5] Neither of these strategies work when taken to the extreme in Chinese to English translation. One approach, in

4 Friedrich Schleiermacher, "Extracts from 'Uber Die Verschiedenen Methoden Des Ubersetzens' ('On the Different Methods of Translating'), Published in 1813," in *Translation/History/Culture: A Sourcebook,* ed. André Lefevere (London: Routledge, 1992), 141–66.

5 John Dryden, "Introduction," in *Virgil's Aeneid,* trans. John Dryden, 1697.

trying to create artificial relatability, erases all that is uniquely "Chinese" about a text and replaces it with a generically Western cultural milieu; the other approach makes Chinese culture seem more foreign, exotic, and Other than it is.

The German Romantics, moreover, had not considered the spread of contemporary globalization and diaspora. Perhaps it was once reasonable—say, in the eighteenth century—to think white Americans were unfamiliar with dim sum and guanxi; today, those terms are firmly entrenched within the English lexicon. Why bring the text closer to the reader, when the reader has already moved closer to the source? And even if there are gaps in the reader's knowledge, why interrupt the flow of the story to explain when Google exists? Information about other languages and cultures is now more readily accessible than ever; the excuse of provincial ignorance no longer makes sense. Why not make the reader work?

The upshot is writers and translators must both carefully consider who they are writing for, and how they represent a culture that is not their own. This is much harder than it sounds, and there are no good answers or hard-and-fast rules; these choices are all context-dependent. Here's an example: In Wang Nuonuo's "The Way Spring Arrives," we chose to add in brief explanations in apposition ("Zhurong, the giant god of fire" and "Chisongzi, the god of rain") where the original simply referenced Zhurong and Chisongzi by name. There is a great deal more to Zhurong than fire, of course—a footnote could have mentioned Zhurong's famous battle against Gonggong, which split the heavens and forced Nüwa to repair the sky. But the story is not about Zhurong, Gonggong, or Nüwa. Zhurong and Chisongzi are only background characters to Goumang and Xiaoqing's story. To appreciate Wang Nuonuo's imagery in that particular scene, one needs only know that Zhurong is associated with fire, and Chisongzi is associated with rain.

There's much more I could say about the technicalities of translation, and how they bleed over into good writing. Though to be frank, the questions outnumber the answers. I am still struggling to figure out how to position myself as a Chinese American novelist and translator, and to navigate the disparities in power and privilege that entails. And I still struggle with balancing my sense of the author's voice and my own authorial voice, which is particularly difficult when one sometimes forgets which is which. The ability to dance between languages and literary environments is a privilege, and one that can harm and offend if carelessly used.

I think about my ability to code-switch a lot these days as I finish the first draft of my next novel, a response to the often blatantly racist and colonialist Victorian canon. I wonder what it signifies that I've chosen English—and in particular the stylistic tendencies of authors like Austen and Dickens—to convey a story about revolution against empire. I think about reform-minded scholars near the end of the Qing dynasty, who were beset with anxieties about Western knowledge and the threat it posed to the Chinese world order, and who regarded English acquisition with a mix of skepticism and apprehension. And this week, as I'm writing this, I'm thinking about the six Asian women murdered by a gunman in Atlanta, and how much power my native fluency in English really affords me, if someone can look at me and still refuse to hear.

I want to bring all this back to the importance and necessity of this anthology, which is written and translated entirely by women and non-binary creators. Of course no one is arguing that translators must always match the precise identities and background of the writer—that is implausible, and misses the point besides. It is not about political correctness or judgments of who is "allowed" to do what, it is about epistemic access. When moving between languages also involves moving between worlds, perhaps it helps that the translators, too, are people who are used to being on the outside, who are used to navigating hidden spaces, and who are familiar with the challenge of making themselves understood.

BIBLIOGRAPHY

Dryden, John. "Introduction." In *Virgil's Aeneid,* trans. John Dryden. 1697.

Gottsched, Johann Christoph. "Extract from Critische Dichtkunst ('Critical Poetics'), Published in 1743." In *Translation/History/Culture: A Sourcebook,* ed. André Lefevere. London: Routledge, 1992.

Schleiermacher, Friedrich. "Extracts from 'Uber Die Verschiedenen Methoden Des Ubersetzens' ('On the Different Methods of Translating'), Published in 1813." In *Translation/History/Culture: A Sourcebook,* ed. André Lefevere, 141–66. London: Routledge, 1992.

von Humboldt, Wilhelm. "'The More Faithful, The More Divergent,' from Introduction to Translation of Aeschylus's Agamemnon (1816)." In *Western Translation Theory: From Herodotus to Nietzsche,* ed. Douglas Robinson. New York: Routledge, 2014.

ACKNOWLEDGMENTS AND CREDITS

The Way Spring Arrives and Other Stories is a collection long in the making that owes its existence to more people than a book can contain. The editors would like to acknowledge the many teams who helped make this project a reality.

Storycom and Friends

Yiwen Zhang, CEO
Regina Kanyu Wang, Producer
Yu Chen, Editor
Emily Xueni Jin, Assistant Producer
Constance Hu
Dong Zhiyan
Ni Xiaoyan
Yu Lian
Ken Liu
S. Qiouyi Lu

Editorial

Ruoxi Chen, Editor
Lindsey Hall, Editor
Sanaa Ali-Virani
Rachel Bass
Irene Gallo
Devi Pillai

Marketing and Publicity

Isa Caban, Lead Marketer

Desirae Friesen, Lead Publicist
Megan Barnard
Alex Cameron
Ariana Carpentieri
Michael Dudding
Samantha Friedlander
Eileen Lawrence
Khadija Lokhandwala
Amanda Melfi
Sarah Reidy
Lucille Rettino
Stephanie Sirabian
Yvonne Ye

Art

Christine Foltzer, Cover Designer
Feifei Ruan, Cover Artist
Jess Kiley

Production

Dakota Griffin, Production Editor
Greg Collins, Designer
Kyle Avery, Proofreader
Zhui Ning Chang, Copyeditor
Michelle Li, Chinese Language Proofreader
Rebecca Naimon, Cold Reader
Lauren Hougen
Jim Kapp
Katherine Minerva
Heather Saunders
Nathan Weaver

Accounting

Louise Chen
Nellie Rodriguez

Audio

Sal Barone, Audio Engineer
Ryan Lare, Audio Editor
Robert Allen
Claire Beyette
Alyssa Keyne
Drew Kilman
Steve Wagner
Emma West

Contracts

Andrea Morales

Digital Production

Caitlin Buckley
Ashley Burdin
Chris Gonzalez
Maya Kaczor
Victoria Wallis

Metadata

Clark Fife
Sarah Lawrence
Margaret Sweeney
Christopher Urban
Paul Wargelin

Operations

Constance Cochran
Michelle Foytek
Rebecca Naimon
Edwin Rivera

Tor.com Website

Emmet Asher-Perrin
Chris Lough
Christina Orlando
Stefan Raets
Leah Schnelbach
Molly Templeton
Sarah Tolf

And a huge thank you to the entire Macmillan sales team, the buyers, and the booksellers who have supported this book. And to our readers: thank you for exploring this season of stories with us. Here's to many more to come.

CONTRIBUTORS

Anna Wu
吴霜

Anna Wu (she/her) holds a master's degree in Chinese literature and is a science fiction writer, screenwriter, and translator. She has won the Golden Award for Best Science Fiction Film Originality and the Silver Award for Best Novella at the Xingyun Awards (the Chinese Nebulas), and her works have been short-listed for the 2019 Baihua Literature Award and nominated for the 2020 Locus Award. She has published science fiction in Chinese and English, and translations in *Clarkesworld, Galaxy's Edge, Science Fiction World,* and other magazines with a total of more than four million Chinese characters. She has also published personal science fiction collections *Twins* and *Sleepless Night,* and translated Ken Liu's collection *The Shape of Thoughts* into Chinese. Her stories have been included in *Broken Stars* and published in the United Kingdom, the United States, Japan, Germany, and Spain. Her works have also been included in more than twenty science fiction anthologies or collections in Japanese, English, and Chinese.

BaiFanRuShuang
白饭如霜

BaiFanRuShuang (she/her) is a writer, CEO, and management consultant. She has published twenty-one books, including fiction, and nonfiction on team management and female growth. She founded Knowbridge, a knowledge-sharing platform that provides high-quality training and socializing services to tens of thousands of paid members.

Cara Healey
贺可嘉

Cara Healey (she/her) is the Byron K. Trippet Assistant Professor of Chinese and Asian Studies at Wabash College. Her research situates contemporary Chinese science fiction in relation to both Chinese literary traditions and global science fiction. Her articles have been published in journals such as *Modern Chinese Literature and Culture, Science Fiction Studies,* and *Wenxue*. She is also an active literary translator, with work appearing in *Pathlight* and *The Reincarnated Giant: An Anthology of Twenty-First-Century Chinese Science Fiction* (Columbia University Press, 2018).

Carmen Yiling Yan
言一零

Born in China and raised in the United States, Carmen Yiling Yan (she/they) was first driven to translation in high school by the pain of reading really good stories and being unable to share them. Since then, her translations of Chinese science fiction have been published in *Clarkesworld, Lightspeed,* and *Galaxy's Edge,* as well as numerous anthologies. She graduated from the University of California, Los Angeles with a degree in computer science, but writes more fiction than code these days. She currently lives in the Midwest.

Chen Qian
陈茜

Chen Qian (she/her) started her science fiction and fantasy writing career in 2006. She is a member of the Chinese Science Writers Association, the Science Literary and Art Committee, and also the Shanghai Youth Literary and Arts Association. Her short stories can usually be found in *Science Fiction King, Science Fiction World, Odyssey of China Fantasy, Zui Fiction,* and more. Her works have been selected as Chinese SF Year's Best, and adapted into comics and broadcast dramas. She has published a short story collection, *The Prisoner of Memory;* a YA novel, *Deep Sea Bus;* and a YA short story collection, *Sea Sausage Bus.* She has won a Silver Award for Best Novella and a Golden Award for Best New Writer at the Xingyun Awards (the Chinese Nebula), the Chinese SF Coordinate Award, and a Golden Award for Best Short Story at the Children's Science Fiction Nebula Awards.

Chi Hui
迟卉

Chi Hui (she/her) is a science fiction writer born in the northeast of China, now living in the Southwest with her cat. She began to write in 1993, published her first story in 2003, and is still writing now. She loves food, games, painting, and nature observation. Her science fiction novels include *Terminal Town* and *Artificials 2075.* She also works as an editor at *Science Fiction World.*

Chu Xidao
楚惜刀

Chu Xidao (she/her) holds a master's degree in literature and is a member of the Shanghai Writers Association. She once worked as the creative director of an advertising company, and is now a freelance writer working on fiction and screenplays. Her novels include the fantasy Meisheng series, Novaland fantasy The Heaven Light and Cloud Shadow series, wǔxiá Tomorrow Songs series, romance *Mr. Crunchy Candy,* screenplay *Young Detective Dee: Rise of the Sea Dragon,* and others.

Count E
E伯爵

Count E (she/her) started as an online fiction writer. She likes fantastic and detective stories and has tried writing in different genres and styles. She has published novels such as *Dance of the Seven Veils,* the Poems of the Purple Star Flowers trilogy and *Stranger,* and the recent *The Mysterious City of Chongqing* and *Void of Light: The Key of Chaos.* Her book *Stranger* won the Galaxy Award for Best Book and has been shortlisted for the Firestone Literary Award, Jingdong Literature Award for Science Fiction, and the Xingyun Award (the Chinese Nebula). Her stories have been selected for the *2010 Annual Best of Chinese Fantasy, 2012 Annual Best of Chinese Fantasy, 2014 Annual Best of Chinese Mystery,* and *2015 Annual Best of Chinese Mystery.*

Elizabeth Hanlon
韩恩立

Elizabeth Hanlon (she/her) is a Boston-based translator of Chinese fiction. She is a graduate of Tulane University and studied Chinese at the Inter-University Program for Chinese Language Studies at Tsinghua University. Her published translations include *Of Ants and Dinosaurs,* a novella by Hugo Award–winning sci-fi author Liu Cixin; *Beijing Graffiti,* a nonfiction work on Beijing's graffiti culture; and several short stories.

Emily Xueni Jin
金雪妮

Emily Xueni Jin (she/her) is a science fiction and fantasy translator, translating both from Chinese to English and the other way around. She graduated from Wellesley College in 2017, and she is currently pursuing a PhD in East Asian Languages and Literature at Yale University.

As one of the core members of the *Clarkesworld*-Storycom collaborative project on publishing English translations of Chinese science fiction, she has worked with various prominent Chinese SFF writers. Her most recent Chinese to English translations can be found in *AI2041: Ten Visions for Our Future*, a collection of science fiction and essays co-written by Dr. Kaifu Lee and Chen Qiufan. Her essays can be found in publications such as *Vector* and *Field Guide to Contemporary Chinese Literature*.

Mel "etvolare" Lee

Mel "etvolare" Lee (she/her) is a wǔxiá translator and period drama scribbler based out of Taipei. She specializes in a variety of Chinese fantasy and has translated roughly nine million characters. Her works include post-apocalyptic xianxia *Necropolis Immortal* (Wuxiaworld) and period drama politics in *Return of the Swallow* (volare novels). Her first series, Sovereign of the Three Realms, can be found on Amazon, and more translation-related thoughts can be found at etvolare.com.

etvolare has a significant background in all things finance: an MBA, CPA, CFA level one, and all sorts of A-related irrelevance. Struck by lightning one day, her soul transmigrated to ancient China and beat up young masters . . . ahem. She swapped career paths seven years ago, and now lives and breathes Chinese web novels.

Gigi Chang
张菁

Gigi Chang (she/her) translates from Chinese into English. Her fiction translations include Jin Yong's martial arts series Legends of the Condor Heroes—Volume II: *A Bond Undone;* Volume III: *A Snake Lies Waiting,* co-translated with Anna Holmwood; and Volume IV: *A Heart Divided,* co-translated with Shelly Bryant. Her theatre translations include classical Chinese dramas for the Royal Shakespeare Company and contemporary Chinese plays for the Royal Court Theatre, Hong Kong Arts Festival, and Shanghai Dramatic Arts Centre. She also co-hosts a regular program on plays and playwrights for the Chinese-language podcast *Culture Potato.*

Gu Shi
顾适

Gu Shi (she/her) is a speculative fiction writer and a senior urban planner. She has been working as a researcher at the China Academy of Urban Planning and Design since 2012. Her short fiction works have won two Galaxy Awards for Chinese Science Fiction and three Xingyun Awards (the Chinese Nebula). She published her first story collection, *Möbius Continuum,* in 2020. Her stories have been translated into English and published in *Clarkesworld* and *Current Futures,* XPRIZE's sci-fi ocean anthology.

Jing Tsu
石静远

Jing Tsu (she/her) is Professor of East Asian Languages and Literatures & Comparative Literature at Yale University. She is an expert of modern Chinese literature, intellectual and cultural history, and science and technology. She has received awards and fellowships from the Guggenheim Foundation, the Andrew W. Mellon Foundation, and half a dozen Advanced Study institutes at Harvard, Stanford, and Princeton. Her newest book is *Kingdom of Characters: The Language Revolution That Made China Modern.*

Judith Huang
錫影

Judith Huang (she/her) is an Australia-based Singaporean multimedia creator, poet, author, journalist, translator, composer, musician, educator, serial arts collective founder, Web 1.0 entrepreneur, and aspiring VR creator at www.judithhuang.com.

Her first novel, *Sofia and the Utopia Machine,* short-listed for the Epigram Books Fiction Prize 2017 and Singapore Book Awards 2019, is the story of a young girl who feels abandoned by her missing father and her controlling/neglectful mother. Sofia turns to VR to create her own universe, but when this leads to an actual Big Bang in the Utopia Machine in a secret government lab, opening portals to the multiverse, she loses everything—her family, her country, her world, and her worldview, and must go on the run with only her wits and her mysterious online friend, "Isaac," to help her. Can she save her worlds and herself?

Judith counts bunny-minding, human-systems-hacking, Harvard-alumni-interviewing, hackerspace-running, truth-telling, and propaganda-dissemination as her hobbies.

Judy Yi Zhou
周易

Judy Yi Zhou (she/her) is a writer, translator, and CEO of Cantos Translations, which helps publishers, production studios, and anyone else to connect with people who don't speak their language. Literally or figuratively. Judy is also currently working on a blended memoir/reportage.

Judy's work has appeared in the *Financial Times* and *Foreign Policy* and on NPR and WNYC. Her interpretation for sci-fi author Liu Cixin (*The Three-Body Problem*) was noted in the *New Yorker,* and her other interpretations/translations include work for novelist Ge Fei (*The Invisible Cloak*), *New York Times* bestselling author Kai-Fu Lee (*AI Superpowers*), and Constantin Film (*Resident Evil* and *Monster Hunter*).

Judy graduated *cum laude* from New York University with a BA in English and American Literature and a French minor. She's trying to learn Spanish.

Ling Chen
凌晨

Ling Chen (she/her), board member of the Chinese Science Writers Association and member of the Chinese Writers Association and Beijing Writers Association, writes popular science and science fiction. She has been writing science fiction for many years, covering topics such as aerospace, ocean, biology, artificial intelligence, and more. She has written more than two million characters so far, and her representative works include the novel *The Back of the Moon* and the short story "Sneaking into Guiyang." Of her works, the short stories "The Messenger," "The Cat," and "Sneaking into Guiyang" won the Galaxy Award. The short story "Sun Fire" and novel *Sleeping Dolphin Wakes Up* won the Xingyun Award (the Chinese Nebula). The novella *Sea Fighting* won the "Big White Whale" Original Fantastic Children's Literature Award.

Nian Yu
念语

Nian Yu (she/her) is a science fiction writer born in 1996 in Shanghai, also interested in illustration and comics, and currently working as a paralegal. After publishing her debut story, "Wild Fire," she has been surprising readers with her talented writing in science fiction, fantasy, and fairy tales. She has published multiple stories in *Science Fiction World* and *Science Fiction World YA*. She is the winner of the Silver Award for Best New Writer for the Xingyun Awards (the Chinese Nebulas) and has published a short story collection, *Lilian Is Everywhere.*

Rebecca F. Kuang
匡灵秀

Rebecca F. Kuang (she/her) is a Marshall Scholar, Chinese-English translator, and the Astounding Award–winning and Nebula, Locus, and World Fantasy Award–nominated author of the Poppy War trilogy. Her work has won the Crawford Award and the Compton Crook Award for Best First Novel. She has an MPhil in Chinese Studies from Cambridge and an MSc in Contemporary Chinese Studies from Oxford; she is now pursuing a PhD in East Asian Languages and Literatures at Yale.

Ru-Ping Chen
陈汝平

Ru-Ping Chen (she/her) is a fiction writer and Chinese-to-English translator who resides in California (Northern or Southern at any given point in time) and spends most of her time at a nine-to-five day job, doing barre/yoga/pilates, and writing a soon-to-be-completed novel. Many of her creative writing pieces have been published in the *Daily Californian*'s online magazine (*The Weekender*). You can find her seeking book recommendations on anything and everything about the world and follow her on Twitter @eriasop.

Shen Dacheng
沈大成

Shen Dacheng (she/her) is a column writer and fiction writer. She lives in Shanghai, China, and works as an editor. She has published the short story collections *The Ones in Remembrance* (2017) and *Asteroids in the Afternoon* (2020).

Shen Yingying
沈璎璎

Shen Yingying (she/her) is a doctor of medicine (MD) and a major representative writer of mainland Chinese new wǔxiá in the early twenty-first century. She has published numerous wǔxiá short stories and novellas, and is famous for her female perspective and elegant writing style. She is also one of the major creators of the Chinese fantastic shared universe Cloud Desolate, with major works like *The Story of the White Deer of the Green Cliff, Cloud Scattering Gao Tang, The River and Mountain Never Sleeps, The Cloud Born Knotted Sea House,* and others.

Wang Nuonuo
王诺诺

Wang Nuonuo (she/her) is a science fiction writer. She has won the 2018 Best New Writer of Chinese SF Galaxy Award, the 2018 First Prize of Lenghu Award, the 2018 Third Prize of Lenghu Award, and the 2019 Special Morning Star Award. She has published her short story collection, *No Answers from Earth,* and her stories have been included in *Best SF Works of China Anthology,* published by People's Literature Publishing House, three years in a row.

Xia Jia
夏笳

Xia Jia a.k.a. Wang Yao (she/her) is an Associate Professor of Chinese Literature at Xi'an Jiaotong University. So far, she has published a fantasy novel, *Odyssey of China Fantasy: On the Road* (2010); and the three science fiction collections *The Demon Enslaving Flask* (2012), *A Time Beyond Your Reach* (2017), and *Xi'an City Is Falling Down* (2018); as well as an academic work on contemporary Chinese science fiction, *Coordinates of the Future: Discussions on Chinese Science Fiction in the Age of Globalization* (2019). Recently she has been working on a science fiction fix-up, entitled *Chinese Encyclopedia*. Her first English collection, *A Summer Beyond Your Reach: Stories,* was published in 2020. She is also engaged in other science fiction–related work, including academic research, translation, screenwriting, editing, and teaching creative writing.

Xiu Xinyu
修新羽

Xiu Xinyu (she/her) is a writer living in Beijing who enjoys collecting stones, swimming in the sea, and gorging on chocolate. She mostly uses her master's degree in philosophy to make up tragic novels. She has published more than fifteen SF stories, including the collection *Death by the Night of Glory.*

Xueting Christine Ni
倪雪亭

Xueting Christine Ni (she/her) was born in Guangzhou, during China's "reopening to the West." Having lived in cities across China, she emigrated with her family to Britain at the age of eleven, where she continued to immerse herself in Chinese culture alongside her British education, giving her a unique cultural perspective. Xueting has written for the BBC and the Guangdong Art Academy, as well as lectured on Chinese film and literature. She alternates between fiction and nonfiction works, with books on Chinese mythology and religion (*From Kuan Yin to Chairman Mao*) and science fiction (*Sinopticon*) currently available. She lives in the suburbs of London with her partner and their cats, all of whom are learning Chinese.

Yilin Wang
王艺霖

Yilin Wang (she/they) is a writer, editor, and Chinese-English translator. Her writing has appeared in *Clarkesworld, The Malahat Review, Grain, CV2, carte blanche, The Toronto Star, The Tyee,* and elsewhere, and has been longlisted for the CBC Poetry Prize along with other awards. Her translations have appeared or are forthcoming in *Asymptote, LA Review of Books'* "China Channel," *Samovar, Pathlight,* and

Living Hyphen, while her research on martial arts fiction has been featured on various podcasts. She has an MFA in creative writing from the University of British Columbia and is a member of the Clarion West Writers Workshop 2020/2021. Website: www.yilinwang.com.

Zhao Haihong
赵海虹

Zhao Haihong (she/her) is an associate professor, science fiction writer, and translator, working at the School of Foreign Languages, Zhejiang Gongshang University. She has a master's degree in English and American literature from Zhejiang University and a PhD in art history from the China Academy of Art. Besides doing research and translation, she has been publishing SF stories since 1996 and is a six-time winner of the Chinese Science Fiction Galaxy Award. She has published seven collections of short stories and a novel, *Crystal Sky.* Her self-translated stories, "Exuviation," "Windhorse," and "Starry Sky over the Southern Isle," have been published in English magazines like *Asimov's Science Fiction Magazine;* her short story "1923, A Fantasy" has been translated and included in the 2018 anthology *The Reincarnated Giant: An Anthology of Twenty-First-Century Chinese Science Fiction.*

EDITORS AND STORYCOM

Storycom
微像文化

Storycom is dedicated to providing good content and production management solutions for the science fiction industry, as well as introducing Chinese science fiction to a broader audience internationally. Science fiction films produced by Storycom include *The End of the Lonely Island* (Silver Award for Professional Dramatic Feature at the Raw Science Film Festival, Winner of the Best Drama Award at the fifth Philip K. Dick Film Festival), *The Mailbox* (first place at the Waterdrop Award for Best Film and short-listed for the Golden Goblet Award at the Shanghai International Film Festival), and *Deep In* (Best Design at the Boston Sci-Fi Film Festival). The company has also organized the SF Film & TV Venture Capital Summit at China SF Con since 2019. In the past five years, Storycom has collaborated with overseas partners to translate and publish more than seventy Chinese science fiction stories into English, Italian, Spanish, German, and Romanian.

Regina Kanyu Wang
王侃瑜

Regina Kanyu Wang (she/her) is a PhD fellow of the CoFUTURES project at the University of Oslo. Her research interest lies in Chinese science fiction, especially from a gender and environmental perspective. She is also an award-winning writer who writes both science fiction and nonfiction. She has won multiple Xingyun Awards (the Chinese Nebulas), the SF Comet International SF Writing Competition, Annual

Best Works of the Shanghai Writers Association, and others. She has published two science fiction story collections, been translated into ten languages, resided in Writing in Downtown Las Vegas Residency, been supported by the Shanghai Culture Development Foundation, and been a contracted writer of the Shanghai Writers Association. She has also been actively introducing Chinese science fiction to the world and vice versa. When she is not working on science fiction–related projects, you can find her practicing krav maga, kali, and boxing, or cooking various dishes.

Yiwen Zhang
张译文

Yiwen Zhang (she/her) is the CEO of Storycom, film producer and presenter, external expert of the China Science Fiction Research Center, and vice secretary-general of the China Science and Film Exchange Professional Committee of the Chinese Science Writers Association. Her representative film works include *The End of the Lonely Island, Deep In,* and the blockbuster *My Best Summer.* She established the Shimmer imprint of science fiction books, and has published various science fiction novels, collections, and anthologies, as well as the best-selling *Handbook of the Wandering Earth: Behind the Scenes and Film Production,* of which the English version is coming out with Routledge. She has also established publishing projects of Chinese science fiction overseas, cooperating with publishers and magazines like *Clarkesworld, Future Fiction, Kapsel, Galaxy 42,* and others.

Yu Chen
于晨

Yu Chen (she/her), born in the 1980s, is a senior literature editor. She has participated in a number of major publishing projects and been working with science fiction for more than ten years. The science fiction books she has independently edited and published have won the Best Original Book Award at the Chinese SF Galaxy Awards and been selected for the National Grant for the Chinese Academy Book Translation. She has also published a personal essay collection.